NOAH RISING

ALSO BY HARRY SLACK

Lost in the Surf

NOAH RISING

HARRY SLACK

H. SLACK JR. BOOKS

Published by H. Slack Jr. Books, Bandon, Oregon

Edited and designed by Girl Friday Productions
www.girlfridayproductions.com

Cover design: Emily Weigel
Project management: Kim Kent
Editorial production: Katherine Richards
Image credits: cover © Shutterstock/Amir Bajric, Shutterstock/rdonar

ISBN (hardcover): 979-8-9921470-2-5
ISBN (paperback): 979-8-9921470-0-1
ISBN (ebook): 979-8-9921470-1-8

Library of Congress Control Number: 2024926747

First edition

ONE

Noah Jeremiah North, age seven, four feet, eight inches tall and weighing ninety-one pounds, stood ankle deep and alone in a slow-moving mountain stream in the Siskiyou National Forest. It was a hot August day, and the cool water felt good as it moved over his tattered tennis shoes with the area around the toes worn and cut off. He was standing motionless, wearing threadbare, ill-fitting clothes from a Salvation Army shop. The cool shade of the towering fir and cedar trees near the little stream felt good. He had no mother or father and not one close friend, just Uncle Willis, a man without any parenting skills and with none on the horizon.

Noah was eagerly searching the gravel and sand in the creek bottom for small, bright pebbles and agates. He thought of the little stream as his stream. He was now alone. He was usually alone wherever he was and no matter what he was doing. The stream was partially covered with stream-side low-hanging boughs, vines, brush, and fallen small trees. It was difficult for an adult to walk up and down that stream. It eventually merged with a larger one that was seldom fished or explored because its banks were steep and rocky and unattractive to most people, and there weren't many fish. Noah came to this creek almost daily. It was a short walk to the little stream from the shack where he lived with Uncle Willis.

He was four years old the first day he played in the stream. He had found a bright yellow pebble and showed it to Uncle Willis. Willis took it from him and told him that it would be Noah's job to bring home more yellow pebbles. That was OK with Noah; he liked playing in the stream. The first few days he waded in that cool water, he was barefoot and the gravel hurt his feet. He begged Uncle Willis for wading shoes and didn't get them until he refused to go to the stream. The shoes were worn-out tennis shoes, and when Noah asked Uncle Willis where he got them, Willis wouldn't answer.

Noah stood motionless in the clear water, watching a crawdad walk by his feet with big pincers held high as if it was hungry or crabby like its cousins in the sea. A school of tiny fish fluttered around the toes on his right foot. Noah started to move upstream. He kept going until he reached its headwaters at a large, seeping landslide. It took him about twenty-five minutes to get there, and on the way he found no bright yellow pebbles. After a rain washed through the landslide, it was easier to find the bright yellow pebbles. It had not rained for a month, and Noah knew he would find few if any bright pebbles. Uncle Willis would be upset about that, and dinner would be meager. There was something about Willis receiving the bright pebbles that temporarily improved life in the shack. Uncle Willis was absent most of the time, and Noah never knew where Willis was or what he was doing, and when asked, Willis would say, "That doesn't concern you."

Noah had questioned Willis about their way of life. Noah remembered running into the shack one morning and saying to Willis, "Felix is going to school, why aren't I? I just talked to him, and he was on his way to his second year in school and told me I should be going to kindergarten school. I need to do that."

"You're only five, maybe next year. Besides, you're needed here."

Fishing for bright pebbles afforded Noah quiet time to consider his life, and when he was six years old, he asked himself, If those yellow pebbles are valuable, why am I the only one looking for them? Two years before he'd discovered the little stream, a torrential rain had caused a landslide, resulting in the upheaval of a huge rock formation and moving the stream channel to its ancient bedrock channel, whose crevices and seams were filled with sand, gravel, and some of the yellow pebbles. Apparently no one, including Noah, knew about the change that had occurred to the little stream. Noah was wise to keep the stream's riches to himself.

Noah continued his search without finding the pebble he wanted, so he waded downstream to the big river to leave. High on a ledge above the river stood two boys watching him. He knew one was Felix Bronson but didn't recognize the other boy who was Felix's friend, Gary Allen. Felix and Gary were growing up in the same neighborhood and were classmates. Gary was the only child of a single working mother, giving him considerable time alone, time to be with a friend and time to do what boys do, such as bother Noah, the boy they were watching. Felix had a mother and father, lived in an attractive house, and had a bicycle and a family life and things Noah didn't have. Neither knew that in a few years, an unexpected friendship would blossom.

Noah could see the boys talking.

Felix said, "That's the kid that lives in the shack I showed you."

Gary said, "Let's go down there and find out who he is and what he's doing."

Felix said, "I know who he is. My mom says the boy has no mother or father and no real family."

Continuing to watch Noah, Gary bumped Felix with his elbow, saying, "I've heard about him. Look at him, he's just standing there. He doesn't have a fishing pole, and I heard he has no bike or friends or anything."

Felix put his right hand on Gary and shoved him slightly. "We'll leave him be. He's got enough problems. The kid has nothing, and we shouldn't bother him, so let's head home." Felix was a good person and was uncommonly small. He did not like confrontations. Not because he was afraid but because when angered, he sometimes lost his self-control and would start swinging his little arms and fists at his antagonist, resulting in his nose being bloodied or an eye blackened. He did occasionally scare off a bully with such behavior. Today he would not bother Noah, and neither would his friend.

Noah was happy to see the two boys leave. He didn't want anyone knowing or even suspecting what he was doing in the stream.

TWO

Noah's mother, Virginia Porter, was eighteen years old when she married Buster North. Noah was born one year later, and Buster disappeared. Buster's friends were not surprised; nor was Virginia, who secretly welcomed Buster's absence but was also dismayed by his behavior. It would be years before Noah would know what normal was. Buster had contributed nothing to the marriage except Virginia's pregnancy. Where he was or if he was alive was of little concern. Virginia did not speak to Noah about his father, say who he was, or divulge anything about him. She did know that Buster's family was in New York, that his father was in the shipping business, and that Buster had brothers and a sister. If she learned more about Buster's family, she would tell Noah.

Virginia worked as a waitress in a family-style restaurant. She provided and cared for Noah until she was hospitalized with injuries sustained in a late-night vehicle accident. At that time, Virginia and Noah were living in a small apartment in Grants Pass, Oregon. The apartment was ground level with a combination kitchen/living room and one bedroom. Virginia had accumulated enough household goods and ware to make the place livable.

When Virginia was hospitalized, Willis was the only family member to step forward to care for Noah, which, incidentally, gave him occupancy of Virginia's apartment and a better place to live. No one objected, and no other person or family member offered to help.

Virginia fought to stay alive, but her injuries could not be repaired and would not heal. She finally accepted her coming demise, and while

clearheaded and responsible, she summoned to her bedside Morgan
Reynolds, an attorney she knew as reputable and competent. She explained to him that her husband Buster, before he disappeared, had
deeded to her a piece of land that wasn't worth much. She handed a
recorded deed to the lawyer with instructions to prepare and record a
deed of the property to her son, Noah.

The lawyer prepared the deed for Virginia and returned to her
hospital room for its signing. The lawyer notarized her signature, and
he recorded the document with the county clerk. Virginia told the
lawyer that she did not want her family to know about the transaction.
She didn't trust any of them. She instructed the lawyer to have the
recorded deed mailed to his office where she could pick it up. Virginia
wanted the property tax statements mailed to the lawyer's office where
she could always get them. She intended to tell Noah that the property
was his, but died the day following the signing and recording of the
deed.

Before she married Buster North, he'd talked about the small
house he owned in Rock City, but she had never seen it. Brother Willis
was present and overheard that conversation.

Noah had been alone in the hospital, and he clung to his mother
as she died. The hospital nurse comforted Noah and then called Susan
Porter, the person named on Virginia's hospital admittance form.
Willis Porter, Virginia's brother, came to the hospital and took custody
of Noah, and he and Noah then occupied Virginia's furnished apartment until the next month's rent was overdue. Noah was a sensitive
boy and was profoundly distraught, barely able to cope with the loss
of his mother. Willis provided some comfort, but while in the small
apartment, he would paw through Virginia's few personal belongings.
He found nothing of interest except River County real property tax
statements addressed to the owner, Virginia North. Taxes were a year
delinquent, but each statement had the property description and its
address in Rock City.

Uncle Willis Porter was uneducated, had never had steady employment, and had no assets or money. He did have a driver's license when
it wasn't suspended, and he had a car that would run occasionally—a
crippled horse would have been as reliable. He was irresponsible to
himself and others, never repaying small loans and always grasping on

to a situation that would benefit him. Recently he'd offered to house-sit for a friend and trashed the house with his beer-drinking friends. He looked unkept and was. Some might say there were times when he didn't know whether to sleep in the rain or in a dumpster that had a lid.

THREE

Uncle Willis kept a rumor of Buster North's death to himself. Why say anything if the rumor was not true? Besides, Noah didn't need more bad news. Sooner or later he would tell Noah if the rumors were correct.

He did know enough to visit the Department of Human Services for assistance in caring for Noah. The caseworker assigned to his case was Mary Edison, and she was quick to grasp the situation. She had seen it before. Who was going to benefit the most, the uncle or the child? She saw Willis's ploy, but Noah would have his $150 monthly benefit if a few phone calls confirmed Willis's story. She could monitor the situation infrequently.

It was Willis's plan to stay in the Pacific Northwest. He could start a new dissolute life in some county where no one knew him. He liked the mountains and the Pacific coast. Never mind what Noah might want; Noah wasn't old enough to know what was going on or to make decisions. Willis was awarded $150 per month by the DHS for Noah's care. That would help keep Uncle Willis in food and business, whatever that was.

The morning of Virginia's funeral, Willis had said to four-year-old Noah, "I am leaving this place, and you are coming with me."

Noah's eyebrows crinkled up. "I'm not going anyplace with you. I'm staying here."

"You have no choice, no one wants to be bothered with you. So it's either me or an orphanage."

"Doesn't my Grandmother Porter want me?"

"Yes, but your grandfather won't let her take you."

"Where are you taking me?"

Willis shrugged. "Maybe to a place in Rock City."

After Virginia's graveside service at the Porter family graveyard plot, Willis loaded Noah and his meager things and a few of Virginia's possessions into his car and motored off to Rock City, Oregon. Willis hoped that Virginia's property would be vacant. He had no place to live, so it was worth the risk to drive to Rock City on the chance that he and Noah could occupy the property. He had no better opportunity anyplace else. This was vintage Willis. The address on the tax statement took them to the end of a street at the edge of Rock City. He didn't know that Virginia had deeded the property to Noah, making Noah the owner.

They found the property with an unoccupied shack on it. Noah didn't realize that the next few years of his life would be miserable and that, with his own initiative, he would eventually rise in stature and freedom from distress.

Willis said to Noah, "We got lucky, I think."

Noah did not know why they were lucky. The place looked like a wreck.

"Are we really going to stay here?" Noah asked.

"Let's look inside."

Noah was looking around and saw uncovered inside walls with the studs showing and some rough boards attached as shelves. The floor was a plywood subfloor covered with stains, a few paint splatters, and one dirty throw rug. The ceiling was open with the roof joists uncovered, and the only light was at the end of a cord hanging from a roof joist. There was a bedroom with usable twin beds, a wood kitchen table with two chairs, and a tattered matching chair and davenport near a wood stove.

"Uncle Willis, this place is a dump."

Willis waved a hand dismissively. "Ah, it's fixable, and we'll be OK, just give me a little time."

This was good for Willis. He just might be able to feed, clothe, and house himself and Noah on the small stipend granted by Human Services, and best of all, he might do it without having a job, and there would be no rent to pay! Willis thought he was capable of the fancy footwork needed to accomplish that objective, a marvelous coup. He would pay the city water bill, the electric bill, and other necessities from the DHS monthly benefit.

FOUR

During the last three years, Willis's plan to take care of himself had prevailed, but Noah became uneasy and concerned as he realized that his life in the shack with Willis was far from normal. No friends and no school. Willis forbade Noah to be in town without him, but Noah ignored that rule, and eventually Noah observed what he believed to be normal interactions of children with their parents and others. Now at age seven with no mother, no father, no real social interaction, and the realization that his life was a mess, Noah made a solemn pledge to himself: I'm going to do everything I can possibly do to climb above the life I'm now living. I don't know how I'll do it, but I'm gonna do it.

Noah spent another day in the little stream and did not find a single bright yellow pebble. He was on his way home to the shack where Willis would be waiting for the delivery of a pebble or two. The walk home covered about a mile, partially on a wooded trail, but it was mostly a walk along unimproved streets and a couple of concrete sidewalks ending on a dirt path to the door of the shack. It was five o'clock, and Willis was waiting. He immediately asked if Noah had found anything. Noah's answer obviously disappointed Willis. Noah had hoped that he might smell a dinner cooking, but he detected nothing. Noah had been so distanced from normal social life that he had no concept of what people did with their daily lives.

Noah often asked himself, Was Willis supposed to do little or nothing all day, every day? Or was he supposed to actually have a job and work? How can he just receive my check every month and do so little to take care of both of us?

But this evening he had more immediate concerns. "Are we having dinner? I'm really hungry."

Willis didn't answer. Noah looked around at the interior of the shack and saw walls with two-by-four studs exposed, a ceiling of two-by-six rafters supporting a corrugated sheet metal roof, a doorway to the only other room, where he and Willis slept, the white electric cookstove and the green refrigerator on one wall, the wood stove, and a wood table in the center of the room covered with stuff. The bathroom was an attachment to the shack, with a toilet, a metal shower stall, and a water heater in the corner with toilet paper stacked on top of it. Noah did not want to continue to spend his days in the shack.

Noah took a deep breath. "I'm seven. I want to be in school this fall. Are you going to help me or stop me?" When Willis didn't answer, Noah continued, "I'm going to school this fall whether you like it or not."

Willis thought, This kid is getting some backbone. When he realizes I've derailed his schooling, he is really going to be pissed. Willis had not allowed Noah to attend preschool, and now he told Noah that he could not go to school until next year. Last year he'd missed the first grade.

Noah then knew that Willis wanted him bringing home bright pebbles and doing nothing else. He also knew there would be no school unless he went to school without telling Uncle Willis, and that was exactly what he would do. Upset, Noah walked to Felix Bronson's house and found Felix in his front yard playing with the family dog. Noah summoned up a little courage and walked to Felix.

"Felix, I need your help, but you gotta keep a deep, dark secret. Can you do that?"

"Yes."

"OK, here's the problem. My Uncle Willis will not let me go to school, but I'm going. He won't go there to register me or anything. Will you take me to your school and show me the office where I would register?"

"Sure. Let's go."

They walked into an office and waited in line behind a parent and child registering, and soon Noah was asked by the clerk what he wanted.

"I want to register for the first grade, but I need to take the form to my Uncle Willis to fill out. Uncle Willis has my custody, but he is ill and can't leave our house."

"Here's the registration form and a list of a few supplies you need for school. Make sure he answers every question and completes the form. He should be here with you. Return the form tomorrow."

Noah gently took hold of Felix's arm and said, "Felix, you can't tell anyone about this. I'm registering myself for school without Willis knowing. If I don't, I'll never get to school."

"I won't say a thing."

Noah was accumulating a quart jar of bright pebbles that Willis knew nothing about. If Noah found one pebble for Willis, Noah would keep all the additional pebbles. He'd realized they were worth something because every time he gave Willis a bright pebble, Willis would go to town and bring home groceries, a bottle of wine for himself, and sometimes clothing for Noah. If it was a new month, Willis would put money in an envelope for the power company. Willis never had a bank account.

Noah attended school, the first grade, the grade he'd missed last year. Kindergarten was optional. For several weeks, Willis believed Noah was searching for bright pebbles. Noah left the shack at 8:30 every weekday morning. Willis was usually still in bed when Noah left the shack. Noah no longer believed he was fooling Willis, and it didn't upset Willis's non-employment plan, so Willis said nothing. Willis was weak and would avoid a confrontation.

Noah liked school and did exceptionally well. As disingenuous as Willis was regarding the education and wants of a grade-school boy, Willis had tried to mitigate his failure in the early education of Noah. When Noah was five, he taught Noah the alphabet, how to barely read, and how to add and subtract. This gave him an edge in the first grade, and he would be ripe for advancement before his time. However, Noah knew, if he was to stay in school, he would have to confront Willis.

As the end of December approached, Willis gradually became upset about the tiny number of bright pebbles Noah was bringing home.

Willis stopped Noah on the driveway to the shack. "What's going on with you? Your shoes and pants are not wet. You're not working that stream for the bright pebbles. So where have you been and what have you been doing?"

"Willis, I have been in school every day this school year. I registered for school by forging your name on my registration papers."

"That's illegal."

"What's illegal is a relative with custody of a five-, six-, or seven-year-old child preventing that child from attending school. Taking valuable property, such as gold, from that child is stealing. Likewise, using my DHS funds for your own personal use is no doubt illegal."

"I've done all that for your benefit."

"The state police won't see it that way. You've dirtied your nest, Uncle Willis."

"I've taken care of you. You wouldn't do that to me."

"I will not say a word as long as you participate in keeping me in school and act like you care. That means attending parent-teacher conferences and school functions when parents are invited. If you do that, I may even bring you a bright pebble."

One morning Noah dressed, ate cold cereal, and, when leaving for school, said, "Uncle Willis, I'm going to school and will never stop. I have no idea what you do during the day, but I know what I'm doing, and I'll continue to help on weekends—OK?"

Willis said, "OK."

When Noah arrived at school that morning, his teacher met him at the classroom door and said, "We are making some changes for you today, so go to the principal's office and get squared away for the rest of the school year." Noah did and moved to the second grade. He felt out of place, but the schoolwork came easily and he prospered. He would be eight in February. Skipping the remainder of the first grade was unusual, but he succeeded and was with students closer to his age. Within three months he was one of the top students.

FIVE

The big mysteries in Noah's life were, how long would the little stream produce the bright pebbles, and what was Uncle Willis up to, and what would his eighth birthday have been like if his mother were still alive? She would have had a present and a little cake with candles for him. It had always been just the two of them.

The winter rains and muddy water had restricted his search in the stream except on a few occasions when the stream briefly cleared, and then unbelievably he nearly filled his pocket. The rains must have washed more of the landslide into the stream. When that happened, and it never had before, he would give Willis one pebble. In only three months, mostly on weekends, he filled another jar with the extra pebbles. How long could this last, he thought. Noah knew that sooner or later someone would discover his secret, and that would be the end of it.

That's when he decided that he would have to make a plan. For himself. Noah reasoned, with his eight-year-old intellect, that he and Willis were not a real family, at least not like the real mother-and-father families. So one afternoon, after school on the little stream, he said out loud to himself, "I'm gonna be taking care of myself one of these days, and I'd better be ready, because it'll just be me."

Friday evening he gave Willis a bright pebble. Saturday was not a school day, and he would stay close to Uncle Willis to learn the secret of how he turned the pebbles into goods they could use around the house.

Willis walked to the door and said, "While I'm in town today, you can spend some time on your little stream, and maybe you'll get lucky."

Noah thought, No way—I'm going to follow him!

Noah followed and watched. Uncle Willis walked into Zimmerman's Jewelry Store. Noah hurried to a side window and saw Willis hand Mr. Zimmerman a bright pebble. Mr. Zimmerman placed it on a little scale. Mr. Zimmerman then opened his cash register, counted out some paper money, and gave it to Uncle Willis. Noah had always suspected that the bright pebbles were gold, but not until now did he cease to speculate about it.

While walking back home, Noah was busy asking himself questions about what he should do. He first decided that his jars of pebbles were very valuable and no one must know about them or know they were hidden in his back yard at the base of one of his large fir trees. Also, he must find out what they were worth.

Walter Zimmerman was the jeweler's son and was in the third grade, a year ahead of Noah. Maybe he would ask him about the price of gold. No, the best way would be to take a pebble to the jeweler and sell it. Several weeks passed. Noah's days were spent in school, and he liked what he was doing and didn't want to cause any problems by revealing that he possessed a piece of gold. He would have to find its value. His life was, as he saw it, sort of a messy problem anyway with no solution in sight, so why invite another problem?

It was now March 1966, and school was out for a week. He had gleaned another ten or twelve pebbles during a brief clearing of the stream's water. With time on his hands, he again pondered selling a pebble. If asked where he got the pebble, he had a story.

Noah walked into Mr. Zimmerman's jewelry store and looked around to see what a jewelry store looked like. It was in an old frame building but very clean and with glass-covered counters filled with all kinds of jewelry. There were watches and bright things in the window for people on the sidewalk to see. The inside walls were covered with some kind of colored paper full of pretty designs. There was a man and woman looking at rings under the glass case on the wall opposite Noah. It was very quiet. Mr. Zimmerman was standing behind a counter next to a big silvery cash register. He was watching the couple looking at rings. While subduing his nervousness, Noah put the pebble on the counter and told Mr. Zimmerman he wanted to sell it. Mr. Zimmerman knew who Noah was, knew about his

Uncle Willis, and had heard rumors about their unfortunate living conditions.

Mr. Zimmerman wanted to be sympathetic in dealing with Noah and in a friendly manner said, as he held the pebble in his fingers, "Noah, I really need to know how you happen to have this."

"After my mother died I found two little purses hidden in her dresser drawer, each with gold pebbles in them. Uncle Willis took one purse without knowing about the other purse. I think he sold the pebbles in the first one to take care of us." Noah was upset with himself. He had never lied like that to anyone except to Uncle Willis. He thought, The gold is making me do this.

Mr. Zimmerman said, "Noah, I'm sorry I had to ask you that, but private citizens are not allowed to possess gold. I have to sell it to the government, and they will usually want to know where I got it. I hope you understand."

Mr. Zimmerman then placed a small scale on the counter, did some adjustment to it, and placed the bright pebble on the scale.

He adjusted his glasses, looked closely at the scale, and said, "That is 0.5234 troy ounces." After he punched the buttons on the little black calculator lying on the counter, he said, "At $30 an ounce, I owe you $15.70." Noah didn't know what a troy ounce was, but he would certainly find out, and he wasn't going to embarrass himself by asking Mr. Zimmerman.

Mr. Zimmerman took the $15.70 from his cash register, and as he counted it, he said, "Noah, the government has fixed the price of gold at $35 an ounce. I am paying you $30 an ounce because it is in raw form and needs smelting to clean it. I gather a little bit here and there and then melt it and sell what I can't use as a jeweler. I also must tell you that it is illegal for citizens to own gold. They must sell it to a bank, which turns it over to the Federal Reserve, which is the US government. The bank will pay you $35 an ounce."

Noah was puzzled and said, "Mr. Zimmerman, I don't understand. Does this mean you won't buy any more of my pebbles?"

Mr. Zimmerman delayed his response and then said, "As a jeweler I can hold and deal with a small amount of gold, but it needs to be smelted and refined for sale or for me to use it in my business. You should sell to a bank what little gold you may have. I will continue to buy your pebbles, but you will be paid more if you sell to a bank. I told your Uncle Willis the same thing."

"My Uncle Willis doesn't always do the right thing."

Mr. Zimmerman thought Noah might decide what was best and sell to a bank.

Noah left the jewelry store, surprised at the $15.70 in his pocket. He knew little or nothing about money, prices of goods, or their good or bad features, but he now knew that he might be able to care for himself without Willis's or anyone else's help. He had thanked Mr. Zimmerman, and as he was walking back to the shack, he was thinking about the number of ounces in his fruit jars and what those ounces were worth.

SIX

Noah was home when Willis arrived, and he knew he had to get things right with his uncle. At age eight, Noah knew that he and Willis could not go on hiding what each of them was doing or not doing.

Noah waited for his uncle to sit down in his usual chair before starting in on the little speech he had prepared and practiced. "Willis, I sold a pebble to Mr. Zimmerman today after I saw you sell him one a couple days ago. The state pays you $150 a month and you sell the pebbles I find. Are you earning any money yourself, or are you living off me?"

Willis was stunned. He didn't answer.

Noah took a deep breath and bravely said, "For three years or so you tried to keep me out of school so that I could support you. I'm not doing that anymore. I'm going to school full-time, and there will be no more pebbles for you! I have never told you where they were coming from, so you're stuck with nothing."

Willis stood up, walking around with his arms moving up and around, confronted with the truth and searching for words that weren't there. Finally, he meekly said, "But I've been taking care of you."

"Well, yes, you're here in the evenings because you have no other place to be," Noah scoffed. "The only support going on around here is my support of you here at this shack! You have no job or money of your own. What do you do all day every day?"

"What I do is my business!"

"You were the only one that has helped me and I thank you for that, but your reason for helping me seems to be for your benefit."

Willis said nothing, threw some of his things in a sack, walked to the coat rack, put on his coat and hat, and walked out the door. Noah heard Willis trying to start his old car. It finally started and could be heard driving off. Noah immediately decided to do nothing. He could care for himself. No one would miss Willis. He was now alone, more alone than ever and even more disengaged from any semblance of a family. Noah pondered for a moment and wondered what had happened to his Grandfather and Grandmother North, who he had never met, and what had happened to his Grandfather and Grandmother Porter, who he'd met when he was two or three years old. Now his mother's brother, Willis, was gone. He could support himself, but could he protect himself and his treasure buried beneath a fir tree?

Willis had been gone a week when Mary Edison of the DHS knocked on his door for one of her infrequent visits.

Sitting at Noah's only table with an open file folder before her, she asked Noah to sit down.

"Noah, we believe that your Uncle Willis is gone, leaving you alone. He was not here on our last visit and he's not here now."

"I told him to leave and he left."

"At your age you need to have an adult with you."

"No I don't. I took care of myself and Uncle Willis, and I ran him off because he was useless."

"Our rules won't allow an eight-year-old to live alone."

"Look around here. This is a shack, but it is clean, there's food in the refrigerator, wood for the stove, my bed's made, my clothes are clean, I have my own money and don't need your monthly payment, and I'm a straight-A student."

"Noah, I don't have much of a choice here."

"You're not moving anyone in here with me, and I'm not going to a foster care home."

"Foster care is a good thing. It could be here in Rock City."

"I'm in charge of my life and it's going to stay that way. When I need advice or help, I'll ask for it. I don't want to be told what to do and what not to do. I can figure that out myself."

"OK, Noah, I'm leaving you now and I will review your situation with my regional office. My report to them will not be unfavorable. In the meantime DHS social workers will pay close attention to your living conditions and your personal behavior. Part of the reason for this is the fact that there is not a foster home available in this school district."

"You want to review something? Ask around this town about me."

"I plan to. I must admit, your situation and your care of yourself is better than many of my public charges."

SEVEN

Noah finished the school year, and it was summer vacation in Rock City. Because of his age and proficiency in reading comprehension, spelling, and arithmetic, he had been promoted to the second grade and had completed that grade. He was now with his age group. The last twelve months had been a big awakening in his young life.

He had not seen or heard from Uncle Willis since he left. Moreover, spring freshets had renewed the treasure in the little stream, but the last time he was there he had seen movement in the brush away from it. He was only eight years old and would not be able to defend himself if attacked and robbed. More important, had his secret been discovered? He knew it couldn't last forever. He had worked the stream nearly every day all summer. He didn't have to share with Willis. For nearly four years he had waded that little stream and accumulated nine hidden quart jars of gold pebbles. Mr. Zimmerman continued to buy the pebbles from Noah and kept the transactions confidential. Noah hinted that they were still coming from a purse he'd found with his mother's belongings. Noah was becoming increasingly fearful that he might not be able to care for himself if he had to move.

One day in the jewelry store, Mr. Zimmerman said, "Noah, I hope you are OK. I know Willis has been gone for months, but I've said nothing. I also know that you are alone and that no relative or anyone is there for you. There are nice families that would take you into their home and care for you. They are called 'foster parents.' Would you think about doing that?"

Noah replied, "I'll think about it, but I have made it for about six months on my own, and I'll keep going alone as long as I can. No one shares their life with me and I'm not ready to share my life with anyone until I have to."

Halted by the response, Mr. Zimmerman paused while examining Noah and said, "I don't know much about you. What I do know is that you are very young and you seem to be fiercely independent, you look and act well cared for and healthy, and you are not in any sort of trouble. If any of that changes, I'll have to ask DHS to review your situation. You get what I mean?"

"I understand what you are saying. You need to know that DHS knows nothing about my sale of a gold pebble to you or a sale to anyone else, but I will tell them."

"Also, I need to warn you: Soon I will have to stop buying gold pebbles from you. You should melt and smelt whatever gold you have and sell to a bank; you will be paid five dollars more an ounce than I am paying you."

Noah thanked Mr. Zimmerman for his concern and left with money in his pocket, enough for another month.

Noah walked out of the jewelry store and sat on a sidewalk bench, depressed. He examined his life after Uncle Willis. Is it better? It isn't worse. Am I doing something wrong? No. Did I ask for help? No. Did I get help? Yes. Many times. Many surprises. There's the Rock City Cafe waitress. After Willis left, I had some lunches there. Now at lunch, she brings me an extra-large sandwich and I take half of it home. The grocery clerk follows me around the store, throwing healthy food in my basket while she explains good and not so good food. Ten days after Willis left, I received a letter from the city and one from Pacific Power Co. because the monthly payment to each of them was past due. Mr. Zimmerman bought a few more pebbles, and I went directly to the city office and the local power company office and paid the balance, and now, every month I pay on time. There's an old washing machine in my shack. If I don't put too much in, it works. I hate doing laundry, but I keep clean.

Standing up and walking away from where he was sitting, reviewing his life, he whispered, "Nobody really knows the mess I'm in, and they are not going to hear it from me."

EIGHT

On Noah's last trip to his little stream before school started, he found nothing. It hadn't rained for months, and the bright pebbles had just petered out. That unhappy observation caused him to leave the stream, and in so doing he saw two strange young men watching him where the little stream joined the Salamander River. He had seen them before at that place, and it now frightened him. They each held a fishing rod. Fishing? Maybe. He walked by them on the opposite side of the river. He worried about his safety and the safety of his treasure. He had better do something about that. His treasure was no small matter. Having it buried by one of his fir trees was not the answer.

Noah knew that, sooner or later, the wrong person would learn that he was selling gold nuggets, and he wasn't going to stop, because he needed the cash. That person could be trouble. Only Noah had seen his pebble jars.

Noah recalled that Mr. Zimmerman had cautioned him, "You should know that the gold would be worth more if those pieces were melted, thereby removing any impurities. What I mean is, if you have very many, you could melt them down and mold them into flat pieces or, for additional safety, something that does not look like gold. The gold would be more pure, more valuable, less recognizable, and it would be safer for you and the gold."

Noah, as bright as he was and as alone as he was, knew that he should listen to what a smart adult had to say, at least if it might help him in some way.

The next day Noah wandered into Rock City Hardware, a store that, once inside, appeared to sell everything small and useful.

He asked the clerk, "Do you sell something that I might use to melt something?"

The clerk, amused, motioned for Noah to follow him, saying, "You mean something like lead?" The plumbing section of the store was interesting. He saw stuff he never knew existed. He was looking at what appeared to be a small stove with a little heavy steel pot sitting on what was probably a burner.

The store clerk pointed. "Do you know what that is?"

Noah shook his head, and the clerk said, "Plumbers use it to melt lead to connect soil pipe."

Noah didn't know what soil pipe was but asked, "How much is that thing and what does it burn?"

"It's $39.95 and it burns kerosene."

Wow, Noah thought, and wandered away to the sporting goods section where he immediately spotted a stack of lead sinkers next to a little printed sign set near an object he had never seen. The words on the sign were "Sinker Mold—10% off—$9.95." He could mold his own fishing sinkers from a half ounce to one ounce to one and a half ounces, all the way up to eight ounces. Noah thought, Perfect. He had just sold two nice pebbles and had almost $60 in his pocket. He walked out of the hardware store with the biggest and maybe the most questionable purchase of his life, including a gallon tin of kerosene.

Noah walked out of downtown Rock City to his shack carrying two heavy packages. He was continually asking himself, Did I do the right thing by spending that much money? My plan might not work. He had left town, and as he approached the shack, located at the edge of an open field, two persons ran away from the shack to the nearby forest. They were young men, maybe nineteen or twenty years old, decent looking, wearing nice clothes; one needed a haircut and the other had short, cropped hair. They disappeared into a small patch of timber in the direction of town. In any event, it was frightening to an eight-year-old living alone in a secluded area away from the small town. Noah had no one to talk to or seek advice from concerning this turn of events. Like everything else in his young life, he would have to deal with it himself. He needed to be alert, be smart, and have a weapon of some sort. Noah walked into the shack, and nothing looked disturbed. The door had no lock, and now he would fix that. He then looked at a large fir tree and its base on the edge of the field, and nothing had been disturbed around it. That was the burial site of numerous jars.

Now in the shack, and still a little shaken, he unpacked his purchases and proceeded to study the instructions for the burner. Later he opened and heated a can of chili and ate that with some bread for his dinner. The electricity was still on, and the old electric stove still worked, dirty as it was.

Noah could not stop thinking about his life. He lay awake in bed that night, thinking about Uncle Willis and if he had made a mistake running him off. Oh, well, he mused, in a few days school will start, and I'll feast on free lunches in the school cafeteria. He thought about molding gold sinkers, but that could wait.

NINE

School started in 1966 on the day after Labor Day, and Noah was there, unusually freshly showered and wearing clean clothes he'd set aside for the big day. Staying in school and getting an education was supposed to be the path to a decent life. Never mind that he also had the task of living and protecting his treasure. He knew he would be in the third grade. His grades through the first and second grades had been mostly A's. Report cards needed to be returned to his teacher after they were signed by a parent. Noah hated doing it, but he had forged Willis's name on the card numerous times. He looked forward to the free school lunches and wondered why they didn't serve breakfast. Noah's mind was never at rest. It couldn't rest.

The Rock City Grade School was located next to the Rock City High School. Noah had few friends. At the school entrance he saw Felix Bronson, who he had come to know in the first grade.

He walked to Felix, who was smiling, and said, "I barely saw you this summer. Maybe I'm too busy taking care of myself."

"My family was away on a long vacation. Let's get together after school today."

"I'm good with that."

Finding Noah leaving school for the day, Felix tapped him on the shoulder, saying, "Let's watch the high school boys practice football."

"No, Felix, follow me. I want to show you something."

Twenty minutes later they were standing in Noah's grove of tall magnificent cedars with Noah pointing and saying, "Those are my incense cedars, also known as pencil cedars, used to make pencils. I'm never going to sell them or cut them down. They're my friends."

"Noah, those trees are beautiful but don't get weird on me."

"Felix, you can come here and enjoy those trees anytime you want."

Noah and Felix parted at Noah's shack with the remark, "Felix, you're a good guy. I will not get weird."

"I know it. See you tomorrow."

On the walk to school the next morning, Noah saw two older boys in front of the high school who clearly resembled the boys he'd seen running away from the shack. Later he pointed them out to Felix and asked if Felix knew who they were.

Felix shrugged. "One of them is Jason Hanley. I don't know the other one, but I know that they are not high school students, and they are always hanging around the school at opening and closing hours."

"Could you . . . maybe find out about these two guys without mentioning me? I really need to know about them."

Felix nodded. "Sure, I can do that, and I won't mention you. What is it you want to know?"

"I just want to know who they are and who do they see and talk to. Do they have jobs?" Noah added, "This might be too much to ask. Just do what is easy for you, OK?"

September sped by, and at the beginning of the second week in October, while he stood in front of his school locker, two boys next to Noah were talking about deer season. Having discovered the subject of that conversation, Noah stopped listening and was jostled by Felix.

Noah looked at him with a test paper in hand and said, "Hey, you know that combo reading/spelling/geography test? I got an A, the only A on that test."

Felix snatched the paper from Noah and saw the big red A at the top of the page.

"How'd you do that?"

"Maybe I'm smarter than the average bear."

"You shouldn't say that out loud."

"I think that happened because I have nothing to do at home except read."

"My folks are always shoving stuff at me to read, but I can't get interested, and if I stumble across a couple of words I don't understand, I give up."

"Sometimes I can't understand what I am reading. I found an old dictionary that belonged to Uncle Willis. It's about one quarter the size of a regular dictionary. Sometimes the word's there, sometimes not."

"Felix, you've got to have an education, and maybe you should use your dictionary."

"Noah, I have something to tell you about those two boys. One of them, Jason Hanley, is the son of Jonathan Hanley, who has the only real estate office in Rock City. The other boy, Martin Groves, is a nephew of Mr. Zimmerman of Zimmerman's Jewelry. I saw them both in Zimmerman's store talking to Mr. Zimmerman. Does that do it for you?"

"Yes," Noah said as his mind started laboring from brain cell to brain cell, trying to concoct a simple reason why those three people would be together. The reason could be either harmless or dangerous. He desperately wanted it to be something innocent.

Later that day, Noah gathered all his young courage and walked into Zimmerman's Jewelry Store when it was closing and stood in front of the tall jeweler.

"Why are Martin Groves and Jason Hanley going onto my property? I think you know."

Surprised at Noah, Zimmerman stepped back.

"I don't know, but I'll talk to Martin. He's just visiting us, but he could have overheard some dinner-table talk about me buying gold from you."

"That's what he and Hanley are looking for. Tell them to stay away from me and my place. Jason Hanley is not a good person. I should go to the police."

"Noah, I no doubt created the problem. I apologize for that and I'll fix it. OK?"

"You need to do that immediately."

Noah left for home, wishing people would stop complicating his life.

TEN

Noah was nine years old when school started in September 1967. Martha Webb was his new teacher, and he instantly liked her. The fourth grade was going well, with good grades and friendly classmates, but he was burdened with problems not of his making. Noah counted his troubles: Where is Willis? He didn't really care but wanted to know what was happening to the rest of the $150 a month of government support. He knew some of it was being used for his support, but what about the remainder? Is my gold secret safe? What if I get kicked out of the shack?

He had little or no choice. He could go to Human Services and end up in a foster home not of his choice, he could go to his grandparents, who didn't want him, or he could continue what he was doing and tackle one problem at a time. First thought: I'm not doing anything about the $150 with Willis gone. They might put me in a foster home. Second: If I get kicked out of the shack, I'll find something else. Third: I'll hide my gold somewhere else. February 1967, along with his birthday, had swept by and no one except Noah knew it. He felt more mature at nine years of age.

After school that day, after reading the instructions, he filled the kerosene burner and fired it up, and it made a muted roaring sound. He set up the sinker mold according to the instructions. He did this on some bare ground outside, where he couldn't be seen and wouldn't burn down the shack. He placed some pebbles from the jar in the steel pot sitting on the burner flames. Noah had a broad smile on his face when the melting started. There was a scum on the top of the melted metal that Noah scraped off with a spoon. He grasped the pot's long handle with an old leather glove and carefully poured the liquid gold into the sinker mold. He turned off the burner, went inside, and had hot dogs and a glass of milk for dinner.

After he ate, Noah went back outside, and he dismantled the sinker mold, which was still warm. There were four half-ounce, four full-ounce, four two-ounce, and two four-ounce sinkers. The mold had a section for a six-ounce and an eight-ounce sinker, but he did not have enough molten gold to pour those sinkers. Each sinker had to be trimmed slightly. Noah put the trimmings back into the pot for the next melt. He had twenty-two ounces in sinkers that he knew were not exactly accurate, and yet he had used only a fraction of the pebbles from one jar. He gasped out loud when he realized he had about $700 or $800 in gold, if he sold it to a bank. He had forgotten that gold was a little less than twice the weight of lead, and that gold was sold by the troy ounce, whatever that was.

He thought, Do I just walk into the bank in Rock City and say, "I want $800 for these sinkers," or do I first walk in and ask them if they buy gold? Noah decided to go to the bank and ask them. He had never been in a bank, but he did know that it was where money was kept and that lots of people used the bank. Wouldn't they ask questions like, "Where did you get this?" Or, "Do your parents know what you're doing?" Or, "What are you going to do with all that money?" Noah decided to ask someone who might know, but who? He pondered the question. Should I ask Mrs. Webb, or maybe Mrs. Edison, the woman from the Department of Human Services? Noah decided to ask his teacher.

Noah lingered after school, remaining at his desk while he watched the room empty. It was a large room with a high ceiling and large windows with small panes on the north side of the room. While gathering courage, he focused on the room-width blackboard behind Mrs. Webb's desk and on the rows of empty seats beneath the neon light fixtures hanging from the ceiling. Noah knew that Mrs. Webb was married to Joseph Webb, a sawyer employed by Black Dog Lumber Co.

Noah stood before Mrs. Webb at her desk. She was dressed in a conservative matching brown jacket and skirt, and she had a smile for Noah. Noah said in a feeble voice, "Can I talk to you about something?

It involves my private life and needs to stay that way. Are you OK with that?"

"Of course. What is it?"

"I have a little bit of gold that I want to sell. Can I sell it to the bank, and if I do, do I have to tell them where I got it? Also, if they do buy it, do I have to leave the money in that bank, and if I do, how do I get to use it?"

The astonished Mrs. Webb said, "Oh, Noah, I can help you, but why can't your Uncle Willis help you?"

Noah looked around the room and then said, "Uncle Willis left me some time ago. I'm getting along just fine, but I need to ask how to do things once in a while. Will you help me?"

"Of course I will help you. But, Noah, there is something personal to you that we must discuss."

"OK."

"Do the folks at the Department of Human Services know you are living alone?"

"Yes, and they visit me more than I like since Uncle Willis left. I have had some difficult meetings with my caseworker, Mary Edison. They don't like it, and I'm so difficult to deal with, they say they have me under review. I've been under review for months. I think they are waiting for me to stumble big time, and then they'll move on me. I'm not going to stumble."

"Noah, as your teacher, I'm thinking I have some responsibility to you beyond the classroom. Tell me how you are living and what your day is like."

"Well, I live in a one room shack, I keep it clean, I'm not messy, I do my grocery shopping, cook my meals, study at home, pay my bills, and try to do what is right. I thought I needed someone, but I don't."

Shaking her head, surprised at what she had just walked into, and looking at Noah, she said, "I need to talk to DHS and it will help if I let them know I'm your teacher keeping an eye on you beyond the classroom."

"I guess I understand that. Please let me know what you can do."

Noah left, and Mrs. Webb walked to the school office and phoned DHS and, having introduced herself, talked to Mary Edison.

"Will you talk to me about Noah North?"

"Yes," said a surprised Mary.

"You know he's living alone."

"Do we ever. And he's not going to have it any other way. We just now finished a multiple-person examination of his case, and we're leaving him alone for now. He can only get better as time wears on, but if he screws up, we're moving in. I'm going to make an extraordinary request. Will you please keep Noah's personal living circumstance to yourself? I really believe it is in his best interest and my colleagues agree with me."

"Have you told him?"

"Mrs. Webb, I have a visit planned for tomorrow. I'm looking forward to it. I must say, he's the most unusual, responsible young man any of us have ever encountered."

The next morning, Noah was at school early. Mrs. Webb motioned Noah to her desk.

"I talked to Mary Edison, and I'm good to help you this one time. I need to find out if there is a way to help you on a regular basis."

Martha Webb put a hand on Noah's shoulder. "You're getting a visit from Mary Edison today."

Noah said, "Thank you, I am really happy you talked to her. But, Mrs. Webb, about this business of mine, you can't tell anyone. My gold is mine and always has been, and you, Uncle Willis, and Mr. Zimmerman are the only people that know about my gold, and they know very little. So, can you tell me what to do?"

"Noah"—Mrs. Webb was looking directly at Noah—"the bank will redeem your gold and in return will pay you, and if you want to keep what you need and leave the rest in the bank for safe keeping, you can do that. What you have left in the bank, you can take out as you need it. However, your age might be a problem when it comes to withdrawing the money left in the bank. If that is a problem, we'll do what we can to solve it."

Martha Webb had known since the first week of Noah's attendance in her fourth grade class that Noah was not the typical fourth grader. There was something important missing. He was a loner with few friends, at the end of the school day no one ever picked him up, and he quickly disappeared, apparently to his home, wherever that was. He was intelligent and perceptive and, something made her think, maybe a little shrewd. His first report card did not surprise her. She knew from Noah's first week that every subject would be an A, and it was. She would help this mystery child.

Noah walked directly home after school, and Mary Edison of DHS arrived at four o'clock.

Noah invited her in. Mary saw that his home was neat and clean.

"Noah, asking your teacher to help you and having her interested in your welfare is a huge plus in our decision not to interfere in your life. Treasure that friendship."

"You didn't have to tell me that."

"You're right, I didn't need to say that. This visit is routine only. I'm leaving, but I'll continue to see you on a regular basis."

"I'm good with that. In the meantime, I'll try to stay out of trouble."

ELEVEN

Martha Webb and Noah North walked into the Rock City National Bank. Noah had some sinkers in a cloth sack. It was late afternoon, and Noah saw six other customers in the bank. He looked around and saw two women at a granite counter helping customers from behind a fence-like barrier. There were men sitting at desks at the far end of the room behind a short, polished wood fence. This was Noah's first time in a bank, and he marveled that everything was in one big room beneath a very high ceiling. Then he looked at that big steel door at the other end of the room, thinking: I bet that's where they keep the money.

Mrs. Webb took Noah by his free hand and led him to Wilson Marston's desk behind the little wood fence. He wore a dark business suit and matching tie with a white shirt. Marston had been with the bank for fifteen years. He liked his customers and they liked him. He was good at business development but not so good at managing commercial loans. He was adored by his high school sweetheart wife. He had two popular children attending Rock City schools.

Wilson said, "Hello Martha," and invited them to sit down in the two chairs in front of his desk.

Martha said, "This is one of my students, Noah North, and he has some business to transact with you."

Martha nudged Noah, who sat up in his chair and said, "I have some gold I want to sell," and he emptied the sack of sinkers on Mr. Marston's desk.

"My goodness, Martha, what's going on here?"

"He wants to redeem his gold for cash, which you know he's required to do."

"OK. But we need to know if this is gold, and I can confirm that. There is a new gadget called a spectrometer that is now available to banks. We also have the old nitric acid test for gold. Noah, bring your sinkers and follow me. You must always keep a watchful eye on your gold." Mr. Marston carried with him a record keeping book. He asked another bank employee sitting at a nearby desk to accompany him. They walked to a small room that Mr. Marston unlocked. The room was empty except for a table with a black box and a scale sitting on it.

Noah watched Mr. Marston place one sinker in the small box-like device that was about a foot square. Then he moved a couple of switches and looked at a small lighted screen built into the top of the device.

Mr. Marston said, "This thing is an XRF spectrometer, and it will tell me if a metal substance is gold and how pure it is." He squinted at the screen's readout and then announced, "That sinker is indeed gold and is 98.3518 percent pure, and that's plenty good." All of Noah's sinkers tested the same percent gold.

Mr. Marston then placed all of the sinkers on the complicated-looking scale and announced, "That is troy 41.1435 ounces. Noah, there is something about this business that I must explain to you. Gold is not weighed at sixteen ounces per pound. Sixteen ounces per pound is an avoirdupois ounce. The weight of gold is measured by the troy ounce, which is twelve ounces per pound. This does not mean you will be paid less per pound. The weighing system is just different. Also, gold is almost twice the weight of lead, so your one-ounce sinker is actually slightly less than two ounces. I know this is confusing, and I'll tell Martha about this so that she can hopefully assure you that we are treating you fairly."

They returned to Marston's desk, where Martha had remained seated. The other banker removed printed forms from a drawer in a side cabinet, slipped carbon paper between the three forms, and filled in the numerous blank spaces. Mr. Marston and the other banker then signed the form with copies.

Mr. Marston sat down, used his new handheld calculator, and said, "At $35 an ounce, we owe Noah $1,440.02. How old is Noah?"

Martha knew this was coming and said, "He is nine years old, exceptionally bright, and knows exactly what he is doing. He wants to leave his money in a savings account in your bank and take some with him. Can you do that?"

"He should really have a guardian."

"I believe that he has no family—maybe grandparents, but they wouldn't take him when his mother died, and his Uncle Willis has disappeared and is untrustworthy. So what can we do?"

Marston looked at Martha and said, "Except under some circumstances, a contract with a minor is usually unenforceable by either party. But if there is such a contract, neither party will be allowed to commit a fraud against the other party. Here's what I'll do: If he has any more gold, the bank will buy it, actually *has* to buy it, and most of the money from the sale can go in his savings account. We'll agree that he can walk out with not more than $100. If he wants money from his savings account, you must countersign the withdrawal request. If I believe the withdrawal is improper, I will not allow it. In the meantime, get a guardian appointed, because this plan does not yet follow bank rules!" Marston then had Noah write his address and sign the printed form that he and the other banker had signed. Noah was given a copy, and then he and Martha left the bank. Noah also had the receipt for the gold he'd sold. Martha was frustrated, and Noah had never felt so rich. He now had a little black book in his hand that said he had $1,340.02 on deposit. He also had $100 in his pocket. He thought, This does it. DHS is not going to control me. I may have the means to better my life and living conditions. I don't know how that will work, but I'm gonna do it myself. I need to tell Mary Edison about this.

When leaving the bank, Noah looked into the room behind an enormous open vault door. He said, "What's all that in there?"

"Well," Martha said, "that is a room full of safe-deposit boxes where bank customers can keep their valuables. The bank keeps its money in there."

Noah asked, "May I call you Martha when you're not being my teacher?"

"Yes."

"Thank you, Martha, for everything. I'll try not to annoy you again."

TWELVE

The law office of Morgan Reynolds was located in Grants Pass, Oregon, in the second story of a forty-year-old two-story building with a bank occupying the entire first floor. The law office was a corner office with old double-hung windows on two sides overlooking the streets below. File cabinets lined a wall behind two secretarial desks. Two other walls were lined with glass-fronted bookcases filled with law books. The high ceiling and wood paneling made the waiting area comfortable. A secretary walked into Mr. Morgan's office and handed him a tax statement from the Big River County treasurer showing Noah North as owner.

Reynolds looked at it and muttered, "Crap. I knew I shouldn't have agreed to receive that. Did he ever give us his address?"

"No, so shall I send it to the address on the statement?"

Reynolds nodded. "Yes. Make a note of that address."

It was November 1969. Noah was now eleven years old and in the sixth grade, leading his class in grades but not involved in school activities and not very sociable. One afternoon when he arrived at his shack, he saw a letter in the old mailbox nailed next to the door. The only thing that was ever in that box was junk, but this looked real and it was. A letter from Morgan Reynolds, a lawyer! He thought, What have I done?

He opened the envelope and out came a letter, a deed, and a tax statement for $595.00. The statement said the property would be sold for nonpayment of taxes unless the taxes were paid by November 15. Noah shook his head. Someone has made a mistake. He read the letter from the lawyer, and it explained the purpose of the deed and the statement. Noah didn't understand much, but it had his name on it, and the part that seemed to describe the property stated something about . . . the northwest corner of the southwest quarter of Section 11 . . . "Do I own this place? I guess I do, but really?" He said those words out loud to the sky. He gave the deed a closer look. His mother's signature was on it. He'd check with Martha.

The next day after school, Noah went to Martha and showed her the letter and deed.

After perusing the documents, Martha said, "You need a guardian like Mr. Marston suggested."

"What's that?" Noah asked.

"There is no lawyer in Rock City, so we'll go to Mr. Reynolds in Grants Pass. He will explain what that is and why you need a guardian. But the first thing we need to do is go see Mr. Marston and withdraw $595 and pay these taxes."

The next day after school, Martha and Noah explained the problem to Mr. Marston, and they left with a cashier's check for $595 payable to the county treasurer. Martha mailed it. Martha discovered that Noah's property taxes were about $150 a year.

Two days later they were sitting before Mr. Reynolds, and he explained guardianship and the necessity. Noah partially understood.

Mr. Reynolds asked, "Who will be guardian?"

Martha, while looking at the ceiling and fearing what was to come, spoke. "There is no one in his family that gives a damn, so you tell me."

Looking squarely at Martha he asked, "Will you do it?"

Noah turned to Martha with a plaintive look and said, "Whatever the guardian is, please do it."

She quietly said, "I knew this would happen. Yes, I'll be your guardian, whatever that really means."

Mr. Reynolds explained, "It will be a guardianship of Noah's estate, meaning property and assets he owns. You will see to it that his property is cared for and protected. Annually you are required to make an accounting to the court appointing you, showing that all receipts and expenditures have been accounted for and were proper. You give me the receipts and expenditures, and I will do the accounting document.

"One more thing. Noah's closest relatives will be notified of your application to be appointed guardian. Do you know who they might be?"

Noah stood up, surprised. "The Porter family that lives near here is my mother's family. According to Uncle Willis, my mother told him that my father's family lived in New York. My grandmother, Susan Porter, can probably tell you more."

"Mrs. Webb, I'll call you when I have things ready for a signature."

Mr. Reynolds then explained that the guardianship funds would pay his fee, compensate the guardian for her services, and pay guardianship expenses and a fidelity bond premium, but all subject to prior approval of a probate judge.

Mr. Reynolds got up and sat in the empty chair next to Noah and said, "I know this all sounds strange and maybe unnecessary, but it is essential to protect you and your property. There is another kind of guardian that can control you and your activities, but we are not doing that. We want you to live the life you want and to continue to be the good citizen you are. We still have some things to do for you with the Department of Human Services, and that might not be easy. I have to get Martha officially appointed, so don't do anything with your property in the meantime."

Neither Martha nor Mr. Reynolds knew what Noah had buried in his yard.

THIRTEEN

Martin Groves, nephew of the jeweler Zimmerman, and Jason Hanley, whose father owned Hanley Real Estate, were seated together in a booth in the Rock City Cafe. The booth afforded privacy. The restaurant had a counter, booths, and tables. The chairs had worn fabric seat coverings, and a counter with stools was in front of an open kitchen where the cook could be seen working. The big windows facing the street were a little foggy. It was a good place to visit and eat. One waitress was old and the other young and pretty, and the boys knew her. She brought them each a Pepsi.

Jason waited until the waitress was out of earshot and said, "My dad wants that forty acres."

"Yeah, but I thought he was going to pick it up at a tax foreclosure sale or something like that," Martin said.

"He was going to do that, but—" Jason paused as a couple walked by the booth. He lowered his voice to continue. "But it turns out someone paid the taxes. So it's time for plan B."

Martin frowned. "What's plan B?"

"Some woman named North owned it. Obviously Noah's mom, right? Well, she died several years ago, and Noah's there now. So Dad thinks we should convince him that the property is worthless and should be sold. So . . ."

"So . . . what?"

"So maybe we could antagonize him on the property, and then maybe he'd want to sell and live someplace else."

"Man, I don't know." Martin shook his head. "My Uncle Abe said the place was a gold mine, but I was all over that place when it was vacant, and there ain't a gold mine there. There's nothing but an awful shack in a little clearing, and the rest of the property is kind of rocky ground that slopes off to the north. That hill on the north has nothing but a bunch of old red cedar trees on it that are hard to get to, and I don't know why anyone would want them. Some guy by the name of Buster owned it, but he was never home. Anyway, I don't want anything to do with this." He fixed Jason with a stare and added, "You shouldn't either, so count me out."

Jason knew when his father was serious about something, and his father was definitely serious about somehow getting that property. He thought, Maybe a threat of some kind. It must be scary to live alone in a shack at the edge of town. Maybe a fire or rocks through windows. He is only ten or eleven years old, and this shouldn't be too hard. I think I'll just tell him that to be safe, it is time for him to live some other place.

After school recessed for Thanksgiving, Jason Hanley saw Noah North on the sidewalk in front of the grade school. He walked up to Noah and said, "I think for your own good, you should move from Rock City."

Noah replied, "Who the hell are you?"

"I'm actually doing you a favor," said Jason.

Noah thought, I've been ignored and pushed around my whole life, and this big guy scares me. He's not going to bully me. Uncle Willis told me that most bullies are cowards. Noah said, "I'm not going anyplace. Get away from me."

Jason was not surprised at the response—what else could he say?

Noah knew that he must talk to Martha about Jason Hanley. He wondered if Martha was now his guardian, whatever that was. He would need her.

After Noah ate a can of chili and drank a glass of milk for dinner, he walked in the dark to Martha Webb's house. It was a well-kept typical 1920s one-story bungalow with a well-lit big porch. The yard was neat and orderly, just like Martha. Martha answered the door to find Noah standing under the porch light. She invited him into a pleasant living room filled with comfortable furnishings. She knew he would not be there or bother her if it wasn't urgent and important.

Noah, not at ease, said, "There's a big kid named Jason Hanley who has threatened me, wanting me to leave my place or this town, or something."

That was not the only reason Noah needed Martha's help.

Martha said, "I'll have a word with his father."

Noah said, "This Jason thing is bad enough, but I'm not receiving the monthly $150 that Mary Edison at DHS gave to me. It is paid to Uncle Willis, he is no longer here, and I know he's using it for himself."

Noah eased himself into one of Martha's chairs and quietly, almost to himself, said, "How can all of this stuff be happening to me? All I want to do is eat, sleep, go to school, try to earn a little money, take care of myself without help, and maybe have a friend sometime."

Martha leaned over and hugged Noah in his chair and said, "I'm going to help you."

Noah said, "I'm going to help myself as much as I can. I think I understand you being my guardian a little better. I know I will need your help."

Martha looked at Noah and reflected on this grade-school student, and she surmised that he had used his intelligence to know that his problems might get solved.

Noah said, "I feel beat down, but even though I am only eleven years old, I feel stronger in at least one way. I'll take care of the bully thing myself! The other stuff, you'll have to help me."

Martha said, "Come on, Noah, I am taking you home." She drove Noah to his shack, and before Noah moved in his seat to leave, Martha motioned for him to stay seated.

"Noah, you must call Mary Edison and tell her Willis is keeping all of your DHS $150.00 monthly payment. I will also call her."

"I'll do that."

Martha waited until Noah was inside and his lights had come on. She left thinking, What a miserable, unhappy way to grow up. I'll see if DHS can place a foster parent with Noah. He won't move to a foster home, that's a certainty.

FOURTEEN

In December, Martha received a certified copy of her Letters of Guardianship for Noah Jeremiah North. The document was dated December 12, 1969. She was now his guardian and legally on a bank account with Noah. She was required to be in full control of that guardianship account. She left his name on the account to give him a sense of control. She was unable to get DHS to vary from their foster care rules and place a foster parent with Noah, so Noah was still alone, attending school, and otherwise he seemed OK. She did persuade DHS to pay to the guardianship account $150 per month to be used exclusively for Noah's care. She was not to be compensated from this benefit. It solved several problems.

Noah was feeding himself. That was nothing new. About once a month, after neglecting his clothes washing at home and accumulating a huge pile of dirty laundry, he took the laundry and coins to a laundromat. He hated sitting in that place, but it had a big, efficient washer and dryer. He had done that with his mother and then Willis.

It was March 1970 and school spring vacation was coming. No one was helping him. He was twelve years old. He knew where things were located in the grocery store, what tasted good, what was bad to eat, and how to conserve his money Martha gave him. That guy Jason had not bothered him, but he was still mindful of what Jason had said. Noah reflected on Jason's threat and decided that he was as ready as he could be.

The situation that bothered Noah was his stash of gold in buried jars. He remembered the safe-deposit boxes in the bank. He thought,

I'm a customer, I can keep my jars and sinkers in there. I'll ask my guardian. He smiled. What I need to do is turn those pebbles into sinkers so I know what I have and then put those sinkers in my bank. He went to the wood apple box where he kept the burner and crucible and sinker mold and decided to wait until the coming school vacation to change more of the gold into sinkers. He was shoving the box back under the counter when he heard a sound outside.

Noah had eaten dinner and it was dark. He walked to the front door of his shack, where his baseball bat was leaning against the doorjamb. He eased the door open, but there was no outside light and he couldn't see much. There was some ambient light from the stars and town lights and he stepped outside with his black painted bat in hand. He heard a shuffling sound to his left, and he moved to the corner of the shack and saw someone moving.

Noah yelled, "Get out of here."

The person moved quickly toward Noah and shoved Noah down on the ground. Noah immediately jumped to his feet, looking at the person, but couldn't see his face in the dark. The stranger came at Noah again, but Noah knew he had to stand in place and didn't move, and, as viciously as a twelve-year-old boy could swing a bat, he hit the stranger in the knee. When the stranger reached for his painful knee, Noah hit him with the bat on his cheek and again on the side of his head. The stranger went down and cried out softly while getting on his feet, running and limping off Noah's property. Noah was not quite certain that the stranger was Jason, but the next time he saw him he would know. He had surprised himself and the bat had felt good in his hand.

The next morning Noah stepped outside to see if he could determine what the stranger had been doing. Next to the shack to the right of the window he found a newspaper wadded up with dry brush and twigs piled on it. It was a real fire threat, and he suspected Jason had done it. Noah decided not to talk about it because he did not want a lot of people knowing his private life. Also, he did not want police or any strangers on his place looking around and thinking that he shouldn't be there by himself. This is my place. I want to stay here, and I don't want to be bothered, especially by a numbskull.

FIFTEEN

It was Friday, the last day of Noah's spring vacation. He had been very busy casting sinkers in the mold, and he had walked into the Rock City National Bank and straight to Mr. Marston's desk where, with a thud, he placed a heavy sock. Mr. Marston invited him to sit, and he did.

"What do we have here?" asked Mr. Marston.

"I have a sinker I want to sell, and I want to put the other sinkers in one of those safe-deposit boxes."

"You can redeem a sinker and you'll be paid cash, but it is illegal for an American, such as you, to store or possess gold."

"I don't want to sell. I like it better than money!"

I think this kid is too smart for his own good. I better call Martha.

"There's one hundred twenty-eight ounces in sinkers in that sock, so, if I can't own or possess my gold, buy those sinkers and give me $100 cash and put the rest in my account. You may never see me again with gold, and please don't tell anyone about this."

"You should know that the US Treasury Department is enforcing our gold laws with fines and jail sentences, so be careful."

Noah pondered. What does he know anyway? I still have nine buried jars of pebbles, and that is where they will stay.

Noah followed Mr. Marston and his colleague to a spectrometer in a room where Noah was eventually given a receipt for 255.4369 ounces of gold. Three of them signed the document recording the sale, the deposit of $8,940.29 to Noah's bank account, and the payment of $100 cash to Noah. Mr. Marston was having a phone conversation with Martha as Noah walked out of the bank with his receipt and $100 cash.

Noah heard him say, "Martha, there is something mysterious about this business with Noah. We just now paid him $8,940.29 for some gold sinkers. The kid is uncommonly adult like, and when leaving the bank, he grabbed a stack of old *Wall Street Journal*s. He said he needed them to start fires in his wood stove."

Martha said, "I believe that's why he first took them, but if I know Noah, he'll read some of them before burning them and soon start asking me about articles in the financial sections of the newspaper, advising where money should be invested."

Mr. Marston squirmed around in his chair. "Martha, how can a twelve-year-old do that?"

"Wilson, the word *precocious* falls short of describing this young man's drive. Between your paper's news articles and listings, he'll learn where to put his money. He has money to invest and will have more."

"Does he have friends? Is he involved in school activities? Does he have a hobby?"

"You have to understand that he is busy caring for every aspect of his life."

"He's getting to be more than a bank customer."

"Wilson, consider this. He wants to know what the president is doing about Vietnam because he doesn't want to end up in the army at that place."

"Does anything that affects his life get by him?"

"My guardianship of Noah could be interesting and it will be supervised to ensure that it's by the book. You need to know that Noah has been basically alone for the last four years. He is personally responsible for all of his needs, even his support."

"I'm only his banker, but if he wants non-banking advice, I'll accommodate him."

"You need to know that his Uncle Willis was using him and taking from him."

"Where's Uncle Willis?"

"A while back, Noah ran him off."

"A kid did that?"

"Noah is more of a force than is apparent."

"I obviously don't know much about my young customer."

"Wilson, I think Noah is being bullied by Jason Hanley for the purpose of driving Noah from his place and forcing him to sell. For what reason I know not. None of this needs to be public knowledge. You and your bank need to treat Noah's business with confidentiality in the highest sense. Noah likes his privacy. He probably never thought he would have to worry about privacy."

"Martha, you might be one of the best things that Noah has going for him, and I think he will soon know it."

SIXTEEN

January 5, 1970

Chief trust officer Wendall Dollar and Richard Johnston, the Shoreline Bank's legal counsel, a member of a thirty-person law firm, sat at the head of a large table in the conference room of the Shoreline Bank in Buffalo, New York. Wendall Dollar was five feet, six inches tall and overweight, he was never married, he knew the trust business, he wore rimless glasses, and he was fastidious in every aspect of his appearance, business, and personal life. His job was his life. Wendall did not like anything contentious. He hoped everything would go smoothly today. By the time the North Trust was settled, he might not like the trust business.

Lake Erie was plainly visible through the room's tinted windows. Also seated at the table were two of the beneficiaries of the Alexander Noah North Trust. Alexander North had made his fortune in the Great Lakes marine shipping business. He was an aggressive competitor hated by his business adversaries, and he was personally crusty and obnoxious to most of his family. Alexander died in December 1969 following six years of failing mental health. During those six years, North Marine, Inc., was mismanaged by senile Alexander and his grandson Thomas. Alexander remembered all of his bodily heirs in his trust signed and dated January 31, 1950. The Shoreline Bank's trust department was named trustee of Alexander's estate. On Alexander's death, his will placed all of his assets in his trust that then came to life, and Shoreline Bank took over.

Tricia, Alexander's second wife, whom he'd loved as much as life itself, had been receiving $3,000 per month directly from Alexander until she died in 1968. Thomas had been writing the checks to Tricia for Alexander, whose dementia never let him overlook Tricia. When Alexander died, his surviving sons or their descendants would share equally in the assets and accumulated income, and the trust would be closed. Those three children were Steven, Richard, and Buster. Steven had died childless in 1958 in a boating accident. Richard had died in 1959 and was survived by his two children: a daughter, Margo, and a son, Thomas. They would take their father's share equally.

Buster had left his family in 1950, joining the US Navy during the Korean War. When discharged from the navy in 1956, he visited his father Alexander North and brothers Steven and Richard in Buffalo, and then all contact ended. His mother, Grace, died a month prior to Buster's enlistment in the navy. She had been a firewall between Buster and his intolerant father. Buster knew nothing about his father's estate plan, and neither did anyone else except his trustee, his lawyer, and Thomas. Buster disliked his father, who didn't nurture him or treat him like a son, even after Buster lost his mother. That is what caused Buster to leave and join the navy. Disparaging words coming from his father about almost everything Buster did or didn't do alienated Buster. The same reproachful words were passing between Richard and Steven and their father, but they stayed, with the relationship finally mellowing.

The 1956 visit by Buster to his family in Buffalo was unpleasant. Before departing, he told Richard and Steven that he would be living someplace in southern Oregon. A sailor buddy had told him it was a great place to live.

The heirs in the room were Richard's daughter, twenty-two-year-old Margo North, and his twenty-nine-year-old son, Thomas North. Their father, Richard, hadn't said anything about the size of the trust assets because he didn't know. Thomas knew. Richard's incompetence in failing to advise his father to replace or rebuild depreciated marine equipment was a mistake. The $3,000 monthly payment to Tricia reduced cash and securities to extinction. The only asset left of any value was the twelve thousand shares of North Marine, Inc.

Trustee Dollar then said, "North Marine, Inc., is in decline, has been for years, and, if you want me to sell it, it may be difficult." Dollar then added, "I can't sell North Marine shares piecemeal. No buyer would do that. We need one hundred percent of the shares ready for sale with consent of the owners."

Margo asked, knowing the answer, "Steven had no heirs, so aren't there just two beneficiaries, my father's children and Buster or his children?"

Attorney Johnston said, "That is correct."

Margo sat up in her chair and asked, "Is Buster dead or alive? Does he have children? We're talking about half of these trust assets floating around in the air. Looks like someone should find out."

The trustee, Wendall Dollar, hurriedly said, "We are already looking."

The attorney Richard Johnston added, "We shouldn't distribute shares to anyone until we find Buster or his bodily heir, if he has one. If he has not been heard from for seven years, we can start a procedure to legally presume he's dead. If he has no child, his heirs will be his closest relatives, namely Margo and Thomas."

Thomas murmured to himself, "Holy crap."

Trustee Dollar said, "You of course probably know that the body of the trust is the corporate shares of North Marine, Inc. North Marine, Inc., continues to struggle profit-wise. It has been poorly managed since the onset of Alexander's illness. Since Alexander's death, I have had difficulty hiring competent management. I've given some thought to selling the company by sale of all outstanding shares. If a buyer doesn't show, I would merely liquidate its assets. The heirs need to review those issues and tell me what you think. I want you to know that I have recently hired a person with experience in the Great Lakes marine shipping business, and he thinks he can make North Marine, Inc., profitable. If that happens, we will have plenty of time to decide the fate of North Marine, Inc., namely keep it or sell it."

The meeting ended with two people pondering their good fortune. When Margo and Thomas stopped at Margo's car, instead of saying goodbye, Thomas said, "If Buster North is dead and has no children, his share will be ours. Maybe we should do something about that."

Margo carefully examined Thomas and his spooky suggestion and said, "You are not doing anything, and I am not doing anything remotely linked to what you are suggesting. You got that?"

Thomas had been untruthful with Margo too often, and she hated herself for believing it, but Thomas, with major stakes involved, might be corruptible.

Thomas, turning and walking to his car, said, "You are not as bright as you think you are."

Margo replied loudly, "I do know the difference between right and wrong! Apparently you don't."

Margo had reason to believe that Thomas was concealing something. She did not know, and neither did anyone else, that Buster had told her father and Uncle Steven that he would be living in Oregon. Evidently it was not of interest to anyone at the time and that information went no further, although Thomas had asked his father about Buster. Richard had told him that Buster was in Oregon.

SEVENTEEN

The 1969–70 school year ended. Noah remained top student in his class, but he never thought about that. He recalled the Monday after spring vacation when he passed Jason while walking to school. Jason had four butterfly Band-Aids stretched across his left cheek and a big lump on the side of his head, and he was limping. Noah had said, "You dumb shit!" Jason remained silent. Noah was acquiring some foul language from the playground boys.

He had been busy since the beginning of the summer vacation remodeling and repairing the shack. Martha helped him hire a roofer to fix a leak.

Noah heard the roofer say to his laborer, "I don't know *why* I'm doing this job. This entire piece-of-shit building needs to be torched." Noah mused, Well, that's exactly what I saw Jason doing. Noah was making another improvement. He had cut and nailed up some plywood panels covering exposed two-by-four wall studs. Martha insisted that he replace his ancient washing machine and buy a modern washer and dryer. An electrician and plumber had to be hired. Noah had never lived in a place with a television set. He now had a Motorola TV sitting where the roof leaked, one of the reasons the leaky roof was being fixed.

Late one warm afternoon the roofer shouted, "There's someone here to see you."

Noah walked outside with a hammer still in hand, and a nice-looking young man wearing a trim baseball cap with the name Black

Dog Lumber Co. on it said, "Hi, my name is Bud Cooper. Could I speak to the owner of this property?"

"I am the owner," replied Noah.

"No, what I mean is, I would like to speak to the person in charge of the property."

"I'm the person in charge," said Noah.

"You sure?"

"I'm sure."

"OK then, can I talk to you about your timber?"

"What timber?"

"That timber over there on the downslope to the north."

Noah said, "I've never really been over there. All I can see from here is a bunch of red cedar trees and red cedar treetops."

"Well, come on, let's look," insisted Cooper. "How old are you anyway?"

"I'm twelve."

"You sure you're in charge here?"

They walked north into approximately thirty acres of forest. Noah didn't know the boundary lines, but Cooper knew generally. It was park like under the canopy of big trees with little underbrush, with a few long-limbed wild rhododendrons recently out of bloom. Surprisingly, there were numerous small snowdrifts remaining from heavy winter snows slowly melting in the shade of the tall trees.

Cooper said, "See those snowdrifts? That happens on north slopes, and their moisture accounts for the size and number of trees in here."

"Why are you here?" asked Noah.

"I buy a particular species of log and standing timber for the Black Dog mill, which mills the logs into lumber for the Ticonderoga Pencil Company and a company that makes cedar chests. The tree is incense cedar, also known as pencil cedar. There's not much of it, so it is a valuable tree. This is a very nice stand of *Calocedrus decurrens*."

Noah flinched and said, "Huh, I'm not so sure that I want to sell my trees, whatever they are, but I'll talk to Martha."

"Who is Martha?"

"Never mind. What are these trees worth?"

Cooper said, "Well, there are about thirty acres of good pencil cedar in this stand, but I need to walk through your little forest to tell you what we would pay if you wanted to sell."

Cooper seemed like a good guy, and Noah left him in the forest and walked back to his shack. He'd talk to Martha about Cooper. Cooper cruised Noah's timber, counting and measuring trees, thinking, That kid is in charge?

Noah's summer of '70 was over. He had improved his living conditions, he'd become aware of some valuable trees on his land, his gold pebbles were still buried, Martha was helping him with his banking business and DHS benefits, and he was twelve years old and in the seventh grade, looking forward to every school lunch, the only meal he didn't have to prepare. Martha's guardianship gave her control of all of Noah's assets, and she was very careful to inform Noah of every transaction she intended to make with Noah's funds. Martha moved funds from Noah's savings to a guardianship checking account, and she paid his monthly expenses.

Martha and Noah were together in the Rock City National Bank when Noah quickly walked over to a table in the customer waiting area and grabbed up part of a stack of newspapers and walked back to Martha.

"What was that about?" asked Martha.

"They throw them away, so I might as well have them. I see the weekly *Rock City Newspaper*, and there is not much in it. These papers have everything, but I don't understand most of it. I am starting to understand some things that are going on in our country, but much of it is hard to understand. Besides, I need the paper to start fires. But, Martha, I need to talk to you."

"What is it?"

They sat down in the customer waiting area. It was open, with cushioned chairs and plenty of room for private conversation. No one was paying any attention to them.

"Martha, there are too many things bothering me. I'm afraid I'll mess things up. Someone says there are valuable trees on my land and I think they want me to sell them. I have a feeling that DHS will be told by someone that I shouldn't be living alone, and Mr. Marston is telling me to sell my gold, but how does he know I have any left? It's bad enough living alone without help. Also, I don't understand what I'm reading in the newspapers. There are articles about the government changing rules about buying and selling gold. Also, are we in a war with a place called Vietnam? I see it on my new TV, but it is so awful it can't be real. Just tell me that DHS is not going to take me away, and nobody is getting my trees."

Martha thought, Wow, I really don't have time for this, but I'll make time. Martha looked straight into Noah's wide-open eyes and said with the grit of a mother lion, "I'll never let DHS take you away, and no one is getting your trees! I'll talk to you about that other stuff another time." Noah was relieved and thanked Martha, but he would keep reading those papers and try to figure out that other stuff himself.

Jonathan Hanley sat in his office in the Hanley Real Estate building, an old one-story frame building expertly repaired and remodeled into an attractive commercial structure. From his partially glassed office, Hanley could see his firm's desks, file cabinets, map table, chairs, copy machine, and two typewriters. A couple of salespersons sat busy at their desks. Sitting in front of Hanley was Bud Cooper.

Hanley, with a friendly smile crafted with nefarious intent, said, "How are we doing with the Noah North timber? We should make every effort to acquire that timber. The price of timber isn't going down. So really, where are we on that?"

Cooper said, "We may be no place. The kid told me he won't sell, but he could change his mind when I tell what we'll pay."

Hanley cautioned, "Remember, the price must be carefully set so that on resale to Black Dog Lumber Co., there will be a nice profit for us.

"You know, Bud, your employment with Black Dog has been an exceptional thing for us. Landowners seem to favor selling to a private individual rather than to a mill. They hope we'll do something nice with the land, such as not remove the timber, and they think that because of our elusive purchase conversation about the beauty of the property. We do these purchase and sale deals infrequently, but the mill will continue to know nothing about our arrangement, and they will get their timber. Are we good?"

"We're good, but your son Jason may have messed up any kind of a deal with Noah North. You do know that when Noah caught him messing around his place, Jason charged at Noah, but the kid picked up a baseball bat and beat the crap out of Jason. If we want the North property, we may have to go through a different buyer. Better give that serious thought."

"Wait, wait, wait," said Hanley. "That plan won't work with the kid. He's reluctant to sell the timber, and he certainly won't sell the land *and* the timber. Something needs to be done to motivate him to sell."

Cooper thought about that for a while and said, "I was nice to the kid and have some sort of rapport with him. I'll see what I can do. There is around $30,000 worth of standing cedar on that place."

EIGHTEEN

Bud Cooper was standing at Noah's front door, knocking lightly. It was the first Saturday in December, two weeks since meeting with Hanley, and a decent day for a visit and a talk. The sky was clear, the temperature cool, and the sun warm on his back. He had delayed this visit in hopes that events of the recent past had faded in Noah's young mind. Noah opened the door, a little surprised to see Cooper.

They exchanged hellos, and Cooper said, "We are still interested in your cedar, and there are some things about owning timber that you should consider, just as all timber owners do. Much of the land around you is logged-off timber land highly subject to forest fire. It's a long shot, but you could lose your cedar in a forest fire. A way to avoid that would be to sell the timber. You don't need to believe or rely on what I say. Take your time and talk to whoever you need to and let me know what you want to do."

Noah said, "I think I'll do that." Goodbyes were said and Bud Cooper left in his old Ford pickup.

Days passed and Noah was busy with school and doing the things necessary to live even half a life. He constantly mulled over Cooper's advice. He thought, I really don't want to sell anything, but I better talk to someone who knows about this stuff. Martha can help me with an answer for Cooper. She's a smart lady and probably knows the right timber owner to consult.

Noah called Martha and recited the Cooper conversation and the issue about fire danger to his trees. She would ask a timber owner about selling because of fire danger. He was particularly interested in knowing about DHS bothering him about living alone. She did not say anything to him about those things. He would ask again.

There were few articles in the old newspapers that seemed worthwhile, but two were of interest. President Johnson didn't want to keep the gold standard that President Roosevelt had put in place whereby Americans couldn't privately buy and sell gold, and President Johnson didn't like spending millions on the war in Vietnam that was killing Americans. Noah read another article about boys graduating from high school and being taken into the army without their consent, and it startled him. What is that about? Am I gonna end up in the army? That can't be right! He knew it was right, but he also believed it was wrong.

At twelve years old, he knew he wouldn't let important things slide away. It was December 1970, and he was sitting in school at his desk, thinking he had seen Martha frequently on the walkways common to the grade school and to Noah's middle school and she had said nothing about his concerns. That very day in the hall she said to Noah, "I need to be at the bank after school, so please meet me there."

They were seated in the customer area, and following a very friendly interchange of sincere niceties, Martha said, "I recently talked with Mary Edison, your DHS caseworker, and DHS is not really interested in anyone who is surviving adequately and not in any kind of trouble, probably because they have more urgent business. Mary is to discuss your case with other DHS employees only if there is a substantial change in your living circumstance. So keep things as they are, and even as young as you are, you'll be OK for now."

"Well, that's good news, but what's with those articles about changing the gold laws?"

Martha, in a compassionate manner, slowly examining Noah, thought, Here's a twelve-year-old worrying about the gold market. I don't know any adults that even know about the gold market. Martha responded out loud by saying, "Yes, Congress is considering changing back to private ownership of gold."

"Is that good or bad?" asked Noah.

Martha said, "I do not know. Just keep reading old newspapers and you'll know sooner or later."

Noah decided he had bothered Martha enough, so he wouldn't ask about the Vietnam War, but he did have to ask, "Are any of the boys in school talking about having to go in the army?"

"I have not heard any boys talking about that, and you are way too young to be concerned about you and the army," Martha admonished.

"I am also wondering about my cedar timber."

Martha said, "I talked to a timber land owner in Klamath County, and he said that fire is always a danger but usually not a reason to sell. He also said that there has not been a forest fire in our county for thirty years. It is an issue without a perfect answer, so why don't you hang on to your timber and land and let those fellows find cedar elsewhere."

"I can do that," replied Noah.

Martha thoughtfully said, "I'm giving you this advice as your guardian, and as your guardian, I would not sell any of your timber or land unless you agreed or desperately needed money."

NINETEEN

January 1971 swept by in several snowstorms. The elevation of Rock City was 1,100 feet, and it caught considerable moisture during winter months. The snow didn't last long on open ground, but it held on in Noah's little forest, aiding growth and lessening fire danger.

Noah was on his way to school when he saw Jason Hanley alight from his father's Mercedes sedan in front of the high school. Noah's brain skipped into high gear. Jason is not in school so what is he doing here? I can only think of one reason that Jason did what he did—it was to scare me into selling. For some reason Mr. Hanley wants my place, but I don't know why. I'm sure Jason's father put him up to that stunt at my house. I wonder if Mr. Hanley knows that Bud Cooper is trying to buy my trees for the Black Dog Lumber Co. All of them are wasting their time.

The 1970–71 school year was the first time that Noah had more than one teacher. He and his classmates moved from room to room, each with a different teacher with a different subject. It was a change, and Noah liked it and continued to excel.

Martha called Noah early one morning and asked him to meet her after school in the grade school parking area. Noah was waiting beside Martha's car when she arrived with her car keys in hand. "Please get in." He did, and as Martha drove, she said, "I've overlooked some things as your guardian. You need to file state and federal tax returns for last year, and I'm pretty sure you are not eligible for the $150 monthly benefit from DHS. I hope you understand that we need to be very careful about these things. I want you to go with me to my tax guy. He is a CPA and knows what he is doing. Do you have a Social Security number?"

"Don't think so. I'm guessing I'll be getting one."

Noah was sitting in a big chair next to Martha, facing CPA Roy Sang across his desk. Martha opened the conversation, saying, "Roy, this is Noah North, and Noah, this is Mr. Sang. Roy will help us with your taxes."

Martha explained her guardianship of Noah, Noah's missing family, and her teacher relationship to Noah. She carefully asked Roy if he had any kind of relationship with Jonathan or Jason Hanley, Bud Cooper, or Black Dog Lumber Co., professionally or socially. He said he knew who they were but had no business with any of them.

Martha cautioned, "None of those people or anyone at that mill, or anyone for that matter, can know anything about our business here. My husband is a sawyer in that mill, but he knows nothing about Noah's business. As you may find out, I am not being paranoid about this. I am nervous about something that someday I, as Noah's guardian, or Noah himself, on his personal returns, might have to reveal."

Sang said, "Martha, I couldn't be in business if confidentiality went out the window."

"OK, for starters, Noah has no income except for sales of gold bullion. He sold $1,440 in 1969 and $8,940.29 in 1970. There will be more gold sales. He has been receiving $150 monthly from DHS. He lives alone, and he's my ward and student and my friend, so I sort of look after him. DHS overlooks this non-troublesome situation and gives him a benefit through me as his guardian. He also owns forty acres with valuable timber land and a shack of a house. Also, Noah will be thirteen years old on February 28, and I think he has never had a birthday party, birthday cake, or a birthday present! We have to acknowledge and record his gold sales and source in complete confidence, so don't even think about asking Noah about his gold! I'd prefer it if your office help never sees his tax returns." After a brief silence, Martha said, "Roy, there is one more thing you need to do. Please find out if Noah is actually eligible for the DHS benefit. A hypothetical question to them would probably do it. They know who my ward is, and I don't want to be the one to stir them up on this."

Roy had leaned back in his fancy leather swivel chair, trying to assimilate what he had heard, and said, "Holy crap, did you make that up?"

"You can't make up a yarn like that," Martha insisted.

Sang leaned forward in his swivel chair and asked, "OK, Noah, do you have a Social Security number?"

"No."

"I'll help you get one. Do you have a birth certificate?"

"Not that I know of."

"Where were you born?"

"Grants Pass, I think."

Looking at Martha, Roy asked, "Does he have a receipt for the 1969 and 1970 gold sales? I'll do returns for both years and spread the 1970 income over the past five years, and there shouldn't be any taxes to pay, but returns need to be filed."

"Yes, he has receipts. You will be paid from Noah's funds by me as his guardian, so send the statement to me and see to it that you are as charitable with your time and charges as I am."

"Martha, come back in two days with Noah and those receipts, and if you don't have his birth certificate, I'll have an application for a Social Security number ready for signature."

When leaving, Noah asked, "Is he Chinese?"

"Maybe a little. I think his Chinese ancestors probably built the west end of the transcontinental railroad."

Martha dropped Noah off at his bicycle in the school parking area.

TWENTY

The Arcade Tavern and Pool Hall was filled with after-work-before-going-home beer drinkers, mostly men. Two women were seated by themselves and not looking for company, and they were not going to get any. Two pool tables were in use, the bar was crowded. There were a few empty tables, and it was noisy. Jonathan Hanley and Bud Cooper were seated at a table, deep in conversation. Earlier the tavern owner, Bill Walstrom, had served them beers and heard the name Noah North mentioned. Now he was serving them two more beers. He again heard the name Noah North as well as the words "the kid." Walstrom knew about a little kid, Noah North, living alone. Willis Porter was one of Walstrom's beer drinking customers and had told Walstrom about Noah. Walstrom also recalled hearing some gossip about the kid living alone and hitting Jason Hanley with a baseball bat.

Walstrom thought, Why are these two guys talking about the most vulnerable kid in town? Jonathan Hanley isn't interested in anything but real property, and Cooper is a log buyer, so are they really interested in this kid? Anyway, knowing a little about Hanley, whatever they may be planning can't be for the kid's benefit. I'm going to talk to Martha Webb again; she seems to care about the kid.

Bill Walstrom was well known and well liked by his customers and by people who actually knew him and consequently were his friends. His tavern business and the lesser qualities of some of his customers didn't put him on a glimmering pedestal for most of the townsfolk. Twenty years ago he arrived from someplace on the East Coast with money in his pocket. He was a young man. He paid cash for Walt's

Place, a trashy mess of a bar that sold all types of alcoholic beverages and terrible food. Walstrom remodeled the joint, installed a modern kitchen, built new restrooms, furnished the place, and served only beer and wine.

No one in Rock City knew that Bill Walstrom was a high school dropout who had worked with miscreants and petty criminals in New Jersey until he sickened of it and disappeared. He was smart and tough and had experienced some encounters with men no one should be with. He did know right from wrong, and "right" was the life he would live in Rock City, a place he'd never heard of until he saw the name on a highway marker. For twenty years he accumulated the respect of people who knew him.

Bud Cooper leaned back in the old wood bar chair and said, "Why don't we forget about this kid and his cedar trees and land. You don't need any more property, and my mill can get along without the kid's trees. It's like you have a landowner to deal with but you really don't. This kid's not only smart, he's stubborn as hell!"

"Bullshit," said Hanley. "That kid's not gonna last here very long because I am going to go into the Human Services office in Grants Pass and bitterly complain that they've got a little kid living all alone with no family, no friends, no money, and no support. Hopefully they'll put him in a foster home someplace, and that will put him on the dole from the state. The state will sooner or later recognize the value of his land and may want it sold to pay for the kid's care. Another scenario is that DHS will not cut his monthly benefit, but each payment will become a lien against his land. The kid will not like any of this, but what can he do? With no benefit, he doesn't eat! The state will eventually sell the property or foreclose on the lien, and we will buy."

Cooper laughed and said, "That is a bunch of stupid conjecture, and it really leaves me cold, but I don't care. I've cooled off on this deal with the kid, so count me out. Besides, what the hell do you know what the state will do or not do? I'm leaving. The drinks are on you."

Cooper was a graduate in forest management from Oregon State College and eschewed dishonesty and, in this case, conniving petty individuals. Any timber he bought would be a fair arm's-length transaction.

The next day, a Saturday, knowing Martha Webb was a

schoolteacher and would be home, Bill Walstrom called her. After identifying himself, Bill Walstrom asked her if she was still looking after Noah North.

Martha said, "Yes, I'm helping him. I am one of his teachers, and I am also the court-appointed guardian of his estate. Is there something I'm missing or something I should know?"

"Yesterday evening Jonathan Hanley and Bud Cooper were in my tavern having a conversation about Noah. I was amused when I heard about Jason Hanley getting whacked with a baseball bat by Noah. But I can't believe any good could result from Hanley and Cooper's conversation. It may be nothing, but thought you should know."

"Thanks, Bill, I'll be on notice."

Martha was reluctant to bother Noah about the Hanley and Cooper tavern talk. Noah is too young to have more worries dumped on him. She would soon, as a caution, slip that info into a conversation with Noah.

That evening, Martha's husband Joe handed her the Medford newspaper and pointed to a news article describing how a man escaped certain injury or death by hurling himself into an open doorway to avoid a speeding car that had jumped the curb onto the sidewalk. The man was identified as Buster North, a Douglas County resident. According to the written police report, the car that fled the scene was a late-model Buick with dirty out-of-state license plates.

Martha handed the paper back to Joe and said, "There's something amiss here, I just know it. I'm calling Noah and asking him to come here."

With Noah in her living room Martha showed him the March 16, 1971, newspaper story about his father's sidewalk near disaster.

The following Tuesday, Jonathan Hanley walked into the regional office of the Department of Human Services. It was a new one-story light-blue and dark-blue metal building covering half a block of land on the edge of town. It was a busy place with many offices. Hanley walked into the large reception area and asked the fiftyish woman at the reception counter if he could talk to someone about a neglected child.

"Are you related to the child?"

"No."

"Have a seat, someone will be out."

Twenty minutes later, Mary Edison walked up to Hanley and said, "Please follow me to my office."

Mary's office wasn't a regular office. It was a big room with many windows, a table was near the center of the room, and a secretary was busy at a desk by the windows. Numerous file cabinets formed a line back-to-back in the middle of the room. Seated at the table, Hanley and Edison faced each other.

Mary said, "Did you want to tell us about a neglected child?"

"Yes, I'm Jonathan Hanley. I live in Rock City, and there is a boy, I think maybe thirteen years old, that lives alone in a shack of a house. He apparently has no family, no close friends, and who knows if he feeds himself properly. His clothes and shoes are old, and he has no adult or parental guidance. He should probably be in a foster home or something like that."

"Wow, that doesn't sound good," blurted Ms. Edison. "Do you have children at home?" she asked.

"I have one."

"May I ask about your occupation?"

"I'm a real estate broker with my office in Rock City."

Mary Edison looked at Hanley and asked, "What is the name of this child, and where does he live?"

"He lives on the east edge of Rock City. I don't know his address. His name is Noah North."

Mary said, "Could his address be 600 East Cedar Street?"

"Yes, that would be it."

Mary Edison carefully examined Jonathan Hanley, who had just antagonized her, and said, "We happen to know all about Noah North because we provide him financial assistance. We have a comprehensive written report in our file detailing Noah's living circumstances and living conditions, a report that is private to Noah. You will never see that report. Noah has a guardian that cares for his assets and looks out for him. If you know him, you know his health, physical and mental, is good, and he is the top student in his class and always has been. By the way, we know about the trouble your son had while trespassing on Noah's land."

Jonathan Hanley gradually closed his eyes and thought, What the hell am I doing here? I'm a damn fool.

Closing her file folder, Mary asked, "I'm ready to record on this pad the matters of neglect you know about, and I'm not interested in any gossip, so are you ready to tell me your firsthand knowledge about the various events of neglect of Noah?"

Jonathan Hanley, reeling from Mary's broadside, stood up and muttered, "I think I'm in the wrong place." He then hurried out of the DHS offices to his Mercedes and left for Rock City.

TWENTY-ONE

The school year ended for Noah. The last three months had passed, and nothing remarkable had happened in Noah's life. He filed state and federal tax returns with Martha's guidance but had no tax to pay. Roy Sang and Martha obtained a copy of Noah's birth certificate. He was thirteen years of age. He was born on February 28, 1958, and he now had a Social Security number. CPA Roy Sang warned him that if his gold sales were greater this year, he might be paying taxes.

Summer vacation was beginning, Noah was still alone and providing for himself and getting better at it.

Noah was not letting the world slip by unnoticed. TV news was good or bad. Other programs were either good or stupid. His weekly visits to the bank provided him with old but relevant *Wall Street Journal* newspapers. He still didn't understand 90 percent of that paper, but the news articles kept him informed about the war in Vietnam, as did President Nixon's statements about ending the war. There were also articles about President Nixon wanting the country to leave the gold standard and allow citizens to own and buy and sell gold. Noah was educating himself on what those changes might mean to him. He reasoned that the changes could benefit him, but he wasn't sure. An article in one of his old newspapers grabbed his attention. It explained the method of measuring the weight of gold, and that knowledge would be important in coming years if the US left the gold standard and entered the free market. The banker was right about the troy ounce. Among other things, it compared the weight of gold to other metals. Noah was surprised to learn that a quart of gold weighed 40.225 pounds. He flinched mentally and whispered to himself, I better get my sinkers to the bank. Now there was no question: Noah knew that he must smelt his gold pebbles and get the resulting sinkers to a bank safe-deposit box. His gold would then be safe and ready for sale. No one needed to know what he was keeping in his safe-deposit box or what he had in the ground. If President Nixon had his way, possession of gold would soon be legal.

Noah was standing in his shack with all of his thoughts and concerns coursing and plowing through his mind when he suddenly slumped down in a chair like a person surrendering. I'm just a kid. Why am I involved in all of these problems that should have nothing to do with a thirteen-year-old kid? Those other boys in school are all buddies playing around together, involved in sports, swimming and fishing in the summer, some sitting around doing nothing. I hear some of them talking about girls, and most of all, they are usually free to do anything. Do they have any serious responsibilities? I spend most of my time looking after myself. I guess I have no choice. Maybe someday I will have a choice. I know one thing, the last thing I'm going to do is feel sorry for myself. If I do that, it will be the end of me. Noah sat straight up, thinking, Enough of that, I've got things to do, things that I will do with no help!

Under the kitchen counter Noah found his apple box containing his burner, crucible, and sinker mold. He visited his cache of quart fruit jars, picked up and carried a full jar into his shack, and set it on the table. He then reached under the kitchen counter and picked up the partially filled jar of pebbles remaining from the first two smelts. Now that he knew gold was nearly twice the weight of lead, and that a quart of gold weighed about forty pounds, smelting a full jar and half a jar would give him about sixty to sixty-five pounds of gold. He was concerned about secrecy, so he decided to do the smelting inside. His wood stove was sitting on a large square iron pad for fire safety, and there was plenty of room for the burner and sinker mold on the stove pad. It didn't take long to melt enough gold pebbles to fill the sinker mold, totaling thirty-six ounces, but that was lead sinker weight. If he'd read the newspaper article correctly, which echoed what his banker had told him, gold was a little less than twice the weight of lead, so he might have about sixty-five or seventy ounces of gold per full mold. Maybe making these sinkers wouldn't take too long. While the mold was cooling, Noah kept up the smelting process, and as soon as he cleared the new sinkers from the mold, he filled the empty mold with the molten metal.

The process was proceeding so nicely that he decided to reduce the gold in all of his jars to sinkers. He calculated that, at eight sinkers per mold, it was going to take a long time, maybe two or three hours. He had started the smelting after lunch. By 4 p.m., all nine of the jars were empty, and there was a dirt trench outside filled with cooling bright gold sinkers. The trench was covered with dirt, concealing the sinkers. They were too hot, even on the stove iron, to risk leaving them in the shack. He carried each batch of sinkers outside in an iron bucket, maybe over three hundred pounds of them. Before Noah went to bed, he felt the dirt covering the sinkers, and it was still warm. The newly minted sinkers would be cold in the morning. While falling asleep, Noah was contemplating the sinker move to the bank.

TWENTY-TWO

Fortunately, the summer of 1971 ended with few complications for Noah. He decided to rent a safe-deposit box in his bank on a day when Mr. Marston was not working, thus avoiding an explanation to Mr. Marston. He wasn't sure how that rental would be done. After gathering his courage, he walked to a woman at a desk near the vault door. She knew Noah was the bank's most unusual customer. She rented him a box and described the box visit procedure.

After three trips to the box with sinkers in his backpack, the large safe-deposit box became too heavy to freely move. When in the bank, Noah occasionally encountered Mr. Marston and said hello to him. Strangely, nothing was mentioned about the safe-deposit box that Noah was tending. Noah decided to rent another large box, and he soon filled it with sinkers until it became too heavy to deal with. Still no admonitions or scoldings from Mr. Marston. Noah rented two more large boxes and filled them with his sinkers. His monthly box rent was now $20 a month. He needed a fifth box but decided to keep and hide the remaining sinkers at home.

Mr. Marston had obviously seen him in the bank and surely knew what he might be doing, but Mr. Marston didn't say anything to him. The last time Noah was in the bank, he plopped down in a chair in the bank's customer waiting area where he had sat with Martha, and he reasoned, Something's happened without me knowing. Most of my sinkers are now safe. I might as well ask Mr. Marston what is going on.

He stood up, saw Mr. Marston alone at his desk, and walked over and said, "Can I ask you a question?"

"Sure," replied Mr. Marston.

"Why haven't you said something to me about my business in the safe-deposit box area?"

"Sit down, Noah. I'll tell you what I know, and I'm sure it has something to do with your sinkers. Since 1968 there has been a strong movement in this country to move away from the gold standard rules that you are familiar with. Some gold is being traded on the private market, some at $40 an ounce. We are not participating in that market. Since 1969, no one has figured out if President Nixon will remove us from the gold standard law and allow the free trade and ownership of gold by US citizens. I think we are headed in that direction, and our bank is neutral on the subject. So, Noah, stop worrying about me or your sinkers in your safe-deposit boxes. Also, I noticed that you are regularly taking our old *Wall Street Journals* and I'm sure that is where you get your news. If you want to know the price of gold, look for 'Commodities' in that paper. Does Martha Webb know about your recent visits to the bank?"

"No. I'm leaving now, and I may not see you for a while, except when I need a newspaper."

Noah felt a degree of contentment now that his gold sinkers were in a safe place. He did have a few left at home, but that was OK; he could easily use them as needed.

TWENTY-THREE

Noah was standing in the boys' restroom at school, looking at himself in the mirror. It was February 1972, and in a few weeks he would be fourteen years old. He was bigger and taller than a year ago and was happy with his appearance, something he had never considered. His teeth were straight. His posture was good, and he needed a haircut. He was thinking about his life alone. I'm a loner but not by choice. Somehow, without my spunk and strength, I might not like myself, but I'm the only one that can do anything about it. I think my life is as good as life is for a lot of people. He walked out of the restroom happy with himself, not realizing that hardship had made him a stronger person. He disliked holidays because they called attention to the fact that he had no family and really nothing to celebrate.

Valentine's Day had come and gone. He had never sent a valentine, but he received a couple from classmates. Maybe next year he would deliver one or two. Last year and the year before, he'd spent Thanksgiving Day and dinner at Martha's place, and he avoided Christmas by shying away from anyone he knew. Martha asked him about his Christmas and he told her he was good. It was becoming more and more difficult to avoid or explain away his solitary life. Even the girls were starting to look different and better, and some emotional energy was starting to creep into that observation.

Noah kept himself informed on events related to the war in Vietnam. Articles in his old newspapers reported what was happening in Vietnam, but it was not understandable to a thirteen-year-old. He was seeing the fighting in Vietnam on his TV but never knew why the US was there. He didn't know about the congressional Gulf of Tonkin Resolution following a US Navy warship incident that gave President Johnson reason to continue to escalate US involvement in the Vietnam War.

One morning Noah looked at himself in the bathroom mirror and asked the face, "Am I overthinking this Vietnam thing? I gotta ask someone my age what they're thinking." That day at school, sitting in the lunchroom with Felix, who was being ignored by the girl next to him, Noah waved his hand in front of Felix, getting his attention.

"Felix, I need to talk to you."

"OK."

"Are you worried about Vietnam?"

"My parents will not let me be in the army. They can't stand the war news they see on TV and said they would move our family to Canada where the army cannot get me. I don't know what to make of that. What are you going to do?"

"I'm not going to stop worrying about it. That war should be over by the time we are old enough to be involved, but I don't like any of it."

"Noah, there's nothing we can do about it, so find something else to worry about."

Spring break gave Noah an opportunity to consider an important issue that was bothering him. His shack was a structural and visual mess. He had $8,000 in the bank. Maybe he should rent a decent place in town. Maybe he could build a little house. He had cedar trees to sell, but that would mean messing up his land. He would ask someone he could trust. Maybe Martha or Mr. Marston or even the guy who did his taxes.

Friday, the last day of his spring vacation, Noah walked into the Rock City National Bank, straight to Mr. Marston's desk, and said, "I need some help or advice. Do you have time for me?"

Marston was busy with some paperwork but put his pencil down and nodded a yes.

Noah proclaimed, "I live in a shack that is a mess and an embarrassment, and with the wood heat and jumble of electric wiring, it is probably dangerous. Can I build a little house, or should I rent a place in town? How much does a house cost?"

Wilson Marston scratched his head and said, "You will have to sell a few more sinkers if you build a house. Is living in town around people something you want to do? Probably not, but then, it might be good for you." Marston thought, as he had previously, This is something a fourteen-year-old shouldn't have to be dealing with, but here he is. Where is his god damned family? Fortunately, this kid is as bright as they come, and he is smart enough to get advice when needed.

Marston looked at Noah and said, "You know you need to talk to Martha Webb about this."

"I know that and I will."

Marston said, "Let me think about this over the weekend. Come back Monday after school."

Noah asked, "Is the bank still buying gold?"

"No. There are buyers out there, but I don't know who they are."

"The other question I have is about the newspapers your bank gives me. All those papers are mainly about money and big companies and businesses I've never heard of. There may be an article about a company and how its shares have increased in value or how a company's shares have decreased in value. There may be an article about a company's profits or its losses. There are articles about missing a good buy in shares or how smart someone was to buy a certain stock. What are shares? One article went on and on about how shares in the stock market, whatever that is, are better than owning gold. They say gold pays no dividends, but shares in a company pay dividends, giving the owner of the shares an income. Please tell me what all that stuff is about."

Marston leaned back in his swivel chair and thought, Here's a fourteen-year-old reading old *Wall Street Journals*, wanting me to explain our whole capitalist system. Well, why not?

"Noah, you have asked me a question with a very complex answer, so I'm going to make this simple for now. A person will pay money to a company, and the company will use that money to run and expand its business. The company will give that person a written document called a stock certificate, which is a bit of ownership in that company. The certificate bears the share owner's name and entitles that person to share in the company's income. The amount of income that a share owner receives depends on how many shares he or she owns and how much money the company makes. A share or shares can be sold to anyone willing to buy them. If the company is successful, a share may go up in value. If not successful, a share may go down in value. Are you following me?"

"I guess, sort of."

"OK, here's an example. The Coca-Cola company probably has thirty or forty million shareholders, and most of that company's net income is paid out to all those shareholders. That company is so successful that its shares increase in value. Another successful company is International Business Machines. All those Ford cars you see, they are made by a company with millions of shareholders. But you should understand that there are a thousand or more companies that have issued shares. It can be risky business buying shares in a company, especially if you don't know what you are doing."

Marston picked up *The Wall Street Journal* sitting on his desk and opened it up and said, "Look at this. See all these companies listed? That column gives the daily range of price or share value of a company's share. Down here you can see a chart about a few companies with big increases in share value and a few companies with big decreases in share value."

"Mr. Marston, that's pretty interesting. I'll look more closely at my newspapers so that I can get a better understanding. Right now I'm wondering if I should have some shares because gold gives me no income. But if I sell my gold, it's gone forever. But will shares in a company always be OK? Thanks for spending so much time with me. I'll get out of here."

Noah did study his old newspapers, especially the constant flow of articles about gold and how some members of Congress wanted to drop the longstanding objection to private ownership of gold. Another article in an old newspaper said that President Nixon was not making any serious objection or comment on that subject, and to the surprise of many, in the summer of 1971 he asked the Treasury to "suspend temporarily the convertibility of gold into the dollar or other reserve assets." The secretary of the Treasury didn't do that, so late in the summer of 1971 President Nixon instructed Secretary John Connally to suspend temporarily the purchase of gold by the US Treasury. Noah did not understand, but it was about gold, and that interested him. He finally figured it meant that if you wanted to sell gold, you had to find a private buyer, and the price was no longer fixed by the government.

He soon read that the price of gold on the private market went to $43.40 an ounce. Noah owned a lot of gold. Any news about gold grabbed Noah's full attention. By the start of the 1972–73 school year, Noah knew that something was happening with gold. He saw the gold price change. He had no idea where gold was bought and sold, but he was going to find out. The bank was not buying. Many times he said to himself, I am not selling my gold, not even the few sinkers that are buried in that little trench, and as I understand it, I am no longer required to redeem my gold for dollars. He was fourteen, in the ninth grade, and he had recently spent considerable time trying to understand a little more about gold. He was hopeful that he could have a school year without distractions. Someday he was going to have to better his living conditions.

TWENTY-FOUR

The fall semester swept by without additional distractions. Noah had another Thanksgiving with Martha and her husband, and he avoided Christmas by staying home. Noah's friendship with Felix Bronson was growing. Felix and Noah had bicycles. On New Year's Day in 1973, they happily pedaled around town for hours. He could get to the school, the bank, the grocery store, and anyplace in town in minutes.

Months later, Noah was on his bicycle and had just slowed to turn into his driveway when he saw two men sitting on his front steps. He stopped and put both feet on the ground. He soon recognized Uncle Willis but not the other person. He had locked the door to the shack—otherwise Willis would have walked in uninvited.

Noah didn't move. He was angry. He was busy un-complicating his life. Even though Willis had helped him, Willis's other side of his character was offensive. Noah knew exactly what he was going to do.

He parked his bike, and after gathering some emotional strength, he walked up to Willis and said, "What are you doing here?"

"We came to visit."

Noah looked directly at Willis and said, "I don't want you here, and I don't want to visit with you or any stranger. I don't see a car, so you and your friend can start walking out of here!"

Willis countered, "Don't be like that."

Noah pointed down his driveway. "I am like that and you need to leave, now, and take your friend with you!"

Willis said, "My friend is my former brother-in-law and your father."

Noah examined Willis's friend and said, "I don't have a father, and with my mother gone, you are no longer my uncle, so leave, both of you!" Willis's comment about the other guy being Noah's father, whether true or not, made Noah furious, but he controlled himself. He had always been angry with his father for abandoning him and his mother. What a rat, Noah thought. If I had my baseball bat, I might do something terrible.

Noah asked Buster, "If you are my father, who is your family and where are they?"

Buster North said, "My father, who is your grandfather, is Alexander Noah North. He owns North Marine, Inc., in Buffalo, New York, engaged in shipping on the Great Lakes. My father and my two brothers, Steven and Richard, all live in Buffalo, New York. My mother is dead. I haven't seen or talked to them since I was discharged from the navy in 1956."

Noah asked Buster, "Where do you live?"

"I don't have a permanent address. I can usually be found in Jackson or Douglas County."

Noah asked, "Can't your father help you get settled and maybe offer you a job?"

Buster said, "I can't go back. My father is a mean, cantankerous person and is unhappy with me for leaving him and my brothers. He would make my life miserable. The one saving family trait he has— even though he never showed it—is his loyalty to his family. He is a wealthy man, and he may show his family tie to me by including me in his will."

Noah, agitated, said, "Are you serious? Waiting around for your father to die is insane!"

Noah, now mad and gathering strength, knowing he couldn't let this man derail his life like he had his mother's life, again pointed down the driveway, saying, "Please leave or I may call the police. I can't have you arrested for being what you are, but I can have you arrested for trespassing."

Noah was surprising himself with his bad-tempered behavior. Maybe he had grown enough backbone to stop the older, bigger high school boys from shoving him around. Maybe just being firm was enough. Uncle Willis, and what may have been his father, walked down Noah's driveway and disappeared. He wanted to talk to Martha about what had just happened.

Hoping Martha Webb would be home from school, Noah pedaled to her house. He needed to tell her about his visitors. He did something he had been wanting to do for a long time. He brought with him a one-ounce sinker on a gold chain. He had polished the sinker until it shined like a golden star. He knew that a gift to her was long overdue. When he bought the gold chain from Mr. Zimmerman, the jeweler gave him a small paper gift box. Mr. Zimmerman did not know about Noah's sinkers.

Martha was home and invited Noah inside. Martha's husband was sitting in a big chair reading a newspaper. They sat in comfortable chairs facing one another. Noah recounted the meeting with Willis and the man Willis said was Noah's father.

Martha carefully listened and said, "My advice is to stay away from those two. They've already proven themselves to be irresponsible. I think you already made that decision."

Noah glanced about the room with a serious meaningful look and came to focus on Martha. "My father said I have relatives in New York, maybe uncles and aunts and cousins. I still have a grandfather and maybe a grandmother. I can't ignore that. But what can I do? I'd go there, but I'd only be a burden, and I don't want to be with my father. Besides, I like it here. When I am older and learn my way around, I might look for my North relatives in New York. But I'll never go there for help of any kind."

Noah was about to leave and he said, "Martha, I almost forgot, I brought you a gift to thank you for all your time spent on my problems."

He handed her the little box and she opened it. Martha was delighted with the gold sinker necklace and said, "It's beautiful and has deep meaning to me."

She immediately put it around her neck and fondled the little sinker. Thereafter, Martha would frequently wear the necklace and treasure the unusual gift and its mystery. When worn, it never went unnoticed.

On his way home Noah whispered to himself, "I hope Willis and his friend left town. They must want something from me, but I never want to see them again. Besides, if that was my father, how could he face me? And Willis, I supported him and he stole from me month after month!"

Noah arrived home, and he was relieved that Willis and his friend were not there. He resolved, I cannot let those two upset me, but what can I do? Willis knows about the gold pebbles and is probably thinking that I'm still finding them and have kept them around here someplace. Or maybe my father thinks he still owns the shack. Whatever it is, I'll have to stand my ground and fight them. Or maybe I'll get lucky and they will leave and I'll never see them again.

Noah couldn't sleep that night. His conversation with Buster North was troublesome. The next morning he wanted to know about his relatives in New York. He picked up his phone and asked the operator to help him get North Marine, Inc., in Buffalo, New York, on the phone. Someone at North Marine, Inc., answered, and Noah asked to speak to Alexander North. He was told that Mr. North had died in 1969, but his grandson Thomas was there.

Thomas answered and after pleasant conversation discovered he was talking to Buster's child.

Thomas asked, "Where is your father?"

"I don't really know. He lives here in southern Oregon. I hardly ever see him. Actually, I just discovered that he exists."

Thomas asked, "May I have your address and phone number? If you know your father's address and phone number, I would like that too."

Noah gave Thomas his address and phone number, but he had no information about Buster. Thomas intentionally omitted saying anything to Noah about his grandfather's trust estate. It had been open for three years, and Thomas wanted it to stay that way as long as Buster and Noah were alive. He would keep the information about Noah and Buster to himself, saying nothing to the trustee or the bank's lawyer or anyone.

Fifteen-year-old Noah North was nearly as bright as Thomas but with little social or business experience. Thomas's request for his address and phone number told him there was something happening in Buffalo.

Noah raised his voice and said, "Why are you suddenly interested in our phone numbers and addresses? Something has happened back there. What is it?"

Thomas now realized that Alexander's death and trust could not be kept a secret.

Thomas said, "Your grandfather Alexander North died, and your father is one of the beneficiaries named in his trust."

Noah said, "Have someone send me all the paperwork connected to that business."

When the call ended, Thomas looked at the North Marine secretary and said, "That kid can take care of himself."

Margo North, in Buffalo, New York, was sitting in Wendall Dollar's waiting area in front of Wendall's secretary saying, "Is Mr. Dollar actually in his office? His door is closed, and I can't tell if he is there working or sleeping."

During her young life, Margo had been denied little or nothing, and she was forever unwittingly making it obvious. The North Trust had been open and not closed for three years. Just then Dollar's door opened and Dollar walked out with a customer.

The secretary said, "Miss North, do you have anything nice to say to Wendall?"

Ignoring the secretary, Margo asked, "When can we get distribution and close this damn North Trust?"

"When you people give me Buster's address or his death certificate, find out if he has children, and give me their names and addresses. I've tried, now you try."

It was 1973, and the school year ended in late May. The last months in school had occurred without unusual or surprise distractions for Noah, except for one very important thing: The military draft had ended April 30, 1973. Noah was delighted. No army for him.

He had not seen or heard from Willis or his friend. He worried a little about the sinkers buried next to his shack, and he worried about the war in Vietnam and what was happening to US soldiers. The newspapers he read began mentioning something about a private market in gold.

At the bank, he asked Mr. Marston about it, and although he had heard about it, he didn't know where the market could be found.

Mr. Marston said, "Ask the jeweler, Mr. Zimmerman, about a private market."

Noah thanked Mr. Marston for his time, picked up some old newspapers, and left thinking, No way am I letting Mr. Zimmerman think that I have more gold to sell. His nephew Martin and that guy Jason Hanley are buddies. I saw them together before I caught Jason creeping around my place.

TWENTY-FIVE

Uncle Willis and Noah's father, whom Noah had seen once in his lifetime, were holed up in a tiny room in a Motel 6 in Grants Pass. It was the last week in July, and they were asking themselves what they were doing, and thinking maybe they should just forget about taking something valuable from Noah. Buster thought he deserved something because he was responsible for Noah having the shack and the land. Willis thought he was owed something because he took care of Noah for years. Willis was looking for ideas on how to better himself without really trying.

Looking out the motel room's single window, Willis declared, "I am almost certain that Noah has accumulated a substantial amount of gold, and it is hidden on that property. He brought home pieces of gold for years, and he might still be doing it. We should search his place and do it—of course when he is not there. It might be worthwhile."

Buster responded, "I feel crappy about this whole thing, but I'm with you. Noah actually owes it to me because I am responsible for his ownership of that shack and the land it sits on."

"Listen to me, Buster. Are we going to search Noah's place or aren't we? It would be easier if it wasn't his school's summer vacation keeping him home most of the time."

"Willis, if you're certain he has a sizable amount of gold on the place, we should go for it."

"Maybe you, as his father, could get him to meet you someplace to keep him away from home, giving me time to make a search."

Willis, displaying a trace of conscience, said, "Wait, this is all foolish talk, and nothing that we have said is right or sensible or worth any effort. As a matter of fact, it is wrong to take anything from Noah. Unless Noah wants me to stay, and I'm certain he doesn't, I'm finished here."

"I agree. I'm no father. What the hell's the matter with me? We are nothing but potential albatrosses for him."

Feeling good about one of the few decent choices in his life, Buster walked out of the motel room to congratulate himself in a tavern across the street and was struck by a speeding car that disappeared into the night. Willis heard the *thump*, ran to the motel door, and saw Buster lying in the street. Buster did not need an ambulance or a hospital.

The local sheriff and the state police came to the scene and found no physical evidence and no witnesses.

The next morning, Willis was standing facing Noah, who was by his open front door.

"Noah, I have some bad news. Last night your father was struck and killed in a car-pedestrian accident. I'm sorry."

Noah sat down in one of the chairs on his porch with his head down. Following an awkward silence, Willis sat down.

Noah raised his head and sat straight in the chair. "Willis, I don't know how to feel about this. Tell me about the driver of the car."

"The car never stopped. Apparently no one saw it happen."

This event jolted Noah. He thought, The request by Thomas for phone numbers and addresses for me and Buster was not an unusual request from a close relative, or, in this case . . . was it?

Willis stayed with Noah for a few hours, and when Willis was leaving, Noah asked, "Do you think Buster's death was not an accident?"

Willis frivolously said, "Who knows?"

Willis went with Noah to the coroner and then to a funeral director to provide for the cremation of Buster and for a graveside service. Noah paid the costs.

Ten days later he and Willis attended the graveside service. They and the person furnished by the funeral director to pronounce the last rites were the only attendees. Then Willis was gone.

Home alone that night, Noah was happy the day was over. He mused, What else is going to be piled on me?

The next morning, after an intermittent sleep, Noah lay in bed continuing to absorb recent happenings in his life. He needed to call Thomas, the cousin he had never met, and tell him about Buster's death. Five minutes later, Noah quickly sat up, wide-eyed, on the edge of his bed and looked out the window at the bright sunshine. With Buster dead, I could be an heir in my grandfather's estate. If Buster was murdered, I could be in trouble. Funny thing is, I don't want anything from my grandfather, don't need anything, and don't want to be involved in any of that, but I am.

Noah called North Marine, Inc., from Martha's and asked for Thomas North. He was not there and the receptionist didn't know when he would be. Noah did not have Thomas's home phone number. He left his name and a number with a message for Thomas to call him. When the call ended, Noah was upset. He was fifteen years old with no family, caring for himself and his property and his education, and troubled with things a fifteen-year-old should not have to endure. He would talk to Martha.

Thomas immediately returned Noah's call. Martha did not eavesdrop.

Thomas said, "I was in the building when you called. What is happening?"

"You need to know that my father, Buster North, is dead. He was killed in the street by a hit-and-run driver. Thought you folks in Buffalo should know that."

Thomas said, "Your Uncle Steven died without a wife, children, or a will. Your share of the estate is now one-half, and the other half belongs to my sister Margo and me. You'll hear from the trustee of the estate."

Noah's reaction was, I don't want any part this. I am too young and have too much going on in my life.

Sitting in Martha's living room, he related the misfortune of his father, Buster, and being an heir to his grandfather's estate. Noah's privacy was important and he did not want this matter known by anyone except him and Martha.

Noah said, "I think my father was murdered, and now I don't feel safe. My father was to inherit from his father's estate. I will now inherit one-half of the estate. If I die, my one-half will go to my cousins, Thomas and Margo, who will then have the entire estate. I'm not liking this, and it's a huge burden for me, as if I didn't have anything else to deal with. I think I'm in danger. Would you take me to the Grants Pass Police Department?"

Martha said, "It seems more than a coincidence, but from the little I know about your father, he was probably careless crossing the street, and there are hit-and-run drivers out there. I'm not sure you should get the police involved. As a precaution, just be aware of what is going on around you."

"Martha, I'm in high school, and I've been a pretty good judge of what I should or should not do. I really want to see the police and get their reaction."

Martha said, "I'm calling your lawyer, Morgan Reynolds, and you tell him what has happened and make sure you know who inherits your share if you are not alive."

Noah talked to lawyer Reynolds, and following a full discussion of Noah's inheritance and the other heirs, Noah said, "My father may have been killed and now it's possible that the same thing could happen to me."

Reynolds said, "If what you have told me about your grandfather's trust and family is true, your two cousins, Thomas and Margo, may inherit from you if you have no will."

Noah said, "Don't want that to happen."

"Noah, what about your mother's side of your family? Did your mother have any brothers or sisters?"

"Yes. I have an Uncle Josh Porter and an Aunt Elizabeth Porter and a Willis Porter."

Reynolds said, "They are more closely related to you than your New York cousins. They would inherit your share."

"That can't happen."

"You have no will. So make a will and leave your property to whoever you name."

Noah said, "How soon can I see you? I want a will."

"Just show up here and I'll make room for you. It won't take long. In the meantime, figure out who your heirs are. Also, I should have a copy of your grandfather's trust."

Martha took Noah to lawyer Reynolds's office where a will was written and signed in front of witnesses. His sole beneficiary was

Martha Webb. He could change the beneficiary as his life changed. Noah filled Martha's gas tank and bought her lunch, and she let him off in Rock City at his bank, where he placed his will in a safe-deposit box on top of numerous gold sinkers.

Later he mailed a letter to Trustee Dollar telling him about his will that did not include any of his relatives in New York. He asked that he let Thomas and Margo know about the will.

When leaving the post office, Noah thought, I hope that distraction is gone. I can't live with any more distractions.

Jason Hanley was sitting in his room in the Hanley family home, reviving a painful memory and smarting at the remembrance of his beating at the hands of Noah North. His room was a mess, cluttered with clothes on the floor, girly magazines here and there, an unmade bed, outdated calendars on the wall picturing automobiles, and a picture of his former girlfriend, who terminated the relationship because of his boorish, borderline illiterate conversational skills. He needed to redeem his forlorn performance with Noah North, but how? He was still upset about Noah telling him he was a "dumb shit." Beating up the kid would only worsen things. He needed to humiliate the kid in some way or take something from him that the kid could do nothing about. Better yet, he could do something that could get Noah in trouble with the police. That idea was simple and amused him, and he thought, Yes, that is perfect, and the sooner the better.

Mr. Hanley and Bud Cooper, Black Dog Lumber Co.'s timber buyer, were each maintaining a continued but separate interest in Noah's timber. Cooper decided to go to Noah's doorstep, asking Noah's permission to again cruise his timber and maybe make Noah an acceptable proposition that involved selecting and agreeing to the harvest of specific trees. Bud Cooper, having lost interest in Hanley's schemes, drove to Noah's house.

Noah answered the door, and as always, he was apprehensive as to who or what he might be looking at.

Noah said, "Hello. I think you're here to ask me about my trees, right?"

Bud paused momentarily before saying, "You are correct. I would like one more opportunity to check your trees, and I may present you with a plan that will, with your consent, allow the removal of some select merchantable trees that will be used exclusively for the manufacture of pencils. The logging debris will be cleaned up and young trees planted."

Noah's silence made Cooper uncomfortable, but Noah said, "OK, but get your plan to me. I'll think about it, and if I approve it, the work must be done quickly and while I am home."

Noah knew that there was little chance he would approve the plan. Cooper left in his pickup, saying madly to the windshield, "Crap!"

TWENTY-SIX

Noah would soon enter tenth grade in September to commence the 1973–74 school year, and he wanted to devote his time and energy to his education. His experience with his banker and one of his teachers, his intense interest in gold and its price, and his slight perception of the meaning and value of some of the articles appearing in the bank's old newspapers told him to get educated. He was increasingly aware that his interests were vastly different from those of his classmates. He would endeavor to minimize the difference. He was aware of potential distractions such as the reappearance of Willis, his unusual living circumstance drawing attention, and further requests to sell his timber. He was fifteen years old, and nothing could be worse than the problems of the past that he'd dealt with.

Noah was sitting in the shade on a rock beneath the beautiful canopy of boughs high in his incense cedar trees. The August weather was warm, with a slight breeze moving the cedar bows and making a pleasant, soothing sound. He looked around at the park-like scene enhanced by the shade of the trees preventing the growth of most underbrush. He decided that it would be a crime to ruin his parkland. Noah needed the tranquility that allowed him to consider and to correctly make some decisions.

Quietly organizing his thoughts in his very discreet place, he whispered to himself, "I need to sell the gold that is still buried in my yard and ask Mr. Marston to give me the name of a private gold buyer. I also need to ask him how I can go about buying a share of one of those companies I read about in the bank's newspapers. My gold is sitting in his bank, and I get nothing from it unless I sell it. Maybe I can sell what I have buried and buy a share in a company that would pay me enough to keep me going without having to sell any more gold. I'm not smart enough to do those things without help. Maybe by the time I get out of high school, I will be."

Sitting in front of Mr. Marston, Noah looked at the approving expression on Mr. Marston's face and said, "I have decided to do a couple of things that I can't do without your help. Your bank can no longer redeem gold for dollars. I need to sell some gold that I haven't yet stored in your bank. You need to help me find a gold buyer. The price is now around $103 an ounce, and after I sell some gold, I want to buy a share in one of those big companies I read about in your newspaper. I understand that shares might grow in value or lose in value, but that is what I want to do. The thing is, I don't know how or where to buy a share, so I would like you to show me how to do that. I talked to Martha, and she is OK with it, but she will have to write the check to pay for the share."

Mr. Marston stared at Noah and thought, My God, this kid is only fifteen years old, and he is uncommonly bright and well versed in some significant matters of which many of my customers have zero knowledge.

"Are you really only fifteen?" Marston asked.

"I was fifteen last February. I will be in my second year in high school in September. You surely realize that I have no family and not much to do except look out for myself and my future, so I have plenty of time to think about this stuff."

Mr. Marston said, after a pause to look over the bank lobby to see if a customer was waiting to see him, "Noah, you could be the most interesting customer in the history of this bank. What you have just said and asked me is something many of our adult customers know nothing about. Yes, I will help you find a gold buyer and a stockbroker who is also a good financial advisor."

Noah left the bank wanting to hear from Mr. Marston.

Noah was in his shack, sitting with his elbows on the table with his chin resting in his hands, looking at his phone, and wondering if anyone would ever call him. Two people had his phone number: Mr. Marston and Martha. Martha had helped with the phone company's paperwork and paid the installation cost from Noah's guardianship trust funds. Noah decided that Martha should not be bothered with such matters and he persuaded Mr. Marston to let him have a checking account. Mr. Marston taught Noah how to write a check and keep the checkbook ledger balance. It was agreed, because of Noah's age, that the checking account balance would not exceed $1,000 until he was older. He could now pay his monthly expenses without bothering Martha. Martha, as guardian of Noah's money and property, agreed to maintain a decent balance in Noah's checking account and, as his guardian, if she approved, to pay from his guardian funds extraordinary expenditures. She wanted to be aware of any unusual activity in Noah's checking account, and Noah agreed to show her his bank statements. Noah was gradually gaining more control of his life and he liked it.

It was a week before school started. Noah had just eaten a breakfast consisting of a bowl of Corn Flakes and a piece of toast when his phone rang. It could only be Martha or Mr. Marston.

Mr. Marston said, "I located a gold buyer that has an office in Medford. The buyer's business name is Kaplan and Graves. They are in your new phone book. Call for an appointment."

Noah asked, "The price of gold is high, and I want to sell quite a bit, so how should I be paid? A check doesn't sound good, so should I ask for cash?"

Mr. Marston asked, "Well, how much are we talking about?"

"Well," Noah said, "over $40,000."

The response was slow in coming. "Did you say $40,000?"

Noah said, "Maybe a little more than that."

"How do you plan on getting to Kaplan and Graves in Medford?"

"I haven't figured that out yet."

"What do you plan on doing with the money?"

"First I thought I'd put it in your bank, and then invest in my future."

"I think I'd better help you. Medford isn't that far. Be at the bank at two o'clock this afternoon."

"OK, thanks, I'll be here."

Noah had dug up the remaining sinkers he had at home and was sitting in the bank lobby with about forty pounds in a sack. He had in hand that day's *Wall Street Journal* belonging to the bank and was reading the Commodities section when Mr. Marston stepped up and said, "You ready?"

He was, and they were soon entering Medford. Noah had his sack at his feet and *The Wall Street Journal* in his lap. Mr. Marston drove downtown to one of several small storefront businesses located in a well-kept red brick building. A stylish plain gold-lettered sign, Kaplan and Graves, hung over the full glass entrance door. When Mr. Marston and Noah walked in, it looked to Noah as though they were in a jewelry store. The shelves and showcases were elegant oak and glass, filled with grand silver and gold bowls, service ware, teapots, gold and silver coins, and some pieces of raw gold and silver. There were two leather customer chairs against one wall. Mr. Kaplan introduced himself, and Mr. Marston told him that they were there to sell gold.

"Well, Kaplan and Graves are buying, so what do you have?"

Noah put his sack on the counter without letting go of it and said, "I have about forty pounds here." Noah pulled out a six-ounce sinker, and Mr. Kaplan looked bewildered.

"If that is gold, we'll buy," said Mr. Kaplan. "I'll need to test it first," he said as he picked it up and turned around in the direction of a back room.

Noah said, "Wherever you go with that, I go."

"Certainly," said Mr. Kaplan, and Noah followed. The back room was well lit, uncluttered, neatly kept with tools and merchandise in place and a clean workbench with a spectrometer sitting on it. Noah watched Mr. Kaplan test and then weigh the six-ounce sinker. He even tested it with nitric acid. It tested as gold with purity nearly the same as the bank's test, at 95.71 percent. It weighed 11.8763 troy ounces.

Mr. Kaplan looked at Noah, a little puzzled, and asked, "How much gold do you have?"

Noah said, "I think I have around four hundred and eighty ounces. Can you buy that much?"

"I think so," said Mr. Kaplan. "Go get the rest of it and we'll see what we've got here."

When every sinker was tested and weighed, the purity was 96.03

and the total weight was 486.4552 troy ounces. Mr. Kaplan had placed all the sinkers in a wood tray, and Noah carried it back to the front counter where Mr. Marston was waiting in one of the customer chairs.

Mr. Kaplan said, "Noah, how much do you want for the four hundred and eighty-six ounces?"

Noah said, "I want $103 per ounce."

Mr. Kaplan immediately said, "I can't pay $103 an ounce!"

Noah, slightly upset, said, "Why not? That's the price of gold."

Mr. Marston handed Noah the latest issue of *The Wall Street Journal*, and he opened the paper to the Commodities section and handed the paper to Mr. Kaplan.

Kaplan looked at the paper and said, "As a dealer, I cannot pay full price. I need to discount that price so that I have room for profit when I resell."

Noah said, "You and I both know that the price of gold is on its way up and that is where you will make your profit, so forget about the discount."

Mr. Marston and Mr. Kaplan were astounded by this boy's firmness and audacity in dealing with an adult.

Mr. Kaplan said, "Nobody knows that the price of gold will rise."

"Yes, they do," Noah countered. "For several years before 1971, the government had been talking about making our dollar no longer redeemable in gold, and in 1971 the Treasury made it happen, and you know that Congress will make it official. You also know, when that happens, private ownership of gold will send the price up. The Bretton Woods system is ending and you know it. $103 per troy ounce is my sales price, and you will make plenty at that price. I can wait for the price increase just as you can, but I have some expenditures I would like to make now, and that is why I am selling."

Mr. Kaplan started writing a check.

"Mr. Kaplan, I don't want a check, I want cash."

"You don't get cash, you get a check."

Mr. Marston stepped in, addressing Mr. Kaplan. "You'll never have a more unusual customer.

"Noah, take their check."

Noah and Mr. Marston walked out of the Kaplan and Graves store with a check payable to Noah North in the sum of $50,104.88.

Reluctantly, to appease Noah, they drove straight to the Medford bank Kaplan's check was drawn on and bought a $50,104.88 cashier's check. On the trip back to Rock City, Mr. Marston couldn't stop talking about Noah's grasp of what was going on in the gold market.

Noah finally said, "The gold thing has been my life for many years. I've learned more about gold, and what's going on with it, by studying the articles about it in your papers. I've not had much else pleasant to think about. No family. Only one good friend my age. Taking care of myself from day to day doesn't take up much time. My good friends, you and Martha, are adults thinking and speaking with me with adult thoughts and language. I suppose I'm not much of a child anymore. How I dealt with Mr. Kaplan was the only way I knew. Besides, money is money, and not knowing where my life is going, I may need it. I'll tell you this; I am not planning on doing anything stupid with my money."

TWENTY-SEVEN

Noah deposited most of the proceeds of the Kaplan and Graves payment in his guardianship account. Mr. Marston insisted on using that fund, although he believed that fifteen-year-old Noah would be sensible about a huge balance in his checking account, and it would be available to Noah with Martha's good sense and guidance. $4,000 was deposited in Noah's personal checking account.

The 1973–74 school year was about to commence, and there was one more thing Noah needed to do before school started: purchase shares in a company that would give him some income. He called Martha on his new phone and asked to meet with her.

She asked, "Is everything OK with you?"

"I'm OK," Noah said. "I want your help in buying some company shares. I kinda know what I want but don't know how to do it."

Martha suggested that they meet at the bank in an hour. Noah was sitting in the bank's customer area and Martha sat down beside him.

She said, "What is this really about?"

"Like I said, I want to buy some shares in a company or companies that I see in this paper." He was holding the bank's latest copy of *The Wall Street Journal.* Martha looked at Noah, a little surprised, and said, "Is this something a fifteen-year-old should be doing?"

"Yes, it is. It's only my body that's fifteen years old. According to many articles I read in this paper, now is a good time to be buying a company's shares."

"How do you know what to buy?"

"I don't know, but according to this paper there are people that can tell me."

Martha said, "Yes, there are such people and they are called stockbrokers."

"Well then, help me get one, and please explain to him that I know what I'm doing."

Mr. Marston saw Martha and Noah seated and talking, so he walked over to them and sat down. "Anything going on here that needs my help?"

"Yes," said Martha, "Noah needs a stockbroker. As his guardian, I'm not real comfortable with this, but I'm not going to deny him a shot at the stock market."

Marston said, "If you could have seen him yesterday dealing with a gold buyer, you wouldn't question his competence and determination in money matters. His performance with the gold buyer was classic. If he wants a stockbroker, let's get him one."

They moved over to Marston's desk, and Marston got Marty Woods, a broker for Smith, Morgan and Wiley, on the phone. Smith, Morgan and Wiley was one of the largest brokerage firms in the country. Marston told Marty Woods that he had Noah North, a fifteen-year-old, and his guardian sitting by his desk, and they wanted to open an account and get into the market.

Woods said, "I'll send you our brokerage agreement that Noah and his guardian need to read and sign. I'll get it in the mail to you today. By the way, what size of an account will we be starting with?"

"Upwards of $50,000 or so."

Woods said, "As soon as I receive the agreement, we'll get busy on this."

Martha said, "What was that about $50,000?"

Noah said, "That's what I got for the last sinkers I had at home."

"Good grief," uttered Martha, "I had no idea that we were dealing with that much money."

Noah said, "You ain't seen nothing yet!" Noah was thinking about all the sinkers he had in his safe-deposit boxes. He didn't think about what might happen in the stock market.

"Oh, I almost forgot," proclaimed Noah. "I want to be able to draw at least $1,000 from my checking account without asking anyone."

He had his checkbook with him and carefully wrote a check to himself just the way Mr. Marston had taught him. Marston said it was all right with him, and Martha agreed. Noah had so far proved himself to be financially responsible.

Marston said, while arising from his chair as an invitation for everyone to leave, "I'll call you when the brokerage agreement gets here." That was the end of the meeting.

The first week of school was a surprisingly agreeable experience for Noah. He'd imagined that his solitary life on the edge of town would bring on some bullying words or acts from some of the older boys, but that didn't happen. Noah and his friend, Felix Bronson, were happy to be together, giving them the opportunity to discuss teachers, girls, college plans, the military draft, and personal issues. Noah knew Felix's parents and liked them. He had been in their home, at Felix's invitation, for dinner. His parents were warmhearted, sympathetic, and inquisitive about their son's new friend.

Noah remembered Mrs. Bronson placing his dinner plate in front of him, saying, "Please feel at home here, and maybe before the evening is over we'll know a little bit more about each other."

"Mrs. Bronson, there's not much to know about me. I live alone, have no parents, take care of my needs, and go to school. It embarrasses me a little, but I'm getting used to it."

"Noah, I'm glad we are close by."

The evening had ended with friendly goodbyes.

Noah of course knew that Felix had lived in Rock City his entire life, that he had many friends, was an average student, had few worries, and wasn't bothered with decisions about his well-being and the course of his life. Noah instantly cast off the thought of jealousy. Noah wanted to invite Felix to his place but avoided inviting him to his shack. It was an embarrassment that he needed to fix, something that he was about to do.

Noah had seen, many times, half houses being towed down the highway. He knew that they were manufactured homes, and he carefully reasoned, as well as a fifteen-year-old could reason, that a small manufactured home would be less expensive than a regular house, and he could probably have one with only a short wait. He could afford one, so he called Martha at home and asked to see her, and he was immediately on his bicycle headed to her house.

Seated in her living room while her husband watched TV, Noah said, "I have decided to buy a small manufactured home and get rid of my shack. Are you OK with that?"

Martha was silent for a moment, knowing the shack was uncomfortable for Noah, and with a smile said, "Sounds good to me, but do you think you can manage the whole project? There's more to it than buying the house."

Noah said, "I know where I want it placed, and I'll hire someone to do that work. I'm pretty sure I haven't thought of everything, but I'll manage. Trouble is, no one sells them in Rock City so, as my guardian, will you help me find one?"

"Of course. Can you be ready to go to Grants Pass on Saturday?"

TWENTY-EIGHT

It was a nice day, and Noah was sitting in the warm November sun on the top step of the porch of his new house. His house project was conceived a year ago, and it had happened with some problems with the plumbing, electric service, and cosmetic corrections to the house's exterior that took months to fix. The manufactured-home seller had its own installation crew who did everything, including the concrete work. It was a two-bedroom house with no garage. That could come later. The shack was gone, with no evidence that it had ever existed. The cost of the whole project was $26,340. Noah added some new furniture, and he had a bedroom that had direct access to the one bathroom in the place.

Sitting in the warm sun made him dreamy, and he was thinking, Now I won't be embarrassed about my living conditions. I feel very good, and maybe lucky, about the $50,000 I invested with Smith, Morgan and Wiley. They knew what they were doing when they told Martha that the commodity market was presently the place for me. I now own some Chevron, Getty Oil and Houston Oil, and mineral shares. I also own some shares in Holly Sugar Co. Funny thing is, all that is now worth over $57,000, and it even pays me some income. Maybe the news I see about coming gasoline shortages has something to do with all that. Knowing something about the commodity market, because of my interest in the price of gold, takes the mystery out of some of this. I better go to the bank and update my newspapers. He moved inside the house and sat in his living room.

Noah's life was getting better. He looked around the room with the slightly vaulted ceiling and big windows facing south with a view of distant mountains and a clear view of the roadway to his house. The kitchen and dining area were part of the living room, and he liked that. The longer he lived alone, the more normal it became. He could never quite avoid the thought that he might be doomed to live alone, and unless things changed, he might be alone forever. What the heck; I'm only sixteen. Everything can change, but I've got to keep control, if I can. I don't have to be alone forever. He would be seventeen in February. He was five foot ten and his clothes were getting too small. Every morning, he looked at himself in the mirror and thought, I'm not bad looking, but I'm sure no movie star! Maybe Rose Marie Simpson likes me. She sits across from me in our algebra class and speaks to me. Noah didn't realize he had reached a minor crossroad in his life. He would spend more time talking to Rose Marie.

After school, Noah bicycled to his bank and grabbed some old *Wall Street Journal*s. Noah's attention was focused on an account about the stock market's biggest loss in nineteen years. He was rattled a little until he compared the stock prices with the schedule of his shares that Smith, Morgan and Wiley had purchased for him. Apparently, commodity shares were not down much, but he now was a little more educated on the subject. He noticed that gold was currently $106 an ounce. He was constantly learning about things they didn't teach in school. He would soon be reminded that learning about unprincipled people is not taught in schools.

Noah met his friend Felix Bronson in town. They had tooled around on their bicycles for an hour or more when they pedaled off a sidewalk, over a curb, and into the street, and when that happened, the frame on Noah's bike cracked and separated at the front forks. Noah almost stopped, with both feet on the ground preventing a fall. He looked at his nearly new but ruined bike. He had never been happy with the bicycle, even though it was the most popular brand. Turned out it was too heavy, the seat wasn't comfortable, the shift sometimes failed, there was no choice of color, and the handlebars were difficult to adjust. He would return it to the hardware store that sold it to him to have the frame fixed.

He said to Felix, "This bike, Road Victor, is the most popular bike in the country, but it is a piece of crap. I think I can walk it home, and that is what I'll do. See you at school."

Noah made the long walk home. When his house came into sight, he saw a car parked in his driveway. It belonged to Willis. The passenger's side door was a mismatched color, clearly a pickup from the wrecking yard. He peeked into the car and saw an unrolled sleeping bag in the back seat along with the debris of a dozen car meals. Uncle Willis was sitting on the porch steps. Noah pushed his broken bike to his front steps and confronted Willis. He was decent looking, wearing clean but worn pants and a shirt just off the rack at Salvation Army.

"What are you doing here?" he demanded.

"I just came for a friendly visit."

Noah was upset with the bike problem and more so with his visitor. He rested his broken bike against the side of his porch and said, "We are not real friends, so please get in that junker car over there and leave!"

Willis stood up and said, "I apologize for abandoning you, but some of that was out of my control. You are all alone, but you should have some family with you to help you in your early years."

Noah couldn't respond quickly enough. "If anyone needs help, it is you. As far as I know, you have no job, no education, no property, probably no bank account, and little responsibility, even to yourself. You are thinking that you might, somehow, gain a foothold here and help yourself to whatever you can. I want you to leave now, and don't return."

Willis said, "OK, I'll just stay for a while and then leave."

"Please leave now," replied Noah. "And if you don't leave now, I'll call the Rock City police. You are trespassing!"

Willis was now shaken but responded, "I'll go to the Department of Human Services in Grants Pass and let them know that I am your uncle and, because you are only sixteen and alone, you need an adult with you to care for you and see to your well-being, but I can't help unless I live with you permanently."

Noah was not only disgusted, he was now mad. "You are as phony as you sound. Going to the DHS won't work. It was tried before when I was younger and it didn't work. A greedy person wanted my land, and DHS told that person that I was secure with protection and help from my teacher and guardian, and with my ability to support and care for myself. So now, just get the hell out of here."

Willis was shaking his head while walking away. He turned around and asked, "Is that house all yours?"

"It is, and you will not get close to setting foot in it! The only person you can fool is yourself."

Noah stood shaking his head and watched Willis's car disappear down his driveway. Willis was furious with the encounter. His vanity, to the extent that he had any, was wiped away, but only Willis and Noah had seen its demolition.

Noah pondered the event. I wonder if there is any other sixteen-year-old in the world that has to confront crap like this?

Willis looked back through his side mirror at sixteen-year-old Noah standing on his front porch and said to the world, "I can really be an asshole."

Noah then looked at his broken bicycle. Now I have to deal with this. If the hardware store doesn't fix it or replace it, I'll figure out something. Noah did not know that someday soon he would "figure out something" and a lot more.

School was moving along smoothly. Noah remained after his last class for the day. He was seated at his desk, thinking about the past nine or ten days. Mr. Jenkins, his English teacher, was seated at his desk.

Noah had not been successful in his request to the seller of his bike to fix it or replace it. He knew the difference between right and wrong, and he knew he was right.

He walked to Mr. Jenkins's desk and asked, "Could you help me with a personal matter?"

"Certainly." Mr. Jenkins knew, like most of his teachers, about Noah North, his lack of family, and his success at school. Noah told him about the bicycle problem and poor design and said that all he wanted was for it to be fixed or replaced. Fixing by welding would make him happy.

"What is the name of the company that makes the bike?"

"Road Victor."

"I'll help you for sure in a couple days."

"Good," said Noah, and he returned to sit at his desk. Now I have to figure out how to ask Rose Marie Simpson to the dance after the game on Saturday. I think I just walk up to her and ask her. I'm sure I'll screw it up. Maybe I better forget it. No, I'm not like that.

He again walked to Mr. Jenkins's desk and asked, "May I ask another question?"

"Sure, what is it now?"

"You can't tell anyone I asked you this. It is personal. OK?"

Mr. Jenkins quickly examined Noah and said, "Your secret's mine."

Noah paused uncomfortably and uttered, "What's the right way to ask a girl for a date?"

Mr. Jenkins thought, He does need somebody sometimes, and he has the guts and smarts to ask. He doesn't know I can't even prevent my fiancée from running off.

"The proper way is in person, privately and sincerely. Do not ask on the phone, through a friend, or by message or letter. Instead of saying, 'Would you go to the dance with me?' say, 'I'd sure like to take you to the dance.' Have you got all that?"

"I sure have, thanks much." Noah hopped and skipped out of the classroom.

TWENTY-NINE

Jason Hanley was still smoldering from his physical and verbal encounters with Noah North. Bud Cooper knew precisely where he stood with Noah and understood that there was zero chance of buying timber from him. He did want to know where the boundary lines separated Noah's lands from neighboring land. Giving that information to Noah might improve his relationship with the young man. Surveyors and their necessary employees had, in Oregon, a right to enter lands for surveying purposes. Bud hired a surveyor and drove to Noah's place to survey some lines. Noah was not home. Bud left a note on Noah's front door stating that he was on the property to make a survey. It should not take long. He hoped to see Noah before he left, and if Noah had any questions, he should please call him. The permanent property corner marks were all in place, and within a couple of hours, Bud and his surveyor were walking out of the timber when they saw Jason Hanley place a bicycle behind Noah's house and hurry away down Noah's driveway.

Bud said, "What the hell was that about?" Bud and the surveyor left and thought nothing more of the incident.

Pretty Rose Marie Simpson was elected freshman class princess to the Royal Rock City High Homecoming Court. It required her appearance at the football game and the school Thanksgiving dance. Noah had not foreseen the horror of maybe in some way having to be involved with her at the homecoming football game. He had decided to ask her to the dance anyway, but his resolve always faded when he was about to ask.

Now he was annihilated, dead in the water, and because she was pretty and popular and now a princess, she would have a hundred invites, all from David Cassidy types.

He walked into his algebra class early and was startled to see Rose Marie Simpson sitting at her desk across from his desk.

He said, "Hi," and sat down, looking straight ahead with blurred eyes, saying nothing. No one else had entered the classroom, and he said to himself, Screw it, I'm asking her anyway!

Noah turned, catching Rose Marie's attention. Gathering all his nerve and strength, and looking her in the eye, he said, "I would sure like to take you to the dance Saturday."

"And I would like to go with you," she replied.

"Wow, really?" Noah partially gasped. "I'll pick you up at seven. We'll have to walk, but you live close to the school, so it's a short walk."

They talked about nothing much until the class started. He didn't hear or see anything for the first ten minutes of the class. He had been thinking, Holy shit, did that really happen? Holy shit, did that really happen? Holy shit, did that really happen? If he'd had a mom and dad, he would've liked to tell them about his first date with a princess.

Noah was walking home from school knowing he had errands to accomplish but still thinking about Rose Marie Simpson. He was very happy that he had asked her to the dance that morning. He needed some new, decent clothes and was headed to the new Fred Meyer store on the edge of town. He missed his bicycle. He knew he should buy a new one but a different brand. He did his shopping. The lady in the Fred Meyer store learned from Noah why he needed new clothes, and she helped him like a mother. He walked into his bank on the way to the hardware store, withdrew several hundred dollars, and then walked into the hardware store and bought a bicycle. It was not a Road Victor. It was a Blue Streak. He still had business to settle with Road Victor.

He rode his new bike with the new clothes in its basket. He saw a police car parked in front of his house. The policeman told Noah that he needed to talk to him. Noah put his new bike and packages on his porch and walked back to the policeman. There was an old bicycle on the ground by the police car.

The policeman looked at Noah and said, "Is this your bike?"

"No," said Noah.

"I knew that. You are under arrest for the theft of this bike."

Noah was upset, mad, and surprised that such a thing could happen to him. He told the policeman that he had not stolen that bike or anything else, ever!

The policeman said, "Well, we have a witness who saw you take the bike and followed you to see you ride it up your driveway."

Noah was quick to say, "Whoever told you that is a liar!"

The policeman loaded the bike in the back of the police SUV and said to Noah, "Get in the police car."

Noah pleaded, "This is a terrible mistake."

The policeman replied, "I've heard that before."

"Not from me."

Noah pleaded, "Look, this is a new bicycle I bought an hour ago and the tags are still on it. Why would I steal some kid's bike? You're doing the wrong thing here."

The policeman said, "Get in the car before I handcuff you!"

Noah was led into the police station in the Rock City Hall. The clerk in the police station was also the clerk in the City Recorder's office. She knew Noah was taking her daughter to the Saturday school dance and knew little else about him. She recorded his name and address and phone number. He was charged with petty theft of property worth less than $250. She declined to fingerprint Noah. She read from the bail schedule set by the municipal judge and said bail was $500. She also told Noah that the County Juvenile Office would be notified.

The clerk looked at the policeman and said, "We don't usually require bail for a minor this young."

The policeman said, "I'm new on this job, and the chief said bail in all cases."

"We can't put them in jail with adults."

"Well, we don't have any adults in this jail, so what's the problem? This is the theft of a bicycle, and there's too much of this going on, so I insist on bail."

The clerk said, "Noah, do you have bail money?"

Without answering and still madder than ever, he counted out five

$100 bills on the counter and returned several $100 bills to his wallet. He was glad he had stopped by his bank. He'd planned on replacing most of the crumbling furniture in his house, but that was now on hold. He picked up the bail receipt and left the building with a speechless clerk and policeman in his wake. The clerk and the police officer looked at one another in disbelief.

The officer said, "What the hell was that? A sixteen-year-old packing maybe a thousand dollars in his wallet?"

The clerk said, "He's an unusual kid, and I've never heard anything bad about him. You may have made a big mistake."

When Noah arrived home, he sat on a chair to try and get control of whatever in him needed to be controlled. He was furious about the wrong committed against him, and to imagine what Rose Marie would think about him was indeed painful. He stood up, looked at his phone, and decided to call Rose Marie and tell her what had happened.

As soon as she answered, he said, "Rose Marie, something has happened to me that I must tell you about."

"I know what you did; my mother is the court clerk," was her immediate reply. "I can't go to the dance with you." The phone clicked in Noah's ear, and she was gone. Noah plopped down in his chair, and tears emerged in his eyes. Noah was down but still very much alive, and he wasn't walking away from it. The next day was Thanksgiving, and he was invited to Martha's house for midday dinner.

Noah related the whole sorry mess to Martha and her husband. They believed him, and Martha told him to get a lawyer. He would call Morgan Reynolds, the lawyer who was his mother's lawyer. It might be expensive. Fortunately, after the last gold sale, he had deposited enough money in his personal account that he didn't have to trouble Martha for funds from the guardianship account.

Noah was back in school on Monday after the disastrous Thanksgiving holiday. Rose Marie was not in her seat opposite him. She had moved far away to another seat. Few classmates talked to him, but that was normal. He told Felix that the theft charge was a mistake, and Felix may have believed him. After his English class he spoke to the teacher, Mr. Jenkins, who he had asked for personal advice. He told him what had happened, and he wanted him to know that he had stolen nothing, never had and never would.

Mr. Jenkins said, "I believe you, and if I hear any conversation to the contrary, I'll try to stop it."

After school that day he went to Mr. Marston at his bank and had the same conversation as he'd had with Mr. Jenkins. Mr. Marston had the same response as Mr. Jenkins.

It was the second week in December when Mr. Reynolds called Noah to say his case had been transferred to the juvenile division of the circuit court in Grants Pass, a hearing was set for Monday, January 13, 1975, and he wanted to see Noah in his office after the holidays.

The day Rose Marie Simpson said she would go to the dance with Noah had been the happiest day of his life ever. Now he was experiencing the unhappiest day ever.

Bud Cooper was sitting at the bar in the Arcade Tavern, reaching for his third beer. There were Christmas decorations festooning the back bar in a less than spectacular manner. There were a half-dozen wood tables with chairs near the bar; few were occupied. Pool tables filled a larger room behind the table seating area. A game was on at one table. The bartender was the owner, Bill Walstrom. The only other person at the bar was a spectacular brunette Bud had been eyeballing, and he was about to do something in that arena when Bill Walstrom, who was a friend of Bud's, said, "Have you heard anything about that orphan kid, Noah North, and the trouble he is in?"

Bud replied, "I know that kid, and he's the most independent, competent kid I've ever known. He knows who he is, where he is, and what's going on around him. Tried to buy his timber, and he has sense enough not to sell. He even put a new house on his property. So what's going on with him?"

"Well, he was arrested for stealing a bicycle. Strange thing is, he had just purchased a new bike the day he was arrested."

Bud said, "Wait a minute, my surveyor and I were on his property the other day, and we saw Jason Hanley place a bike behind Noah's house and leave. We remarked about it and thought it strange. I'll bet a million dollars Jason intentionally made trouble for Noah."

Bud finished his beer and was ready to leave when he quietly said, "Bill, who's the sexy gal sitting at the other end of the bar?"

"That's my wife, you idiot!"

The next day Bud Cooper walked into the Rock City Police Station and asked the clerk, Mrs. Simpson, if he could talk to the officer who arrested Noah North. "He's on patrol" was the response.

"Maybe you could tell the officer that Noah North did not steal anyone's bicycle," urged Bud.

"What do you mean?" she said, almost demanding a response.

Bud told the clerk the whole story and added, "Rumor has it that some time ago, Noah caught Jason Hanley trying to burn the old shack that Noah lived in, and when Noah caught him in the act, Jason tried to attack Noah, but Noah clubbed him good with a baseball bat and Jason ran away. Even with Noah having no family and living all alone fending for himself, he has to put up with this bullshit! Didn't Noah tell you he was innocent?"

Bud turned and quick-stepped out of the police station. Mrs. Simpson gasped, drew a deep breath, lowered her head, and audibly said, "Oh my God," and while considering Noah's shocking misfortune, officer Ray Martin walked in.

Mrs. Simpson looked up at the officer and said, "How did you know Noah North stole a bicycle?"

"I got a phone call from a guy who saw the theft. I went to Noah's house, but Noah wasn't there, so I looked around and found the bike behind Noah's house, sort of concealed."

"There are two witnesses, Bud Cooper and a surveyor, who saw Jason Hanley put it there."

"Holy shit, I'm gonna get sued, the city is gonna get sued, and Jason Hanley is gonna get sued."

"Is that all you can say? What about poor Noah?"

"I gotta check this out with Bud Cooper and the surveyor. If it checks out, I'll ask the city attorney to have the case dismissed."

"You do that and do it now! You ruined his Thanksgiving, don't ruin his Christmas."

Christmas Day 1974 was cold and clear. The light snow from days ago glistened on the tall trees in Noah's cedar forest. The best of his few Christmas presents was the dismissal of the theft charge against him, thanks to Bud Cooper. With no close friends and no brothers or sisters or cousins or mother or father or aunts or other family he might have known, there was no one to give a present, especially since Uncle Willis's last vestige of integrity had decomposed in his driveway.

He was invited to Martha's for Christmas dinner, and he had another highly polished one-ounce sinker for her. He thought about a present for Mr. Marston and Mr. Jenkins, but it didn't happen.

Martha was excited about her second sinker. It matched the first. Noah thought he might have bettered her husband's gift. They reviewed Noah's skirmish with the law. The turkey dinner was super, and he wanted to stay late, but his innate good manners told him not to. At the polite time, he left for home on his new bike.

Noah spent most of the remainder of his Christmas vacation at home. He had been exonerated in the bicycle incident, but it continued to be an embarrassment, and he wanted to avoid any conversation about it. However, when in the police station asking for the return of the bail money, he had to talk to Rose Marie's mother, the clerk who would see to the return of the $500. She was upset and Noah was upset. She handed him the previously prepared court check and said, "I can't tell you how sorry and sad I am about this awful mistake."

Noah immediately responded forcefully, "Explain why Jason Hanley hasn't been charged with filing a false police report. Is it easier to arrest a sixteen-year-old with no family and no support—is that it? Mrs. Simpson, I apologize if I've been rude. Anyway, I am still polite and nice to your daughter, and that is important to me. She is a good friend, and now that may be over."

Noah didn't tell Mrs. Simpson that he had considered bashing Jason Hanley again with the baseball bat. He wouldn't do that because the townsfolk now had confirmation that Jason Hanley was a bully and a fool and a liar, and that was his punishment.

THIRTY

One constructive thing Noah had done during the short vacation was read with care, for the purpose of educating himself, *Wall Street Journal* articles about the development of improved and innovative products by successful companies and articles explaining the failure of a company or the failure of its product. He had subscribed to the paper and used it to his advantage. There was a lot of other good stuff in that paper that was entertaining.

He was upset with his treatment by Road Victor, Inc., which would not repair or replace its flawed bicycle. He had the time and he thought it would be a good exercise to challenge that company. He found the company on the American Stock Exchange. The price was a "Bid," "Ask," and "Last," so which one of those was it? It must be the Last at $5⅛. What the heck is that? We don't have any one-eighth coins.

The gold price was now $106 an ounce. He hadn't called Smith, Morgan and Wiley recently, so he called his broker, Marty Woods, and asked if he should sell some gold at $106 and buy Road Victor, Inc., at $5⅛. Marty Woods had been in the financial services business for twenty years. Marty lived in the west suburbs of Portland with his college sweetheart wife and his three children. He thought he knew teenage children, not only his own but their close teenage friends. Marty Woods thought, Is Noah North really a teenager? He has no father. Should I be one in this instance?

Marty Woods paused and said, "Noah, you're sixteen years old. Please tell me, what are you doing? You don't want that company—they are poorly managed and unprofitable."

"I figured you'd say that, but they have an old, respected name, and I want to buy a few shares and get financial info about them. Can you do that for me?"

"Yes, but for what purpose?"

"I may cause them a lot of trouble, more than they caused me, or I might not. As you know, I'm alone. Shit is dumped in front of me every time something good starts to happen. I'm sick of it. People need to know that if they knock me down, I'm gonna get up. I know the bike is a small matter, but it is an opportunity to stand up, even if I'm just a kid. *The Wall Street Journal* says that if I want to know about the management of a corporation, I need a copy of its by-laws, whatever those are. Can you get that for me too?"

"You have enough money in your cash account with us to buy a hundred shares, so don't sell any gold. I think you know that on December 31, 1974, the US opted out of the Bretton Woods Agreement, and US citizens can now own and sell gold. You're probably the only sixteen-year-old that knows anything about that. If that happens, you will be happy you hung on to your gold."

"I know that you think I'm strange, and maybe I am, but I have never had a family, hardly any friends, but plenty of time to screw around with this stuff. I'm not bragging about this, but I am a straight-A student, and that doesn't make for a lot of school friends. In fact, I think I have a couple of enemies. Also, if I make a big mistake, it will be my fault, and it will not be because I followed someone else's advice."

Marty Woods said, "OK, we'll make the buy and get those other things to you. I'll also get their annual report. Just so you know, when a customer makes a dumb stock purchase like this, we have him sign a statement that the buy was against our advice. I'll send that to you immediately for review and signature by you. You return it to me, or I won't make the buy."

The first day of school in January 1975 was unremarkable except that Rose Marie again sat at the desk across from Noah. There were only a couple of other students in the room. Without looking at him, she whispered, "I'm sorry," but she said nothing else.

Without looking at her, Noah said, "Is that all you can say?"

"What am I supposed to say?"

"You can apologize for your rudeness on the phone."

"OK, I apologize for my behavior."

Noah got up and, in a couple of short steps, moved a chair next to Rose Marie. His leg was against her leg, and she didn't move.

"One more thing—a friend does not abandon a friend in trouble. I wouldn't abandon you if it meant throwing myself in front of a speeding locomotive."

"You're too good with words, Noah. I hope you mean them."

"I carefully choose my words, especially the important ones."

She turned her head, now inches away from Noah's friendly gaze, and with watery affectionate eyes focused on him, she tenderly said, "Noah."

It was a new experience for both of them, and for a moment they remained silent, warm, and blissful.

"Noah, can we put all this behind us?"

"Yes, it would be the smart thing to do. Can we meet after school?"

"Yes, but I don't know anything about you, and neither does anyone else, except I like what little I do know about you. Are you concealing bad stuff?"

"Yes, I'm concealing good and bad stuff. I'm wanted by the law in several states. What about you?"

Rose Marie said, "Class is about to start. Let's continue this after school." Noah nodded in agreement. Noah fell deep in thought and wondered, Did that handsome muscle-bound football player take her to the dance?

Later, Noah walked Rose Marie to her house. They held hands until they were at her front door.

"Noah, my mother is in Grants Pass today and won't be home until late. Please come in."

"Rose Marie, where are we now after that big mess with the bicycle?"

"Noah, I'm more committed to a close, personal, affectionate relationship with you than ever."

Standing pleasantly close together in Rose Marie's living room, Noah slowly put his arms around her, and she responded.

"Rose Marie" was the only thing he could gently say as they cautiously inched together.

They kissed until they were breathless.

"Noah, that was exactly the right thing to do."

Noah left Rose Marie, overjoyed with their renewed relationship.

The last week in January was filled with cold rain, and Noah was riding home on his bike. The mailbox on his driveway entrance was stuffed with a large brown envelope. He tore it open while walking into his living room. All of the materials he wanted about Road Victor, Inc., were now in hand. He placed all of them on the table, then quickly looked in the freezer to make certain he had a frozen dinner. He had the 1972, '73, and '74 financial statements, balance sheets for the same years, and the 1974 annual report. The annual report was written in simple language so all stockholders could understand. He also had the by-laws. He didn't understand the documents, so he called his tax man, Roy Sang, and made an appointment for the next Saturday morning. Martha said she needed to go to Grants Pass and would be happy to take Noah.

Noah continually asked himself if it was wise or stupid to go after the bike company. He had been giving considerable thought to what his life's occupation should be. He had settled on either business management or something like Marty Woods's stockbroker occupation. Either way, attacking in a lawful way a crummy but potentially good company would be an education for a sixteen-soon-to-be-seventeen-year-old. Right now he had to go to the grocery store and figure out what he needed and what not to screw up for dinner. Shopping by himself with money in his pocket was better than shopping with Uncle Willis with no money. He had read the list of a hundred chemicals on the frozen dinner package and put it back. He would go fresh and live.

It was Saturday morning, and Martha and Noah were sitting at Roy Sang's desk. Martha had brought him there each year for the preparation of his income taxes. Roy Sang was annually astounded at Noah's gold sales and the bright kid who made them.

Roy was anxious to know why this extraordinarily affable, bright kid was sitting in front of him. "So, what can I do for my favorite sixteen-year-old client?"

Martha said, "Noah wants you to teach him how to read and

interpret a corporate balance sheet and a corporate financial statement. He also wants to know what to look for in an annual report."

Noah reached in a large brown envelope and put the contents on Sang's desk. "I'll pay you for your time. I really want to know these things."

"Why does a sixteen-year-old boy need to know how to read a balance sheet and a financial statement?"

"Because I'm a shareholder in the Road Victor company. I want to do something to let the world know they can't treat customers like dirt, or maybe I want to save it, or maybe I want to quicken its death. Most of all, I want to cause a lotta trouble when I do that. Besides, I'm almost seventeen and in the eleventh grade."

"My God, you're serious. OK, I need a fun breather from my regular work. Here's a pad and pen for notes. Martha, if you have something to do while in town, you'll have time."

Martha left and Roy said, "This is college stuff, but I'll try and make it simple." Roy picked up the balance sheet and said, "See this? Everything the company owns is on the left side, and everything the company owes is listed on the right side. Items on the left are assets, and items on the right are liabilities. The bottom line on each side must have the same number, or something is wrong. That's why it's called a balance sheet. Are you OK so far?"

"I guess."

Roy was a good, patient teacher and he had an exceptionally bright and willing pupil. When Roy was explaining the balance sheet, he spent considerable time on the meaning of long-term liabilities and short-term liabilities. Roy emphasized that short-term liabilities could be a problem without good income or good cash reserves.

"This balance sheet means nothing but trouble," Roy said as he put the document on his desk. "This is an important statement. Most companies issue it every three months because it provides information about the company's ongoing expenses and income. It contains vital information, and if a company's shares are traded in the stock market by the public, all of these statements are required to be published and made available to the public. The price of the company's shares can be affected, either up or down, or with no effect. In my view, your Road Victor company may have a problem. Something else you should know, and I can't help you with it: A company can pad its balance sheet by overvaluing assets and understating liabilities or not stating possible or contingent liabilities such as known probable claims against them for a faulty and defective product, or maybe an underfunded employee retirement plan."

Roy looked at Noah, who had a slightly puzzled expression, and said, "Noah, what you've learned is a tiny fraction of what there is to know about corporate finance. An example of what you know of this subject would be like knowing all about one rock in a pile of gravel and thinking you know every rock in that pile. I hope you get what I am saying, because the financial officers and accountants at Road Victor will be familiar with each rock in that pile of gravel. I don't know what you're planning, but you don't stand a chance of succeeding unless you have shareholders holding a majority of shares on your side."

Noah responded, "I'm going forward. My ammunition is in hand, and there may be more."

Roy said, "I would like to talk you out of your mission against Road Victor. It's impractical, complicated, and unachievable for one sixteen-year-old boy."

Noah looked around the room and said, "If I have to criticize the company officers, I will, if I have the guts! I plan to attend a shareholders' meeting and tell them that the company's failing because of rotten management. I want to tell them that their bicycle is faulty and outdated, and the competition with new and better bikes will put Road Victor out of business. They need to know that Road Victor is on death row. I have their by-laws, and shareholders are allowed to speak and change the company directors. I guess the directors are responsible for everything. Martha told me about directors on the way down here. She doesn't think much of my plan." Noah sensed that Roy wanted him to leave, but Noah said, "There's one more thing I need to know. I don't understand about shareholders. Why does a company have them?"

"OK, I'll make this quick. A corporation is formed, but it has no money. It sells shares to get money. It uses the money to buy buildings and machinery and hire employees to get its business going. It is not a loan. It never has to repay the money to the shareholders, but they share in the profits and losses, and they can, as you know, sell their shares. Road Victor needed more money, so it borrowed, and it has to pay it back, and that is one of their problems. They had to borrow because no one would buy new shares from a failing company. Did you get all that?"

"You see me making notes, so I've got plenty to think about. I'd better get out of here."

Noah's advanced education had started at 10 a.m. and ended at 12 noon. Martha was in Roy's waiting area when he walked out with Noah.

Martha asked, "Well, Roy, how did it go?"

"It couldn't have gone better. It was easier with the financial statement, but he seemed mad and upset when we reviewed the annual report, and I don't know why, but I think he knew what I was talking about. Anyway, he's paid me and you're ready to go. Good luck, Noah, and I'll soon see you with your tax material."

Roy walked close to Martha and said, "I tried to talk him out of his assault on Road Victor. It's impractical and will fail. You need to talk sense to him about this adventure that can only fail and embarrass him."

Martha said, "You don't know him. I'd be wasting my time."

Riding in Martha's car with her was pleasing because Noah had many things to discuss with her. He kept thinking, Why couldn't she have been my mother? He told her about Rose Marie and how they'd patched things up. He also said he wanted to landscape his yard and would be asking her to write a check if she agreed. He wanted to tell Martha about his scheme to attend a Road Victor shareholders' meeting. He decided to keep that info to himself for the simple reason that he hadn't figured out how he was going to do that. For a tough, experienced adult, it would be a David and Goliath thing. For a sixteen-year-old it would be a David and three Goliaths thing! He also decided to give more thought to developing a plan, but also thinking that the plan might be developed while suffering a form of temporary insanity. He'd heard of that—maybe that was what it was?

When Martha let him off at home, she said, "Nice house."

Noah said, "Thanks. It needs a nice grass yard. I thank you for letting me wreck your day."

Martha drove away, thinking, If he keeps forging ahead like this, he'll end up another Henry Ford or president of General Motors.

THIRTY-ONE

February could be a decent month for Noah. He would soon be seventeen years old. No one troubled him. Was his path ahead clear of land mines? If Noah was lucky, Willis was hopelessly lost someplace, and maybe he was not as evil as he once thought. Jason Hanley was around and about but was probably walking up the back alleys out of sight. The coolest thing in Noah's semi-seclusive life was his renewed friendship with Rose Marie, but he wasn't her charming prince. He discovered that neither was anyone else, not even the football player. So, his path to Rose Marie was clear, at least for a while. Recently something had been oozing into his bloodstream, causing him to think about Rose Marie in romantic terms. Visiting with her in school every day was good, and a real date would be better, but there was no place to go except the ancient Rock City Movie Theatre. It was open on weekends, and of course there were a couple of restaurants in town. She could come to his new house, but everyone under the sun would veto that. He would soon have a driver's license and maybe a car. It was an embarrassment that he lived alone. These were Noah's thoughts in his algebra class. He was awakened by the class bell and realized he had hardly heard or seen a thing in that class.

Rose Marie passed by him and said, "You can't be doing that."

"Doing what?" he asked.

"You looked like you were unconscious in class."

"Correct, I was. Walk with me."

Martha invited Noah for dinner on his birthday. He didn't want a birthday party. It forced people to maybe applaud him for no worthwhile reason. Martha of course didn't know. She would have had a party for him regardless, just as a real mother would. Noah pedaled there, thinking he should have a car, and when he arrived, he was startled to see Rose Marie and his friend Felix.

Noah said hi to Felix and walked to Rose Marie and said, "Rose Marie, I'm really happy to see you, especially after my big sleep in class and your comment."

She said, "Happy birthday. Martha called my mom, and I got the OK to come. Here's a little present for you." She handed him a small box and said, "Something every boy needs."

Noah looked around the room and said, "Shall I open it?" She nodded. It was an expensive pocketknife. Noah thanked her.

Felix said, "Noah, I didn't have enough sense to get you a present."

Martha said, "My gift is this party." Noah thanked everyone. He was now seventeen and eager to go forward. He actually enjoyed his birthday party and particularly the birthday cake and ice cream. The party was a first for him. Noah walked Rose Marie and his bicycle in the direction of her home. Before they reached her house, he had developed a terrible desire to say or do something to make it clear that they were more than friends.

"Rose Marie, let's stop for a minute. Seventeen-year-olds don't fall in love, do they?"

"Noah, what are you trying to say?"

"I wish I knew."

"That would be nice, and then I'd know if we're thinking the same thing."

"OK, Miss Simpson, I know I sorta love you."

"I may sorta feel that way too. I think it's something that just happens."

When they reached her front steps Noah said, "Step over here with me behind that rhododendron bush."

She did, and he said, "If it's OK, I am going to kiss you." He moved to her and she to him, and they kissed. He looked at her, she at him, both pleased with themselves.

Noah said, "Wow" and "Good night," and he walked and skipped to his bicycle and pedaled home with his mind everywhere except his bicycling.

THIRTY-TWO

Smith, Morgan and Wiley sent Noah Road Victor's letter setting the place and date of its annual shareholders' meeting. The meeting was at the large conference room in the Seattle Hilton on June 5, 1975, at 10 a.m.

How am I gonna do that? He'd think about it. He then wondered, Am I letting this bike thing take over my life? It was early March, and he had time to make a decision. He picked up the meeting notice and began reading it. The company had five directors. He knew that from the by-laws. Two of them were up for election. Noah held back a laugh and thought that maybe he should be a director. Mr. Sang had told him that a majority of corporate directors have total control of the corporation. Noah then thought, A seventeen-year-old kid on the board to tell them what kind of bike to make. How's that gonna work? Actually, they need someone on the board to tell them what a bunch of screwups they are. Could I do that? Can it be that hard? I wonder. But crap, I gotta go to school—but wait a minute, I think their board of directors meets once a month. If I'm not a nitwit, I can do it! I'm only forty minutes from the Medford airport, and a day's absence from school once a month is nothing. I've never been on a plane, never even been close to one, don't even know how to get a ticket. Martha will help me.

Noah received from Marty Woods copies of Road Victor directors' meeting minutes for the past twelve months. Most of the minutes dealt with falling sales receipts, how to deal with company debt, and a falling capital base. He wasn't clear on what all of that meant. Mr. James Swanson was the CEO. There was no mention of plans to fix the lack of capital and, most important, nothing was discussed in any of the minutes about guaranteeing their bike or improving, changing, or adding a new bicycle. Sang had explained to him the importance of a good capital base. The minutes had recorded suggestions about renewing and enlarging the long-term debt that was secured by a mortgage on the manufacturing plant, its equipment, and everything else worth two cents. He didn't know what a mortgage was, but he'd find out. Fortunately, Roy Sang's two-hour lecture had proved essential and gave Noah a grasp of what Roy Sang saw as a failing business. Noah took copious notes. Minutes of three directors' meetings recorded suggestions to reduce monthly directors' fees from $2,000 a month to $1,000 or $1,500 per month. Each of the past three years, the CEO had received a year-end bonus of $75,000. Payment of monthly meeting transportation, lodging, and out-of-pocket meeting costs to directors would remain unchanged. Noah was not inclined to use profane language, but standing in his new living room, still smarting from his worthless Road Victor bike and those directors' fees, he was mad and exclaimed loudly, "What in the hell is going on there? Is this sort of thing really supposed to happen? I'm going to that meeting, and I'm getting myself a director's job, seventeen years old or not, and I'm gonna change all that. I hope the price of gold stays up—I may need it!"

Noah didn't know it but he had just set his life's trajectory in business and in love. He would never regret it.

March would soon be over, and Noah continued to be an exceptional high school student. He couldn't figure out if Rose Marie was more than a girlfriend. They were frequently together, and he wasn't interested in any other girl. But what about Rose Marie—was she OK with him? After considering the issue, he decided not to worry about something like that. He couldn't do anything about it. Besides, he'd already decided his path was clear. Anyway, that mystery was as old as civilization.

Noah was sitting in the cold on a folding chair on the front porch of his new house, thinking about the terrible frozen dinner he had just eaten, and the fact that he'd even eaten it, when he saw a new white Ford pickup roll up his driveway and park. Noah stood up as Bud Cooper approached him. Noah thanked him for telling the police about Jason putting the stolen bike on his land.

Bud said, "I'm here to suggest something that you should do." Noah nodded and Bud continued, "When my surveyor and I were here, we found the original survey stakes marking your northeast corner and your southeast corner."

Pointing northerly, he said, "All that cedar timber over there is on your land but close to the boundary line. There is some merchantable timber on your neighbor's property to the north and east, and some loggers don't care much for property lines if there is valuable timber just across the line. Boundary line markers can disappear, and loggers claim honest mistakes were made. So, mark those corner stake locations well, and be vigilant if logging operations commence on your neighbor's land. You need to keep this conversation to yourself. You don't want your neighbor thinking poorly of you because you think he is a potential trespasser."

Noah planned on doing what Bud suggested. Noah thought, If you have nothing to worry about, I guess you're not alive. He watched Bud turn his pickup around and drive away. Noah would later find those corner markers and know where they were, what they looked like, and where their witness trees were located that gave the compass direction and exact distance to the corner markers. Noah thought, I know Bud Cooper's employer wants to buy my timber. I also believe Bud is secretly looking out for me and doesn't want me to sell.

Roy Sang had given Noah a Saturday appointment in March for his 1974 tax returns, and after he overheard Mr. Jenkins tell another teacher that he was going to Grants Pass Saturday, he asked Mr. Jenkins if he would take him to Grants Pass the next time he went. Noah was now in Roy Sang's office and had given him the tax info he needed.

Noah said, "I'm going to tell you something that I don't want anyone else to know. Can you do that?"

Roy told Noah about a CPA's rules of confidence. Noah then briefed Roy Sang on his plan for Road Victor's annual shareholders' meeting. Roy was astonished but not really surprised.

Roy said, "Holy shit, you're really going to do it, aren't you? I'll tell you one thing: They will try to stop you from speaking, and when they

try, you take a sharp step in their direction and tell them that you are
a shareholder, that this is a shareholders' meeting, and you won't be
bullied, so just listen and please don't interrupt. You be sure and tell
them that your CPA, your stockbroker, and your banker have reviewed
with you Road Victor's financials and directors' minutes. That will add
strength to your statement. The first thing you do when you get there
is get someone to nominate you for director. To do that, you must convince that person that you know what is wrong with management and
what you plan to do. You may have to talk to more than one person.
When nominated, you make your big speech. You find out who might
make a good director for the other position and you nominate him
or her. A woman would be good, especially if there are a number of
women shareholders present. If some director wants to stop shareholder comments by talking a lot, interrupt him and say loudly, 'This is
a shareholders' meeting, not a directors' meeting.'"

The day was clear, bright, and warm for March but cool beneath
the huge cedar trees in Noah's little forest. He was pleased that he had
not sold his forest, and out loud he said, "And I never will sell you." He
was sitting on the ground, leaning against the base of one of his cedars,
wondering if he could pull off his big plan for Road Victor. He didn't
know it, but his rough-and-tough life raising himself and protecting
himself and doing all those things for himself that should have been
done for him had made a seventeen-year-old an adult in some ways.
He was bothered by a column in his newspaper that made a joke about
minority shareholders knowing little and causing the most trouble at
shareholders' meetings. He dwelled on that and swiftly concluded that
that was him. I'll fix that right now. I'll be there with 5,100 shares or
maybe 10,000 shares. Marty Woods will have a fit. He walked out of
his forest to his phone. His strong character was always there, and cou-
pled with his rough living circumstance, he had been shaped for life. If
Noah had the inner strength to carry it off, Road Victor management
might not be prepared for what he believed was the bloody truth.

The response of Marty Woods to Noah's buy request was not
as expected because Noah's idea that 5,000 shares or 10,000 shares
would end his minority shareholder status was wrong. Marty lectured,
"Road Victor has been in business for over ninety years and has over
four and a half million shares of common stock outstanding. Many of

those shareholders will not be at the annual meeting in person, but they have given a shareholder at the meeting written authority, called a proxy, to vote their shares. Many of the old shareholders or their heirs probably hold a huge number of shares and will vote the proxies of others. If you think you're going to do what you want to do, you'll have to conjure up some magic! Get to the meeting early and convince the right shareholders that you are real, and they need a bright kid who knows about bicycles on the board and knows about the company's financial march to death."

Noah still had school to deal with. His social studies class was, for Noah, interesting but maybe not very important—or was it? European history and events flowing from that eventually gave us the United States. Wow. The workings of the US government were boring but important. He supposed that knowledge of various peoples around the world was OK, but study of the inner actions of people in their relationships was nonsense. Sitting in that class he realized that he was too fully engaged in the Road Victor business. He needed to be in school physically and mentally. He wanted to spend some time with Rose Marie, and he had not. He wanted to spend time and effort making his new house more livable, and he had not. Even now, his mind was everywhere but on social studies. He said to himself, No more Road Victor stuff until the week before the meeting. My education is the key to everything, and it will happen here and in college. He had solicited applications from the University of Oregon and the University of Washington and had done nothing with them. Noah would try to keep that vow.

Some news articles in his *Wall Street Journal*s were of keen interest to him, especially the attempts by President Nixon and Secretary of State Henry Kissinger to end the war in Vietnam. The military draft had ended two years ago, and he would not be drafted into the army when he finished high school. Like thousands of college students and draft-age men, he hated the war. Some articles found on the opinion pages of his newspapers claimed that all the North Vietnamese wanted was to have their country to themselves and be a nation among nations, and no foreign country should interfere with that. Seemed right to Noah. He didn't want anyone interfering with him. Maybe he understood more clearly than some. He also read an article about the

FDA recalling diet drugs containing amphetamine because some people were using it for recreational purposes. Noah thought, What the hell is that?

It was still quite clear that Congress had not done anything about getting off the gold standard, but gold prices were pretty good. Most of *The Wall Street Journal* writers predicted that the price of gold would rise as soon as the gold standard ended.

Noah would hang on to his gold. He had sold a few sinkers to increase his shares in Road Victor. He could still hear Marty Woods calling the buy uninformed and stupid. He had signed the broker's paper called a "disclaimer." The Vietnam War ended April 30, 1975.

That was good news.

Something strange was beginning to happen with some of his high school classmates. He did not have a confidential relationship with any classmates except Rose Marie and Felix, and they were not a part of any of the unusual conversations he was hearing. Their conversations were intentionally quiet and private. A small number of students would, at times, act bizarre. The word he kept hearing was "pot."

He sought out Felix Bronson and said, "What is this talk about pot that I'm hearing?"

Felix said, "You don't know? It's been around awhile, but it's just now come to Rock City. It's dope. You smoke it and it makes you crazy."

"Have you smoked it?" demanded Noah.

"Yes, once. I don't smoke cigarettes, and that pot was terrible."

"That stuff is marijuana, isn't it?"

"Yes. I read about it. It contains a drug that is mind-altering."

Noah wondered out loud why anyone would do that.

"I don't, and it is expensive," was Felix's response.

"Well, it's illegal to have it, isn't it?" asked Noah.

"Yes, it is, and it's unlawful to sell it. That's why those guys are being so quiet about it. Stupidity tops too many things."

"I'll talk to Rose Marie about it. She may know about pot, and she may not know who is the sleaze-bag dealer or user to avoid, and, if we know, we'll tell her. It could be dangerous for us to act on this. Let the police deal with that stuff."

Felix became unusually serious and went straight to the point, saying, "Noah, I hear that some of these people who sell pot also grow it. Our climate is perfect for the cultivation of marijuana, and creepy people have a reputation for growing it on other people's land. They apparently do a good job hiding their plants. Three or four acres of your land slopes off to the south and can't be seen from your house. It even has a pretty decent spring at the head of that little creek running off your property. That makes your place perfect for growing that stuff. You need to keep an eye open for trespassers."

Noah said he would, but he was thinking, That's not going to happen, but I'll pay attention. There can't be anyone like that in Rock City. Noah didn't realize that those thoughts were naive.

Noah had reached a point where he could not afford to be distracted from his schoolwork or from his scheme about Road Victor. His commitment to go after Road Victor was not a normal response to its crummy bicycle, but Noah was beyond normal in many ways. There was no distraction from the bike business until the pot thing arrived at his school. He might or he might not do something about that. For now he would not let that problem interfere with his life.

He was continually preparing himself for the shareholders' meeting. He studied the nomenclature of a bicycle, and he studied the bylaws and found nothing that prohibited a seventeen-year-old from being a director. Nominations for director were made at the meeting. He suspected that some nominations were already planned. The bylaws mentioned that a proxy was allowed. He checked the meaning of *proxy* in his Merriam-Webster.

Martha had taken him to Medford and to a travel agent. She assisted him in buying a round-trip United Airlines ticket and a three-night stay in the Olympic Hotel. Noah laid three $100 bills on the agent's desk. Martha could see he had a few more of those bills in his wallet, and she again thought, This young man is unique, never to be doubted. On the way home she took Noah into the Medford airport terminal and acquainted him with the place and how things worked. He soaked it up.

She said, "When you get to Seattle, go to the front of that terminal and take a taxi to your hotel. The taxi will charge you around $20, so be ready to pay. Do the same thing at the hotel to get you to your meeting and back. Take a taxi every place you go in Seattle. It is much safer, and you won't get lost. You are only seventeen and untraveled. Don't flash your money when opening your wallet. The wrong person might be watching."

Noah looked at Martha for a brief moment as she started her car. Then he said, "Martha, go to Seattle with me. I will need your help. I'll pay all your expenses. Turn around and go back to the travel agent's office, please." Martha turned the engine off and sat bewildered and silent.

Noah said, "Please. I can't go alone, and you're the only person in my life that has actually cared enough for me. No one but Mr. Webb would need to know, if that is important to you. I'll be walking into the wolf's den, but I'm gonna do it. Your presence at the meeting would help."

This was the first time in his life that he had begged anyone for help, and he didn't like it. He somehow knew that it was the right thing to do, and Martha knew it.

She glanced at Noah, who knew what was happening, and said, "OK, I'll be happy to go to Seattle with you. School will be out for the summer, and you are indeed a special person that hardly needs looking after, but I'm going with you anyway."

They returned to the travel agent's office.

On the way back to Rock City, Noah said, "I can't thank you enough, Martha. Please stop at my bank, I'm out of cash."

The last week of May, Noah attended the Rock City High School graduation rites with Rose Marie. He watched a couple of strange-acting boys graduate that must've been involved in the pot thing. He hoped that would be the end of the problem in this school.

THIRTY-THREE

June 3, 1975, arrived and Noah and Martha were seated in a United Airlines Boeing 737 at twenty-five thousand feet over Oregon and halfway to Seattle. Noah was excited to be on an airplane, and he was all eyes and ears, checking out everything including the land below. There was plenty to talk about, but at first there was not much conversation.

Noah was busy examining a tiny sack of nuts he had been handed by a nice lady wearing a United Airlines jacket. His thoughts wandered away to what he was traveling to and to his relatives in New York.

Noah turned to Martha and said, "Is it more important for me to be in Seattle with people I don't know or for me to be in Buffalo, New York, with my relatives?"

Martha said, "That's for you to decide and you have plenty of time to do that. For now, you concentrate on Road Victor."

Martha then asked what Noah was going to wear to the annual meeting. His response was vague and sounded like, "About what I have on."

"There is a men's store at the Seattle Airport, and I'm taking you there."

He thought, Wow, I'm thinking this is what mothers do.

The landing gave Noah a good look at the Seattle skyline, the huge seaport facilities, and the surrounding area. The landing of the monster airplane without crashing relieved his fright, and before he knew what had happened, they were on their way to claim their baggage with a new sport coat and white dress shirt in hand. His shoes barely passed approval. On their way to the hotel, the tall buildings amazed him, and their hotel—it was enormous. Two single rooms had been reserved. He explored a bit while looking for the sign-in desk. The Olympic's dining room was immense. It would be a new experience eating there considering the fact that he had never eaten in a hotel dining room or anything like it. The room's ceiling was covered with six- or seven-foot squares of dark wood paneling separated with molded wood beams and was at least two stories high. The walls were paneled with similar wood up about eight feet from the floor. There were twenty-five or more wood tables with thick white table cloths and wood chairs matching the tables and a row of paneled wood booths along one wall. The tables were set with many utensils and some glassware. Noah hoped that Martha would help him with the menu and the choice of forks and spoons.

The cost of dinner that evening was entered on his room bill. The expense of his adventure was starting to bother him. He said to Martha, "Good thing I went to the bank! Martha, I would be a mess if you weren't with me. I had no idea of what I didn't know."

Martha replied, "A bright Athenian four hundred years before the birth of Christ thought the same thing, but he said, 'I know nothing.'"

Noah said, "I can't always understand everything you say."

It was 8 a.m. and they were on their way to the 10 a.m. meeting. It was several blocks away in a large conference room of the Seattle Hilton Hotel. Noah was dressed in his snappy but conservative new sport coat and new white Van Heusen dress shirt with no tie. Martha was wearing her stylish camel hair coat. The Seattle weather was cool. He was totally focused on the business set before him. They walked into the meeting room where numerous rows of folding chairs had been set out for the meeting. Facing the chairs was a slightly raised area with a long table with folding chairs set on one side facing the expected audience.

Noah stepped up to a desk where a sign said Register Here, and he identified himself and picked up a printed meeting agenda. The stock register book held his name and the number of shares he owned. The stock register book and the registration of shareholders were necessary for identifying them and the number of shares they could vote. The public was not allowed to attend the meeting. They walked to Margaret, the woman registering shareholders, and he introduced

Martha as his guardian. Martha had a certified copy of her guardian-ship papers in her purse and showed it to the lady at the desk, who approved her presence. They obviously wanted shareholders only at the meeting. Fortunately, she had never removed that document from her purse since the day lawyer Reynolds had given it to her.

The refreshment bar was behind the registration desk. Noah was at the refreshment bar helping himself to a small goodie from the end of a toothpick when he heard a shareholder at the registration desk give her name and number of shares held. That was important information, and he spent a great deal of time at the refreshment bar occasionally popping tasty bite-size things in his mouth as any teenager might do. He was there off and on until the meeting started. So far there were only forty-five or fifty shareholders present, but he had heard many people declare to the registrar whose proxy he or she held and the number of those shares. He would remember the shareholders who controlled a large number of shares plus a proxy and the names of some other shareholders who held a large number of shares. He also saw and overheard two very young shareholders register. Of course, Noah suddenly realized, the directors had always had most of that shareholder information at their fingertips. Have they been counting votes of shareholder friends, believing that they know who will continue on as a director?

There was sufficient time before the meeting commenced to talk to a few shareholders, particularly those who would be voting many shares. He walked over to Lila Jameson, who was maybe sixty years old, was smartly dressed, looked to be straight from the hairdresser, and had a warm, sparkling look about her. He sat down next to her and introduced himself. She didn't know why she had the attention of this nice-looking boy, but she would soon find out.

He said, "I heard you register, so I know who you are, and I would really like to talk to you about this company. I'll be quick. Will you listen to what I have to say?"

She looked him over with a disapproving expression on her not-so-young face. "OK, but be quick."

He told her he was a seventeen-year-old shareholder, and based on what his CPA, his stockbroker, and his banker had told him, Road Victor had been oozing life for years and was about to fail, but it might be saved if drastic measures were put in place. He squared around in his chair and, facing her directly, said, "Do you want to hear more?"

"Yes," she quickly responded.

Noah reviewed the balance sheet he had in hand and how it was probably tweaked to not look so bad. He said he had been told that it was so bad that new capital was needed but could not be raised by the sale of common stock, and no banker in his right mind would loan more money to Road Victor. He talked about the last quarterly financial statement that showed insufficient income to pay the mortgage that covered every fixed asset owned by the company. He told her that all five directors were overpaid and had been sleeping on the job for at least five years. Recent directors' minutes that he had in hand proved that.

He continued to have her direct attention and said, "But worst of all, the Road Victor bicycle is a piece of crap. Walk into any bicycle shop and they will tell you. Mrs. Jameson, I am a straight-A student, I am an orphan who never had a parent, I've never asked anyone for anything except my guardian, who is here with me, and I'm upset because the only bike I ever had broke almost in two. It was a Road Victor with poor workmanship, and the dealer wouldn't fix it or give me a refund, and there was no warranty."

The woman raised an eyebrow at him. "Well . . . what could I possibly do about all of that?"

Noah sat up straighter in his chair. "Nominate me for director. They need a bicyclist on the board, not a bunch of old men. I may know more about this company than most of the shareholders. Oh, by the way, the board gave the CEO a $75,000 bonus for each of the past three years. We have a chance to get two new bright directors and tell the CEO to find a new job. There are many women here that hold many shares and proxies. Please tell them about this conversation and make me a director. My only task will be to save this old company. Your shares have fallen to five dollars a share. If the company fails, our shares will be worth nothing. This is truly the last chance the shareholders have to save this ship. Help me do this and help yourself and everyone here. Mrs. Jameson, are we good?"

"Yes," she replied.

Noah then pointed across the room and said, "See that lady over there with the camel hair coat? She is my guardian; she was also my fourth-grade teacher. Her name is Martha Webb. If you want to know the good and bad about me, ask her, and if you talk to any of the other ladies about me, tell them about Martha."

Noah then found young Bobby Shaffer and sat next to him. Noah introduced himself, and Bobby Shaffer was thinking, What does this kid want? Bobby Shaffer had inherited his 110,000 shares from his late widowed mother. He had no siblings, lived alone in a decently furnished three-room apartment, and was about to receive his master's degree in business from the University of Washington. He was sitting on four job offers but wanted to horse around for a year or so. Besides, his current girlfriend was too clingy and serious.

Bobby Shaffer gave Noah a disapproving stare and said, "Who are you?"

"I'm nobody."

"Well, what can I do for you?"

"You can vote for me for director. The other thing you can do is accept the nomination when I nominate you for the other director's position."

"Are you crazy?"

"Look, Shaffer, I know more about this company than most people in this room. My CPA, my stockbroker, and my banker studied the company's financials, and the company could be belly-up in a year. Also, their bike is a piece of shit. With you and me as directors, we'll replace the CEO, get rid of some expenses, and redesign the bike that hasn't been redesigned in eight years. The bike competition has trashed us. You have 110,000 shares today worth $540,000. If something isn't done almost immediately, this time next year your shares will be worthless. Two years ago, they were worth nearly $2,000,000. So what brilliant thing did you do at the last five shareholders' meetings? Maybe you should just sell and let some other brilliant shareholder take the loss."

"OK, Noah North, what the hell; I'm with you. Why is a seventeen-year-old interested in this business?"

"I raised myself without parents with little help, and I don't like being cheated or pushed around, and Road Victor did that to me, so I informed myself about them and came after them. When I was doing all of that, I learned about corporations, their shareholders, and a little about management. I may be in over my head, but I'm not a quitter. I'm hoping that I can accomplish something for myself and the other shareholders."

Shaffer gave him an appraising look. "You're a gutsy kid, but being a kid may be the weak link in your plan."

Noah told Shaffer that he had known that from the beginning and then said, "My age hasn't prevented me from doing anything I wanted to do. If it had, I would be down and out and nowhere! I have been lucky to have wanted the right things."

Noah had been occasionally looking over at Mrs. Jameson, and he had seen her talking to Mrs. Woodson and, later, Mrs. Latimer. Both looked to be in their sixties. I wonder if the right things are being said, he said to himself. Then he saw all three of them walk over to Martha. It looked like they were introducing themselves. He knew they were asking Martha about him.

Martha said to them, "Noah North lives in Rock City, Oregon, where I teach school. He is an orphan and I am his guardian. He has been the top student in every class following a late start in school. He had a foolish relative keep him home from kindergarten and the first grade."

Sylvia Latimer, the owner of over a half million Road Victor shares, asked, "How is it that he is knowledgeable about corporate business?"

Martha said, "He has had a real interest in the commodity market and the stock market since he was eleven years old, but I'm not telling you why. He wasn't interested in reading a newspaper until he started reading *The Wall Street Journal*, which his banker was giving him. Later he subscribed, and he has gradually acquired a business-like vocabulary and a half-smart sense about the way companies function. His advisors understand him, and Noah understands them because they are usually speaking in a business and money vernacular tied to that business. He is a quick learner. He's a smart and gutsy kid who doesn't like the word 'no.'"

Mrs. Woodson said, "That's all we wanted to know. We thank you."

The folding chairs in the Hilton conference room were filling up, and Road Victor directors were starting to sit down at the long table.

Their names were plainly visible on nameplates facing the audience. The three-year terms of directors William Moore and Jerry Monson had expired, and they were seeking re-election. Apparently Stanley Clarke was chairman of the board, and he opened the meeting. He introduced himself and the other directors, as well as the chief financial officer, John Sims, and the chief executive officer, James Swanson. The CEO and CFO sat in chairs set apart from the directors' table. A secretary who sat at the directors' table read the minutes of last year's shareholders' meeting, and they were approved.

Stanley Clarke was seventy-five years old, an apartment complex owner, handsome, three times divorced, and four times married, with five children by his first two wives and two children who hated him as he hated his wife's springer spaniel. He was a businessman without a vision, and he didn't like change or anyone telling him what to do. He tumbled into the category of "the less you know, the more you know," thus giving his fourth wife second thoughts. If it were not for his beautiful house and grounds and the society he lived in, she would leave him.

The CFO gave a financial report that didn't say much and didn't mention looming failure. The CEO gave a lame and gloomy report of the company's bicycle business and falling sales but made no mention of a plan to increase sales, except that when the economy improved maybe bicycle sales would too. For an hour or more, questions were asked by the shareholders, and vague responses were made by the CEO and some directors. Most of the questions asked were made by obviously upset shareholders.

Noah was getting uneasy and nervous about the election of directors. The questions kept coming about sales and projected income, plans to contain expenses, plans for a new product, and plans, if any, to repair and modernize the production process. Noah didn't hear a single positive response. The final item on the agenda was reached, and Chairman of the Board Stanley Clarke announced that the meeting would proceed with the election of two directors to replace those whose terms had expired. Nomination for the expired term of Jerry Monson was now open. Immediately a shareholder stood up and nominated Jerry Monson, and instantly another shareholder stood up and seconded the nomination. Lila Jameson rose and nominated Noah

North. Bobby Shaffer stood and seconded the nomination. Noah was surprised in several ways. First, he had never seen a nomination event, and second, Mrs. Jameson had surprised him, although it was exactly what he wanted her to do. Maybe if it were not for her, all of his time and plans would have evaporated. Bobby Shaffer then moved that the nominations be closed, and Director George Newton seconded the motion, and on the vote it passed.

Chairman Clarke then announced that nominations for the expired term of William Moore were now open. Immediately a shareholder arose and nominated William Moore. Another shareholder unknown to Noah started to second the nomination, and before he could say anything else, Noah arose and nominated Bobby Shaffer and moved that nominations be closed. Lila Jameson seconded the motion, and it passed.

Shareholders accustomed to uncontested director elections, dreary financial reports, and optimistic CEO speeches were now silently and politely twitching in their seats, looking at each other while grasping and assimilating the curious nomination of two youngsters for directors. Soon they were noisily questioning and talking as if they didn't know what to do. Chairman Clarke stood and requested silence. He said that blank slips of paper would be given to each shareholder present with instructions to write their name and proxy held, the number of shares they represented, and the name of the nominee to receive their vote.

Seventeen-year-old candidate Noah gathered all his emotional strength, stood up, and in a clear voice, said, "I wish to speak to the shareholders about myself and tell them why I want to be a director."

Chairman Clarke, with a faintly amused grin on his face, visibly matching similar expressions on the faces of the other directors, looked Noah over and said, "Go ahead, the floor is yours."

Noah stood erect, getting nervous and uneasy while looking over the room and his audience and thinking, If I can confront Uncle Willis and Buster North and that idiot Jason Hanley, and raise myself, I can do this.

Grasping the back of the chair in front of him for balance, he said, "First, you need to know who I am. I am seventeen years old, I am an orphan, I am a straight-A student, I own my own house, and my tutors for this meeting were my CPA, my stockbroker, my banker, my law-yer, and my guardian. I have, with help, studied this company's latest balance sheet, latest financial statement, and the minutes of the last few directors' meetings, and I have reviewed the bicycle market. I had never owned a bicycle until last year. I bought my first bike, a Road Victor, because like every kid, I knew the name, it must be good. Ten days later I rode it off a sidewalk curb into the street, and the bike's top tube separated from the head tube and the down tube almost sep-arated from the head tube. I scratched my knees and an elbow. I took the bike back to your independent dealer, who would not fix it or re-fund my money, and there was no warranty. I asked around and dis-covered that Road Victor bikes are now a piece of crap. I have never taken anything lying down, so I bought a few Road Victor shares, and here I am. I bought those shares for the purpose of coming here and causing trouble. My broker wouldn't buy your shares for me without making me sign a paper that said he had advised me not to buy Road Victor because it was a terrible investment. After meeting some of you shareholders, I changed my mind, and now I want to help save Road Victor because it is worth saving."

There were audible gasps followed by murmured conversation coming from the audience. A few seconds later, things settled down. Noah looked around the room, standing straight and erect, and said, "You ain't heard nothin' yet."

Chairman Clarke, who had scrambled to find out who the hell this kid was—no one at the directors' table seemed to know anything about him—weakly said, "Noah North, you sure you want to continue this?"

"I certainly do, and the by-laws give me that right." Again looking over his audience, he continued, "I'm here to help you save this old bicycle company. This company has been around forever but has been headed downhill for maybe ten years because other bike companies have a better bike. We have not changed our design for, I think, nine or ten years, and the worse things got the less we did. The directors' min-utes that I have show no mention of improving our bike and no men-tion of fixing the lack of capital. Without new capital, we can't fully fix anything. Worst of all, repaying the company's debt is taking all the income, so there is no money for making a new and modern bike. There is nothing in the directors' minutes about cutting expenses or selling unused property. If we don't start to gradually and continually increase our income, our shares will lose more value." Noah picked up his file from the seat of the empty chair next to him and slammed it back down on the chair. The shareholders were silent.

He then said to them, "I'll be finished in a minute or two. The most immediate thing to do is to stop selling a bike that is an outdated piece of junk. Throw away all the steel material used in our bike and replace it with the new super-strength lightweight aluminum. That will not be expensive, and it will be an honest change to advertise. It will be a start to an all-new Road Victor bike."

Noah walked closer to the directors' table but still facing the audience and said, "These directors have been sitting at that table for term after term. Some for twenty-five years, others from fifteen to twenty years. They have all been directing our company on a downhill slide for at least fifteen years. Every quarter they see a balance sheet and a financial statement usually worse than the last one. The CEO has been handing them those papers most of those years, and his financial officer has been preparing them. I don't know what they have been telling you at these meetings on how to fix things. They certainly didn't tell us at this meeting. It looks to me that all of these directors are old and haven't bought a bike or ridden one for twenty-five or thirty years. A director should know all about his company's product. A seventeen-year-old knows about bikes. There are more ways to cut expenses. Each of these directors has been receiving $2,000 for each monthly directors' meeting he attends. I passed arithmetic, so that's $120,000, plus travel, plus lodging expenses for five directors for a year. Also, the CEO has been given a bonus of $75,000 a year for the past three years. If I am elected, all that will stop if I have my way, and I usually do. The travel and lodging expenses for directors will be paid. If you want to save your investment and maybe see it grow a little, start the change and vote for Bobby Shaffer and Noah North." Noah sat down and sighed with relief.

Chairman Clarke said, "If any other candidate wants to speak, now is the time."

Jerry Monson stood up and said, "With all due respect to Noah North, we should not be electing a seventeen-year-old to this board of directors. We need mature and experienced businessmen to guide Road Victor through our current problems."

Monson sat down and Bobby Shaffer arose and said, "The present board took at least twelve or thirteen years to get us into this mess, and suddenly these five brilliant, financially wise, modern-thinking, innovative old guys are going to save us. This isn't Disneyland, Mr. Monson. Miracles ain't gonna happen!" Bobby Shaffer sat down.

"Anyone else want to speak?" asked Chairman Clarke. No one else spoke.

Several women handed out a small blank white paper to each shareholder while Chairman Clarke repeated instructions to write their name, number of shares, the name of any proxy, and that number of proxy shares to be voted.

The room was alive with near-muted conversation. Some shareholders were walking around asking questions and some were giving advice while others simply voted and gave their ballot to the one collecting ballots.

Noah and Bobby heard a nearby voice say, "I'm not voting for some kid."

Twenty minutes went by, and Clarke asked for all the ballots. They would be counted by the secretary to the directors and two shareholders she selected at random. The votes were being counted at a large table behind the directors' table.

Noah walked to the reception area and to Martha, who was pacing around, obviously impatient and unsettled.

"Martha, I'm going to be a director, so take it easy. No one challenged what I said. It's in the bag!"

After thirty minutes, Chairman Clarke asked the secretary what was happening. Chairman Clarke announced that the tabulation was slowed by incorrect figures on many proxies, and their correction from the stock register records was taking time.

The room became silent when the board secretary walked to Chairman Clarke and handed him a single piece of paper that contained the vote tally. A close look at Clarke revealed a subdued gasp. Chairman Clarke announced that Noah North and Bobby Shaffer had become Road Victor directors. The room was filled with applause. Noah and Bobby Shaffer stood together.

Noah looked at Bobby and, quietly joking, said, "Now what do we do?"

Shareholders lined up to meet Noah and Bobby, urging them to fix Road Victor's decline. Many said they would now hang on to their shares.

A glance at people sitting at the directors' table showed surprise, disbelief, and what looked like worry on the face of the CEO. The CEO was concerned because at least one of the two new directors seemed as fearless as he was young. Chairman Clarke called for a directors' meeting to start in thirty minutes.

Martha, who had witnessed the whole meeting, rushed over to Noah and hugged him. "Congratulations, you might be famous." Before he could respond, Lila Jameson congratulated him by giving him a hug that ended up with his head buried in her generous breasts.

When she let go, Sylvia Latimer hugged him and said, "Noah North, I have over two million invested in this company. I don't know why I still have it, but please save it and maybe add a little for me."

"I will if I can," he replied.

Jerry Monson walked by Noah and said, "I hope you know what you are doing."

"I do too," Noah responded.

More shareholders introduced themselves to Noah and Bobby and wished them success.

Noah, in a brief melancholy mood brought on by fleeting thoughts of his life without a family, said to Martha, "I have no way of telling you how happy I am and how much I love all the things you have done for me. If I could have a mother and had my choice of all the mothers in the world, I would choose you."

Martha thought, Noah is still a little boy, but he'll never let anyone know it.

Then she said, "Well, Noah Jeremiah North, that would be OK with me."

Noah and Bobby sat at the directors' table in the Hilton meeting room. The other three directors were also seated. Some shareholders were still hanging around the refreshment table. The woman who took minutes of the shareholders' meeting was seated at the directors' table, prepared to record the minutes. She read the minutes of the prior directors' meeting, and they were approved. Congratulations and handshaking had gone around with little or nothing being said.

"This meeting won't take long," announced Chairman Clarke. "There's not much we can do today. But first I congratulate Noah North and Bobby Shaffer as new directors. We are so entrenched in the same business model that change may be difficult. Directors Hedges and Lancaster and I are old, and a new direction for Road Victor will not be easy. We're not immovable."

Noah, expecting Clarke's comment, said, "It will take a while for Bobby and me to get used to how things are done or not done."

Chairman Clarke said, "We are going to skip old business and go forward with new business if there is any."

Noah immediately moved that all steel frame parts on their bike be replaced with high-quality-strength aluminum and that it be done immediately. No discussion was held, and the motion passed three to two with director Oliver Hedges voting aye. Clarke was wrong. Things would get done. Bobby suggested that at the next meeting there be a report on the change of material for the bike frame and a report that the change had been made, and whether or not new bikes were headed to the dealers.

Bobby then said, "We also want in that report the names and experience of our people designing our bikes."

The motion passed three to two with Director Hedges's help.

Noah looked across the table at Mr. Hedges, clearly catching his gaze.

"Mr. Hedges, I'm glad you are with Shaffer and me on these small matters, and I hope you are on the big ones to come. If you are, there will be a turnaround."

Bobby then made a motion that within ten days, the directors be furnished with a report on the change of materials and the status of the remodeled bike and the engineers' names. The motion was not discussed. The motion passed. Noah made a motion that minutes of all directors' meetings be mailed to shareholders owning over a hundred thousand shares. There was no discussion on the motion. The motion passed three to two. Noah then made a motion that directors' fees be eliminated. Noah and Bobby smiled as three directors squirmed in their chairs. The three old directors wanted to discuss the motion, and the three complained that they needed to be paid because of time away from their regular employment and business. Noah wanted to respond, but he knew it would be useless. Noah's motion failed three to two. Bobby moved that the meeting be adjourned. The motion passed. The old directors had had a long uncomfortable day and were anxious to get the hell out of there—so anxious that they didn't realize that now all the big shareholders would see from the minutes that the old guys had voted to keep directors' fees at $2,000 a month.

Bobby Shaffer found Noah walking out of the hotel with Martha. Noah introduced Martha to Bobby.

Bobby said, "We gotta talk. I need your address and phone number, and you need mine. We need to figure out how and where we're going with all this." Martha dug a notepad and pen out of her purse, and they exchanged phone and mail info.

Noah said, "I don't have time now. I have a plane to catch. We can sort things out by phone and by mail. OK?"

"Sounds good," said Bobby. "We'll be in touch."

Noah again sat next to the window on the 737. Martha said, "You know, there was a *Wall Street Journal* reporter at that meeting, and he was furiously writing when you were speaking. You are going to see your name in the paper, maybe more than you like. A seventeen-year-old director of a well-known company is news. I'm saying this to you because you must choose your words carefully if you are interviewed. Most of all, don't criticize people, but if you have to, just politely question what was done or said, and be truthful as you always have been."

Noah, still looking out the window, said, "I can do that," and turning to Martha, said, "You know those one-ounce sinkers I gave you? They're more than one ounce. They are each about seventy percent heavier by volume than lead. If you ever weigh them, gold is weighed in troy ounces, or twelve ounces to the pound."

Martha laughed out loud and put her hand on Noah's shoulder and said, "What a funny thing to say. Surely you know that is not why I treasure them, and I'll have no reason to weigh them."

"Well, I'm thinking about giving you another one."

"Please, Noah, you don't have to do that. This whole trip has been a joy and a pleasure, and I wouldn't have missed it for anything."

THIRTY-FOUR

Noah was back home with the whole summer vacation ahead of him. He hired a landscaper to plant a lawn and a few shrubs and to install an irrigation system. No one in Rock City except Martha knew what had happened in Seattle or that Noah had even been there. His *Wall Street Journals* were an education and his entertainment. Knowing what was happening in the world was interesting, but the world of business was important; the Thursday, July 3, 1975, issue had an article that had his total attention. It was printed on an inside page, but the headline was large—you couldn't miss it:

TEENAGE DIRECTOR AT ROAD VICTOR

A Seattle, Washington, company that hadn't had a surprise in 15 years got one at its shareholders' meeting June 5. Seventeen-year-old shareholder Noah North ousted 20-year incumbent director Jerry Monson with a clear majority vote. North, in a blistering criticism of the present management and calling the company's bottom line a free fall, won the vote of several large shareholders wielding proxies. He attributed his knowledge of the public corporation to tutoring by his CPA, stockbroker, and banker. The other new director, Bobby Shaffer, nominated by North,

showed his colors at the directors' meeting
that followed the shareholders' meeting. The
first major change to their front-line bike
in 15 years was ordered at North's urging,
whereby aluminum replaced all-steel frame
parts. He said that was only the beginning.
North lectured that bicycle manufacturers
should have a director or two who rode bicycles. Road Victor now has two. We know
nothing more about Noah North except that
he's a winner. Road Victor's shares did not
move, but they might.

Noah was not surprised at the newspaper article. Martha had told
him on the way home that it would happen. He hoped that it would
not cause him problems. He was accustomed to privacy and liked
it. Because of that newspaper article, people in Rock City who knew
Noah North would now know more about him. I don't know if that is
good or bad, but I'll find out. I certainly don't want everyone knowing
all about me. Trouble is, I've been spending all my time with adults,
and maybe I'm becoming one. Why can't I just be a kid? I'll call Felix.
Better yet, I'll call Rose Marie.

He dropped his new Blue Streak bike in Rose Marie's yard, and she
appeared on her front porch with a can of Pepsi in each hand.

They sat together on her front steps, and Noah asked, "Have you
heard about my trip to Seattle?"

"No."

"That's good," he said.

She looked puzzled. "What are you saying?"

"I am saying that after what happened in Seattle, people are going
to look at me and not see a teenager when I want to be a teenager and
be with you."

"I still have no idea what you are talking about."

"OK," he said. "I was elected to be part of the management of Road
Victor, Inc., and I'll be in Seattle once a month. Explaining the whole
thing is too complicated. Right now I want to listen to you about your
life."

Rose Marie said, "Why are you acting so mysterious?"

"I am really happy with my Seattle trip, and I just want you to know that, and I don't want it to interfere with our friendship, whatever it is." Noah placed his hand on her hand, saying, "We still have two months of the summer, and I would like to spend a lot of it with you."

She said, "I'm good with that."

He looked over at the Blue Streak bike lying in her yard and mumbled, "What am I doing with that?" They talked about the coming school year and being in the twelfth grade. Noah thought he might try to get on the baseball team, and Rose Marie wanted to be a runner, but there was no girls' track team or any girls' sports in their high school.

Noah suddenly stood up and said, "I gotta go," and quickly kissed Rose Marie on the cheek, jumped on his bike, and rode away. Rose Marie was left thinking, What was all that about?

Wilson Marston, banker, was sitting at his desk, catching up on his reading, when he read the article about Noah North in the July 3, 1975, issue of *The Wall Street Journal*. He silently said, Holy shit. The kid actually did it. We actually have a celebrity customer. He then showed the article to nearly every employee in the Rock City National Bank. Some bank tellers are seasoned gossips, and soon many bank customers and their friends knew about Noah North.

Rose Marie Simpson was enjoying dinner with her parents when her father asked her if she had heard the news about her friend Noah. Mr. Simpson had read the article. He said, "It is interesting to know that Noah has a CPA, a stockbroker, and a banker. He must be a rich kid. Rose Marie, do you know anything about that?"

She said, "I know a little bit about that. Noah is a very bright straight-A student and also modest and quiet about his life. He did tell me a little about his Seattle trip and that he will be going there once a month to help manage Road Victor, Inc. I think it's neat. I don't know about any of the other stuff."

Wilson Marston and Rose Marie's father were not the only ones to read that article.

In Buffalo, New York, two weeks after the July 3 *Wall Street Journal* publication, Margo North walked past Trustee Wendall Dollar's receptionist and his secretary and into his office. She was very noticeable, and Wendall, with his office door wide open, couldn't take his eyes off Margo's strident high-heeled march into his office. She slammed the July 3, 1975, issue of *The Wall Street Journal* on his desk. He knew she was not to be denied. She was beautiful, with her dark hair pulled tightly back to a sloppy knot. Her eyes were big, bright, and almond-shaped with a little cosmetic help, and they actually looked friendly. Her red lips framed a large mouth full of white teeth all in perfect alignment. Her figure complemented everything. It wasn't possible for her to always be friendly, but she was always beautiful.

Margo unpleasantly said, "Does anybody work here? There's enough info in that article to inform you about everything you need to know to wind up and close the North Trust."

Before Wendall Dollar could answer she was gone.

Noah occasionally considered learning more about his New York family, but he wasn't interested in going there, not yet, anyway. He was interested in happenings in Rock City and Seattle, and he was interested in knowing the truth about his father's death. He would talk to Bill Walstrom at the Arcade Tavern and get his opinion about any connection between Buster's death and relatives in Buffalo.

Marty Woods, stockbroker, who read the July 3 article, called Noah and said, "Well, you did it. Now what are you going to do?"

Noah replied, "I've learned a lot. I know how to get airline reservations and tickets and how to navigate airports, how to get a hotel room, how to buy clothes, how to get elected to the board of a failing company, and how to possibly save the life of a near-dead company. I also made some nice friends with a lotta shares in Road Victor. Other than that, I'm trying to enjoy the summer. When school starts, I'll be anxious to see if my classmates react to me peacefully. Do you have any advice for me? Do you want me to tell you when to buy Road Victor?"

Marty said, "You've just reminded me to send you Securities Exchange Commission rules about insider trading. Employees and management of public corporations like Road Victor cannot privately give out information about their company that will affect the value or price of their shares unless that information has previously been made public by the company. Likewise, you cannot buy your company shares until after that company information is made public. It is a crime to violate that rule. Be sure to read and know those rules and to abide by them."

"Thanks, Marty, I didn't know anything about that."

"Anyway, Noah, I wish you the very best."

The previously unnoticed Noah North was now noticed, mostly by people he didn't know, and he happily fielded many friendly hellos. When he walked by the Arcade Tavern, the owner Bill Walstrom saw him and walked out and stopped Noah and said, "Noah, congratulations on your connection with Road Victor. I want you to know that people are talking about it, and ninety-nine percent of the talk is good, but there are a tiny few that are envious or don't understand such things. I want you to call me if you have any trouble or problem with such people. I'll be there for you."

Noah said, "I need to talk to you. You've just said what I wanted to hear."

Seated in Bill's office, Noah said, "I came here today to see you. I think I have a problem. Can I call you Bill?"

"Yes."

"OK. I think someone may want to kill me. I think they killed my father, but I don't really know. It's all about an inheritance that was coming to my father, and now it's coming to me. If I am not alive, all of it passes to some relatives. I talked to one of them, a cousin, Thomas, on the phone and told him where my father was and gave him my address. Then my father was run over and killed by a hit-and-run driver. Before that happened, someone drove a car onto the sidewalk and nearly hit him."

Noah handed Bill a large envelope that the bank trustee, Wendall Dollar, had sent him. It contained a copy of Alexander's trust document and info about all the beneficiaries, including their addresses and phone numbers and a general statement concerning when the trust would be ready for disbursement and closing. It disclosed that Noah owned one half of the outstanding shares of North Marine, Inc., and that Thomas and Margo owned the other half. Noah said, "My cousins Margo and Thomas North may believe they will inherit my share of the North Trust and anything else I may own. I've made a will that should solve any inheritance problem. They don't know much about me, but I can't let them be a threat. If you hear of any strangers showing up around here that I should know about, please call me."

"I'll look out for you, Noah, and I treat all this as confidential."

"Thank you."

Bill said, "Do you know anything about these relatives?"

"No."

"You need to call Thomas's sister, your cousin Margo. She may be the one to give you some answers, if there are any. It's four o'clock back there. Maybe she's home and wants to talk." Noah had her phone number in his wallet.

Bill offered the use of his private phone. Margo answered.

"I'm Noah North, your cousin in Rock City, Oregon."

"Yes."

"I need to talk to you."

After a pause, Margo said, "Sure, go ahead."

"Margo, I'm going to be direct. Buster North, your uncle, my father, was recently killed. I won't explain why we suspect it, but we think he was murdered, and now I'm concerned about my safety. What I have said has to be related to the terms of Alexander North's trust."

Margo was on the verge of exploding verbally.

"If there is any truth in what I have said, you need to know that every beneficiary named in that trust is either a suspect or in danger. If you know what I'm hinting about, you might do the right thing. You need not say anything now. After you've had time to ponder my message, I'll call you for your response. Please keep in mind that I have a will that names a beneficiary that is not related to the North family."

"I got the message."

"You OK with another call from me?"

Margo said, "Yes," and hung up.

Bill said, "I know you've eliminated them from benefiting from your death, but they need to be on notice."

Noah sat with Bill for a few minutes in silence and left.

Regardless of his various personal matters and the North Trust problem, Noah was having a decent summer. Rose Marie was good company. No one was unfriendly to him except maybe his Buffalo relatives. He had to stop riding his Blue Streak bike because, if people knew him and his relationship with Road Victor, they might think he was disparaging Road Victor bikes. He bought another Road Victor, thinking, *What a waste of money. I won't ride it on rough ground.*

He received his Road Victor directors' meeting notice for the July 26, 1975, meeting. He called the travel agency in Grants Pass and discovered that they would make all the reservations for the Seattle trip. He wouldn't bother Martha except for a ride to the airport.

When he arrived at the directors' meeting, he was handed an agenda. It had an item for appointing a new director. Donald Lancaster was pissed off about the change in directors and had resigned. Noah sat next to Bobby Shaffer. Directors Clarke and Hedges had not arrived.

Bobby pointed at the director agenda item and said, "This is important. I'll bet Clarke and Hedges have already cooked up something to fill Lancaster's seat."

Noah said, "They can't do anything without three votes. We need to delay this to the August meeting. I'll take care of that, but first, let's see if someone is nominated and see if the behind-the-curtain boys have been busy."

Directors Clarke and Hedges arrived. Minutes of the previous meeting were read and approved. Clarke, the chairman, went directly to the appointment of a fifth director. Hedges nominated Martin Kinzly, an educated sixty-five-year-old successful owner of a lumberyard. Bobby Shaffer moved to table the matter until the next meeting. That motion failed, as did the motion to close nominations.

Clarke said, "I guess we won't accomplish anything today."

"If you want to prevent us from producing a new bike, you'd be right," asserted Noah. "And while we are at it, let's go to rim brakes and disc brakes. Our only brake is a hub brake, and it's almost bike history. So I move that we add rim and disc brakes to our bike-braking system."

Shaffer seconded. There was a little discussion asking the CEO, James Swanson, if that could be done, and he said it was possible. The motion passed three to one.

Shaffer said, "Why hasn't the letter to the directors and major shareholders containing a copy of the directors' minutes gone out?" Swanson said it was about ready to be mailed.

Noah, mad and clutching the edge of the directors' table and digging in his fingernails, said, "It is my understanding that when the directors order you to do something, you do it, and, Mr. Clarke, why aren't you doing this instead of me?"

"I was about to," he fraudulently stated.

"Also, where is your report to us about the status of the frame material change to our bike?"

"We haven't completed the change."

Noah said, "We didn't ask for a report after the change, we asked for a report on the status of the change and the names of our engineers working on the change. So where is the report?"

"I'll have it next meeting."

Noah said, "You should start looking for another job."

Chairman Clarke hurriedly said, "Now, now, let's not have any of that around here."

Noah looked at Clarke and said, "There hasn't been enough of that around here. Lack of real management is Road Victor's problem. Your old soft touch to problem-solving is out the window." Noah continued, "There is one more piece of business to cover. I move that from this date forward, no director shall be paid for his services as a director, and that includes his services at this meeting." Bobby Shaffer seconded the motion. Chairman Clarke said, "Anyone want to discuss this?"

Mr. Hedges asserted, "We need to be paid for our time and services. I'd be willing to drop it to $1,500 a month."

Noah said, "No director should be paid for leading his company to its death. Let's vote now." The vote was two to two.

Noah said, "Mr. Swanson, a copy of these minutes go to directors and major shareholders."

The meeting ended on a sour note. He and Bobby left together, agreeing that they were shaking things up.

Noah said, "I sometimes surprise myself. Popeye is my hero; I am who I am."

They agreed that Bobby should find a candidate for director. He knew a couple of young shareholders.

The next morning, Noah flew home, hiring a taxi to take him to Rock City. He mailed his expense vouchers to John Sims, CFO of Road Victor.

He then called Bill Walstrom and said, "It's time to call Margo again. I am uneasy and worry about my New York relatives' behavior. I want to call them from your place so you can remain informed."

Sitting in Walstrom's office, Noah looked around at the dismal setting. There was no shelving, and the space was littered with pasteboard boxes, coats, and other stuff forgotten by customers, open boxes of new beer glasses and mugs, piles of new Arcade Tavern sweatshirts and hats, old beer advertising, a dozen or more bowling trophies, and some unidentifiable junk.

Noah said, "This is different than sitting in a corporate boardroom."

Ignoring him, Bill said, "You don't need to call. I've again talked to Margo. She said her brother Thomas probably knows what happened to Buster North. She wasn't the least bit hesitant in saying that about him. She also said that she confronted Thomas with your accusation and he denied it. She told him she would talk to the police if anything else happened out here. She's gotta be a gutsy woman."

Noah said, "Thanks, Bill. Hope that ends it."

THIRTY-FIVE

Noah and Rose Marie were spending much of August together. They were sitting in lawn chairs in front of Noah's house actually watching grass grow in his new lawn. He knew that it would be a big mistake to invite her into his house. Her parents would have a fit, and the innocence of it could never be explained. He was now taller than Rose Marie at six feet. He did not realize that he needed the growth to match his adult-like intellect and life. His kid image was disappearing. His relationship with Rose Marie was still schoolgirl and schoolboy, but Noah's conversation, convictions, and choice of words were more adult than schoolboy. He realized the change and asked Rose Marie to stick with him. She saw the change coming, and yes, she'd stick with him. Events in Noah's life in the past several months had convinced her that he was unique and special. He told her that his next directors' meeting was August 23. She knew he would be gone two or three days. When she picked up her bike to pedal home, Noah held her gently by her shoulders and kissed her. She returned the kiss and then headed home.

Noah received the CEO's letter declaring that the change of steel to aluminum frames had been accomplished, and Russ McCormick and Steven Kraus were Road Victor engineers. The letter indicated that some of the new bikes had been shipped, and dealer comments were excellent. It also contained a copy of the last directors' meeting minutes. The letter showed copies sent to major shareholders.

Two things were bothering Noah, things that he had time to consider and maybe resolve before the August directors' meeting.

One, Rose Marie complained that there were no girls' competitive sports between schools, that the boys had competitive sports with other schools, with school money spent for them. He remembered the conversation:

"What are you saying?"

"I'm saying that an article I read in my father's *Sports Illustrated* magazine stated that any school with boys' competitive sports had to have competitive sports for girls."

"I don't know anything about that, but I'm too crazy about you to not help you and find out about it. I'll call my lawyer."

"Your lawyer?"

"I'll explain that sometime."

Noah had called lawyer Morgan Reynolds and asked about women's sports in schools. His answer was mixed.

"Noah, why are you bothering me about this?"

"It is important."

Lawyer Reynolds told Noah everything he needed to know about Title IX requirements. If a school had boys' or men's competitive sports, it had to have girls' or women's competitive sports equally in every respect. Federal funding could be withheld for non-compliance.

"Noah, that law is mandatory for schools."

"Will you represent me?"

"No. It's a social or political issue, and I'm not interested. Something tells me you are capable of doing this, but first talk to the school and the district. If they don't act, then I'll give you the names of a couple of competent lawyers."

Two, Felix had told him that some people were smoking marijuana, and it made them dopey, and that it was illegal to possess the stuff. It seemed like a very strange thing to do. He decided not to involve himself trying to stop that stupidity. The school authorities or the police could do that.

Noah walked into the Rock City High School office. It was weeks before school started, and the principal, Philip Robards, was there and said hello to Noah. He then said, "Noah, you're the most unusual student we've seen in this school."

Noah said, "Thanks. There's something I need to talk to you about. I've been to the library in town and read parts of what they call Title IX of an act of Congress that requires schools that have men's organized sports to have women's organized sports, and to fund the women's sports and provide equipment, facilities, and coaches comparable in money and facilities provided for men's sports. I think I've said all of that correctly. That law was passed June 23, 1972. Rock City High School has done nothing required by that law. I believe some of the girls here are upset. Can you tell me if the girls will have organized sports and competition with other schools this year? They have it in Grants Pass, Medford, Ashland, and I don't know where else."

Principal Robards looked at the seventeen-year-old standing in front of him, knowing that any kind of an excuse would not fly. He said, "This school has done nothing, and there are no plans to do anything. The district school board refused the necessary funds and in effect decided that they were not going to follow that law."

Noah said, "You tell the school board that if they don't act immediately, they'll be hearing from my lawyer. Don't let them think that they are dealing with a seventeen-year-old that is not their equal in this matter. Mr. Robards, this is just business, nothing personal." Nothing more was said, and Noah left. Noah was on his bike headed home and was again asking himself, Why am I getting involved in adult matters? Maybe it's because I've never really had a childhood and I'm still not having one. I can't be somebody I'm not. It's true, I am what I am, can't change that! Besides, if I can right a wrong for a friend, why not?

Principal Robards hurriedly sat down at his desk and called Charlie Morton, chairman of the Rock City School District Board. "Listen, Charlie, we got a problem. The district needs to abide by the mandates of that Title IX law."

"The hell we do. Those bastards in Washington, DC, can't tell us what to do."

"Oh, yes, they can," responded Robards. "And they will. There has been a serious complaint that can't be ignored. Remember, there are federal funds involved for some of our basic needs. Those funds will not be overlooked in any enforcement action by the feds."

"Ah, shit, Robards, who's complaining?"

"Noah North."

"Is that the kid involved with Road Victor bicycles?"

"That's him, and you'd better pay attention. He already has a law-yer on the case. You and the board had better take Title IX seriously, or none of you will ever get another woman's vote."

"Who in the hell does that kid think he is?" Morton asked.

"You're going to find out if you do nothing."

"OK, we'll cut funding for the boys' sports by half and start up girls' sports. That will make Mr. North quite popular."

Robards said, "That will backfire, and we'll say goodbye to present board members. There are many things that Title IX requires us to do, and we have done nothing. We are required to designate a person to monitor, by written public record, our compliance with that law."

Morton said, "We'll see what happens."

The next day, Principal Robards stopped Noah downtown and said, "I talked to the chairman of the school board, Charlie Morton, and they will not do anything."

Noah said, "You know, I really should not have taken this shot at looking out for the girls, but they need to be treated fairly, and that's not happening. So, does a seventeen-year-old kid have to do your job? I am busy with a couple of business things and trying to take care of myself. Tell you what I'll do, but that will be the end of it. I will call Mr. Morton. Better yet, where can I find this guy who wants to keep the girls in their cooking classes?"

"He owns that farm equipment business south of town."

"Thanks. I will have a conversation with him, but don't alert him!"

The next day, Noah pedaled south of town, wondering why he'd gotten involved. He walked into a large metal building, and after look-ing around, he saw a man in an office located next to an equipment showroom. Two of the office walls were solid glass. Noah asked and was pointed to Mr. Morton sitting at a desk in his office. Noah stood in the open doorway and asked, "Are you Charlie Morton?"

Morton acknowledged that he was, and Noah introduced himself and said, "I need to talk to you."

Morton said, "OK, have a seat."

Noah looked Morton over and said, "You know why I'm here. Title IX is an important law. It means a lot to the women in this country and the girls in our school district. Please don't ignore it a day longer. If you haven't read it, read it, and you might be surprised at what can happen if you don't follow the law. You can find that law, nicely printed in a pamphlet, in the Rock City Library. If our school district doesn't immediately start complying, I intend to notify every federal authority I can think of and make an effort to have major newspapers in Oregon print an article about this school district and Title IX. Want your federal funding to disappear? If all of that happens, you will have poked every woman in this state in the eye. Once that happens, you and your school board members will look foolish, and soon you will no longer be school board members. It's now your move."

"You can't do that," uttered Morton.

"I can and I will without hesitating!"

When Noah walked toward his bike, he was thinking, This is the last truly adult fight I'm getting into. I've got to try and get away from hearing about adult responsibilities and getting myself involved. But I did do this for Rose Marie and her girlfriends. If I could help, why not?

Charlie Morton remained seated at his desk, barely saying out loud, "Holy shit, did that really happen? A seventeen-year-old kid walks into my office and chews my ass! I guess he really did bite that bicycle company in its ass. Maybe Principal Robards is right about him. It wouldn't hurt to revisit this issue and maybe do what the law requires, damn it!"

THIRTY-SIX

Noah was sitting in the Rock City Cafe on a date with Rose Marie. The summer of '75 was ending, and important things were happening in Noah's life. Rose Marie was in his life, and it was increasingly important, because the attraction was gaining strength and causing Noah to feel less alone. He had to know if she was attracted to him.

With his elbows and forearms on the table, he leaned forward and whispered, "Rose Marie, I'm attracted to you big time. Are you attracted to me?"

With a nice smile across the lunch table, she said, "Of course I am, you fool."

"Good, now I don't have to worry about that. I'm too young to say this, but I will. I want to be with you as much as our lives will allow and maybe forever."

"Noah, that's too much. We'll just have to see what happens. I'm with you, but we are not at any important crossroad."

He would soon be leaving for Seattle, and he had to know what their relationship was. Now he kinda knew, but he also knew that he should back off a little.

The waitress placed their lunches on the table, and Noah, while looking at his hamburger, said, "There's something I need to tell you. You and your girlfriends will soon be able to participate in interscholastic sports."

Noah, still looking at the delicious hamburger and then at Rose Marie, said, "The last time I was with you, you made me realize that tons of money is spent on boys' sports and nothing on girls' sports and that it was wrong."

As she dangled a french fry between her fingers, deciding what to do with it, Noah heard her quietly say, "I forgot about that conversation."

"Well, I didn't. My lawyer told me what the law required, and you are right."

"That's nice to know."

"He didn't want the case. He told me to take care of the problem myself."

"You don't have time for this."

"I don't like seeing people doing the wrong thing. I went to the town library, and I read the law called Title IX. I'm sure I didn't understand everything. I then had a talk with Principal Robards about his failure to follow that law."

"You told our principal he was doing something illegal?"

"I guess you could say that."

"He's going to be happy when you're gone."

"In the meantime, he blamed the school board for ignoring Title IX. I'm pretty sure Mr. Morton, chairman of the school board, knew I was coming. He was in his office and, to make a long story short, in a respectful business manner I let him know that all hell would break loose if the school board didn't immediately follow the Title IX law. I thought he might do the right thing and he did. He was more shocked by getting chewed out by a seventeen-year-old than anything else. Rose Marie, please keep this to yourself. Mr. Morton doesn't need any further embarrassment."

School classes were going to start soon, and the summer was whizzing away. It was time for the August 23 meeting of Road Victor directors. Noah's yard was looking good, and his life was definitely busy and interesting and under control because he was in charge of it. Nevertheless, he was never certain that Uncle Willis was out of his life.

The flight to Seattle was pleasant. It gave him time to plan his moves. He had mailed letters to shareholders Lila Jameson and Sylvia Latimer about the new director selection. He asked them to contact Chairman Clarke and make it plain and clear that the nominee he and Bobby

Shaffer chose was to be the third new director. He hadn't heard from them.

Noah enjoyed staying in the Olympic Hotel and eating alone in their dining room. When eating there he would muse, Someday I'll have company with breakfast, lunch, and dinner.

Noah and Bobby met early outside the directors' meeting room. Bobby said, "I've talked to two young shareholders, and each is willing to be a candidate. One is Cecil Newman, who was at the shareholders' meeting and voted for us. He is a bank operations officer and owns a few shares. He has a bike but not a Road Victor bike. He claims Road Victor bikes are a piece of shit. He would like to be a director. The other candidate is Samantha O'Leary, a twenty-two-year-old engineering graduate from Oregon State University. I've seen her at a couple of shareholders' meetings, and I met her at last year's shareholders' meeting. She happens to be beautiful and owns around fifty thousand inherited shares. She is employed by Boeing and jumped at the idea of being a Road Victor director. She rides a Schwinn bike and said that a Road Victor bike is a piece of shit. She wants to change that."

Noah eagerly said, "O'Leary would be perfect." Bobby agreed.

Bobby said, "After we fix Road Victor bikes, our advertising can be: A Road Victor bike is no longer a piece of shit."

They walked into the directors' room together and said hello to Chairman Clarke. The other two directors hadn't arrived. Noah asked Clarke if he had been contacted by Lila and Sylvia.

Clarke said, "Yes, thanks to you."

Noah said, "We'll soon see how that works out."

Ten minutes later, Chairman Clarke called the directors' meeting to order. Following the preliminary business, he said, "We might as well start with old business and get the election of a new director over with. So, nominations for director are open."

Bobby Shaffer nominated Samantha O'Leary, and Noah moved that nominations be closed. The vote was two to two, then Clarke added a yes vote that closed nominations. Noah was thinking, Lila and Sylvia did call him.

Clarke said, "Anyone want to discuss this?"

Oliver Hedges asked in feigned disbelief, "You want a woman on this board? This is no place for a young woman who knows nothing about business matters. Clarke, you can't possibly go along with this, and you two young boys are going to crash this company. We need a seasoned businessman like Martin Kinzly."

Noah said, "Hedges, are you aware of the fact that women buy bicycles and they even ride them? I actually know a girl that has a bike, as does every one of her girlfriends. One woman engineer among us and you're upset? Women customers will benefit, and women shareholders will love it. Just give it a try, and if you can't stand it, there are plenty of sidewalks and roads leading out of here. Stay with us and you won't regret it."

Samantha O'Leary was elected three to one with Clarke's vote.

Bobby said, "Now we need to get down to business and nurture the fortunes of our grand old company. We asked for names of our engineers. Mr. Swanson, do we have them?"

CEO Swanson said, "Yes."

Noah asked, "Are you happy with their work and qualifications? Also, do they have the time and freedom to develop new and unique innovations for our bike?"

Swanson answered, "I'm good with their qualifications. They both have mechanical engineering degrees. They are busy seeing to production and efficiency on the manufacturing line. They've never been directed to devote a separate effort to innovate or re-invent our bicycle."

Noah said, "That is why this company is drowning, and this board is the reason, loud and clear. Bobby, you, me, and our new director are going to save Road Victor, and we would like Clarke and Hedges to join us, wouldn't we? I think we should have an additional engineer devoted solely to development of new products. We'll need to discuss that."

Noah then made a motion that no fee or compensation, including compensation at this meeting, be paid to a director. Hedges said, "Director compensation is common practice in nearly every sizable corporation, and Road Victor directors should be paid for their time and services."

Bobby Shaffer said, "If we get this company rolling and profitable, I will agree, but in any event, $2,000 per month is too much. Make this vote unanimous, and you previous dissenters will save face."

Noah's motion passed three to one with Hedges's vote. Clarke was shaken.

Chairman Clarke asked the board to fix the date of the next board meeting.

Noah said, "Could we have it on the nineteenth or the twenty-sixth? I'll lose only one day of school." Clarke fixed the twenty-sixth of September as the next meeting date.

Oliver Hedges responded, "My God, we are being run by a schoolboy."

"Get used to it, Mr. Hedges, because I'm not going away," responded Noah.

Noah and Bobby were walking out of the company offices when Noah stopped and said, "You know what we just did? We elected a director we've never seen or talked to about anything really important. How'd we do that?"

"We're really good at what we do, and especially you, but we'll keep it a secret," countered Bobby.

Noah was informed by the hotel clerk that the hotel had an airport shuttle, and he used it the morning after his meeting. He had the window seat for the fifty-minute flight to Medford. After Noah boarded the plane, a man with a briefcase and newspaper sat down in the aisle seat across from him and commenced reading *The Seattle Times* newspaper, and about halfway to Medford he said, "I'll be damned."

Noah asked, "Something wrong?"

"No, nothing. I own an employment agency in Portland, and this article puts a new slant on who's employable. It seems that Road Victor has a seventeen-year-old running the company."

Noah, as a prank, said, "Something wrong with that?"

"Could be. That company's shareholders should be upset," said the man.

Noah seriously said, "The shareholders elected him director, so why would they be upset?"

"Well, they probably didn't realize what they were doing."

Noah said, "Do you know anything about that company and what has happened to its management and direction since that seventeen-year-old went on board?"

"No."

"Then you really can't have an opinion, can you?" asked Noah.

"I suppose not. I shouldn't be thinking out loud."

They sat silently until they were in the landing pattern at Medford, and Noah looked at the passenger next to him and said, "I'm that seventeen-year-old."

The man, obviously surprised, said, "Sorry about that. I'm Gus Ireland, Western Employment. I don't usually go on like that, but after our conversation, I think Road Victor is in good hands."

"I am Noah North. Could I have your card? I might need it soon."

Noah arrived in Medford, and later a taxi dropped him at his doorstep. His house was in order. He always worried about leaving an empty house. He washed his face and, looking in the mirror, asked the face, "Now, can I be a teenager for a while?" It was too late to call anyone, so he ate a terrible frozen dinner laced with fifty chemicals, watched a terrible TV program, and after he read what interested him in the last three issues of his newspaper, he went to bed happy with the past two days' accomplishments and the price of gold at $105 an ounce.

School was starting in a couple of days. The first day of school was going to be interesting and Noah knew it. He wanted to hug Rose Marie but didn't. It was good to see Felix. It seemed as though everyone had grown a little bit, and the girls were looking better than ever, especially Rose Marie. He also knew that the publicity about him might cause a few comments that would be difficult to ignore or deal with. He hoped they would be kind comments. When he chose a seat in the higher math class, Rose Marie sat down in a seat across from him.

Noah said, "I'm glad you sat there. Can we meet after school?"

"That would be nice. You can tell me all about yourself," she whispered.

Annoyed, Noah said, "I've told you, I don't like talking about myself."

"Noah, I didn't mean it that way. I'm sorry."

Noah said, "I'm too young to be involved in Seattle, New York, and Rock City. I should be shedding New York soon, and maybe then I won't be so testy."

The higher math teacher, Frank Yates, who had taught first- and second-year algebra, was commencing his twentieth year of teaching and was no longer excited about teaching. All last year when Noah was his best student, Yates had never had a conversation with Noah. Something was bothering Yates about Noah, but he didn't know what it could be. Yates didn't look at Noah or say anything when he walked into the room. The room had filled, and Frank Yates stood and welcomed everyone to the new school year. He said in a cynical tone, "You all might be surprised to know that we now have a celebrity, a captain of industry, in this class, Noah North."

Noah stood up and said, "Please, that is an important part of my life, and I am very serious about it. I own shares in a company that has problems, and some other people and I are trying to fix that. We found the problem, and it's being fixed, so please don't joke about it. If you have anything else to say about me or my life outside school, please be nice."

Considering the difficult speeches and verbal encounters Noah had recently experienced, this one was easy.

Frank Yates said, "I didn't mean to hurt your feelings."

"You didn't hurt my feelings. You seemed to cast doubt on my competence in business matters." Noah was prepared for such comments, and he wanted to stop them in their tracks. This exchange might do it, as it was certain to get around.

Frank said, "I think we'd better let it go at that."

Noah thought, Am I ever going to be a teenager?

When leaving that class, Rose Marie playfully bumped into Noah and said, "Wow," and hurried away to her next class. After his last class he was eager to be with Rose Marie and to see if she would be there. As he hurried by Principal Robards's office, Robards was standing by the door and said to Noah, "I need a minute."

Noah stopped, and Robards said, "You mustn't talk to a teacher the way you talked to Mr. Yates."

Noah caught Robards's eye and said, "If they talk about my personal life that I have outside this school, I'll show them no quarter." Noah had recently heard that expression on TV, and it seemed to fit. Robards was speechless. Noah was in a hurry to see Rose Marie, and he left Robards, who seemed paralyzed verbally. Noah guessed that his exchange with Robards might not be over. He didn't know whether having the last word was good or bad.

Rose Marie was waiting. He wanted to kiss her but didn't dare and instead said, "I really miss you."

"Well then, why do you stay away?"

"I've been busy out of town, and I apologize."

"You certainly had it out with Mr. Yates. You gonna get away with that?"

"I already have, I think. You didn't want me to let him get away with that, did you?"

"I didn't know what you'd do, and I don't know anyone that would do what you did."

Noah put his hand on Rose Marie's shoulder and said, "Please try and understand me. I am alone without parents and have no one to back me up here, at school, or anyplace except maybe my guardian, Martha Webb, and possibly Mr. Jenkins, the English teacher. A parent would not like a teacher making fun of their kid. I am what I am. I know one thing, I wouldn't stand by and let a teacher or anyone make fun of you or hurt you, so now you know how I feel about you. Is that too serious for a seventeen-year-old?"

"Maybe, just don't complicate things," she allowed.

"Give me your hand. I'm walking you home."

That evening, Martha Webb called Noah and said she wanted to see him. He hopped on his bike and visited Martha at her home. Seated in her living room, she said, "Noah, I heard about your conversation with Frank Yates and Mr. Robards. Robards called me. I have no idea why Yates did what he did or why Mr. Robards would say anything to you when the matter was settled. Anyway, I'm merely suggesting that you tone things down a little when confronting a teacher or the principal, something most students wouldn't think of doing. You don't want to lose the important student-teacher relationship. Hopefully they will have learned a lesson in your case. Otherwise, how is life treating you?"

"I'm living my life mostly as an adult and not as a teenager. There's not a lot of fun in that. I have to constantly look ahead and make certain all my needs are covered when none of my teenage friends have to do that. At least I'm financially OK. Martha, I thank you for calling me this evening. I knew there was something improper with those conversations, but I gave the only response I could. But you're right, I'll tone it down next time. Gotta go. Goodbye."

The 1975–76 school year was underway, and Noah was cultivating his association with teenagers. His frame of reference was in business with adult relationships, and it was difficult for him to set that aside, but he got pretty good at it. Apparently word of his chastising Mr. Yates had made the rounds, and no one mentioned Road Victor to him or anything related. Mr. Yates was acting as if nothing had happened. All of that was OK with Noah. He would soon receive a notice of the September directors' meeting, something he looked forward to. Road Victor had stayed at a 5⅛ bid. Noah was thinking, Once we get one or more new modern bikes on the market, our stock at today's price will have been a good buy.

Later that day, Noah called Road Victor's head office and talked to CEO James Swanson about directors buying shares of their company. James Swanson said, "Directors and management and some personnel must be careful about buying shares when critical corporate information is not generally known to the public."

Noah said, "I kinda knew that. Is it OK for me to buy our shares now?"

James Swanson was happy to have his perceived enemy talking to him; maybe his job was secure after all. He told Noah it was now OK to buy.

A few days later, Martha took Noah to his bank and then to Kaplan and Graves, gold buyers in Medford, where he sold some sinkers. Martha watched and heard everything. She was astonished when she learned the size of the transaction, and it was unsettling to see and hear Noah bargain on the price. He was knowledgeable and unrelenting in demanding $139 an ounce. At a crucial point, Noah asserted, "You know that within a year our private ownership and trading of gold as a commodity will double that price. Don't try and tell me you haven't held gold a lot longer than that to beat the market."

Kaplan and Graves lost the negotiation on that note. Martha had never seen or heard anything like it, especially with a seventeen-year-old being the dominant player. Apparently Noah knew as much about the gold market as the buyer. Martha was invited by Noah, as his guardian, to the buyer's back room to watch the spectrometer grade the sinkers for purity and then to watch the weighing of the sinkers. The total weight was 1428.63129 troy ounces, or $198,579.75.

During the trip back to Rock City, Martha said, "Noah, $198,000 is a lot of money, many people don't have that much in a lifetime. As your guardian, may I ask what you plan to do with the money?"

Noah said, "$110,000 for Road Victor shares, some cash, and I'll be needing your signature on a guardianship check."

Martha now realized that she was a guardian in name only. When the check cleared in Noah's guardianship account, he ordered twenty-five thousand Road Victor shares. Martha signed the check payable to Smith, Morgan and Wiley. He would have about $67,000 left to pay taxes.

Noah said, "There's something else you need to know. I've taken the driver's ed class and now have an Oregon driver's license, and soon I'll be asking you to take me to Kaplan and Graves to sell enough gold to buy a car."

Noah placed his order. Marty Woods, stockbroker, knowing enough about Noah not to challenge him, said anyway, "Do you know what the hell you are doing?"

"Yes. You gonna make me sign something confessing that I don't know what I'm doing?"

"Yes, and you be sure and sign it and return it. I also need your check."

Noah received the directors' meeting notice fixing Friday, September 26, 1975, as the meeting date. This was good timing. Noah would miss some Thursday afternoon classes and Friday classes. No one except Rose Marie said anything to him about skipped classes. It wouldn't have changed a thing if they did.

Noah was now needing transportation. He called Martha.

"Martha, could you drive me to Medford to the gold buyer? I apologize for continually asking you for help. I really need a car, and if I have one, I'll stop pestering you. Could we go before the twenty-sixth?"

"I'll pick you up tomorrow in front of your school at three p.m."

"Martha, you're too good."

The next day, after stopping at his bank, Noah walked into Kaplan and Graves with a small sack of sinkers and came out with a $74,128.65 check.

Noah filled Martha's gas tank, and she drove him to his house.

After breakfast at the Rock City Cafe and skipping some morning classes, Noah walked into his bank and seated himself in front of Wilson Marston and said, "I'm gonna buy a car. It might cost $30,000 or $40,000. Can you increase my credit card limit to $40,000?"

"Good grief, Noah, no one buys a $40,000 car, especially a seventeen-year-old!"

"I don't know exactly what they cost, but I'm getting a good one."

"Well, you always seem to know what you are doing, but you should take it easy on that. Have your checkbook and credit card with you, but I'm not increasing the card limit. Go with the car dealer to his bank and have his banker call me, and we'll make a money transfer from your account to his account. When they do that, they need to hand you the car title."

That evening Noah looked at his cedar forest and, with a heavy heart, thought, I need to call Rose Marie. Most of all, I need to get my life together in one place, but I'm not going to abandon my duty to Road Victor.

The next morning a taxi dropped him at the Medford airport. His tickets were ready for him at the United counter. The return ticket was to Portland, where he would look at cars.

When Noah arrived at the Olympic Hotel, dinner was still being served. He was the only kid in the big room and maybe the only guest without a hard drink. His waitress acted like she wanted to mother him by suggesting a well-balanced dinner. No one had done that for about eleven years. He was thinking, I'm going to be nice. I'm going to be polite. I wanted a nice steak, but I'll order the salmon dinner as she suggested. When you're alone it doesn't hurt to be nice, but sometimes you can't be nice. He had finished his self-evaluation when a stranger asked if he could have a word and sat down across from Noah. The stranger's card revealed him to be a feature writer for *The Seattle Times*. Noah looked him over and said, "I don't do interviews, especially when I'm having dinner."

"This will just take a minute."

"No it won't because you don't get a minute or any part of a minute. Please leave."

He left.

At breakfast in the hotel dining room, Noah was turning pages in the hotel's complimentary edition of *The Seattle Times* when he saw a column headed:

ROAD VICTOR'S IRASCIBLE TEENAGER

Last evening in the grand dining room of the Olympic Hotel, Noah North, a 17-year-old overachiever, one of three new directors on Road Victor's board, sat amid its great patina-enriched paneled walls. He declined an interview and sent one of our feature writers packing with not-so-subtle words ringing in our writer's ears. Having stated that, if anyone can get Road Victor out of the doldrums, this young man may be the person to do it. Mr. North, just be nice.

What the hell is *irascible*? He'd have to look that up. The hotel's bacon, eggs, and pancakes were good. He stood up and left for the directors' meeting, thinking, The best part of that meal was I didn't have to prepare it, and screw that newspaper.

The meeting started with all directors present as well as CEO Swanson and CFO Sims and the secretary. Coffee, soft drinks, and pastries adorned the middle of the large directors' conference table.

After the necessary fundamental business of the board was completed, Noah said, "Could Mr. Swanson give us a report on the status of the braking and other innovations to our bicycles?"

CEO Swanson stood up and said, "They are progressing nicely."

Noah, slightly annoyed, said, "We want a specific, detailed report. Are new brakes on our bikes, are they on the market for sale, and do all of our dealers have the aluminum-frame bikes? We want dates and production numbers, and if there are delays in any of this, we want to know about it. Also, we would like to see proposed advertising for our new bikes. So, specifically, where are we on all of this?"

CEO Swanson stood and reported that they'd had trouble getting brake parts and new wheels with proper rims, but they were starting to arrive, and within a month the new bikes should be arriving at dealers. Some aluminum-frame bikes were being produced and delivered. No advertising was planned.

Noah asked, "Isn't every one of our bikes aluminum framed? Do we employ any advertising people?"

The CEO said, "Nearly all of our bikes are aluminum framed. We contract our advertising."

"Wait a minute, are we still making steel-frame bikes?" asked Noah.

"Yes, we wanted to use up our inventory of steel," said the CEO.

Noah said, "For God's sake, steel is one of the things putting us out of business! Did the board or anyone on it tell you to use up the steel?"

"I asked Mr. Clarke about it, and he said to use up the steel," was the CEO's reply.

Noah said, "Why is it that three new, young directors know more about this business than you two? I move that from this date forward, all Road Victor bikes manufactured must have aluminum frames." Bobby Shaffer seconded the motion and called for the vote. The motion passed three to two. Samantha O'Leary, the new director, was with Bobby and Noah on the vote. The same Samantha O'Leary whose disconcerting good looks seemed to bother directors Clarke and Hedges.

Hedges said, "It seems to me that getting our new bike on the market may be the most important thing that ever confronted this company. So why are we messing around with it like business as usual?"

"Exactly," said Noah, who added, "Is there any reason we can't have a new aluminum-frame bike with full choice of brakes on the market by November first, just in time for Christmas?"

Swanson said, "We can try."

Noah said, "Trying will no longer be good enough for Road Victor or you."

Bobby Shaffer asked the CEO if he would take the directors on a tour of the factory after the meeting and give explanations of what they were seeing and let them meet some of the employees, especially the engineers. Swanson said he would be happy to do that. Noah then asked Swanson if he would furnish each director with a status report on units produced ready for delivery and dealership orders, together with any material or production difficulties, and do so at least five days prior to the next directors' meeting and every meeting thereafter.

Swanson said, "I can do that."

Noah said, "I wish you had said that you will do it, but you know what we want and why we want it."

Noah turned, looking over the directors, asking them if they had any objections to that request, and there were none.

"Mr. Swanson, once we get over a couple of hurdles, we can work together."

"Noah, I'm trying."

"You've gotta hate having to deal with a seventeen-year-old."

"I think I'm a normal CEO."

"You think I should be in my room building model airplanes, but I'm here trying to make this company work, so we are all going to have to live with that."

The factory tour was an education. A huge wood-and-steel-framed building with old baked-on paint curling off the metal and huge un- painted wood beams forming expansive trusses high overhead, the building was nearly five hundred feet long and two hundred feet wide, filled with substantial but worn wooden tables and benches and high overhead fluorescent lights. A paint shop was at the end of the building where the finished bike left the building to go into storage in a ware- house in an adjacent building of similar construction. There were fifty or sixty workers who could be seen at one place or another putting bike parts together. Noah had seen pictures and had read about Henry Ford's mass-production assembly lines, and it appeared that this bike factory might not be mass-producing anything. The directors were in- troduced to the factory engineers, Russ McCormick and Steven Kraus, who followed the group, answering questions.

Noah said to Steven Kraus, "Let's go for a little walk."

That was OK with Steven, and they parted from the others.

Noah said, "I wish I knew more about manufacturing. Is there no assembly-line production here?"

A smile illuminated Steven's face when he said, "No, and that has baffled me since the day I got here four years ago. I have a mechanical engineering degree, and I have fundamental knowledge in the makeup, development, and construction of a mass-production assembly line.

Highly skilled employees focus on their expertise only, and theoretically you get a better product. Keep in mind, you don't have to be a genius to put a bike together."

"So why don't we have assembly-line production?" asked Noah. "They say it gets more production, and a better bike at lower cost. That's true, isn't it?" asked Noah.

"Of course it's true. We could cut our production cost and pricing dramatically and, with our name and a good new bike, beat the competition," asserted Steven.

Noah asked, "What would it cost to install a proper assembly line?"

"With all new tools and machinery, maybe a million dollars."

"Could that be done without screwing up present production?"

Steven said, "Yes, the building is big enough for that."

Noah left the Road Victor building believing the company was on the threshold of a clean recovery.

The next morning, the plane broke through the cloud cover into bright sunshine and started its descent into Portland. Noah was busy thinking that his life could be headed in the wrong direction. He asked himself, Why am I concerned with a bicycle company? I keep throwing myself on its problems. When Road Victor shares double, I'm gone, I think. Noah was now carrying a small smart briefcase. It held the newspaper with the "Irascible Kid" story that he would show to Martha.

When he left the terminal in Portland with his carry-on, he hired a taxi to take him from car dealer to car dealer. He visited the Ford, Buick, Chevrolet, Dodge, Mercedes, and Oldsmobile showrooms. He had to stay in Portland overnight to see everything, and the next morning, Sunday, he revisited a few of the car dealers that interested him. Deciding on the right car came after serious thought and introspection because he might be spending a large sum of money. He'd started life with nothing, and he had lived with the least of possessions. No scooter, no tricycle, no bike until he was sixteen years old, and no parent to haul him around. He was going to lessen that unhappy state of affairs and have a nice car, maybe the best car, and enjoy every moment he spent in it. The dealership only had a black one in the model he wanted. The purchase could not be completed until the next morning because the banks were not open on Sunday. Following another night's stay in Portland, Noah went with the car dealer himself to the dealer's bank and, with Mr. Marston on the phone in Rock City, the money transfer was made. Another new experience for Noah.

With his driver's license tucked in his wallet, Noah carefully drove home in his black 1976 Mercedes 450SL.

Driving home in an unfamiliar car and on the freeway was challenging.

He called Rose Marie and picked her up for lunch at the Rock City Cafe. Before he could alight from his car to ring her doorbell, she walked outside and directly to him. She was beautiful, with long loose hair and a nice figure. He'd recently started noticing those things. He thought, Is she really only seventeen, and is she really my girlfriend?

After hellos, the conversation was going nowhere when Noah said, "I think I love you."

"Noah, we're just kids!"

"I know it, but can't one kid fall in love with another kid?"

Rose Marie looked at Noah and said, "I guess, but still, it's something I have to think about."

"Rose Marie, I just blurted that out almost like my brain was located in my heart. You're right, let's just think about it, and when we do, I'll do more thinking than you."

"Good, that's settled."

During their conversation, she was busy looking at the interior of Noah's car and touching it here and there.

"Nice car, Noah. Did you have to get such a fancy one?"

"Absolutely."

After lunch, Noah drove Rose Marie home. While driving home, he remembered the documents he'd received from North Marine.

Noah was sitting at lawyer Morgan Reynolds's desk in Grants Pass, Oregon. Reynolds was reading the trust and will received from Shoreline Bank.

Reynolds looked at Noah and said, "Looks like you own half of North Marine, Inc. Are you anxious to get into the Great Lakes marine shipping business?"

"You know I'm not!"

Reynolds said, "Well then, sell or give your shares to your relatives, or you and your relatives sell all the shares in one transaction. I'll write the trustee a letter proposing that. OK?"

"Shouldn't I know something about North Marine? My relatives must think there is some value there, because I believe they eliminated my father as a beneficiary, and I'm not so sure they want me around. Mr. Reynolds, please ask the trustee for all the financials on North Marine, including real property tax statements showing valuations."

Reynolds said, "Maybe you should go there and see everything."

"Let's wait and hear their response."

THIRTY-SEVEN

Noah had missed last Thursday afternoon's classes and all of Friday's classes, but on Thursday he had taken home textbooks from each class to be missed, and Sunday he had attempted a catch-up session. Noah again sat across from Rose Marie in Mr. Yates's algebra class. Mr. Yates was still smarting from his last nonacademic verbal exchange with Noah. He wanted to regain what he'd lost in that prior squabble, so he decided to avoid anything personal and directly address Noah with an academic quiz. He said, "I hope you were all able to study and understand that bit of homework I handed to you Friday. It is important for today's subject, first-degree equations. Noah, how do we know when an equation remains an equation?"

"I have no idea," said Noah, and choosing his words carefully, he added, "I wasn't given the homework, and none was delivered to me."

"Do you consider this class important?" asked Mr. Yates.

"It was important that I miss Friday's class," responded Noah.

"You didn't answer my question," said Mr. Yates.

"Did it have something to do with equations, or was it personal?" asked Noah.

Yates was frustrated. Noah quickly said, "Don't worry, I'll eventually know as much about equations as my classmates, and yes, I do consider this class important."

Yates turned away from Noah and proceeded with his planned instruction. Noah glanced at Rose Marie and her facial expression said, You gotta stop doing that to him! Noah and Rose Marie were leaving

Yates's room for the next class when Rose Marie clutched Noah's arm and said, "Being a smart-ass is not attractive, so stop it!"

"You might be right," he answered.

His next trip to Seattle was October 26, and he didn't want to take on anything else, especially the Buffalo relatives, and he hadn't heard from Reynolds.

His mind was on Road Victor. He had been thinking that Road Victor could easily manufacture an additional product, given the size of its plant and workforce. He'd let that incubate in his mind for a while.

The next day, Noah was in his bank, depositing two Road Victor expense reimbursement checks, when Mr. Marston motioned him to come to his desk. Louis Santos, the banker who was with them when Noah's sinkers were tested for purity, was seated at Mr. Marston's desk.

Mr. Marston said, "You remember Mr. Santos. He wants to ask you for a favor."

Louis Santos said, "I understand that you travel to Seattle every month, and I wonder if you could take something to my cousin in Seattle. He would meet you at the airport if he knows the time and gate."

Noah said, "I guess, but why can't you do that?"

"I could, but it would save me airfare and I'd really appreciate it."

"OK, but what am I carrying?"

"Just a briefcase filled with personal family things."

Noah asked Santos for the name, address, and phone number of the cousin, and Santos wrote it on Marston's notepad and gave it to Noah, who said, "I'll swing by the bank the day before I go north."

Noah was walking out of the bank when he said out loud, "I ain't gonna do that," and he walked back into the bank and told Santos he couldn't deliver anything to his cousin, and he should find someone else. Santos said nothing, and Noah left the bank, muttering, "I'm not getting involved in little things anymore, besides, it sounded weird."

The day after Noah's encounter with Santos, Martha Webb was in the bank buying some traveler's checks, and Mr. Marston was asked by the teller to sign them. Martha said she and her husband were flying to Seattle Friday afternoon for the wedding of an old school chum's daughter. Marston asked Martha if she would mind doing a favor for

Mr. Santos, who needed something delivered to his cousin in Seattle. Martha walked to Louis Santos's desk and he explained what he wanted done with the briefcase and how his cousin would be at the airport. Martha had the airline tickets in her purse and gave Santos the information his cousin needed to meet her. Martha was flying in two days, and Santos gave her the briefcase. It was black, very fancy, heavy with brass fittings, and locked. Martha put it in the trunk of her car.

The night prior to leaving for Seattle, Martha and her husband were finishing dinner when their front doorbell sounded. Martha walked to the windowless door and opened it to find two men, each wearing a black hoodie and sunglasses. "Are you Mrs. Webb?" one of them asked. When she answered yes, one of the men slammed the door open, smashing Martha against the wall, while the other man walked in, pointing an automatic pistol at Mr. Webb and telling him to stay seated. Martha was held against the wall by the bigger of the two home invaders. She was terrified, and his foul breath was nauseating. She screamed, "Let me go! Get out of here!"

Her assailant viciously slapped her, and her husband pleaded, "Let her go, get away from her!"

The man with the gun then moved closer to Mr. Webb, saying, "Shut up!"

Martha's assailant now had one hand on her throat, demanding, "Where is it? Just give it to us and we're gone!"

"Where is what?" Martha cried.

"Don't act stupid—the money, you idiot!"

"We don't have any money here. What are you talking about?"

"Come on, hand it over."

"I have some traveler's checks. You can have them. They're in my purse over there."

"We don't want any fucking traveler's checks. Give us the hundred grand or you're dead." The big guy backhanded Martha.

Martha whimpered, "Is it in a black briefcase?"

"Yes," he said.

"It's in the trunk of my car. The keys are in my purse."

The big guy let go of Martha and ran outside to the car. He immediately came back in and said, "I've got it."

When leaving, the man with the gun said, "You tell anyone about this and you're dead!"

They both disappeared, leaving Martha hurt and shaking but thankful she and her husband were alive. Martha and Joe Webb hugged each other fiercely.

As they separated, Martha said, "Do you think we should call the police?" Joe did not respond. Their doorbell sounded, and Joe opened it to see Noah North standing in the semi-darkness.

Noah saw Martha in distress and walked to her. "Martha, what is going on?" he almost demanded.

Joe shut the door and said, "We've just been assaulted and robbed by two men."

Noah said, "Martha, it looks like you are hurt. Are you OK or what?"

"They hurt me, and I'll get over the hurt but not the sight of those two awful men."

Noah said, "I came by here on my bike, taking the long way to Rose Marie's house, when I saw two men run to their car and speed off. One was carrying a black briefcase. Was that yours? Never mind, let's take you to the hospital."

Joe said, "Can't do that. They threatened to kill us if we told anyone."

Noah said, "Come on, you fell off a ladder. The hospital is ten minutes away."

They took Martha's car—its keys had been left in the trunk lock—and before they reached the hospital, Noah found out that the briefcase had come from Louis Santos, the banker, and the robbers claimed it held $100,000. The nurse and doctor in the ER bought the ladder story. Who would question Martha? She'd suffered a few bruises, and her shoulder hurt slightly. Her hurt was more emotional than physical.

They returned to Martha's place around 9 p.m. Noah said goodbye and pedaled home to his phone book. He found Louis Santos's phone number and address, and in a state of rage and revenge, he drove to Santos's address with his baseball bat. The house at the address was white, neat, and small, set in a tiny grove of young twenty-to-thirty-foot pines. Noah was standing in the porch light when Louis Santos answered his doorbell. Noah's bat was held behind him. Noah's anger made up for the difference in age.

Noah said, "We need to talk."

He was invited in, and Noah asked, "Is anyone else here?"

"No," was the answer.

They sat facing each other. The room was comfortable and sparsely but nicely furnished with a sofa, Sony TV, hi-fi equipment, an easy chair, and motel-like prints on the walls.

Louis said, "What's the baseball bat for?"

"In case you try to leave or you don't tell me the truth." Noah was taller and heavier than Louis.

Louis said, "Let's not have any trouble."

"That will be up to you," responded Noah. "To start with, Louis, Martha Webb was beat up tonight by men who took the briefcase you gave her to deliver in Seattle. What was in the briefcase, and was it the same briefcase you wanted me to deliver?"

Louis was silent. Noah slammed his baseball bat down on the coffee table in front of Louis with a resounding crash, bouncing things off the table onto the floor. Louis was frightened.

He said, "I don't know, I was told to deliver it."

"What are you involved in, Louis? All I want are the names and whereabouts of the two that beat up my friend Martha. Tell me that and I'll leave." Noah stood up, assuming a stance with his bat that suggested he was about to slam a home run on Louis's head. Louis looked up at Noah and saw a very distraught young man with tears glistening on his cheeks.

Louis cowered slightly and said, "I don't know, but I may know someone that does."

"Louis, I am not leaving here without names and places! Who gave you the briefcase? Who is your cousin in Seattle?" Noah remained in his batting stance and said, "I can break your shoulder or your head. Louis, you went to college, didn't you? You have a good job at the bank! You could lose all that if the bank knows about bad stuff you must be involved in." Noah didn't think he would hit Louis with his bat, but Louis didn't know that.

"Martin Groves and Jason Hanley gave the briefcase to me for delivery. They are both bank customers and make substantial deposits.

Regulations are coming that will require banks to report certain cash transactions, and it will be interesting to see what those boys do. I figured there was cash in that briefcase but really didn't know and didn't care."

"Louis, there was $100,000 in that briefcase. How could Hanley and Groves have that much money?"

"Wow. They've never had any sums of money close to that amount. I'm sure that most of it was not their money. They might know who beat up Martha, but I honestly don't."

"OK, Louis, how did anyone besides you know that Martha Webb had Jason's briefcase?"

"Two guys came to the bank. They said they were business friends of Jason Hanley and that Jason had told them some time ago that I was Jason's banker. They said they were working on a land purchase with Jason, and they asked if Jason had recently made a large cash deposit. I told them I couldn't say, it was against policy. They became very threatening, and I told them that I gave Mrs. Webb a briefcase that Jason wanted delivered in Seattle."

"Don't you dare tell them or anyone about this meeting, or I'll be back. And one more thing: Don't you get my bank in trouble!"

"The name of that person in Seattle is Rusty Hernandez." Santos gave Noah the address and phone number.

Noah didn't know how to deal with the information about Hanley and Groves. He did know someone who could help. It was still a week before his Seattle meeting, and he didn't want to miss school, so he would have to act after school and in the evenings. He was infuriated by the attack on Martha. Noah drove to his house to consider all that had happened, and with Martha foremost in his mind, he knew his next move.

The next morning, before heading to school, Noah called to check on Martha. Joe Webb said that he and Martha would be taking a few days off at home, using the time they had expected to be in Seattle. Their Seattle trip was postponed. Noah said he would visit later. He then called Bill Walstrom, owner of the Arcade Tavern, at his home.

Noah said, "Mr. Walstrom, I need your help. I don't know who else to ask. Could I meet with you after school today, say about four o'clock?

I could come to your tavern but would rather meet at my house because we need privacy."

"I can do that. I know where you live."

"Thanks, Mr. Walstrom. I'll see you there at four."

Students at the high school that day were talking about Martha Webb, which surprised Noah. Few people knew about the event, but the hospital visit probably created the source.

Rose Marie came to Noah and asked, "Did you hear about Martha Webb? Isn't she your friend and guardian?"

"Yes, and I'm boiling with anger, and I don't want to talk about it. Please forgive me for not wanting to discuss it. I'll talk to you about it later."

During the remainder of the school day, Noah couldn't think about anything except pay back and justice for Martha. Noah drove home after school. Mr. Walstrom's car was in his driveway, and Walstrom was sitting in a folding chair on Noah's front porch. Noah sat down and told Walstrom about the events of last night.

Walstrom said, "Martha Webb is one of the finest persons in our community. I don't know how I can help, but I will."

Noah said, "I want us to meet with Jason Hanley and his father alone and really put it to Jason about his knowledge, if he has any, of drug dealing in our community, and who his enemies are, especially the ones that assaulted Martha. The Groves guy might give up some information. He is a relative of Mr. Zimmerman, the jeweler. But let's go after Jason first."

"I know Jonathan Hanley. I'll set up a meeting and call you."

Three hours after their meeting, Bill Walstrom called Noah, and a meeting with the Hanleys was set for four o'clock the next day in the Hanley Real Estate office. Two days ago, Noah had been pleased with the fact that his life was rather pleasant and, although busy, was stable and free from stress and worry. He was thinking, Here I go again, just like that shareholders' meeting, a seventeen-year-old kid taking on strong adults. I'll be there for Martha, and that's all the courage I need.

Walstrom drove to Noah's house and picked him up, and soon they were in Hanley's office with its two big windowed walls, big desk, and comfortable wood chairs, the commendation awards to Jonathan Hanley hanging on the two wood-paneled walls and a row of filing cabinets probably containing sales documents for every other piece of real property in town. There was, of course, a mounted marlin on the wall behind Hanley's desk. He wanted you to know that he'd been to Baja.

Jonathan sat in his swivel chair at his desk, Jason sat to the side of the desk, and Noah and Bill Walstrom sat in chairs pushed back from the front of the desk.

Jonathan said, "OK, what's this all about?"

Noah sat forward in his chair and said, "This is about the terrible assault on Martha Webb in her home two evenings ago."

"Whoa, whoa. What's this have to do with us?" exclaimed Jonathan.

"You'll soon see." Noah stared at Jason and said, "You gave a black locked briefcase to a banker, Louis Santos, to be delivered to Rusty Hernandez at 15634 Pike Street, Unit 29, Seattle, Washington, phone number 206-397-2003. The briefcase contained $100,000. Martha and her husband were flying to Seattle, so Santos asked Martha, as a favor, to deliver the briefcase to Hernandez at the airport. Two men, who you probably know, beat up Martha and took your briefcase from her. Tell us the names of those two men and how to find them."

Bill Walstrom added, "I don't want to tell you what will happen to your reputation if you refuse. Got that?"

Bill Walstrom looked squarely at Jonathan and said, "This matter has not been taken to the police. The two men threatened to kill Martha. Tell your son to tell us everything. Lies will be noted."

Jonathan meekly said, "This is the first I've heard of such a thing."

Quickly, Walstrom said, "Time is of the essence. Don't waste another second. Tell your son to tell us everything, or after we're finished with him, he'll be in police custody. Tell us, Jason!"

Jason squirmed in his chair and, sobbing, he looked at his shoes, saying, "I didn't plan any of this. I'm sorry about what happened to Martha."

Noah said, "Give us names and addresses, you damn fool!"

Noah then focused on Jonathan and said, "My baseball bat is in the car. Do you want me to get it?"

Jason said, "OK, OK. Those two men carry drugs and money for the dealers. The $100,000 is peanuts compared to what they actually transport. It was with seven or eight bags of money in their Suburban, so I just helped myself. I wanted it to go to my friend in Seattle so we could divide it up and have a good time in the big city."

"Jesus Christ, Jason, what in the hell has gotten into you?" roared his father. "You tell them everything you know about this mess."

Jason said, "Wesley and Toby are their names. I do a little business with them, and I was with them when they picked up several sacks of cash at a rest stop on Interstate 5. Later they came to me and accused me of taking a bag of cash, and I denied it and convinced them that they were wrong."

Noah, with a finger in Jason's face, said, "How could you be so stupid as to put yourself and strangers in danger?"

"They asked me who my banker was, and I told them it was Louis Santos at the Rock City National Bank. That's all I know except that they drive a black Suburban and they live in the Pine Tree Apartments in Medford. That is all I know," whined Jason.

"What were they going to do with all that money?" asked Bill Walstrom.

"I don't know, they never said," said Jason.

Noah, in a near-ruthless tone, said, "Better be careful, Jason. I wouldn't want to be you when Wesley and Toby find you."

Jason thought, Oh shit.

Bill Walstrom tapped Noah on his shoulder and said, "There's nothing left here for us, so let's go."

They sat in Walstrom's red Buick Roadmaster and discussed the path forward. They decided to see Martha and Joe and tell them everything that had happened with Jason and his father. They agreed that the issue would be whether the police should be told about Wesley and Toby and their location.

Martha and Joe were home. Noah and Bill were invited in, and with the four sitting in the Webbs' living room, Noah, who intentionally sat next to Martha on her sofa, said, "Martha, there is no way I can tell you how unhappy and upset I am over what happened to you. I just want you to be OK. Bill and I have discovered why you were assaulted and who did it. We don't know their last names, but we have their address."

"Jason Hanley caused the whole mess," offered Bill, who continued, "Noah and I have just finished meeting with Jason and his father, and we believe Jason told us everything. Apparently, Jason stole a bag of drug money from two drug creeps, who were then upset but who also knew that Louis Santos was Jason's banker. They accused Jason of taking the money, but Jason denied it. They didn't believe Jason, so they went to Louis, who, somehow thinking he was doing a favor for Jason, told those two about the briefcase that he gave you to deliver in Seattle. The guy you were to deliver it to was a friend of Jason's, and they were going to divide the money and have a good time in Seattle."

Noah said, "Martha, one of the reasons we are here is to ask you if I should inform the police about the two that assaulted you and where they can be found. We don't need an immediate answer, so if you want to think about it, that's fine. It is your decision. You might keep in mind that those two thugs got their money, and there would be no reason for their return."

Noah and Bill stood up to leave, and Noah said to Martha, "I wish I were the one that got hurt and not you."

"That's very nice, Noah, but I'm going to be just fine."

Bill said, "You call us if you want those two creeps prosecuted."

When Walstrom let Noah off at his house, Noah said, "They will not report the event to the police."

Walstrom said, "I can understand that. The drug business is a many-headed monster, and a threat made could be carried out by a friend or drug colleague even if those guilty boys are jailed."

"If I can identify those two and find them in Medford, I may use my bat again."

The next morning, after a shower, Noah carefully looked at himself in the mirror and then stepped on the scale. He weighed 180 pounds and guessed himself to be about six feet tall. He was growing fast, and considering the fact that he was acting more like an adult than a kid, the growth spurt was good. In his car on the way to school that morning, Noah made two decisions. The coming trip to Seattle would put him in Medford, where he would find the Pine Tree Apartments and Wesley and Toby, and maybe learn their full names and where they were usually found. The trip would also put him in Seattle, and he would visit Rusty Hernandez on Pike Street. It was impossible to set aside the attack on Martha. Nearly all of the high school students had had her as their fourth-grade teacher. They liked her and wanted to know what happened. Noah decided that revealing the circumstances causing the assault would be a big mistake, fostering crazy interpretations and harming Martha. If there were any, he would put them down. Noah found it difficult to wash Martha's ordeal from his mind. A volcano in his back yard might be the only thing to cause him to forget. Maybe he never would.

A phone call from his lawyer, Morgan Reynolds, helped distract Noah from his concern about Martha's real-life nightmare.

Reynolds said, "I think your interest in North Marine might be worth something, or at least that's what I gleaned from the material the trustee sent me. So what do you want me to do?"

"Tell the trustee that my share is for sale." Noah wanted to say that he wouldn't give his time and energy to save two companies simultaneously.

THIRTY-EIGHT

The upcoming October 26, 1975, directors' meeting was forcing Noah to corral his thoughts. He wanted to talk to the director Samantha O'Leary about production capacity and new products. Bobby Shaffer gave him her home number. When Noah called her, she was pleasant and she liked the idea of a second product being manufactured using the existing uncrowded production line. Wheelchairs, walkers, strollers, and golf carts sounded good to her.

She said, "We'll ask Clarke to appoint our two engineers and you and me to a committee for a recommendation to the board. We should meet in the plant immediately following this coming meeting."

Noah said, "Good idea. We don't want Swanson on this committee. He hasn't had an original thought since he was born."

Samantha liked this literate seventeen-year-old and laughed, saying, "We might not be able to make that call, Noah. Clarke and Swanson are nineteenth-century persons."

Noah said, "See you in Seattle."

Noah drove to Medford four hours before his flight to Seattle. He found the Pine Tree Apartments. Noah walked into the office of those apartments and asked for the apartment number for his *old friends*, Wesley and Toby. Asking for their full names might reveal his fib about friendship. There was a black Suburban parked in front of number 121. Noah thought, Now what do I do? I know what I want to do, but that's murder. I need to be smart about this.

He wrote the license plate number of the Suburban on a file cover in his briefcase.

During the flight to Seattle, he had random thoughts about Samantha O'Leary. He entered his room in the Olympic Hotel at 4 p.m. and picked up the phone. He called Samantha O'Leary at her Boeing number. He called her because he liked her good looks, her obvious intelligence, and her engineering skill, and he wanted company at dinner. She answered, and she didn't seem to be upset about his call.

Noah said, "I'd like company for dinner, could you be it?" The anticipated long pause was a killer.

She said, "Why not? Where will this happen?"

"Could you meet me at the Olympic Hotel dining room at six?"

She knew he was a young, brainy, resourceful man and not timid. "OK, Noah, but I have to drive for an hour to get there, so it better be interesting. Bye-bye for now."

He put the phone down, pleased with himself.

Noah was seated in the Olympic's spacious wood-paneled dining room when Samantha arrived. As she walked to Noah, he saw some men's heads turn toward this good-looking woman, probably wondering, What's with the young guy she's headed toward?

"Noah, this is very nice of you. Do you always stay here?"

"Always and alone. Thought your company and advice would be nice."

She asked, "Don't you have a family member who could accompany you?"

"No, but I have a good friend that was with me on my first trip here. She was my fourth-grade teacher, and she's usually there for me when I need her. I've been alone since I was eight years old, but wait, I'm not having dinner with you to talk about myself."

"I believe your life may be exceptionally interesting," offered Samantha.

Noah said, "You could be right."

Samantha was at once comfortable with Noah. She was an outdoors person who spent much of her free time hiking mountain trails in Washington and skiing in the winter.

When she was younger, she'd done the same thing in Idaho, her home state. Older friends with teenagers were sometimes with her on those hikes. She was a veteran downhill skier, having spent many days on the slopes with skiers of all ages, including skiers Noah's age. This was especially true at the big ski areas, Sun Valley in her home state and Whistler Blackcomb in British Columbia, where teenagers were all over the place, sometimes bothersome. Her older friends in Seattle, mostly Boeing employees, had children Noah's age. Noah was a stark contrast to any seventeen-year-old she'd ever met, and she wanted to discover why.

"Noah, I think we should order dinner."

Their waiter appeared as if on cue, and they ordered dinner.

"May I call you Sam?"

"Yes, all of my friends do."

"OK, Sam, my main purpose here is for us to talk about my idea regarding additional products for Road Victor. I'm thinking you will give me your honest opinion on that subject. Is my suggestion a good or bad idea?"

"It's a good idea that needs to be pursued and explored by a committee of market experts, a director or two, and our plant engineers."

She set her napkin down and took a long look at him.

"Noah, I gotta ask you something personal. What's a seventeen-year-old doing in the business and financial world?"

"I read a statement by a successful man that said, 'Never work for anyone,' and I agree. I never have and never will. I don't like to be told what to do and what not to do. Hopefully, I will always do what's right and be nice about it. Sam, please don't ask anything else about me. I didn't ask you here to listen to me talk about myself."

"Noah, this isn't getting any wheelchairs built, is it?"

"Right. I was thinking four-wheeled walkers with bicycle rim brakes, a horn, and headlights."

"Noah, I think we can work on that."

Noah added, "Remember, we don't want CEO Swanson on that committee. He's never had a thought outside a three-foot circle."

"We are not making the committee appointments," Samantha cautioned.

"I might as well tell you, I'm letting Chairman Clarke know that he will cease to be chairman if he doesn't appoint the right people, but I'll be nice. That's not a bluff. I'll call for the election of a chairman, just as the by-laws allow, and he'll lose."

"Will you really tell him that?"

"I really don't want to, but I will if I have to, and I intend to be respectful to him."

"You know what Stalin and Mao said about revolutions? They said there had to be blood to be successful."

"I didn't know they said that."

Samantha knew that Noah didn't know everything, so she gave Noah a brief international history lesson about people disappearing in communist nations.

"We are not going to cause a million people to disappear, but we may cause a tiny, polite revolution in our ranks."

Their waiter, with a white starched, cut waiter's jacket and black tie and pants, laid two perfect dinners before them.

After the waiter left, Noah looked at Samantha and asked, "Do you have a man in your life?"

"That's none of your seventeen-year-old business."

"You're right, but tell me anyway."

"Maybe."

Samantha realized what was happening. She was about to respond when Noah said, without thinking, "I find myself personally attracted to you. I could not have had a better dinner companion."

"Take it easy, Noah, you're still in high school over three hundred miles from here, I'm four or five years older than you and employed in my chosen profession, and I'm not looking for any changes."

Noah responded, saying, "Forgive me, I'm used to saying what I honestly believe."

He then engaged in some introspection. Rose Marie is the girl in my life. But the sensation of pleasure and passion stirred within me by Samatha O'Leary is overwhelming. It's not just her beauty. It's something I can't describe; I'm not sure anyone can. I've got to take it easy with this. Sidestepping Rose Marie is not an option.

When they finished eating, Noah said, "Thank you for having dinner with me. You're more than good company, and Road Victor is lucky to have you on its board."

"Noah, you're a real gentleman, and I hate to leave, but I have an hour's drive ahead of me, so I'll be seeing you tomorrow."

Noah put the dinner on his room account and walked Samantha through the hotel entrance and to her car.

"Thanks for a nice evening, Noah." She gave him a surprise firm hug and drove away.

Liking that woman was more than a lingering thought.

During her drive home, Samantha was thinking, What was that personal conversation about? He's seventeen, bright, and in many ways a young man in charge. I think I'm liking it. He is good-looking. Am I nuts?

Noah intentionally arrived early at the company's offices for the meeting. He found Samantha and Bobby and reviewed Samantha's suggestion about a committee investigating new products. Noah then found Chairman Clarke in the directors' room. Clarke seemed to be brooding about changes he knew were coming. He would be crusty and stubborn about change and women in business, and he was conservative politically, much the same as Attila the Hun might be.

In the boardroom, Noah said, "We are going to suggest that you appoint a committee to investigate possible production of new products. The committee members should be directors Shaffer and O'Leary, engineers McCormick and Kraus, maybe a market analyst and me, and no one else. I really hope that is OK with you."

"So you're telling me what to do," fumed Clarke.

"Only suggesting," replied Noah, "and so we don't have a long discussion about this, please just make the appointments and you will remain chairman of the board. Otherwise I may call for election of a chairman, as provided in our by-laws, and we will have a new chairman."

"So, a seventeen-year-old is now running Road Victor," howled Clarke.

"Beats not being run at all, Mr. Clarke."

Samantha and Bobby watched Noah as he verbally caused Clarke to come to grips with his future at Road Victor.

Samantha said, "I think Noah just told him the time of day."

Bobby said, "That kid's got more guts than a slaughterhouse."

Clarke called the meeting to order. After finishing housekeeping business, CEO Swanson reported that all production was now for the aluminum-frame bike, and the procurement officer had been successful in contracting for new brake parts that only needed assembly. New rims and wheel sizes had been designed, and machinery was being acquired for their production at Road Victor.

Samantha, after slowly scrutinizing Directors Hedges and Clarke, said, "Road Victor has an opportunity to manufacture and market new products. The size of our plant and experience of our personnel gives us an excellent profit opportunity. We need to seriously explore this matter, and I ask Chairman Clarke to appoint our engineers Russ McCormick and Steven Kraus, Shaffer, Noah, and myself, maybe a market analyst, and no other person to a new products committee."

Clarke invited discussion. Hedges suggested that the CEO should be on the committee.

Noah said, "No, he's too busy getting the new bikes rolling, and we need some new original thinking and imagination. Let's think and imagine like a couple of brothers named Orville and Wilbur, who, like us, made bicycles."

Samantha looked away, nearly choking on stifled laughter.

Clarke then appointed the members as requested, with Bobby Shaffer as chairman, and said, "The committee can appoint a market analyst if they need one."

Bobby Shaffer said, "Mr. Swanson, would you make sure these two engineers know about this and ask them to meet us in the plant after this meeting?" Swanson nodded his approval.

Bobby then said, "This committee should meet in about two weeks and try to reach some conclusions and have a recommendation for our November meeting. Our travel and lodging expenses should be paid."

The committee met with McCormick and Kraus in the plant and instructed them to devise plans for the production-line manufacture of four-wheeled walkers and other similar products such as a baby stroller or golf cart, and if that was feasible, then design them as collapsible for easy transportation and shipping. These products had to be patented, so they needed to make sure they were.

Samantha cautioned, "Keep this stuff to yourselves, we don't want anyone stealing this market opportunity from us."

The directors said their goodbyes, and Noah headed to visit

Rusty Hernandez at 15634 Pike Street. Noah was not forgetting Martha. She was his motherly lioness. Noah couldn't get Martha's ordeal off his mind. The address at 15634 Pike was a pawn shop. Noah told the taxi driver to wait. He walked into a cruddy sidewalk-level pawn shop with last-chance valuables resting in old locked glass display cases. The best stuff was on shelves behind the counter, and other items were in the sidewalk show windows. Each item on display could no doubt tell a story, maybe a story of desperation about the person who'd hocked it. Noah was the only customer. He asked the young man behind the counter with long brown hair for Rusty Hernandez.

"I'm Rusty."

Noah looked at Rusty with a disparaging eye and said, "I'm here for Jason Hanley, who hasn't heard from you. I'll ask you once—did you get the package?"

"No. It should have been here days ago but it wasn't."

Noah said, "Have you been in touch with Wes and Toby?"

"No."

Noah said, "Where is the $100,000?"

Rusty said nothing.

Feigning politeness, Noah said, "This could get real shitty for you."

"If the money is lost, Jason and Martin could disappear," urged Rusty.

Noah demanded, "Now we're talking about Jason stealing money from those guys, aren't we?" Then he added, "Tell me who and where they are and I'm out of here."

Rusty was sick, nervous, and wishing he was on another planet.

"Wesley and Toby of Medford, Oregon. That's all I know," he said, looking as if he were watching a torpedo wake streaking toward his ship.

"Thanks," Noah said as he turned toward his taxi. He had checked out of the Olympic and was on his way to Sea-Tac Airport.

As soon as Noah walked into his house, he called Martha.

She answered, and he said, "I want to see you now."

"I'm here, come over."

For the first time, he hugged Martha, then sat on her sofa and said to Martha and Joe, "I think I have enough info on the attack on you to cause the police to make some arrests and get some convictions if they handle things properly, but it's up to you, Martha," cautioned Noah. "Also, there may be some serious problems between the people responsible for the attack and some of their nasty friends who are upset about the attack."

Martha and Joe decided to forgo any further strife and unpleasantness. Noah agreed, but the facts were stored in his brain. He was thinking, What would Jason's disappearance mean to the community? Maybe like losing the summer mosquitoes. Then there's Jason's accomplice, Martin Groves. I haven't spoken to that insect. He can flit about for a while.

High school had been like a vacation for Noah compared to the other, more difficult obligations in his life. He visited Rose Marie every day. Early on she had been pretty, and now, in Noah's mind, she was bordering on beautiful. Nearly every day, he thought, What about Samantha O'Leary? It must be true, beautiful women can drive men crazy, but what about schoolboys?

Following up on one further thing he'd vowed to do, Noah found Martin Groves with the help of Mr. Zimmerman, the jeweler. He was employed by the Black Dog Lumber Co. Noah knocked on Martin's apartment door. It was in an old highway motel with motel rooms converted to family living units. It was 7 p.m. and dark. Martin cautiously opened the door, saw Noah, and tried to close the door. Noah stuck his bat between the door and the jamb and forced his way in. Martin Groves was older but not much bigger than Noah, and his lack of resolve made him no match for the boy with the bat. They were in a one-room mess with clothes dropped everywhere, the bed unmade, empty pop cans sitting around, and empty grocery packages overflowing in a wastebasket. There was an apartment-size electric stove and a small refrigerator on one wall. The door to the tiny bathroom was open. There was nothing good about the place. Noah said, "You know why I'm here, so start telling me about that drug business of Jason's and yours." Noah held his bat in readiness.

Martin said, "I'm sorry about Martha Webb. Those guys, Wesley and Toby, are suppliers. They wanted their movements and deliveries to go unnoticed, so they asked Jason and me to get Louis Santos to help. Louis had no idea what he was doing, and that's why things went to rat shit."

"Give me the last names of Wesley and Toby," demanded Noah.

"It's Wesley Waterman and Toby Winston."

"Do they drive a black Suburban and live in Medford?"

"Yes."

Noah took his bat off his shoulder and said, "Martin, sane people would say you are behaving like an idiot. Stupid people would say nothing. You have one foot in quicksand and a brain that knows right from wrong, but you haven't used it! Do what is right, and your life won't end up in a dumpster!"

The problem was, Noah had no plan for the people who'd hurt Martha. He wanted to commit several crimes against them and burn the bat, but he knew better. Jason Hanley and Martin Groves didn't know better. Noah left Martin, having no idea how depraved Martin and Jason were.

Jason and Martin had a dimwitted plan they'd conceived after they heard about the assault on Martha Webb. They reasoned that their knowledge of Wesley Waterman and Toby Winston's illegal drug business, Jason's theft of $100,000 from them, and Waterman's and Winston's violent character put Martin's and Jason's lives in danger. Certainly banker Santos would tell Waterman and Winston anything they wanted to know. Jason and Martin believed their lives were in danger, and they made a plan worthy of a sociopath, a plan they thought they would never put into play, but they did.

Three weeks after Noah's visit to Martin with his bat, Martin and Jason found Waterman's black Suburban in Medford. Jason had stolen dynamite from an unlocked logger's truck at a road construction site. They had finished wiring five sticks of 80 percent dynamite with an electric primer cap to the Suburban's ignition when they were discovered by Waterman and Winston, who did not know that Jason and Martin had attached anything to their Suburban. Jason and Martin were badly beaten and put in the Suburban to be dealt with later and buried in the forest. Winston got in the car, as did Waterman, who turned the ignition key, and a terrific explosion killed the four young men. The police investigation revealed nothing except dynamite residue and four bodies. Inquiry was made to loggers' supply businesses, the only sellers of dynamite in southern Oregon, and no sales of dynamite had been made to anyone of interest. A license to buy explosives was required by the state. After the police and sheriff's work was complete, they announced: "We are not even close to having a suspect. It was probably drug related."

Noah drove to Martha and said, "We may know why those young men were killed, but we don't know how it happened. The problems they created for you have ended. We can feel sorry for their loved ones."

Martha looked at her husband and then Noah and said, "We need to mentally walk away from this now." The unfortunate episode in their lives was permanently ended.

THIRTY-NINE

Thomas North and his sister Margo were distressed that their eighteen-year-old cousin was half owner with them in North Marine, Inc.

Thomas said to Margo, "He wants us to buy his shares."

"Well, let's do it," Margo said. "Make him an offer."

"I did, and he turned me down."

"What did you offer him?"

"Five thousand. I was actually talking to his lawyer, who told me not to be foolish."

Margo said, "Smart lawyer."

"His lawyer then offered me $25,000 for three thousand shares. I was so upset that I hung up."

"Thomas, in business you are a dunce. It was you that ran North Marine into near failure, and now we are both paying the price. The trustee told me that Noah has the North Marine financials, even some directors' minutes. He and his people know you screwed things up. He might even think you did it intentionally."

"Margo, his lawyer, Reynolds, told me that Noah will sell his shares to a competing marine shipper if we don't sell him three thousand shares."

"Thomas, you'd better re-read that *Wall Street Journal* article. You're in over your head. Don't you get it? He wants total control. You will have none. He will fix North Marine, Inc., and we will benefit."

"Yes, but he's taking half our shares."

Margo stared at Thomas for an instant and said, "That's life as you arranged it! So accept the deal. If you don't, I'm selling him fifteen hundred shares for $12,250! If you sell him your shares, I will not alert him to the threatening statement you made about Noah and his father. Remember? I told you it was wrong."

Thomas, unhappy with Margo, said, "As long as he has control, he may as well have half of my shares."

Margo said, "Don't say another word. I'm thinking."

Issues with North Marine put Noah to work in Oregon. He sat at CPA Roy Sang's desk in Grants Pass. When he finished the story about North Marine, Roy Sang picked up the North Marine papers Noah had laid before him.

Sang took time to review the North Marine financials and the North Trust and to get some answers from Noah. "OK, why am I looking at this stuff?"

"What should I do?"

Sang said, "You don't have time for this. Get rid of your interest in North Marine and let the trust assets play out. You don't need the money, and you don't need any potential grief."

Noah said, "You're right about that. Trouble is, I have no family ties. I was set adrift in this world with no family and no connection to anyone except my goofy uncle. Now I have one good cousin relative, my cousin Margo in Buffalo. I've changed my thinking about my family ties. They have some importance to me. I'm not sure what it is but I can't pass that by."

As he left Sang's office, Sang said, "Just don't do anything foolish with your money. A dying business is a bad investment, and North Marine is dying."

Noah replied, "Oh yeah, what about Road Victor?"

Noah deposited $25,000 with Reynolds with half payable to Thomas North and half payable to Margo North. He hated doing that for Thomas. They accepted the offer, and Noah received half their shares and control of North Marine, Inc., with nine thousand shares. He called his broker, Marty Woods, and after telling him what he had purchased, Noah said, "I have decided that I made a mistake."

Woods said, "Noah, you don't have time to fix everything. You wanted to fix your relatives' business, and I think that's why you did what you did. You need a quick fix, don't you?"

Noah agreed.

Woods said, "Go back there, hire a good, gutsy CEO, let him revive that company to profitability, then get out."

Noah said, "North Marine cannot be fixed without a loan or new capital, and I'm prepared to do that, if it's not too much."

Marty said, "If you want to benefit from an increase in share value, have North Marine issue new common shares that give existing shareholders the exclusive right to buy those new shares. Do not make a loan to that company. There are limits on deducting loan losses from bad loans, and if you are unlucky, you're headed in that direction. Have the attorney for North Marine take care of the resolution for the issuance of new shares with preemptive shareholder rights for adoption by the directors. Did you write that down?"

"Yes."

Noah sold some sinkers and immediately flew to Buffalo, New York, with a reservation at the Falls Hotel on Buffalo Avenue. Niagara Falls was visible from his room, which was not a luxury suite but was clean. A thousand newlyweds had probably stayed there.

When he was settled, he called North Marine and told a secretary who he was and that he was in town for a visit and would be there the following morning. The next morning he took a taxi to the Lake Employment Agency and told the person in charge, Mr. Grimes, who he was, and he explained the job he wanted to fill and what he expected of the manager of a marine shipper.

Mr. Grimes asked, "How old are you?"

"I'm eighteen, but don't let that fool you. I'm here to hire the CEO I briefly described. I'll negotiate the compensation that could be more than a salary. This hiring is urgent, and I'll try not to be a pain in the ass. Here's my hotel number."

Noah left after a few pleasantries with Mr. Grimes.

As Noah walked out his door, Mr. Grimes thought, No, he's eighteen in age only.

Twenty minutes later, a taxi dropped Noah in front of a near-falling-down wood-frame building on the lake waterfront. There was a weathered sign proclaiming "North Marine, Inc." hanging on a couple of rusty sixteen-penny nails. Inside, things were better.

He walked into the building and was welcomed by Myra Houston, the person who'd answered his phone call. She was a well-dressed, nice-appearing woman Noah guessed to be forty-five or fifty years old. She was married to Philip, an automobile mechanic, and they had two children, one in college and one in high school. Myra was in charge of her family, but her family didn't know it. Myra led North Marine, and the few employees left were happy about it.

She walked Noah around inside the building, which had ample storage areas for goods in transit, and through a covered moorage for ship repair and refitting with adjoining working areas. Large pieces of marine equipment sat about with other machinery used in ship repair and construction. It all looked as if it had been idle, and there were no employees seen. During the tour, Myra related a detailed history of North Marine. She told Noah the purpose and use of every piece of equipment viewed and the use of every building they entered.

Noah and Myra stopped walking. "How long have you been employed here?" Noah asked.

Myra said, "Mr. North employed me a week after I received my undergraduate degree in business at Yale. I was to manage our charter services, which is the backbone of this business. Mr. North managed everything else until his health interfered, and I gradually spent more time with his responsibilities."

"But, Mrs. Houston, why is this company now in such disarray?"

"His grandson Thomas moved me away from management. I am sad to say that our business has been on a downhill slide ever since. Money should have been spent to maintain and replace ships and equipment. The money went to the personal use of those in charge, and income is now so meager that we should close."

"Is there enough demand for the services of North Marine and other companies like it to put us back in business and keep us there?"

"Absolutely."

They walked back into the large office. It was orderly, well kept, and pleasant, with large windows showcasing a three-hundred-foot moorage arranged for mooring ships perpendicular to the large shoreside wharf. There were small wharfs between each moorage. A large loading wharf was opposite the moorages. The cranes located there looked well kept. Many of the berths, all for large ships, were empty, and those with moored vessels, all named North Marine, seemed to be in disrepair. Noah hoped the machinery in those vessels was shipshape.

Soon seven employees showed up in the office. Mrs. Houston introduced Noah North as the new majority owner of North Marine.

Noah stepped forward and said, "Alexander Noah North was my grandfather. I never knew him, and he may not have known that I existed. Yes, I inherited one-half of the outstanding shares, and I bought half of the other shares, giving me control of North Marine. I'm eighteen years old and you'll find that my age is meaningless. My plan is to revive this company by investing my own funds. Once safely revived, I will sell it. I will make certain that all employees continue as employees of any new owner. I will hire a CEO to run this company. He or she will be directly answerable to me even though I live on the West Coast. I need your help as bad as you need my help. I think Mrs. Houston has made arrangements for some refreshments to be served. You can approach me and ask me anything."

Hans Jonsgaard, the only ship captain now employed by North Marine, stepped up to Noah and said, "Hope you can right this ship. The other Norths cannot. Myra Houston can be your new CEO. She knows this business and why it is failing. It is a good business, and we have everything we need except money and a leader. Myra Houston is your leader."

Mrs. Houston stepped close to Noah and Hans.

"Noah, this man knows everything about Great Lakes ships, safe lake routes, when to stay in port, and how to make a profitable bid to carry goods or raw materials."

Noah looked at Hans and said, "I'm going to keep this company afloat, and we need you."

"I'm not going anyplace."

When Myra was alone, Noah walked to her and said, "Myra, I want you to be CEO of North Marine. We'll negotiate your salary later. Will you take the job? It'll be rough at first."

"I'll take the job on the condition that Thomas North and anyone representing him stay off the premises, and that he not be allowed to interfere with the business or any of our employees."

Noah, with a smile on his face, said, "I'll take care of that.

"One more thing, Myra. As soon as I had the additional shares, I had Attorney Johnston call for a meeting of shareholders. Thomas and Margo were given proper notice, and the meeting is in five days at this office. He will have a resolution giving shareholders a preemptive right to buy twelve thousand newly issued common shares, with the number of shares purchased limited to the number of shares presently owned by the shareholder. The price will be $50 per share. Accordingly, I will probably be adding $600,000 capital to North Marine. You need to make a plan to put North Marine back in business. You can send me your plan. I need to leave for Oregon after that meeting. Remember, we are all as close as the phone."

Noah called Mr. Grimes at the employment agency, thanked him, and told him that he'd hired a CEO.

The North Marine shareholders' meeting was held in June 1976.

Thomas North and his sister Margo arrived early. They wanted to know Noah's plans for North Marine.

Thomas was an annoying, obnoxious man with few friends. He felt entitled to a life without interference from anyone, especially an eighteen-year-old.

Thomas stepped up to Noah and said, "Why didn't you talk to Margo and me about your plans for North Marine?"

Noah shrugged. "It was going to happen regardless. We can discuss it now. The plan is to right the ship, make it prosperous and attractive to a potential buyer, and sell. You and Margo will benefit from the sale, and it is my hope that you do."

The shareholders' meeting was held, approving the issue of new common shares that contained the shareholder preemptive rights, and the new shares were offered for sale.

Noah had prepared for his bailout of North Marine with a gold sale. He wrote a $600,000 check at the meeting to North Marine, Inc. Thomas and Margo knew before they arrived at the shareholders' meeting that they were no match for the eighteen-year-old shareholder. Their refusal to buy or order any of the new shares was entered in the shareholders' minutes. It was then that Noah handed his check to Myra for deposit in North Marine's general account. Ironically, Thomas and Margo would benefit from Noah's action. But Thomas felt upended by Noah's power play.

At the meeting's end, Thomas, frustrated, without thinking, said, "You don't know anything about this business, so we all hope you know what you're doing."

"I don't have to know much about this business because I hired someone that does. She was at the shareholders' meeting. I thought there might be some unpleasantness, but I was wrong. The new CEO is Myra Houston, and she has instructions from me that you, Thomas North, shall not enter these premises except by written invitation from me. Your meddling is over."

Noah left Buffalo with twenty-one thousand common shares of North Marine, Inc., believing he had solved major issues with North Marine and that time would increase his equity in North Marine, and he would sell and unburden his life. Thomas and Margo each ended up with fifteen hundred shares of North Marine.

Margo and Thomas left the building together.

Thomas said, "You know, Margo, we are Noah's heirs. We are his closest relatives. If he had no will, and if he died, his estate would be ours."

Margo said, "Thomas, are you an evil person? You might be."

Thomas said, "I'm a practical man."

Margo said, "I'll bet you had something to do with Buster North's *accidental* death."

"I had nothing to do with that. I haven't left New York in ten years."

Margo walked away from Thomas, saying, "You wouldn't have to leave. Noah North is going to know about you!"

Halfway to her car, Margo turned around, walked to Thomas, stood in front of him, and said, "Noah had a mother, and no doubt he has close relatives on her side of his family that can inherit from him, so stop your stupidity about harming Noah."

Five days after arriving home, Noah received a letter from Margo North. The letter was a four-sentence warning: "Noah, you are a decent person. Thomas is not a good person, and he may be a danger to you. Please take this message seriously. My best to you, Margo."

Noah immediately found Bill Walstrom and showed him Margo's letter and reminded Bill of what had happened to Buster.

Bill said, "I'm on it. Go about your life with your eyes and ears open."

FORTY

Home and alone was a good time for Noah to evaluate his life, his accomplishments, and the road he was on. He knew that the North Marine business put too much responsibility on him. He wanted to put that to bed as quickly as possible and, if necessary, get Thomas legally neutralized. Aside from Thomas, his thoughts pleased him, but he could not define his life's direction except that he wanted to be self-reliant and a good person. A knock at his door interrupted his introspection.

Bud Cooper, timber buyer for Black Dog Lumber Co., wanted to talk. Sitting in Noah's living room, Bud informed Noah of Eastern Pacific Timber Company's intent to sell five thousand acres of their logged-over timber lands. All of those lands were contiguous to Noah's land on the east and south. A little stream bordered part of the five thousand acres on the south. That stream arose on land Noah sought to buy. Downstream it eventually flowed onto national forest land. That little stream was the goose that laid Noah's golden eggs. Bud told Noah that Eastern Pacific, the owner that logged off forest land, could be trouble because it had violated the Oregon law requiring reforestation of logged-off lands within six years after harvest. Rumor was that Eastern Pacific did not have the funds to replant.

Bud said, "Noah, you should somehow acquire those lands, if only to protect yourself and your timber. You do not want anyone logging next door to your timber. You can trust the big timber companies, but not some of their contract loggers. Not all of the lands have been reforested, and that is Eastern Pacific's problem. Eastern Pacific might accept any halfway decent offer." Bud had no knowledge of Noah's ability to buy those lands, but he thought Noah should know.

Eastern Pacific's office was in Medford, and Noah was there the next day. He first drove to the county surveyor's office, where he studied a map of the land he wanted to buy, but not carefully, and he bought a copy. He parked in front of the Eastern Pacific Timber Company office. He saw a secretary watching him from her desk in the windowed office, and he walked in.

"Do you have an appointment?" asked the receptionist.

"No, but this is important."

"What is important?"

"I want to buy the timber land you have for sale."

"How old are you?"

"Eighteen."

The receptionist picked up her phone, punched a button, and following a short wait, said, "There's an eighteen-year-old here driving a Mercedes that wants to buy the timber land we have for sale."

She put the phone down, saying, "He said they have a buyer."

"Tell him I'll pay more now and in cash."

She called and relayed the message. She turned to Noah and said, "Go down the hall behind me and to the first door to the right."

Noah entered the office of Josh Horton, who said, "Who in the hell are you?"

"I'm Noah Jeremiah North. Who are you?"

"I'm Josh Horton. Please make this quick."

Noah slowly looked the room over and said, "What's your price per acre for the five thousand acres?"

"Why do you want it?"

"It surrounds me on three sides, and I don't want a neighbor."

"OK. We have a buyer at $10 per acre."

"Let's get this over with. I will pay you $13."

"Do you know that that's $65,000?"

"Yes."

Horton picked up his phone, dialed a number, and soon said, "I have a $13-per-acre offer." Horton held the phone away from his ear and then put the phone down and said, "It's yours. You'd better be real."

"My lawyer, Morgan Reynolds, will be in touch with you."

Noah drove straight to Reynolds's office in Grants Pass. Fortunately, Reynolds was in his office and able to see Noah. When Noah told him the price, Reynolds momentarily lost his breath and asked if Noah had the money.

"I'll have the money when we close."

While in Medford, he stopped at the office of Kaplan and Graves and made arrangements for the delivery and sale of gold sinkers. Nothing was said about price.

Gold was now on Noah's brain. An old *Wall Street Journal* prediction on commodity prices had said that in 1975, gold would end up $180 per ounce or more. That's what it was in late 1974. Noah knew what he was going to do. It was 1976 and, in the gold-pricing business, pricing was not a science. Gold was down, hovering around $130 per ounce. He knew it had to rise; he didn't like the day's price, but he needed the adjoining land.

The next day, Noah visited his bank and emerged with a heavy briefcase holding nine hundred ounces of gold sinkers. Noah struggled to carry it.

Parked in front of Kaplan and Graves, he missed the company of Martha, who had always taken him there.

The price was agreed at $130 an ounce. Then Noah drove to Kaplan and Grave's bank for two cashier's checks. Then he went to the lawyer Reynolds's office, where Noah sat with a $65,000 check for Reynolds to deposit in his client's trust account. Noah had another check in his pocket, payable to him for $52,000, enough to pay taxes and bank the rest.

Reynolds said, "If the seller's title is clear, this sale can close in a couple of days."

Five days later, Attorney Reynolds called Noah and said the transaction had closed, and Noah would soon receive his recorded deed and a statement for attorney's fees and costs. He now owned the land bordering him. That would eliminate any timber theft on his cedars. His new lands had an irregular boundary, something he had paid little attention to, and this time, when he carefully examined the surveyor's map, it confirmed the fact that within one of the sections of his new land was a portion of the little stream he'd waded in when he was four years old. From that stream came his fortune. Noah had a good feeling about that. The opposite bank of a portion of the stream bordering him was in the national forest. That little stream merged with a larger stream that eventually joined the Rogue River.

Felix Bronson and Noah had started to become friends by the end of Noah's first school year eleven years ago.

A few days before Thanksgiving, Noah watched Felix walk into the Rock City Cafe. Noah parked his car, walked into the cafe, and sat next to Felix. Felix had been riding a bus, attending a few classes at Rogue Community College in Medford. Felix seemed fidgety and uncomfortable, which was not uncommon for Felix, who was easily frustrated with small issues. If the issue involved a boy who teased him or bullied him, Felix would start swinging and usually end up the loser. That would be a big issue, and Noah sensed Felix's unease was something different.

Noah put his hand on Felix's shoulder and said, "Felix, whatever it is, I'm with you, so take it easy. Are you bothered with me because of my car?"

"Noah, I know you need a car."

Felix said, "My mom and dad and I want you to have Thanksgiving dinner with us. Can you do that?"

"Sure thing, Felix. When should I show up?"

"About noon would be good."

"Felix, you didn't have to be nervous about the invite."

Later that day, Martha invited Noah for Thanksgiving, as did Rose Marie, but Noah had to decline. As soon as he received the third invite, it became clear to him that Rock City was his home, and it was where his friends were. His business in Seattle was important, and he had friends there that were only business associates. They did not outweigh his connection to Rock City, and he would try to live his life accordingly. North Marine was becoming less important.

After boarding a Bombardier Dash 8 Series 400 at Medford for Seattle, Noah decided that flying with crowds of people traveling between Thanksgiving and Christmas was ridiculous. He also knew that driving his car back and forth to Seattle would be stupid. Driving it to Medford was far enough. Sitting in line with the plane's turbo-driven propellers was unnerving. He'd never been on a prop plane. He thought, If a propeller came off, it would spin through this window, and that would be that! But that can't happen—or can it?

Noah had called Samantha O'Leary from the Medford airport, and she picked him up at Sea-Tac. She drove to the Olympic for dinner with Noah.

When seated, Noah said, "I've caused you a terrible inconvenience today. I wasn't thinking. I won't do that again."

Sam smiled and cocked an eyebrow at him. "Does it make any difference that I wanted to see you?"

"Yes it does, and five years' difference in age is nothing."

"This might be a date," Sam said. "But it's also a meeting of two company officials."

Noah said, "Well, as I see it, we have several reasons to be together, and this is part date."

The dinner they ordered was before them, and Sam, changing the subject, said, "When we meet with the committee tomorrow, what are we looking for?"

Noah, distracted by Sam's charisma, blurted, "I'm looking for a schematic drawing of another production line and an inventory of everything needed."

"Noah, let's go back to the date thing."

"Not yet. I'm looking for accessibility of components for the new product plus a time frame on everything. I want to see a walker design as we requested. I think we might get what we want if Swanson doesn't have anything to do with it."

"We mustn't push too hard," Samantha replied. "These guys have their feet in the mud and aren't interested in anything fresh and untried."

"Samantha, our company doesn't have much time left. We have to force-feed the old troops. I'm anxious to see what happens tomorrow, and hopefully we'll start walking our company away from the gallows."

"That's pretty dramatic, Noah."

"No, but if you own 560,000 shares like Sylvia Latimer and 308,000 shares like George Newton, you and Bobby and I should be in their prayers, asking us for a miracle."

"Noah, you may be an eighteen-year-old captain of industry on the rise, and no one could go wrong by hanging on to your coattails, but you are not the self-appointed savior of Road Victor, so take it easy on miracles."

"Tomorrow may be a sunrise or a sunset for Road Victor," proclaimed Noah as he walked Samantha to her car.

Sam said, "Did you hear what I just said to you about patting yourself on the back?"

"I did and you are right. It is an outright lack of character."

Noah thought, What's the matter with me? I know better.

When Samantha opened her car door to get in, she quickly turned around, gently grabbed Noah's head in her hands, and kissed him on his cheek. Noah turned his head and stole a real kiss. Then they firmly clutched each other in a warm, fierce kiss.

He thought, Was that the writing on the wall?

Samantha drove away in her BMW sedan, smiling at the intellect and boldness of her eighteen-year-old who was metamorphosing into more than a friendly colleague.

The next morning, Bobby, Samantha, engineers Russ and Steven, and Noah met on the factory floor with the bike plant in full operation. Russ and Steven had been briefed on their committee's purpose by Swanson, but they rejected Swanson's negative views and took a rock-solid positive approach. They had a plan for the rebirth of Road Victor. They had the schematic drawing and, most of all, the excitement and will to not only save their jobs but to manufacture a walker, a golf cart, a baby stroller, and a wheelchair.

Russ pointed to the far side of the plant structure and said, "The new production line will be the full length of that space. All those supplies on the floor will be moved onto high vertical steel shelving accessed by a forklift. There will be enough room on that shelving to supply both production lines."

Bobby asked, "Did I understand you to say that all these new products can be assembled on the same production line?"

"Absolutely," responded Russ and Steven jointly.

Noah said, "This is better than we imagined, but what about the manufacture of the component parts? Do we still have room for manufacturing bicycles?"

"No," said Steven. "We need an additional building, and we will need to hire additional employees to train. We will resource component parts from independent companies. Also, good employee skill level will take time."

Russ said, "The cost, including new and additional equipment, will be about $2,600,000."

Noah said, "Samantha, you're an engineer, what do you think about this plan?"

"I'm an aeronautical engineer. I didn't take wheelchair or walker engineering in school, so I will rely on our two engineers."

"Touché," uttered Bobby.

"That is not to say I can't help. We three engineers don't have to be rocket scientists to design and make these new products. We do need something highly durable and marketable."

"Are we all satisfied with the proposal, and do we agree to submit it to the board of directors?" asked Noah.

Bobby said, "I'm good with it, but I'm not so sure that we can pay next month's electric bill. So where do we get the dough?"

Everyone held the same opinion except Noah, who said, "Don't worry about the cost, I've got that covered."

Samantha walked over to Noah. "Noah, I know you're smart but not that smart."

Noah, with a kind smile, said, "I talked to my CPA, my lawyer, and my stock brokerage firm because it was obvious there would be a major cost involved. We just didn't want to admit it, but we don't have the capital necessary to build a mousetrap. I got the idea from a *Wall Street Journal* article about an old company raising new capital."

Bobby said, "We need to have Russ and Steven at the directors' meeting, and they need to put the proposal for the plant, tool, and employee requirements in writing for the meeting. Noah can present his financing proposal."

When the committee was breaking up, Samantha walked in front of Noah and stopped. "Noah, why didn't you skip high school and go straight to college?"

"I had some growing up to do."

Sam drove Noah to the Olympic and parked beneath the portico out of the rain and said, "Do you want me to take you to the airport tomorrow?"

"No, you've spent enough time with me. I'll see you at the next directors' meeting, but, Sam, there's something I need to say."

They surveyed each other carefully, and Noah said, "To be blunt, I'm developing a deep and growing affection for you. Actually, I think I love you."

Samantha was silent.

"Noah, you affect me the same way. I didn't have the nerve to say it."

"Let's leave it at that. Maybe it'll go away."

"Noah, there's something going on here that you need to tell me and that I need to know."

"Sam, you're right. When we met in the Olympic dining room, for me, it was slam bam, an instant affection for you. I couldn't avoid it and didn't. Didn't really want to. Our lives have been hugely different socially and in terms of education, and with your occupation, you have a great future. I have no idea what my future might look like. Our age difference could be a problem. So, romantically, we need to fade. I need to be in Rock City, and you should find someone equal to you."

"Noah, you're the smart one about this, and I'll try. Just remember that love and affection can last forever."

"Sam, seeing each other only once a month will help; working together will not help."

"Noah, I'm changing the subject. There's something I have to ask you. It is personal, and if you don't want to answer, say so. You have a banker, a stockbroker, and a lawyer. Are you a rich kid or what?"

Noah sat in silence and then said, "Yes, I'm a rich kid, and I'm totally responsible for that. I'll tell you enough to let you understand, and you may think it's a fairy tale. When I was four years old, I was an orphan living in a shack in the woods with an uncle. I found a few bright heavy yellow pebbles in a stream, and Uncle Willis took them from me. I soon found out what they were, and for seven or eight years I kept all but a few. No one knew. As years passed, I learned about what I had. I taught myself about gold, its measure and sale. I supported myself, and I still have some of it. I have a car and a decent house in Rock City. That is the short story. I'd like it to be confidential. The full story is long and interesting."

"Noah, I'll keep your confidence. People probably wouldn't believe that story anyway, but, Noah, I believe you."

Noah picked up Sam's hand, kissed it, and said goodbye.

Sam drove away saying, "Whoa, what was that?"

The flight back was pleasant. Drowsiness set in and his mind wandered off considering college. Every day in Seattle he conducted business with college educated people and he did not feel disadvantaged in any way. He thought, Maybe I'm not smart enough to have that opinion. I seem to be as creative and inventive as anyone but maybe not quite as literate. College will take four years or more out of my life and I may avoid that.

The plane ride back to Medford was giving him time to consider many things. Road Victor was a success story, and he was in full control of North Marine, a distant enterprise managed by Myra Houston. He talked to her frequently. She was satisfied with her compensation, and she had North Marine back in business. The new capital injection and her work was the prize. There were so few problems or issues with North Marine handed to him, that Noah, with all the other social and business issues in his life, no longer gave much thought to it. He awaited the day when he could sell that company and keep all its employees happy.

Now at home, he decided to talk to Martha. He drove to her house and sat in her living room. Her husband Joe politely turned off the TV and left the room. Noah thought his visits might annoy him. He was a nice guy, but he was the sawyer at the Black Dog mill, and he probably wanted to saw up Noah's incense cedar trees.

Noah asked Martha, "What should I be doing with my life? I'm just walking into one situation after another, trying to solve every problem."

Martha said, "Your days here might seem empty if you were not fully engaged with business interests that directly affect you. How's it going with Road Victor?"

"I think Road Victor is saved. I think I've saved an old family company in New York that I never told you about. Soon I'm going to shuck all my management connections with business and sit and watch. So what should I do with my life?"

Martha, to sum up, said, "Continue to do what you are doing at a slower pace and be good at it. Don't make enemies, and be careful with the girls. And don't ever be shy in asking me for help."

Noah didn't mention his problem with Samantha or Rose Marie. Time might solve that issue.

Noah's question had gotten a very general answer, and he was back where he started.

"Thanks, Martha, I can live with that. In case you're interested, my next Road Victor directors' meeting is going to be a blockbuster, but keep that to yourself."

Back in Seattle, Noah was alone for Thursday evening dinner at the Olympic. He didn't call Sam. That complication might fade away.

The next day, Noah took a taxi to the Road Victor offices.

Chairman Clarke called the meeting to order with all directors present plus the CEO, the CFO, the secretary, and engineers Russ and Steven. Ultimately the chairman asked for the new products committee report. Bobby handed out the written report, and it was reviewed. Bobby, Samantha, and Noah had no questions. Director Hedges urged that they not deviate from their paramount historical calling, the manufacture of bicycles.

Noah said, "We won't deviate an inch on the bikes, even when we add another product or two."

Clarke nervously shuffled papers. "Your report calls for a $2,600,000 expenditure of money we don't have, and none is in sight."

Noah said, "We have that covered."

CEO Swanson asked if he could say something. Chairman Clarke said, "Certainly."

CEO Swanson pleaded that a plant remake would disrupt bike production.

Samantha answered, "We've determined that there would be minimal interruption, and bringing on a new product far outweighs in value any interruption of bike production."

"We can't afford any of this," CFO Sims whined. "We couldn't borrow that much money if we wanted to, and a new issue of common shares would be unsellable."

Chairman Clarke said, "I wholeheartedly agree."

"We expected that response from the get-go," Bobby Shaffer warned. "Noah, tell them how to bring on new products."

Noah stood up. "Don't look so forlorn." Then with a kind smile, he said, "I talked to my CPA and my stock brokerage firm and my lawyer about this very problem, as a hypothetical. I did that after I read a *Wall Street Journal* article about a money problem like ours, and one company's method of overcoming the lack of capital. Here's what we do. We sell a bond called a convertible debenture that pays six percent interest semiannually. Each bond will cost $10,000, its face value can be converted for common shares only, and when converted, it must be converted in full. The bonds can be converted by the owner at any time for shares of our new issue of common stock at its market value on the day of conversion. The bonds must be converted to shares within five years. They are callable by us at any time for shares at market value, but not less than our share value at the time the bond was purchased, and if they haven't been converted within five years, the bond will be called, and the $10,000 bond will be paid to the bond holder with new common shares issued to the bond holder at their market value but not less than the share value on the date of the bond purchase. Interest will stop when the bond is called or voluntarily converted. The incentive to the debenture holder is to convert when the share price is low. He or she will end up with more shares and benefit immensely when our shares rise in value. If a brokerage firm thought our debentures were good enough, a brokerage firm might buy the whole issue at a discount. I think some of our shareholders might be eager buyers. You need to know, according to my broker, there will be substantial expense in getting this issue to the market with SEC approval. $100,000 was added to the estimated cost to cover legal and other issue expenses so, $2,600,000 will be the total bond issue. I know this is a full load, and I have been studying it with constant good advice for nearly a month. I'm really not all that smart. Go ahead and ask me questions."

"Just how risky is this?" asked Clarke.

"It pledges our full faith and credit, meaning every asset of this corporation, to secure the issuance and delivery of our new common shares to the bond holder. Sometimes a bond holder can look for payment from a specific fund or asset only and not beyond. Those are words right out of my lawyer's mouth."

"What if this doesn't work?" asked Hedges.

"If it doesn't, we can continue to endure the death throes of this great old company."

Clarke said, "That's totally pessimistic and fatalistic."

"Mr. Clarke, when you look up and see a grand piano falling on you and you do nothing, then you will be doing what you have been doing time and again as chairman of this company."

Samantha moved for the approval of the financial plan as presented, and it was approved three to two.

Noah looked at CFO Sims and said, "You need to hire the best financial-services lawyer in Seattle and get him working on this. If the $100,000 estimated legal cost is not enough, tell him the actual cost will be approved by the board."

Clarke and Hedges remained silent and in minor shock. They would have the whole evening to whine and complain to their wives about the young upstarts who didn't know anything about business.

Walking out of the building with Samantha and Bobby, Noah said, "We seem to be getting things under control at Road Victor, but I need to tell you that I may have an important business problem in the making in Rock City, Oregon, and now and then, I could miss a directors' meeting."

Samantha reached her car and offered Noah a ride to the Olympic.

Stopped at the Olympic portico, Samantha said, "I want you to know that your presentation today of the financing scheme to raise new capital was brilliant."

"I appreciate that, but you surely know that my words were those of my CPA, my lawyer, and my stockbroker. They thoroughly schooled me. There is a likelihood that Road Victor shares could be worth $20 a year from now."

For a minute they sat silent in Sam's car, each knowing something needed to be said about their admitted affection for one another. Sam finally said, "Is that personal thing between us over?"

Noah said, "Not with me."

Sam said, "Not with me."

Noah had an early evening flight home, and Sam drove him to Sea-Tac. She parked in front of the terminal, where she stepped out of her car and walked with Noah the short distance to the terminal door and said goodbye.

FORTY-ONE

Noah was now trying to decide if he was happy in Rock City. Opportunities were not there; they were in the big city. Martha was there for him, he loved Rose Marie (or did he?), his house was comfortable, but something was missing. Was it the boyhood he'd never had, though he could never say exactly what it was he'd missed? He couldn't describe the emptiness of being part of a family that never existed, and he was unable to grasp that part. He knew what was missing in that area. He had no family, but maybe there was one in Buffalo, New York. What could an eighteen-year-old do about that? The idea that he shouldn't do anything about it needed to be buried and kept buried like a lousy unexploded bomb. News of his grandfather's trust was another distraction.

The situation with Road Victor was not a worry because he knew that what should happen would happen. The thought that he and two directors had control of that grand old company was frightening. Mistakes can be made. We're not perfect. Road Victor shares were down a dollar. Four and one-eighth would be a good buy. Noah thought, I wonder what a share of North Marine is worth? I'm going to have to deal with that sooner or later.

Marty Woods called Noah and sounded concerned. He said, "There's a rumor that Road Victor is trying an unheard-of scheme to raise desperately needed capital for a new product and that it caused the price drop."

Noah said, "It's the convertible debenture scheme I talked to you about, and you instructed me on how it worked and what was required.

Our securities attorney is putting everything together. We have two directors in opposition, and they probably leaked something stupid."

Noah's brain was working overtime. He decided there'd been a leak of the unannounced confidential financing plan. He called Bobby Shaffer, who'd seen the share price drop and wondered the same thing about a leak. They both speculated that it was Hedges, Clarke, or Swanson.

Noah said, "If you know someone at *The Seattle Times*, see what they know."

Noah then called CFO John Sims and told him, "John, we need to have all the paperwork done on the debenture and share issue for the December board meeting. I'm told that a prospectus will be required, so you hire whoever you need to get that done immediately. Our shares dropped twenty percent in value based on a half-assed leak about our new direction."

Sims said he'd been told that the December meeting would be the seventeenth. He might have the share issue and debenture work done, but it would probably be January '77 for an approved prospectus, meaning there would be no bond sale for at least two months.

Noah cautioned Sims, "Do not let Clarke, Hedges, Swanson, or anyone else interfere with your work on this. Getting our financial plans and paperwork before the board is your job and no one else's. They may try, and if they do, I want an immediate call from you. The Securities and Exchange Commission would not like such interference." Bike sales were increasing, so the two months' delay sounded acceptable.

Noah's double life was again beginning to bother him. Leading the pack was better than being in it; besides, he knew his social life as a schoolboy had been thrown out the window years ago. He should be looking forward to Christmas, but he would rather avoid it and bypass what had never been a part of his life. He was having these melancholy thoughts as plans formed in his mind to stop the misinformation about Road Victor financing.

Noah called Sylvia Latimer, owner of 560,000 shares. She knew he wasn't going to fade away.

Noah said, "Mrs. Latimer, may I call you Sylvia?"

"Certainly, Noah."

"OK, Sylvia, I want to meet with you as soon as I can get to Seattle. I know you live in Bellevue, but I don't know where Mrs. Woodson or Mrs. Jameson or George Newton live. If they live close by, I would like to meet with them at the same time. Road Victor has some real positive action in the works, but the old guys are trying to stop it by leaking partial information. We can't publish it yet because the paperwork isn't finished. You big shareholders need to know what is happening. I want to meet before the end of the year, on Thursday, December 16, with you and the other three shareholders I mentioned. I will be at the Olympic, and we could meet there for lunch. If you could get them to the lunch, we would all benefit. Do not let Clarke or Hedges or Swanson know about our meeting. I think it is one or more of them trying to neutralize us three new directors. Also, you will like our plan to revive Road Victor. Hang on to your hat and your shares—don't sell a single share. Please report to me as soon as possible. Sylvia, are you OK with all of this?"

"You know I am. The dollar drop cost me $560,000, and I want it and more back."

Noah said, "Stay with me and it will happen."

Sylvia called Noah Wednesday evening. She said, "I've got George and Lila coming."

"That's great, Sylvia, I'm flying in the late afternoon on the fifteenth. Noon it is, the next day at the Olympic."

Prior to leaving for the Medford airport, Noah called Sam and Bobby, told them what was happening, and invited them to the Thursday meeting.

Every person Noah wanted at the meeting was present, and they sat at a large round table in the Olympic's magnificent dining room. There were a few guests in the room, and it was too early for the lunch crowd. It was a good venue for this meeting that was vastly important for all of Road Victor's shareholders. As strange as it might seem to anyone who didn't know Noah North, the eighteen-year-old director took charge.

He first thanked everyone for showing up and then said, "This meeting is important. Make no mistake, what we can do at this meeting will benefit everyone connected to Road Victor. What is said in this room stays in this room. Everyone got that? It was a three to two vote of the board of directors that is putting us on a path of survival and prosperity. Our dissenting directors do not want supplemental products or a new capital creation drive. Furthermore, someone in management is trying to derail our efforts by leaking a distorted view of the financial plan we adopted."

Bobby described the convertible debenture, its capital acquisition, and the likelihood that it would be immensely attractive to existing shareholders.

George Newton asked, "So, if I buy ten thousand dollars' worth of debentures, I will get a six percent annual yield, and I can convert each debenture for our new common shares at their market price?"

"Yes," said Bobby, and he added, "there will be a few tweaks, including a required conversion date, but that's it. There is risk as in any investment, but there seems to be confidence in our board, and our investors will like our business plan."

Director Samantha reviewed the plan for additional products. She clearly set forth plans for a new revolutionary walker and an innovative wheelchair as well as a golf cart and baby stroller. She explained that their production would not interfere with bike production and that two of Road Victor's engineers had done some market research, and their planned products would be winners because the market looked good.

The plan called for modifications and building improvements. Availability of component parts was a positive as well as the use of the present manufacturing assets, and eventually there would be a need for additional employees and machinery, but there would be a conservative start.

Samantha finally said, "New capital of about $2,600,000 is needed for the expansion."

Lila wanted to know if all that wasn't risky.

Samantha replied, "The risk is much less than doing nothing. If we do nothing, the bicycle will not save us, and doing nothing won't add value to our shares."

Sylvia asked, "When will the finances be in place? I hope it's before I die."

"It will be." Samantha smiled.

George Newton said, "You three young folks give 'em hell and put those two old bastards in their place!"

Noah again cautioned, "I'm told that the board should not make an announcement about the debentures until the SEC has reviewed the paperwork and has approved the convertible debentures and the issuance of additional common shares. Also, please know that neither one of those securities can be sold until the SEC approves our prospectus covering these securities. However, we will let the public know about our plans as soon as the SEC approves and our lawyer gives us the OK. We need to do this quickly to discredit the gobbledygook leaked by our enemies. You are insiders with info the public knows nothing about, so you must keep it to yourselves, and you cannot buy or sell our shares until all of this plan and issue is made public."

Everyone seemed satisfied with the information handed out, although everyone was probably a little apprehensive about results. Lunch had been served during the ad hoc meeting, and several people who didn't know much about each other stayed and discovered something about their colleagues.

The next day, Friday, Noah walked silently into the directors' room. Every director's chair at the table came with a neat stack of documents in front of it.

He now had his full concentration on Road Victor business. He sat and quickly reviewed the documents before him. They were what he wanted, the resolution for adoption of the approved capital plan. The lawyer who'd prepared the documents was in the room. Every director, the CEO, the CFO, and the secretary were present. After breezing through the usual agenda items, Chairman Clarke called on the securities lawyer, Jack Warren, to present and explain the debenture and stock issue. Warren did, and to Noah it didn't appear to be what the directors had decided at their last meeting.

Noah was not satisfied. He said to Warren, "I assume you had a copy of our minutes calling for the convertible debentures."

Warren said, "Yes," and added, "the minutes are quite explicit."

Noah said, "This is quite a stack of paperwork, and we really won't have a chance to review it unless we spend an hour or so at this meeting studying it, something I'd rather not do. So let me ask you. Did any member of this board of directors contact you with a request or instruction as to the content of these documents?"

Warren looked at Chairman Clarke and said, "Yes, Mr. Clarke contacted me several times."

Noah, glowering at Clarke, asked, "Did you change or add any provision not called for in the board's resolution providing for the debentures?"

"Yes."

"What did you add or change?" demanded Noah.

Lawyer Warren interposed, saying, "He insisted the price of our new shares on redemption of a debenture be fifty percent more than the market value of a share, and I made that change. I told him it would make the debentures unsellable. He said it would raise more capital, and the change wouldn't matter because of the size of the stack of documents—they wouldn't be carefully reviewed, and no one would notice the change."

Noah said, "That condition is so stupid that any knowledgeable investor would think it was a typo! Clarke, I thought you were smarter than that."

Mr. Clarke's face revealed confusion, and he was silent.

Noah, obviously irritated, asked, "Is that the only thing he wanted changed?"

"Yes."

"Did anyone else connected with Road Victor call about this convertible debenture plan as set forth in our minutes?"

"Yes, CEO Swanson called a couple of times to make sure I incorporated the change requested by Clarke. CFO Sims called me to object to Clarke's and Swanson's actions and to tell me to ignore them and not to deviate from the terms set forth in the board resolution. Yesterday Clarke called and told me not to come to the meeting and said that the CEO would present the documents and the resolution for adoption. Apparently CFO Sims heard about that and insisted I be here. I told him that I didn't know where my allegiance was, and I would not speak unless asked a direct question. Sims told me he was going to ask, so I should be prepared."

Noah North immediately had Clarke's mendacity, guile, stupidity, and chairmanship in his crosshairs.

Bobby Shaffer, who was greatly annoyed, said to lawyer Warren, "Will you please change the document or documents to provide debenture redemption value as stated in the resolution in our minutes?"

Warren immediately, with pen in hand, lined out and added text conforming the documents to the wording in the minutes.

When he'd obviously finished with the changes, Noah said, "Did you do it?"

"Yes I did, and I can't tell you how relieved I am."

Samantha said, "I can't believe all this subterfuge crap. I move for the adoption of the written resolution providing for our convertible debenture and share issue plan." Noah seconded and called for questions.

Clarke, who had just seen himself destroyed, sheepishly said, "There will be no debate unless someone asks for it."

No one asked, and the vote in favor was four with one abstention.

Noah said, "Mr. Chairman, will you open nominations for chairman of this board?"

Clarke got up and was leaving the room when he turned and said, "Oh, what the hell." He walked back to the table and, while standing, said, "Nominations for board chairman are open."

Noah said, "I nominate Oliver Hedges and move that nominations be closed."

The vote was taken, and all five directors raised their hands. Stanley Clarke left the room.

Noah had one more onerous thing to do. He looked at CEO Swanson and said, "You need to be looking for a different job." Swanson stood up and walked out of the room. The four directors stood and shook hands all the way around the table, knowing the right thing had just happened.

Chairman Hedges said, "The turmoil that happened here today was enough for one meeting. Unless there is an objection, I summarily adjourn this meeting."

When leaving, Samantha stepped in front of Noah and said, "Noah, you manipulated that directors' meeting like a pro, especially the way you engineered Hedges into the chairmanship. Suspecting that someone had messed with our plan was uncanny."

"Sam, I never did trust those two."

Sam offered Noah a ride to the Olympic. Before she started her car, Noah said, "I have to tell you something. For me there is more than a business relationship developing here. I enjoy every minute I spend with you. I know it's crazy, so let me take you to dinner tonight, and you can explain how our age difference should make my affection for you go away."

"Noah, we both know there's much more to our phase-out equation than age. Why are you now making it hard to deal with?"

"Sam, this has to be one of those things that is unexplainable. I hope I'm adult enough to accept the unexplainable."

Without saying anything, Samantha drove to the Palisade restaurant that overlooked the Seattle Yacht Club.

When seated and looking at Sam, Noah said, "Wanting something at the wrong time and the wrong place and making the right decision might be impossible, at least for me."

They sat in silence for a painful moment.

"Noah, you've just said what I was agonizing about."

"Sam, I may be assuming too much, but you would be miserable living in Rock City, Oregon, and I would be miserable living in the big city away from my magic cedars and five thousand acres of timber land."

"Your eighteen-year-old vision is on the mark. One thing you should know about me is that I have never looked for a man; there was always one there, but each one was missing something."

"Sam, you just hit on a subject that I am embarrassed for not mentioning earlier. I thought it would go away but it hasn't. A classmate of mine and I have been close friends for over a year, and it has been turning into something more than I expected. She's my age but the emotional attachment is a tiny fraction of my overwhelming affection and maybe love for you. I have said this because, in parting, I want you to know who and what I am."

"Noah, I've known the good person you are since our first meeting."

"Sam, regardless of who I might end up with, in my deep subconscious, you will remain the love of my life."

"Noah, my thoughts dovetail with yours. We both thought this dinner together was not a good move, but it was a good move. The right words were spoken this evening. We will remember those words."

"I'm bleeding, Sam, and we've just had our last dance."

"And, Noah, we never ended up in bed together, not even close."

"Sam, it's over."

Sam dropped Noah at the Olympic and the next morning took him to Sea-Tac. During the half-hour drive, except for small talk, they sat in silence. Their plan to end things was now in place. At the terminal entrance there was a hug, and they parted.

Driving home, Samantha was miserable and said to the car windshield, "How can I part with that young man? There is so much to know about a person, and I barely know anything about him, yet I think I love him. How can that be? We had no intimate conversation, no big romance, and we did almost nothing sexually. So, whatever it was, it's over . . . or is it?"

Noah sat in the Alaska Airlines boarding area in the middle of a hundred men and women and some children roaming about, waiting for the call to board. He thought about parting from that bright, lovely woman. He reflected on the events of the past few days. The business conducted at Road Victor had been gigantic, but ending a fine personal relationship that had barely started might be unbearable. Sam needs to make a life for herself in the big city, and she knows it, and I need to make a life for myself in the tiny town I know and like. Except for business, it's over with her . . . or is it?

FORTY-TWO

It was a few days before Christmas, but family life for Noah was non-existent, making Christmas a non-event. He knew it was a religious Christian holiday and that gifts were exchanged, but all that had swept by him year after year. He had a faint memory of his mother and a Christmas tree, and since then he had only seen Christmas trees in stores and in a friend's home. Noah knew there was something good about Christmas, but didn't know exactly what it was.

Noah wanted company, and he invited Rose Marie to have a Coke with him. He parked his car at the Rock City Cafe. The place was nearly empty.

Noah said, "I don't know the meaning or the importance of our relationship or its connection with the future. I'm not even certain about my connection with the past. Time may tell us."

Rose Marie looked at him with approval.

"Noah, I like being with you, and we will have plenty of time to better know each other."

She was special, and Noah drove her home. He hoped that being with Rose Marie would finally bury his thoughts of Sam.

After Christmas, Noah called Oliver Hedges and asked him if Clarke was going to resign.

Hedges said, "I don't know, but I do know that he is really pissed off."

Noah said, "Well, that's his problem, but we need to know. You know him. Could you call him and find out if he will resign? We need to get names and information for director candidates on January's agenda and make the choice. Although you are the only director I've talked to about this, if Clarke doesn't immediately resign, he needs to be reminded that three directors can call a special meeting of shareholders for a recall, where he'd feel like a pigeon at a peregrine falcon convention. His vacant position will be filled by the directors until the next shareholders' meeting. I am not saying anything you don't know, but we need to get information to the directors as soon as possible. We also need to solicit resumes for a new CEO. Sims should probably do that with our office staff."

"Look, Noah, I don't like you telling me what to do."

"Sorry, Oliver. Road Victor is being removed from the cliff's edge, is in transition, has a great future, and we need to quickly and decisively act. We need to welcome all the help and advice we can get, so ditch your vanity. Oliver, I apologize for my pushy behavior. Pretty soon everything will be back to normal, and our jobs will be easy. Are we OK, Oliver?"

"I'm good, Noah, see you in January."

"Oh, Oliver, I almost forgot, and forgive me for asking you, but who is handling personnel issues such as hiring and firing, wages, benefits, and all those things a personnel director is supposed to do? Someone needs to be in charge there."

"Our former CEO, Swanson, was handling personnel with the help of his office staff. Maybe Sims, with the help of the CEO's office staff, could handle it until we have a new CEO. Why don't you manage that any way you want, and the board will no doubt confirm it next meeting." Noah figured Oliver was now really pissed off.

Noah called Sam on New Year's Day. "Sam," he said, "I wish you a happy New Year."

"Thanks, Noah. It looks like it might be a good one."

"I would like to say much more to you, but I won't. I talked to Oliver Hedges, and he indicated that he is good with us. I suggested how he should handle the absent CEO problem. I know he was upset with that, but he hadn't done anything. He calmed down by the end of the conversation. What the hell is it with these old guys?"

"Noah, you're ten steps ahead of everybody, except me, so calm down."

Noah couldn't let go and said, "When those old directors want to write their memoirs, they won't have anything to write about."

"OK, OK, I got it," she offered.

"Sam, you know what? I forgot to tell Hedges that our meetings had to be on Fridays. I'll bother him again and maybe ask him if he followed my orders."

"You gotta be joshing me. Otherwise you're acting totally out of character, and that's not nice," cautioned Sam.

"I was joking, I was joking, I would not twist the knife. I never want to give you the faintest hint that I'm anything other than a decent person. I admit, there are times when I'm a little too glib. I may give Oliver a friendly call."

He was now asking himself, was he making the right call on Road Victor, Inc., and its reach for new capital? Was it speculative? He decided that as a director, he shouldn't be recommending Road Victor's debentures without furnishing the issue's prospectus. Martha's broker would have the prospectus and advise her, so he wouldn't worry about her.

Living and attending school in Rock City had provided the environment that shaped his life. The small town had citizens that cared for him, had molded his character and given him inner strength, direction, and meaning. Some of that came from having to protect himself. No one needed to tell him right from wrong; that trait had to have come from his mother, because the rest of his family, if you could call it that, didn't know the difference. These thoughts were streaming through his brain as he was considering Seattle as a place to live. In the meantime, he would be a good citizen of Rock City. Although his thoughts were mainly elsewhere, he knew that life favored an educated person. Anything less could be a mistake. Was Seattle calling?

He had a window seat on the Boeing 737. The days of January had moved sluggishly, probably because he was overly anxious to get to his world in Seattle. Staring out the window at the Willamette Valley farmlands below was no distraction from worries about many things, including an early sale of Road Victor debentures and its new product. Is Clarke really gone, and will new products save his company? What will happen will happen, so quit worrying. Jeez, get over it! I hope everything is prepared and in order for tomorrow's meeting. Did Clarke resign? Next week's papers should have the story. I hope Hedges did as I requested. Actually, it was more of a demand. Those old guys are paying the price for their years of negligence and incompetence, but we can save Hedges.

Bobby didn't know if Clarke had resigned.

The next day Noah was in the directors' room talking to Bobby Shaffer when Sam arrived. She gently brushed by him and sat down. Bobby was happy with the new focus of Road Victor. Oliver Hedges called the meeting to order. Clarke was missing and so was CEO Swanson. CFO Sims, the board secretary, and Attorney Jack Warren were present. Following the preliminary corporate housekeeping chores, Hedges announced that he had Clarke's written resignation in hand as he slipped it to the secretary for the corporate records. Hedges asked Jack Warren if he had approved the CFO's narrative of the company's proposed news regarding the convertible debenture, the proposed new products, and factory modifications.

Warren said, "I gave my approval by letter weeks ago, and my letter cautioned that the securities would not be marketed until SEC approval."

Samantha said, "There's been nothing in the financial news or otherwise about that."

Bobby Shaffer was obviously exasperated and said, "We need a real fucking CEO, and we need one now. That news release is super important, and time is money. Mr. Sims, can you see to it that our news release is sent to *The Seattle Times* and *The Wall Street Journal*?"

"Absolutely."

Noah asked Sims if he'd received any applications for CEO.

"I immediately published the request and have not received any."

Noah asked, "I wonder if it's because of rumors of management upheaval here? If no one here objects, do another solicitation outlining our vision of our future and mention that a generous salary will be negotiated."

Samantha asked Sims if he had the fourth-quarter results.

Sims replied, "I do, and they surprise me. We sold more bicycles that quarter than any quarter in the last nine or ten years. I hasten to add, that's still not saying much, but with all that's happening here, I'm pretty optimistic."

Noah added, "Stalin and Mao were right, blood needed to be

spilled." Sam and Noah may have been the only directors who knew how appropriate that comment was.

Sam noticed that Hedges looked horrified and said, "Oliver, it's only a figure of speech."

Sam was thinking, Why am I letting this bright young man slip away?

Noah asked Hedges if Road Victor was getting along without a CEO.

Hedges said, "Yes, I've checked on that. Sims and McCormick, and one of the plant engineers, are jointly acting as CEOs, and it seems to be working." The board approved the arrangement.

Noah knew the meeting was ending and said, "Let's hope the journalists cast us in the good light we deserve, and one more thing, none of us should be trading our shares unless you clear it with Jack Warren. I'm told that violation of SEC rules is not nice."

Noah added, "As soon as we see that the debentures will be sold, we must begin designing our new product. Sam, you are the director in charge of that, and I'm wondering if our engineers, Russ and Steven, are up to the task. If you were to get into the design work itself, you should be paid for your time. What are your thoughts on this? You're the expert."

Sam said, "I didn't take mechanics for design of baby strollers or golf carts in engineering school. If I tell Russ and Steven what we want, they should be good to go. They nicely redesigned our bike brakes and frames."

Noah said, "One thing that's really important is that regardless of whether it's a walker, baby stroller, wheelchair, or little push-or-pull golf cart, they must be collapsible and easily packed into a mail-ordered paste-board box and into the trunk of a car. Our expertise must prevail on this, even against a new CEO. I have a feeling our bikes will even sell better but may become obscured in the wake of our other product sales."

"Noah, you have a business sense that few people have. Let others get involved with details."

Noah said, "You are correct."

He was not saying anything to Sam about his inheritance of North

Marine shares. She would know that he had no time for other business problems. He would properly divest himself of his North Marine shares.

Noah left Seattle in the rain and, as on other flights home, melancholy set in, now exacerbated by the gloomy weather. His Rock City life and his Seattle life were not converging; instead the disconnection was growing. He had been a baby cared for by his mother for the first four years of his life, and he was alone for many years thereafter. He did not grow up as a child, and socially he was more like half child and half adult. He'd made his fortune in Rock City, he'd gotten his education there, his few friends were there, and he'd gotten rid of Uncle Willis there. But where was his future, and where was his love? He decided to keep those thoughts to himself lest he alienate some people in Rock City and drive himself crazy. He would always keep his land and his cedar trees. His forlorn mood ended when his plane touched a dry runway in Medford.

The Medford taxi dropped him at his doorstep, and there was no one to meet him, especially not an Olympic doorman. He was lonely but comfortable in his house, and he started reading *Wall Street Journal*s. Gerald Ford was president but had lost the next term's election. Gold was $133. Road Victor was steady at $5⅛. Noah mulled, I wonder what my normal high school classmates are thinking this Saturday night?

He visited Martha on Sunday as if she were now his ward. Among other topics she was anxious to discuss was Road Victor stock she had purchased, and she said, "But it hasn't done anything."

"Martha," Noah advised, "all shareholders are waiting for the effect of a corporate announcement that should come this week from *The Seattle Times* and *The Wall Street Journal*. My friends and I have caused a revolution in that company, and gun smoke is still in the air." He ate a piece of Martha's rhubarb-strawberry pie.

Noah stayed seated and said, "There's something I need to tell you that for now needs to be kept confidential. I'm a beneficiary with two first cousins, and we are the sole beneficiaries of my Grandfather North's trust. It seems my father was one of my grandfather's three children, all boys. I have been to Buffalo, and I acquired a controlling

interest in my grandfather's marine business. I need to return to
Buffalo and make certain that North Marine, Inc., is functioning and
prospering. I hired a new CEO and I think I will be happy with her
performance. Nevertheless, I have no idea of what I have done or what
I may run into."

Martha said, "Isn't your business and personal life too full to get
involved in something two thousand miles from here?"

"Yes, but I need to know my relatives. Hopefully they are a level
above my mother's family. Please know that my Grandmother Porter
is a good person."

Martha examined Noah and said, "Be careful to square away your
close personal relationships before you disappear to the east!"

Noah said, "I'm not hurrying off to Buffalo. I do need to get there
soon so I can make a decent decision about keeping or selling my interest in a shipping company operating on the Great Lakes."

Noah left Martha and drove straight to Rose Marie. Visiting with
Rose Marie was nice, but the future of that relationship might be com-
promised. His business interest in Seattle was the main culprit. Noah
reflected on that sad thought. Should I let my romance with Rose
Marie slip away? Why can't I get Samantha O'Leary out of my head?
He owed every consideration to Rose Marie and to his friends in Rock
City. He was a young man bothered with the intrigue of romance.

The Road Victor shakeup, capital plan, and new product announcement appeared in the February 15, 1977, issue of *The Wall
Street Journal.*

> Young lions of the venerated Road Victor,
> Inc., bicycle manufacturer infused their
> sensible skills into that company following a
> coup that later led to a little bloodletting. The
> net result was three new youthful directors:
> the ringleader, 18-year-old Noah Jeremiah
> North, Bobby Shaffer, and Boeing engineer
> Samantha O'Leary. Chairman of the board
> Stanley Clarke was ousted, and CEO James
> Swanson was asked to find another job. Old

director Oliver Hedges was elected chairman of the board. When approved by the SEC, debentures will be issued bearing a 6% rate that must be converted to company shares at beneficial prices within five years. $2,600,000 capital will be raised for plant modifications for the manufacture of new products. Improvement of their bicycles is ongoing, and bicycles will continue to be the company's premier product. Debentures will be sold as soon as the company's prospectus is approved. The competence of the young board is on full display. Road Victor is born again. Note: They are seeking a CEO and a fifth director.

Noah accepted the article as partially flattering and was anxious to have the other directors' takes. Getting the prospectus approved quickly was imperative.

He would be nineteen years old on February 28. He hated birthdays. They reminded him that he had no family. He wouldn't remind anyone. Uncle Willis had had a birthday party for him, and Martha had had one for him. He didn't like people giving him presents. Hopefully no one would remember.

Noah was reading an article in his *Wall Street Journal* about a woman named Patty Hearst, who'd been forced to rob banks by her kidnappers, when his phone rang.

"Noah, this is Martha. You are invited to your birthday party at my house next Saturday at three o'clock. Will nineteen candles be correct? I know your birthday is Monday, but that day doesn't work."

"Thank you, Martha, you are too good. Nineteen candles will be just right."

The birthday party he didn't want was perfect. Martha greeted Noah and facetiously said, "Do you know any of these people?" Rose Marie, Felix, and Felix's classmate and secret love, Jennifer Moss, were there, as well as Mr. Marston. It was a small group, all happy to see and visit the new nineteen-year-old. The chocolate cake was superb, and when Martha handed him a second helping, he thanked her. "Martha, you always do the right thing."

The guests gave Noah birthday cards. He drove Rose Marie home, and at her door, they kissed.

Noah was in Seattle the evening before the March 4, 1977, directors' meeting. He had arrived at a difficult time in his personal life. He was dealing with his affection for two women.

Noah called Sam from his hotel room. "Sam, I need to see you. Tomorrow, can you pick me up early, giving us an hour or so before the meeting?"

"Certainly."

The next morning, parked in the company parking lot, Noah said, "We agree that our personal relationship should end simply because it is the right thing to do. I can't be in love with you and my high school sweetheart in Rock City, and that's what is happening."

"Noah, you're being very adult and I hear you."

"Trouble is, my relationship with you is a difficult relationship to end. My guts and my heart tell me so. Rose Marie was my first love, my high school sweetheart, my age, a beautiful hometown girl, and I think she loves me. Social convention almost demands that she be the one. It tears me up to say these things to you."

"For the sake of both of us, I one more time agree with you, and friends we will be, but know this, you have a solid reason to end things and I don't."

Walking together to the directors' room with their agreement in mind was difficult.

The meeting of Road Victor directors commenced at 1 p.m. All were present, with one director's seat unfilled, and everyone seemed to be wearing a smile. On the market, Road Victor, Inc., shares were twitching up, having risen despite the previous brain-dead acts of a CEO and a director chairman, both now ousted from Road Victor.

Before Hedges called the meeting to order, Noah, in a loud voice, said, "Don't get too excited—we still have a mountain to climb."

Samantha looked at Noah with an expression not unlike Rose Marie's when he unnecessarily verbally abused a teacher. Noah looked across the table at Samantha O'Leary and thought, Why is she doing that? She doesn't know any more about the bicycle business than I do, and she's not my teacher or my guardian. Bobby Shaffer had a broad smile on his face, knowing that Noah North was still in control. CFO Sims gave the interim financial report, noting an upswing in bicycle sales and numerous inquiries about convertible debentures. He reported that the SEC had the proposed prospectus and that Attorney Warren was happy with it.

Chairman Hedges and Shaffer each submitted copies of a written resume for a new director. Bobby's candidate was Walter Morrison, a twenty-eight-year-old married University of Washington candidate for an MBA degree. He held one hundred shares of Road Victor, Inc. Hedge's candidate was Fred Iverson, a sixty-three-year-old retired banker with good credentials and a BA degree from Northwestern University, the owner of fifty thousand shares of Road Victor. Samantha nominated Morrison, and Hedges nominated Iverson. The vote was three to one for Morrison.

Noah said, "We had two good candidates, but youth has carried this company away from financial misery, and youth will continue on that road."

Chairman Hedges appeared anxious to speak and said, "I fully agree with the direction of our company, and I ask CFO Sims to stay on top of our prospectus approval. Also, where are we on the CEO vacancy?"

"Nowhere," said Sims.

Noah said, "Advertise in *The Wall Street Journal*," and then he said, "We have a shareholders' meeting coming up. Last year it was June fifth; when do we want it this year? Saturday, June eleventh, would be good. Anyone have any problems with that?"

Bobby moved that the 1977 shareholders' meeting be June 11 at the Seattle Hilton. The motion passed and the meeting ended.

Before they left the boardroom, Sam eased close to Noah and said, "You are never going to let Mr. Hedges run his meeting, are you?"

When they were out of the building, Noah walked to Samantha O'Leary, nudged her, and said, "Hi. At my age I'm not even supposed to be in full control of myself, but I try to be. Actually, I have no alternative. I find myself saying to people what needs to be said. If that is offensive, I apologize. I know no other way, and I can't help it. Any manners I have, I've taught myself, and I probably missed some. Sometimes when my friend Rose Marie disapproved of the way I spoke to some of my teachers, she looked at me the way you just looked at me at the end of the meeting."

Sam looked him over and said, "Don't you ever, ever change." She bumped his shoulder and said, "Follow me, but you gotta let Hedges run the meeting." Without thinking, he did—he would have followed her anyplace. Never mind that he needed a ride. And never mind that they needed to cool their personal relationship.

Seated in her car, she said, "Noah, do you have any friends or relatives in Seattle?"

"None except the people at Road Victor."

"Just remember, you have at least one."

Noah was focused on Samantha when he said, "Something has happened in my life that is a complete surprise. Because of my deep connection with Road Victor, I want you to hear about it from me. I don't want you or anyone here to think I will become less focused on Road Victor.

"My Grandfather North, my father's father, died some time ago, and at the death of my father, I became one of the beneficiaries of my grandfather's trust. I didn't know anything about my grandfather, let alone know that I would inherit anything from him. I have been to Buffalo to see what I inherited and I met cousins that I didn't know I had. I didn't want to be involved in any of that business back there, but I am. It was the smart thing to do and I did it. I know I'm already too involved in business issues."

Sam said, "What you just said is true. You can't be everything to everybody, so make a clean break back there as soon as you can."

"That's exactly what I intend to do."

Samantha dropped him off at the Olympic, and Noah endured the sting of the loss of Sam.

The next morning, while seated on an Alaska Airlines plane with the pilot forcing it to a cruising altitude, Noah thought, Living my life in two different places with a different life in each place is unnatural and difficult. Maybe that is now three places. I've gotta correct my life sooner and not later. Something's gotta go, but what? New York, of course!

"Home again," said Noah as he opened his front door. His house sitter, Felix, was there, and Noah paid him. Getting Noah's attention by holding Noah's forearm for an instant, Felix said, "Noah, why do you spend time in Seattle?"

"I have a job there. It's complicated, and it's not what orphans usually do."

Felix seemed bewildered and a little miffed, and Noah caught that and said, "Sorry, Felix, I don't need to be a smart-ass with you. It really is complicated. I will tell you that I work with Road Victor, Inc., in the bicycle business. They wanted me because I'm young and they think I know what boys and girls want in a bicycle. I happen to like the job, and it was not always easy because it started with people I didn't agree with. Now those people are gone, and the job is pleasant but demanding. I'm needed there two or three days every month, and even when I'm in Rock City, the job takes some of my time. I think you realize that I support myself, and I cannot enjoy my life like a teenager should."

Felix said, "I kinda get it, and I kinda don't get it."

The next day, Noah sat beside Rose Marie in the Rock City Cafe. It was private enough to allow an intimate conversation.

She said, "I'm missing you, Noah, and I do not understand it. Your mind is elsewhere."

"It is," he said. "Road Victor's success is driving me, but make no mistake, I know exactly where I am and what I am doing, and I'm totally in control. That doesn't mean I'm throwing away any relationships. Rose Marie, I intend to be ambiguous about Seattle; I simply do not want to explain everything. Precocious orphans are like that, and childhood experiences make us what we are. I know that not everyone will like me, so I'll take what is offered. You may not understand all of that, but just remember, you are one of Rock City's jewels."

"Noah, I don't understand all of that."

"Rose Marie, it gets worse. I now have business as well as relatives in New York. I plan to end that business connection as soon as possible. Please, don't ditch me."

"Noah, will I ever understand you?"

"Just understand that I love you, and I know what I am doing. Gradually you will understand me, I hope."

Noah was comfortable in his new house, but he was not happy. He was juggling North Marine, Road Victor, Rose Marie, and Samantha. It wasn't simple; it was now complex, but he was doing it.

The Rose Marie and Sam issue involved personal emotions that had to be resolved. He was the one at fault, and he needed to act.

Noah was in Seattle on March 24. The directors' meeting was the next day. The meeting notice stated that the debenture and share issue prospectus had been approved, and he was anxious to know if the sale of debentures was succeeding. He didn't know that John Sims had placed for sale the entire issue with Smith, Morgan and Wiley, a nationwide brokerage firm that was also Noah's stockbroker.

When Noah walked into his room at the Olympic, he immediately picked up the phone and called Bobby Shaffer, who told him the debentures were selling. That was the only information Noah wanted.

The March 25, 1977, meeting was underway with everyone present, including the new director, Walter Morrison. Everyone knew the convertible debentures were on the market and was anxious to know what was happening. Sims, acting CEO, reported that half had sold in three days, and the rest could be gone next week.

Noah said, "I knew it."

"Nobody can stop us now," Bobby Shaffer said.

Samantha chimed in, "We can't let up. It will be a lot of work, but Bobby's right, we're on our way."

"I can't believe it, but our common shares are up to eight," Hedges said.

Noah remarked, "Oliver, you now with us?" Noah looked at Chairman Hedges and said, "Could we talk about a CEO?"

Hedges said, "That's next on the agenda."

Noah looked at Sims and said, "Mr. Chairman, we may want to talk about Sims, so would you ask him to leave the room?"

Sims left the room, and Hedges said, "I think the rest of you may feel as I do. Sims knows this company and its business interests. I can see him as CEO. I'd welcome a motion to that effect."

Walter Morrison, the new director, said, "You people have known Sims ever since you've been here. You knew his competence, so why all the fuss about getting a new CEO and not immediately hiring Sims as CEO on Swanson's departure?"

Sam answered, "We've been involved with deeper issues, and we obviously blew off focus on the CEO vacancy."

Bobby Shaffer made the motion to hire John Sims as Road Victor's CEO.

Noah said, "I call for a vote." The vote was unanimous.

"John Sims is our new CEO," announced Oliver Hedges.

After the meeting, Samantha O'Leary walked up to Noah with a near-serious demeanor about her and once again said, "Are you ever going to let poor Mr. Hedges run his meeting?"

"I've been thinking about it. We should probably talk about something else."

"Might as well, no reason to talk about who should be allowed to preside at our meeting."

"Could you take me to Sea-Tac tomorrow?"

"The only thing I need to do is be at my job at Boeing to assist several engineers in the design of an improved landing-gear retraction system for the Boeing 747."

Noah immediately said, "No, no, I'll take a taxi."

"I'm taking you!"

The next morning, she parked her car with Noah in front of the Alaska Airlines terminal entrance. They silently looked at each other with an intensity that conveyed a hundred messages.

"Sam, this has to be goodbye. I've got to be true to myself and true to you and true to a girl in Rock City, and I haven't been doing a very good job."

Sam watched Noah vanish into the crowded terminal.

Waiting at the gate, Noah thought, Can I really ever end my affection for Sam? I really belong with Rose Marie.

When in the Medford airport, Noah made first-class round-trip reservations to Buffalo, New York. The trip would be in April. Noah picked up frozen dinners on the way home.

He perused his *Wall Street Journal*. An article applauded the successful sale of Road Victor's convertible debenture issue and the coming rise in shareholder equity. Road Victor's price at $8 was welcome, and it might not slow down.

He was excited about Road Victor's turnaround and was anxious to hear if plans were fixed and in place for rebuilding the production lines. Noah knew that he was responsible for saving Road Victor but was not going to say it. Lonely nights in Rock City cast a shadow over his accomplishments.

The frequent trips to Seattle were losing their excitement and were closing in on wearisome, but Noah knew that he would never abandon his venture to plug the holes in the Road Victor ship.

He was with Rose Marie in the Rock City Cafe, spending and enjoying quality time with her. Because of his preoccupation with business matters and trips to Seattle, she hinted about his lack of focus on her.

"Noah. Are you here?"

"Rose Marie, things are winding down in Seattle."

He didn't mention the disenchanted break with Samatha.

When they were leaving the cafe, not caring if they were seen, Noah suddenly and carefully hugged her, saying, "Just know I love you, and you were right. I have been distracted about a business matter."

Arriving home from his visit with Rose Marie, Noah called Myra Houston, North Marine CEO.

"Myra, how are things going with North Marine?"

"I have mailed you financials covering my first year as CEO."

Noah asked, "Are they OK?"

"They're good—actually, better than good."

"How'd that happen?"

"Two of our chief competitors each lost a ship in a storm. We filled the void."

"Why didn't we lose a ship?"

"I kept two of our newly refitted ships in port and the other close to home for a quick refuge. Noah, we only have three ships. We're down four since Alexander's illness became debilitating. With Thomas then taking charge, business reinvestment went to hell."

"You earned your keep, Myra, and I won't forget it."

Noah called Marty Woods at Smith, Morgan and Wiley.

Noah said, "Marty, remember me telling you I was investing in North Marine?"

"Yes."

"Marty, I'm ready to get out now. That ship righted itself and doesn't need me. Do you know someone that can help me find a buyer for North Marine, Inc.? As the majority shareholder, I can assure you that the board and the shareholders will approve a sale. Ten million dollars is the sales price. If you didn't know it, business is booming on the Great Lakes. The auto industry is producing cars like a five-thousand-rabbit warren produces bunnies, and the Great Lakes shipping industry is transporting goods and material for the steel and the auto industry. You'll be furnished with any financials you need."

"Noah, send the financials now, and I'll put an ad in *The Wall Street Journal*, with inquiries to my firm."

Noah was annoyed and distressed as he packed for his trip to Seattle. Leaving Rose Marie, Felix, and even Martha every month was not easy, especially when he had just returned home. Now he would be gone again.

On the plane's quiet slide into Sea-Tac Airport for the April 23 meeting, Noah decided, Now begins a new Road Victor. Nothing can stop us. Thank goodness I am getting out of North Marine.

The next day's meeting at Road Victor's head office found every director happy and maybe a little smug about the upward direction of their company and its share value. CEO Sims called the debenture sale a complete success, with capital funds now on hand for investment.

Chairman Hedges said, "Does anyone want to talk about directors' fees?"

Nothing was said until Noah spoke. "Please get this straight: There should be no such fees until after we have declared a decent dividend. One of the reasons Bobby and I were elected to this board was because of this company's absurd directors' fees, not to mention the idiotic CEO bonuses, all made while this company was dead in the water. Our shareholders deserve the best from us."

Samantha O'Leary said, with a smile, "Thanks for the speech, Noah."

When declaring the adjournment, Chairman Hedges said, "I can't begin to tell you how happy I am with this board."

Walking out of the meeting, and not caring if anyone was listening,

Noah eased up to Samantha O'Leary and said, "I didn't know you were a smart-ass."

"Noah, sometimes you need a little cold water sprinkled on you. But please, don't stop your speeches. Today you hit a bull's-eye."

"I can't leave things to chance—never could, never will," was Noah's response.

Sam said, "Do you need a ride?"

"To the Olympic, thank you."

She dropped him at the Olympic portico.

Noah watched Sam drive away and thought, I didn't want to leave her.

Sam glanced in her rearview mirror and thought, Why did I leave him? Whoa, am I nuts?

Noah left Seattle knowing that Road Victor was now a living, breathing force in the corporate world. He was thinking, Never mind that Bobby, Samantha, and I are responsible. That's not important. What's important is the benefit to our shareholders.

Noah was again home in Rock City on Monday. Rose Marie was aloof, and his friend Felix was having difficulty understanding Noah's absences. He had both of them read the Road Victor article in the old February 15 issue of his *Wall Street Journal*. Felix and Rose Marie read it together, and neither understood and said so.

"OK, the details are complex but, simply put, I participate in the management of Road Victor, Inc., a multimillion-dollar company that manufactures bicycles and, soon, other products."

Felix asked, "Do you help manufacture those things?"

"No, but together with four other directors, we employ experienced people who hire and manage maybe three hundred to four hundred employees to do that."

Rose Marie asked, "Where do you stay in Seattle?"

"In a big hotel, the Olympic."

"Isn't that expensive?"

"Rose Marie, it is, but Road Victor pays those expenses and my travel expenses."

Felix nudged Noah with a push on his arm. "Do you like staying in a hotel?"

"I'd rather be home, but, Felix, I can call the hotel kitchen almost any time and have food delivered to my room. Can't do that at home."

Felix and Rose Marie, surprised, laughed with Noah.

Felix asked, "Are the new Road Victor bicycles good bicycles?"

"Yes, that's one of the first things I insisted be fixed, and it was."

"Wow, you can tell people what to do and they do it."

"Felix, it's done in a nice, professional manner."

Rose Marie asked, "Do you get paid for what you do?"

"Yes, but not much."

"Then why do you do it?"

"I like what I do. I'm a shareholder in Road Victor, and those share values are up and will continue rising, all to my financial advantage and to the advantage of all shareholders. I have educated myself in business matters, and I'm using that knowledge for the benefit of a lot of people."

Felix said, "You must like being in Seattle."

"Seattle is OK, but I will always have my home here. I like my friends here and plan to stay."

Felix asked, "If I wanted a Road Victor bike, could you get me one at a low price?"

"Yes . . . I suppose you want me to get one for you."

"Might as well."

Noah wasn't going to admit that he would like to be a regular, normal teenager and take pleasure in all the usual teenager fun and games and friendships. His hardships had molded him into something different, but he would try to be pleasant about it.

Noah ate dinner at the Rock City Cafe and drove to Martha's home. She was expecting him. It was a warm, bright evening, and they sat on her porch. Noah showed her *The Wall Street Journal* article.

Martha said, "This is amazing."

Noah said, "Martha, my business interests are starting to run my young life, and I am not sure I like it. Going back and forth to Seattle is a pain, and constantly trying to solve problems here and there and in New York is difficult. Would you think about that? Sometime give me your thoughts?"

"OK, here's what I think. Don't change anything. You are one of those people who will have a good life simply because you are smart about doing what you know, and you will be paid for what you know and not for what you do."

Noah said, "Thanks, Martha. One more thing. Buy more Road Victor, but first consult your broker and follow his opinion."

Noah owned five thousand acres of logged-off land that, by law, needed to be reforested. He had agreed with the seller, Eastern Pacific Timber Company, to reforest the land, and the purchase price to Noah was reduced. In April, Noah contracted with Wild Planters, Inc., a group of mostly college dropouts, to replant the five thousand acres in the fall planting season for $50,000, including fir and cedar seedlings. It would be a decent investment if the trees lived. He paid $5,000 to bind the written reforestation agreement. He was now living in a very large forest.

Noah had a window seat on the Bombardier Dash 8, headed for the May 27 directors' meeting, again worrying about a propeller coming through his window.

Noah found Samantha O'Leary in the Alaska Airlines boarding area. Noah had asked her to meet him. He wanted to discuss the May meeting.

Sylvia Latimer and Lila Jameson, two major Road Victor share-holders, had just disembarked from a plane arriving from Portland. They saw Noah North and Samantha O'Leary together. They eased over to Noah and Samantha, with all four smiling at their accidental meeting.

Sylvia said, "I like seeing you together almost as well as my $8 per share. We love you young directors. You make Lila and me feel like born-again capitalists."

"I'm sure we'll see you and Lila at the shareholders' meeting in June."

Samantha said, "With Bobby Shaffer's help, the five of us saved our company, and it's going to get better, much better."

"Can we take you someplace?" Sylvia offered.

"No, I have my car."

Lila pulled on her friend's sleeve. "Come on, Sylvia, they don't want two old ladies hounding them."

Samantha was driving back into town on Interstate 5 with Noah, whose mind was considering his good fortune in not being alone and wondering if his shitty, lonely past should be used as a measure for defining good fortune. That woke him up.

He said, "You know what? I'm not alone today. Where are we going?"

"Are you OK?" asked Sam.

"I can tell you that every neutron in every atom in every cell in my body says I'm OK. I still want to know where we are headed."

"We are headed to the Olympic."

Noah was exiting her car when he said, "Are you taking the whole day off from your job tomorrow because of our directors' meeting?"

"Yes. Why don't I pick you up for breakfast? There's much to discuss about Road Victor."

"Sounds good to me. We are not forgetting our agreement to end affectionate personal ties, are we?"

Samantha said, "No, but if you're like me, you're still working at it."

Noah stood out of the rain under the Olympic Hotel's portico and watched Samantha O'Leary's black BMW disappear. He checked in, ate dinner, and went to bed.

During breakfast at a nearby cafe, Samantha said, "Let's go to the plant and see what's going on with new construction. If there are any problems, board action might be necessary."

The visit saw the framework of the new production line in place and additions to the old line mostly complete. Boxes of components, supplies, and tools for new products were stacked high in the old warehouse. Engineers Russ and Steven were there, pleased with the changes.

Waiting in the anteroom to the board meeting room was one person, George Newton, owner of 308,000 Road Victor shares. Noah and Sam were early.

George Newton stood up and said, "I've had second thoughts about new products, and we are making a huge mistake."

Noah walked up to George and said, "How so?"

"We make bicycles. That's what we do, that's what we've always done, and changing that is a mistake."

Noah was upset but concealed it. "Fortunately, that's not your call. Besides, for some reason I thought you were OK with our new direction.

We're up to $8 a share. That means an over $600,000 increase in your equity, and it's going to get better. So what is your problem?"

Samantha wasn't going to have any part of this conversation.

George said, "I'm talking about the long-run prospects."

Noah said, "Well, for the past fifteen years, you old guys kept old-guy directors who led you to the brink of insolvency, and in less than a year, us young guys saved your fortunes and your asses, and now you want to tell us what to do?"

"Young man, don't talk to me like that—show me some respect," demanded George.

"Don't 'young man' me. When you do that, it means your opinion is not based on reason. Your only chance is at the shareholders' meeting in June. You can explain how saving the company, the substantial increase in share value, the increase in capital for new products, and the market acceptance of our new bicycle are not winners, and how our bright new directors have failed our company. While you're thinking about that, why don't you go home?"

George paused for a moment in deep thought and then left.

Sam said, "Weren't you a little rough with him?"

"I was, but he'll complain about me to some who will not agree with him."

Sam said, "Complaints are bad. I hope you never have to complain about me."

"The only time I could complain about you would be if you ran off with the garbage man."

Ignoring Noah's remark, Sam said, "I hope this directors' meeting is short."

The directors' meeting was indeed short. Corporate business was quickly dispatched. Chairman Hedges applauded the directorship and the meeting ended, fixing June 28 as the next meeting date after the shareholders' meeting.

Sam was driving Noah to the Olympic when she put her right hand on Noah's shoulder and said, "Is this ridiculous? I believe we are falling into a relationship that has no end. I know we have acknowledged it and tried to avoid it, but it's there, isn't it?"

"Yes, you are right. I have just barely started my life, and your life is well underway and loaded for success. I'm five years younger, have no real education, and my affection for you grows every time we are together, but so what?"

Sam raised an eyebrow at him. "Do we want to stop it?"

"The question is, can we?"

Sam slowed, drove her car into a Safeway parking lot, and stopped. She said, "From some of our conversations, I know you have a girl-friend in Rock City, and I have two men, both co-workers, that I've dated, and both want more from me. Because your smarts and energy and character resulted in my infatuation with you, I stopped dating them."

Noah said, "I'll be gone tomorrow, so let's think about our relation-ship for a while. In the meantime, you should start dating those young men just like I'm dating Rose Marie."

Sam said, "I'll be stewing about it while you are thinking about it."

"Sam, you'll recognize a good man when you see him, so make a life for yourself here in Seattle. It will make it easier on both of us."

It was a silent ride back to the Olympic portico. The next day, Sam took Noah to Sea-Tac where, with their goodbyes, their eyes met, with each eye revealing an infinitesimal glimmer silently proclaiming: It should be over, but it's not.

"Sam, I'll be back for the shareholders' meeting."

One hundred twenty minutes later, Noah's plane touched down in Medford. He was still living the sweet and sour of the past two days.

FORTY-THREE

The riddle concerning Samantha was emotional, and dealing with it was akin to picking up quicksilver with your fingers. He needed to deal with both matters. He could not miss the June 11, 1977, shareholders' meeting in Seattle. Successfully burying his romantic attachment to Samantha O'Leary might be derailed every time he was in Seattle. He desired a clean solution to any problem, but a solution to the issue that he and Samantha faced would not be easy.

Noah's trips to Seattle put him in the corporate world where he thrived. He left the Olympic Hotel alone in a taxi, knowing the shareholders' meeting would be a joy and a triumph of new over old. Noah and Sam arrived early at the large Seattle Hilton conference room. Samantha O'Leary looked like Miss Washington, and Noah was a handsome, well-dressed young man looking older than nineteen.

The shareholder presence was a familiar scene, but a different mood prevailed.

Sylvia and Lila, representing over eight hundred thousand shares plus proxies, came to them.

Sylvia said, "What a beautiful couple."

Noah said, "Sylvia, I would rather you said, 'What beautiful directors.'"

Noah and Sam were pleased to see the room filled with happy shareholders.

The directors were seated at their table in front of the shareholders. Chairman Hedges opened the meeting. CEO Sims made the annual "State of Road Victor Address." He finished by saying, "By the way, our shares are up another point today." The applause was the first in twenty years.

Hedges invited comments and questions.

A shareholder stood and asked, "Where is the young man responsible for all this?"

Noah looked different in shirt, tie, sports jacket, and slightly longer hair. Chairman Hedges said, "Stand up, Noah." Noah stood up and listened to friendly applause.

The shareholder said, "Could you say a few words?"

Noah walked to the podium and said, "You ain't seen nothin' yet!" and he returned to his seat.

The place went crazy with laughter and applause. Sam saw Noah wipe a few tears from his cheeks, and she thought, What a marvelous young man.

People were slow to leave. They wanted to talk about their good fortune. Sylvia came to Sam and Noah, who were busy with shareholders. When the chance came, Sylvia invited Noah and Sam to a dinner she was having that evening at her Lake Washington home in Bellevue. It was close to Sam's condo, and they accepted.

"I might be lost with Sylvia's friends."

"You won't be lost," Sam said, and added, "they might be lost."

Sam and Noah avoided mentioning their unrequited personal relationship, and at the first opportunity, Noah said, "Let's let the question about our relationship alone and see if it goes away."

"That's not like you, Noah, but I agree."

Sylvia's place was big and beautiful, overlooking Lake Washington. It was a 1930s white, two-story colonial with a huge, well-appointed living room and large windows facing the lake. Two gorgeous Pakistani rugs covered the floor. There was a discreet bar at one end of the room. Part of a large dining room could be seen from the living room. The front entryway had white wood paneling and an elegant curved banister stairway to the second floor. Sylvia was an experienced hostess, and she was careful in omitting busybody guests who would cross-examine other guests. Sam and Noah were comfortable. They met the mayor of Bellevue and his wife. They met a Washington Huskies assistant football coach, his wife, and a Boeing executive and his wife.

Noah and Sam walked into Sylvia's dining room and sat beneath a large crystal chandelier.

"You need to show me what utensils to use and when," Noah whispered.

Sam winked. "Just follow my lead."

The dinner did make Noah nervous. He had never attended such a dinner and he was not going to talk about himself. He let Sam, who was sitting beside him, know that there would probably be no conversation that he could intelligently join. A fellow sitting next to him asked the mayor across the table if he was still messing around with gold. There was considerable other conversation, and few paid attention to the question.

The mayor said, "Well, I thought the price would move up fast, but it hasn't."

Noah leaned to Sam and asked in a whisper, "Should I get involved in that?"

"Go for it, maybe they won't ask you anything else."

Noah looked at the mayor and said, "Gold prices won't go anyplace until investors and institutional buyers get interested in that commodity. It hasn't been that long since we left the Bretton Woods Agreement."

"Whoa, you seem pretty positive about that."

"Better check it out, Mayor. Not many are buying the stuff," Noah said with a smile.

The fellow next to Noah said, "Gold is around $130 an ounce and a good buy."

Noah said, "For the past year, it has hovered around $139 an ounce. Today it is $133 and a safe buy, if that's what you want."

The mayor said, "At $133 an ounce, a pound of gold is only worth $2,128?"

Noah shrugged. "It is worth about $500 less than that. Gold is weighed by the troy ounce, which is twelve ounces a pound."

Sam leaned over to Noah and said, "Did you really have to correct the mayor?"

"I couldn't help it."

That ended the gold discussion.

After a perfect dinner, the guests hung around for a while. They were more interested in beautiful Sam than Noah, and that was OK with him.

The mayor said to Noah, "Sylvia told me about you, and she is right—you are a bright, resourceful young man. I believe a tremendous future awaits you. My very best goes with you."

On their way back to the Olympic in Sam's car, Noah was reflecting on his personal relationship with Sam and how manageable their age gap might be, but it might not be OK for Sam. He mumbled to himself, "I'll say something to her, but I don't know what or how."

They sat quietly in Sam's car under the Olympic's portico, silently and joyfully reliving the events of the day.

Noah turned and faced Sam, saying, "Am I really too young to be having this very personal affection for you? I have been nineteen since February, and I graduated from high school last year. Are our worlds really that far apart?"

"Noah, you have great mental strength, so apply it to resolve our common private problem and quit fighting it."

Sam then put her hand on Noah's arm and said, "I know exactly what you are saying, and I agree. But for now, an affable business and arm's-length personal relationship is enough."

"No it's not, but I agree."

Noah, as he'd done many times, watched Sam's car disappear into a field of car taillights.

While Noah's plane coasted in the late-morning light over the Rogue River to a Medford landing, Noah continually wrestled with a major issue: Was his life in Seattle or in Rock City? He had good friends in Rock City, which complicated things, and he had graduated from its high school, but was that enough to keep him in Rock City? A great university was in Seattle, as were great business opportunities and financial opportunities; his overwhelming connection to Road Victor, Inc., was there, and Samantha O'Leary was there. He would continue to wrestle with this issue.

The other issue was North Marine, Inc. Fortunately, it was taking little of his time or attention, thanks to CEO Myra Houston, who sent him frequent updates. Income was on the upswing, making a sale more likely, but he had heard nothing from Marty Woods about buyer interest. He was resolute in the effort to sell North Marine, Inc. The distraction with North Marine had to end.

Noah picked up *The Oregonian* in the Medford airport. Three days later he decided to read it while sitting on his front porch, and in the business section he saw an article headed "You Ain't Seen Nothin' Yet." It was a reprint from *The Seattle Times,* and the writer was the guy he had bad-mouthed out of the Olympic dining room months ago. Noah read the article.

YOU AIN'T SEEN NOTHIN' YET

It was the first time in 15 years that Road Victor, Inc., shareholders attending an annual shareholders' meeting in Seattle were happy. Two years ago a 17-year-old shareholder, Noah Jeremiah North, took charge, and he and Bobby Shaffer were elected directors. An upset director resigned, and a young Boeing engineer, Samantha O'Leary, was appointed director. These three young directors, with their management, financial, and new product ideas, and holding a majority vote, saved Road Victor. Noah North's business acumen in creating much-needed new capital was part of their plan. At this year's June 11 meeting, a shareholder asked to see the young man responsible for the remake of Road Victor, and when asked to speak, North rose from his seat, walked to the podium, and only said, "You ain't seen nothin' yet." The applause and laughter in praise for the young man brought a tear to his eye. Road Victor shares are up 35% in one year.

Noah did not like being the focus of attention, especially for his impromptu statements at meetings and in classrooms. Not many in

Rock City who read the piece would know what to make of it. Others would and Martha did. She called Noah and said, "Come see me."

Sitting with Martha on her porch, he said, "You saw *The Oregonian*, right?"

"Please tell me about it," she insisted.

Noah stated, "I'm much more than the person you know, but you will always be my first and most continuous best friend ever. That newspaper article says everything but a million details. The devil is in some of those details."

"Are you staying in Rock City?" she asked.

Noah looked out across Martha's yard and said, "I will always own my house and land here, and I received my high school diploma here. I may be in Seattle, but until I have my college education, who knows where I'll be. I'm not forgetting my roots. I would like to stay here. I plan to die near my little forest of giant cedar trees. That is the only time I've uttered that sentence. I believe in never working for anyone unless I am in full charge, so no telling where that will put me. Also, North Marine in Buffalo is for sale. I should never have gotten involved, but I did save it. No one in Rock City needs to know anything about that business."

Martha said, "That's pretty good insight for a nineteen-year-old. You need to treat your friends with care, especially Rose Marie."

"Rose Marie Simpson and I have a romantic attraction for each other. I have no idea where that will go. If she were to wait around for me, it might be a mistake. I'm a person who may not know where he belongs."

Martha hugged Noah on his departure. Forever without a mother, father, or anything resembling a family, he was now only five hundred family hugs short of what he should have had at age nineteen.

The next day, Noah walked into the Rock City National Bank and to Mr. Marston's desk, and they shook hands.

Marston said, "You're a celebrity, Noah. That was a complimentary article in *The Oregonian*. You obviously have financial and management skills that any bank could use. We have an opening on our bank's board. You could have the seat if you wanted it."

Noah said, "That would be an honor, but no thanks. There's too much going on in my life. What I want is a credit card. My friend tells me that carrying around a couple dozen hundred-dollar bills is not smart."

Noah signed the papers Marston had shoved in front of him.

Marston said, "You can't have a balance on that card greater than $10,000, and if you pay the balance in full each month, there is no interest charge. You'll receive your credit card in the mail."

When leaving, Noah said, "Ask your broker about Road Victor—you could be a winner!"

His relationship with Rose Marie troubled Noah. She needed to know that they were close friends and that she was important to him. Ignoring her would be a crappy thing to do. He pedaled over to her house. She was home and happy to see him.

Sitting on her front steps, he said, "Rose Marie, I have to tell you something that has happened in my life that I didn't plan. As fond as I am of you, I have to be honest and say to you that I developed an emotional attachment to a woman in Seattle. But that attachment is ending for valid reasons. You are the first girl that captured my attention and affection, something that I value more than you know, but I'm moving on in many ways."

Deflated by Noah's comments, Rose Marie said, "Noah, I knew this was coming. A couple of days ago, my father handed me *The Oregonian* with the article about you. When I read it, I thought, Noah and I are no longer in the same world."

Noah, with his usual smile, said, "I won't be in Rock City every day. You know that, but you are in my world, and we'll continue to be together frequently. Our affection for one another may continue to grow. I will do nothing to prevent it from growing."

They hugged each other and Noah left.

Noah was busy gathering his thoughts and plans for the June Road Victor directors' meeting when a call from Marty Woods informed him that they had a $6,000,000 offer for the shares of North Marine.

Noah was surprised and said, "Marty, North Marine is worth more than that."

Marty said, "How do you know that?"

"Three ships, real property, and a going business is worth more than that offer."

"Noah, two years ago you had nothing in New York. Now you can put $5,250,000 before taxes in your pocket and get rid of that business distraction you shouldn't have been involved with in the first place. Besides, you know nothing about valuing Buffalo real property, let alone marine shipping assets."

"Marty, you're right. This is why I have you, in case you didn't know. A condition of the sale that is essential must be the buyer's agreement to retain my CEO, Myra Houston, for at least five years at no lesser wage or benefits."

Marty said, "Thanks. You know you have done your two cousins a favor even though they won't know what happened. So say goodbye to New York."

"You are right. New York is history."

Marty quietly said, "Well, what do you want me to do with the proceeds?"

"Send me a check for about $1,500,000 to pay taxes. Then buy something conservative and safe with a yield."

FORTY-FOUR

Noah was waiting for his plane in the Medford airport, reflecting on his nineteen-year-old complex life that needed to be uncomplicated. Felix Bronson was again looking after Noah's place, and Felix had the Olympic Hotel phone number. Things might be tidied up with Rose Marie. Samantha and business decisions awaited him. He hoped that he was capable of toning down his attraction to Samantha O'Leary. Maybe the summer solstice would bring him luck. Noah walked out of the Sea-Tac terminal to a taxi and later registered at the Olympic.

The next morning, Samantha gave him a ride to the June 28, 1977, directors' meeting. Noah was anxious to discuss Road Victor's readiness to manufacture walkers, strollers, wheelchairs, and golf carts.

Sam said, "We might be close. The designs by Russ and Steven are innovative, functional, and marketable. We have one prototype walker we're trying to damage or wear out, and it's looking strong. We've applied for a patent. Same with the golf cart and stroller. The wheelchair can wait."

"Sam, once those items hit the market, our shares will go over $20. Considering SEC rules, I think it's safe for us to buy, and I'm doing that when I get back to Rock City. I hope we get a positive report on plant modifications and maybe a prototype of the walker or the golf cart you told me about. We've got to forge ahead on those things. Getting new products on the market is imperative, and I don't like building fires under people."

They were two hours early to a 1 p.m. directors' meeting, and they ended up on the main production floor, occupied by one assembly line fully remodeled as specified and the second assembly line nearly completed. This was an important day for Road Victor, Inc., because three new forceful young directors were breathing life back into the grand old company, and today they confirmed that they were fast out of the starting gate.

Sam said, "We're getting there. Steven and Russ, show us what you've done with a walker."

They wheeled in a dolly with a walker on it. Sam carefully looked it over and said, "Perfect, couldn't have done better myself."

Russ said, "Road Victor will manufacture the collapsible frame. Everything else will be purchased in bulk and assembled so easily it can be done by chimpanzees."

CEO Sims was present, and Noah said, "I think we'll be selling most of these by mail order, so we'll need container-board boxes by the time you get the marketing underway. Using publications like the *AARP* magazine and *The Elks Magazine* might be good for walker sales."

The directors' meeting was uneventful. Cautious optimism circled the room, the first such feeling in that room in sixteen years.

Noah said, "We've got our heads above water, but we're not on dry land yet."

Near the end of the meeting, Chairman Hedges said, "My old friend Stanley Clarke is in deep depression over his ouster. His wife thinks it might help if we welcomed him here for a visit. I'm pretty sure he didn't tell her the nuts and bolts of what happened, and I'm guessing he told her he voluntarily resigned."

Noah immediately responded, "I'm sorry for his depression, but under no circumstance is he to set foot on these premises. Forgive me for saying that, but he almost sank this splendid old company, and at his last meeting he attempted a coup de grâce."

When the meeting ended, Noah asked Sam to stay.

When the room was empty, Noah said, "I hope you don't mind me speaking like that about Clarke."

Sam said, "I'm OK with what you said. It needed to be said, but I didn't think a nineteen-year-old would have the courage to clearly say it."

"I'm nineteen, much taller than you, and I'm having trouble ending a serious personal, emotional relationship with you that could really take hold. You need to shoo me away."

"You can say the damnedest things. I do know what you're saying, and I'll do what needs to be done. You are right about a personal relationship, and it is awkward for me."

Sam took Noah to his hotel, and when parting, Sam said, "I won't be taking you to the airport in the morning."

"I understand. Besides, you have a job."

The next morning, he took a taxi to Sea-Tac. Noah was seated in the front row, first class. He was one of only six first-class passengers. He was immersed in thoughts about Sam, Rose Marie, continuing work with Road Victor, and his terminated connection with North Marine. Remaining issues were clear and present.

The pretty flight attendant got his attention by offering him a beverage, and when he declined, she sat down beside him. The name on her attendant's badge was Sophia.

Sophia said, "I know who you are. I see your name on the passenger list every month. You're the young man that saved my father's job at Road Victor."

Noah looked at Sophia and said, "Thanks for saying that. It helps me in making some difficult choices, such as, should I be here or there?"

Sophia said, "I don't know what that means. You sure you're only nineteen?"

"I've been asked that many times, but I have proof. Last year I graduated from high school and nineteen is what *The Seattle Times* said about my age, so I'm sticking with nineteen."

The plane was in a smooth descent into the Medford airport when Sophia returned to her duties, saying, "See you next month."

Felix was leaving Noah's house when Noah arrived.

Felix said, "My visit here today surprised a man on your front porch who looked like he wanted in. Turns out it was your Uncle Willis."

"Thanks, Felix, I'll need to check into that for sure." Noah thought, He must be here because he wants something of value from me. Let him make his move and I'll act. Maybe he'll go away, and unpleasantness will be avoided.

Noah was relieved to be home, the military draft had ended in

1973, Road Victor was saved, North Marine was gone, and he was ready to build on his friendships and the good things in Rock City. Tomorrow he would call Rose Marie for a date and Martha for a visit. However, Noah would never overlook the role that gold had played in nurturing him onward and upward in life from age four. Tomorrow he would see his banker. The price of gold would soon heat up and Noah wanted to be ready.

At 9:30 the next day Noah walked to the desk of bank manager Wilson Marston.

Noah sat down and said, "Can you find someone to help with my safe-deposit boxes?"

Immediately Jackie Shaw, the bank's operations officer, a pleasant dark-haired woman, showed up at Marston's desk, and he asked her to help Noah. Noah handed her his key. Soon Noah returned to Marston's desk. The operations officer stayed.

Noah handed Marston a heavy briefcase and said, "Could you get someone to weigh this for me?" Wilson left with Noah's briefcase and later returned and handed it to Noah with a slip of paper with "1,100.17286 troy" written on it.

Noah got a money pouch from Wilson and put the sinkers in the pouch with the weight slip and, with the operation officer's help, placed the pouch in one of his safe-deposit boxes.

The operations officer saw Noah handle a few of the gold sinkers and turned to Marston, who saw her astonished look and posture, indicating that she wanted to speak.

Marston quickly said, "Noah knows what he's doing and when to do it. So don't fuss about what you saw."

Before Noah returned to Marston's desk, the operations officer said, "I know who that kid is. He's only nineteen. Does he always act like he is in charge?"

"Always," said Marston. "And he is."

Noah returned with his empty briefcase and said, "Wilson, all hell may break loose on the gold market before the end of August, and when it does, I'll be at Kaplan and Graves with that pouch, all weighed and ready to go."

Noah left, and Jackie Shaw said, "How much am I missing here?"

"Only an amazing biography."

The August 1977 board meeting was next on Noah's calendar. He decided to skip it. Attendance at the July meeting had been inconvenient. His good friends in Rock City deserved his attention, and so did the commodity market. Gold was moving up.

Noah stopped at his bank and put a money pouch full of sinkers in his car.

He thought, I should have called Kaplan and Graves first, but I think they can handle it.

He walked into the Kaplan and Graves office and was met by Mr. Graves, who said, "I know why you're here today."

"Of course you do. Just know I want $183."

"We're not paying that."

"I didn't drive all the way over here for less."

Mr. Kaplan looked out the window and saw a black Mercedes parked at his front door and said, "That your black car at my front door?"

"Yes."

"And you want me to pay for it?"

"You already did. I want $183."

"We'll give you $180."

"I can do that."

Noah headed back to Rock City with a cashier's check drawn by Kaplan and Graves's bank in the sum of $198,003.10, and he deposited it in his Rock City National Bank checking account. He was buying Road Victor shares the next day, and he was seeing Roy Sang to amend the quarterly return of his estimated tax.

Monday morning, Noah had Marty Woods on the phone and said, "Buy me fifteen thousand shares of Road Victor. Try to get it at less than eight."

Woods said, "That will cost you $120,000."

Noah said, "Of course it will. I'm sending you a check today, but I want the buy now!"

"You know what you are doing?" asked Woods. "Noah, you still need to sign a disclaimer when buying that stock, but you can sign it later."

"Yes, and please call me back and tell me what you did."

That evening Noah called Bobby Shaffer. He might have an update on Road Victor's new products.

Bobby said, "I have great news! Russ and Steven have designed four new products, all compatible for combined assembly on our new production line. Get this: a golf cart and a baby stroller on the same frame and wheels but barely different in appearance except for their obvious use. Also, they have commenced production of the walker, and it looks great. They are still working on the collapsible wheelchair. The walker, golf cart, and stroller are collapsible and durable, and combining the assembly of those things on the same assembly line is a master stroke. We're on our way, Noah, and these things are going to sell like hotcakes."

Noah said, "I will not attend the August 23 board meeting. Too much going on here."

After breakfast at the Rock City Cafe, Noah drove to his house, and he glanced at his cedar forest and, with a heavy heart, thought, I need to be here. I need to call Rose Marie. Most of all, I need to get my life together in one place, but I'm not going to abandon my duty to Road Victor. I'll miss the August meeting and will not miss the September meeting.

The September directors' meeting was opened by Chairman Oliver Hedges. Every director was feeling good about Road Victor. Sims introduced Tom Martin, mentioned his credentials, and asked that the board make him CFO, and the board did.

CEO Sims reported that production of their new products was coming along, and some would likely be on the market within a month. Not only that but bicycle sales were up.

Noah said, "If we don't have a marketing firm, we need one—one that will get us nationwide coverage. It will cost us, but as they say, it pays to advertise. Mr. Sims, where are we on that?"

"If the board has no objection, that is what we will do."

New director Walter Morrison said, "As soon as all of our new products are coming off the production line, shouldn't we have some sort of commercial celebration, show off our new stuff, and invite the press and public?"

"That's a great idea," Director Shaffer said.

Noah looked at Director O'Leary. "Now we're talking. They can't stop us now."

Sims said, "You need to know about hiring new employees. It is difficult to find employees with enough skill to pick up a dozen different parts and attach them correctly. Once they learn how, they're OK. Some can't learn to get out of bed in the morning, and they don't last. We have around five hundred fifty employees, making our personnel manager a busy man."

Chairman Hedges asked, "How long will it be before we give our shareholders a dividend?"

"Maybe early next year, if we get lucky with sales," said Sims.

The meeting ended at 4:30 p.m., and Noah walked with Sam to her car.

Bobby Shaffer caught up with them and asked, "What's going on here?"

Noah replied, "We don't know."

Bobby said, "Nice," and walked away.

Sam said, "Noah, that was barely OK."

Noah replied, "I know it was. We can barely explain us ourselves, so he got an honest answer. Could you drop me off at the Olympic?"

FORTY-FIVE

The October and November directors' meetings revealed substantial response from marketing strategies, but the production of new products was slow. By the January 1978 board meeting, the fourth quarter profit and loss statement was out; the bottom line was good and production was increasing. The published fourth quarter results were reflected in the stock market.

February was a month that gave Noah an opportunity to develop his relationship with Rose Marie. He would be twenty years old on the twenty-eighth.

Noah and Rose Marie were finishing lunch on Saturday at the Rock City Cafe, watching snow accumulate on a roof across the street and melt on the warm hood of his car. She was attending Rogue Community College in Medford. Their companionship was on its way to permanency without them knowing it.

Noah said, "I hate to tell you this. I have to leave for Seattle on the twenty-fourth and will return on the twenty-sixth. Someday I hope you go with me, and someday I may be finished with Road Victor."

"Hasn't that business been really good for you?"

"Yes. Definitely, and someday I may tell you all about that."

"Well, you don't need to apologize for your trips to Seattle. Not to me, anyway."

Noah, looking seriously at Rose Marie, said, "I haven't said much to you about my relatives in New York or my business with them. I inherited and then financed a business there to save it. I recently sold that business, and I no longer have that distraction."

Noah drove Rose Marie home and said goodbye at her doorstep, and he was soon driving to Seattle. By the time he arrived, he had decided that flying to Seattle was better than driving.

Noah attended the February 25, 1978, directors' meeting.

CEO Sims gave a report on the state of Road Victor. It was the finest such report in the company's long history. Road Victor shares had closed at $20 the day prior to the meeting.

Near the end of the meeting, Sims said, "We have a serious problem with finding aluminum welders."

Noah said, "Maybe we could subsidize a trade school to teach that skill, or better yet, there are many aluminum boat manufacturers in the area; why don't we steal a couple of their welders?"

Sims, surprised, said, "That's not usually done in a gentlemanly business culture."

No one else responded, and Noah said, "Come on, I'm serious. Go to an employment agency or headhunter or, otherwise, get some welders! We're not running a friendship club!"

With the meeting nearly over, Chairman Hedges said, "Our attorney handling the new common share issue told me that facsimile signatures of the chairman and president on the stock certificates are required. We have no president. Who wants to be president?"

Bobby Shaffer said, "I nominate Noah Jeremiah North."

"Are you nuts, Bobby?" Noah said. "A twenty-year-old director is OK, but a twenty-year-old president is too much for the shareholders to stomach. Actually, I won't be twenty until three days from now."

"I know that, but you, on your own initiative, started the entire transformation of our company, and you are seeing it to fulfillment. You deserve this more than anyone who ever had anything to do with Road Victor. Besides, you are qualified."

Samantha O'Leary seconded the motion.

Walter Morrison said, "Sounds good to me. We're now a young company with young ideas, so why not?"

Chairman Hedges said, "I see where this is going. Everyone in favor of Noah North as president of Road Victor, say yes."

There were four yeses.

Noah and Sam walked to Noah's car. It was next to Sam's car.

At the car, Noah said, "Well, I guess every president should have a black Mercedes. You like it?"

Sam kissed Noah's cheek, ran around Noah's car, opened the door, and threw herself onto the passenger's seat.

Noah said, "Sam, you and I have agreed that, if there was a romance between us, it is over—over permanently!"

Sam said, "I'm resolved to a decent, cool friendship only, and that's it, OK?"

Noah said, "I have to admit, it's being difficult for me, because I could be in love with you."

Sam said, "Well, I must admit it. I may be in love with you. We've made it crystal clear, it has to end and it will. An impractical love may be a poison seed in a relationship. We will remember each other, but that's it. You go live your life, and I'll live mine. The hurt will soon end."

"You are a smart, practical woman, Sam."

"Noah, one thing I have not mentioned; I never planned to stay with Boeing permanently. There is a prestigious engineering firm in Boise, Idaho, that continually invites me to join them. I may or may not do that, and my home state and my family are calling. If we were together, I couldn't move and I couldn't ask you to move."

"Thanks, Sam. That does it, but my affection for you remains in place."

Chairman Oliver Hedges walked by the black Mercedes and was surprised to see Noah behind the wheel with Samantha O'Leary next to him. Hedges quickly turned his head away and mumbled, "That damn kid has everything."

Looking at Sam, Noah said, "I can't believe they made me president. Of course, it's honorary only, but it does have a certain appeal."

Sam said, "I'll give you that. You do know there was no other choice."

Sam alighted from Noah's car, walked around to the driver's window, and said, "Goodbye, Noah."

Sam watched Noah's car disappear down the street and thought, Did this really have to happen?

The next day, Noah's heart and stomach could feel the emotional wreckage left by Sam's goodbye. Out loud he said to the rearview mirror, "Why do I feel this way? We were not real lovers. Nothing happened beyond a few kisses. Maybe it's because we wanted more to happen. I guess it's over." The drive home was dreary. Noah parked in his driveway. It was a long trip by car, and he decided that flying was the way to go. He also decided that he needed a garage.

The next day, Noah called Rose Marie and said, "I would like to take you to dinner tonight. Can you do that?"

"Noah, you sure you know what you are doing? It seems like you are always in Seattle, and when you are here, Seattle is on your brain."

"I know exactly what I'm doing."

Rose Marie said, "That was dumb of me; you always know what you are doing."

That night at dinner, they sat in a booth. Marge, the ever-present waitress, took their orders. She wondered what was going on, because boys in Rock City didn't take their girlfriends to dinner except on school prom nights.

Marge asked, "Do you want this on one check or two?"

Noah thought, We're certainly not in Seattle. He politely answered, "One check, please."

Before their dinner arrived, Noah's eyes focused on Rose Marie as her eyes gazed into his, and for a moment nothing was said. He looked away and then put his hand on her hand and said, "There's more at play here than you realize. I've told you before that my interests in Seattle were more than business. My personal relationship with a fellow Road Victor director, a woman, something that should have never happened, has, after a year and a half, ended. Nothing serious or intimate ever happened. Anyway, we remain friends, and I will see her at every directors' meeting, and that's all. However, my relationship with Road Victor is rock solid. I do have a deep affection for you, and if you develop an affection for me, we need to know each other, no secrets withheld. We're young, so who knows where this will go, if anyplace."

Rose Marie removed her hand and put it on top of Noah's hand and said, "We are too young to have complications in our personal lives, so let's keep it simple."

Noah quickly responded, saying, "I think you are nineteen, and I'm about to be twenty. That makes us old enough for anything. Rose Marie, my life has been tangled and complicated since I was four years old. My father had disappeared, and my mother died in a car wreck. I promise I will do my best for us."

At Rose Marie's house, Noah was walking her to her door when he gently took her arm and walked her behind a tall hedge. He then held her by her shoulders and kissed her. She didn't move, and he put his arms around her and kissed her again, and she returned his kiss.

Noah said, "See you tomorrow."

She said, "Thanks for dinner. It was nice, and so was everything else."

Noah drove home to an empty house, where he sat in a comfortable chair reviewing recent events, trying to mark where he was in life. First, he approved of the events of the evening. He then remembered Felix telling him about Willis coming to his house. That was bothersome. He would visit tavern owner Bill Walstrom.

The next day he drove to the Arcade Tavern, where he parked his car and went inside. He knew he was too young to be in there. Bill Walstrom saw him and took him to his office.

Bill asked, "What's going on?"

"I may have a problem that I don't know how to fix. You remember my Uncle Willis. Willis came to my house and wanted money or a handout or something. I ran him off. Recently, when I was in Seattle, he was seen prowling around my house. I think he'll be back and more aggressive. You're the only one in this town that might help me. You may know that I purchased five thousand acres of adjoining timber land from Eastern Pacific Timber Company, and I paid to have it reforested. If Willis came to Rock City, he will probably end up here. Maybe you'll learn his plan and help me end it. When I'm in Seattle, you can call me at the Olympic Hotel."

Bill said, "If there's anyone in this town that I'd like to help, it's you, Noah."

Noah said, "I can't thank you enough for that. If I learn anything, I'll call you. I just can't have any more complications in my life."

Noah knew that his closest friends needed to have a hint of what Noah North was doing. He drove straight from Walstrom's place and parked in front of his bank and walked to Wilson Marston's desk and sat down. He could do that without invitation, and Wilson welcomed him.

Noah said, "Thanks for help with my car. Did you buy Road Victor?"

"No."

"Big mistake. You should trust me as much as I trust you. Oh well, there's always tomorrow to do what you should have done today."

"Happy to see you, Noah. How are things in Seattle?"

"Couldn't be better," said Noah, who added, "I am now the president of Road Victor, Inc. I told the other directors that a twenty-year-old shouldn't be president of anything. They said I was responsible for saving Road Victor, and I was the obvious choice. I am flattered."

"Congratulations, how's the Mercedes work?"

"It'll go a hundred and sixty miles per hour."

Alarmed, Wilson said, "You didn't!"

"Of course not—where's the kid in you, Wilson?"

"Where do you go from here, Noah?"

"I will always keep my house and land here. I have roots here; they're not very deep, but they're here, and I'm planning on staying. Tell me, did you find a director for your bank? If you did, I hope he or she is not afflicted with stump rot."

"We picked Norman Parsons."

"Shit, Wilson, I know who he is, so the average age of your directors is, what, ninety-six? Did they buy a cane stand for the directors' boardroom? I'm guessing there's no one on your board that has had an original thought in forty years. You know what, I'm going to give you some advice that will shape the future of your bank." Noah recited an article in *The Wall Street Journal* that lectured on bank branching and how it was a bank's lifeline.

Noah then said, "There is no bank head office in either Medford or Grants Pass. Put branches in both those towns and do it now, even if you just open a storefront. Get the state OKs, and later build nice bank buildings. Your CEO and board know all that, and it is not a great risk—it's more like a sure thing—but they're afraid of their shadows and won't risk two cents to make a million. Put that before your board and see how many votes and heart attacks you get! People like their hometown banks, and if you push the branching to completion, you may end up CEO."

Wilson had his secretary bring them both a Coke, and they wasted an hour of Wilson's time talking about life in a small town.

Noah said, "Did you notice that I recently deposited a million and a half in my checking account? I'm using it to pay federal and state income tax resulting from the sale of my New York assets."

Winston said, "I saw that but was afraid to ask you about it."

When Noah left, Wilson said, "I wish you were on our board."

Noah flew to Seattle. He took a taxi to the Olympic and called Sam.

He said, "This is strictly a business call. Sam, have you seen the rise in value of your Road Victor shares?"

"Yes, it's kind of outrageous, isn't it?"

Noah said, "See you at tomorrow's meeting."

Noah received a phone call at the Olympic from Bobby Shaffer.

Bobby said, "There's a local *Wall Street Journal* correspondent here in Seattle that wants to interview you. He wants to do a biographical sketch of you. He interviewed me, and I was nice to you. If you want to do that, here's the guy's phone number."

"Gotta think about that, Bobby. Thanks, I'll see you soon."

The Wall Street Journal was Noah's business administration mentor. He needed to give that paper something in return, so the next morning, Noah called correspondent Sheldon Hale, who made plans for the interview.

Noah stayed in Seattle an extra day for Hale's interview. He came to the Olympic for a luncheon meeting. Hale was a correspondent for other news agencies such as the Associated Press and *The Seattle Times*, but this interview was an exclusive for *The Wall Street Journal*. Introductions were made.

Hale said, "Noah, I already know a little about you, and I believe this story will definitely be a feature article, so I am going to want a picture. You OK with that?"

"Yes."

Hale's interview started at the beginning of Noah's life and ended the day of the interview. Hale was thorough, and he was with Noah all afternoon.

When the journalist finished, Noah said, "I gave you an interview but no authority to publish a book. I want you to be kind and charitable to everyone at Road Victor, including those who are no longer there. That also goes for my friends in Rock City. Maybe you should avoid names if you can. Also, I gave you no details on the gold I found, where I found it, or the amount, so don't speculate on any of that stuff. I really want you to go low-key on that. One more important thing. I want to review and edit what you intend to publish. You OK with those conditions?"

Hale said, "Yes. It's no wonder you're where you are."

Hale, with his Rolleiflex, took a couple of pictures of Noah.

Noah sensed that the guy was professional and knew what he was doing. It wouldn't be long before he confirmed that.

After Hale left, Noah said out loud to himself, "I hope I didn't make a mistake, giving that interview."

The next day, Noah left from Sea-Tac. It had been an outstanding weekend.

Noah was home on Monday but would leave again on Friday the twenty-fourth. He was home long enough to keep his home ship on course.

Noah called Felix and met him at the Rock City Cafe. He knew Felix was attending the community college in Medford and that Felix was looking for a part-time job. Felix had told him that he was seeing Jennifer Moss, so it was time they talked.

"Felix, have a Coke or something. I'm buying. You're out of high school now, so what is going on with you?"

"I'm enrolled at Rogue Community College with Jennifer Moss, and things are getting serious with us."

"That sounds really good, Felix. Just keep on track."

"Noah, I'm proud to know you. At twenty, your life is a success."

"Felix, I would trade it all for a loving family from my birth to now, something you know I never had. That is something you have always had. If you think a little wealth makes up for all that, you are mistaken. You are a good friend, Felix, and I want it to stay that way."

Noah dropped Felix off at Felix's house and spent the rest of the day with Rose Marie at her home. He wanted her to have a little insight into his position with Road Victor and what his job was like. He told her about the board of directors and upper management and the interview with Hale.

Noah ended his warm monologue, saying, "Other business matters will not affect our relationship."

Rose Marie said, "You are really an adult and way ahead of the rest of us, because you had to be. Don't you dare change."

"I won't change. I probably can't."

Noah drove home to his usual empty house.

He called Martha early Thursday evening and then visited her. He was greeted with a hug, and they sat in Martha's living room in Joe's absence.

Noah said, "I need some personal, confidential advice. My family on my mother's side, if you could call it that, may cause me some problems. My Uncle Willis visited me a while ago, and I'm sure he wanted money and help from me. I was a little intimidated by him. I asked him to leave, and he left. When I was in Seattle, Felix saw Willis at my house. You know my father left my mother as soon as I was born, and he never showed up until recently, and now he is dead. Am I wrong in not wanting any relationship whatsoever with Willis when he at first helped me but then took advantage of me?"

Martha said, "Noah, you are an adult for all practical purposes." She added, "If you were my son, I'd say, you've asked for no quarter, so you give no quarter—which is to say that you've asked for nothing and you give him nothing. You're your own man with an adult perspective, so go with that."

"Thanks, Martha, I'll not forget your words. I'm off to Seattle tomorrow for another meeting."

Noah left his car in the Medford airport parking lot and arrived in Seattle at 6 p.m. He checked in at the Olympic, and while having dinner there, he thought about Samantha O'Leary and missed her company. He also missed Rose Marie, but it was a different sensation. Mother Nature's force on Noah's libido was not as big a thing with Rose Marie as it was with Sam. He came to his senses with the thought, This is crazy. My affection for Sam is over. She knows it. I know it.

Late the next morning, Noah was in the Road Victor offices. Sam also arrived. They had arrived when most of the office employees were about to leave for lunch. Engineer Russ McCormick was there, and they asked him for a quick look at the production lines. The lines were at a standstill during the lunch break, but you could see products on both lines, unfinished and finished.

Noah said, "That's a beautiful sight."

Sam asked, "Russ, you happy with the way these lines are working?"

Russ said he was happy, and he would be happier when the new employees learned their jobs.

Chairman Hedges opened the March 31, 1978, meeting. CEO Sims was immediately asked by Director Morrison if there was interest in the strollers, golf carts, and walkers.

Sims said, "It's early to say how strong it is. Our marketing is paying off. Numerous orders and inquiries have been received. I think we've got some winners here. I don't have a first-quarter financial, but things are looking good, real good."

Noah said, "Let's fix June 6 for our annual meeting of shareholders and hope that we have good news for them about Road Victor, the likes of which they haven't heard in eighteen years. We're going to do our shareholders a favor and keep this ship hard into the wind. Drifting with the tide almost sank this ship."

After the meeting, Sam went to Noah and said, "You're really running things here, aren't you?"

"Isn't that what the president is supposed to do? Am I being obnoxious with that? It's the last thing I want to be."

"No, you're not. I just like to know if you are still following the same road map."

Noah said, "I think I know what I'm doing most of the time, except maybe I didn't with an interview I gave. Besides, almost every decision I make involves a problem or issue that has never confronted me. But I do try to avoid guesswork. I barely have an education, and I don't have much experience with basic ways of doing business and what's important and what's not important in business management."

"Noah, stop. Make no mistake—you have plenty of time for your higher education, and your business judgment has been excellent. You'll never be without job offers, especially when Sheldon Hale's bio about you is published. You forget that you are twenty, and without much choice, you act as an adult in most things."

The April 11, 1978, issue of Noah's *Wall Street Journal* included Hale's biographical sketch. Noah anxiously read it. It accurately portrayed his relationship and direction with Road Victor, and the personal biographical data about him was also accurate. He was relieved, and under his breath he murmured, "Thanks, Sheldon Hale. If you had to put my life in print, at least, with my help, you got it right."

When Noah parked his Mercedes in downtown Rock City, he drew curious stares. He ignored them. He had drawn curious stares at many a meeting. Curiosity was meaningless and short-lived.

He walked into his bank. It was about to close, and without invitation he sat at Wilson Marston's desk and asked, "Did you buy some Road Victor shares?"

"No, but I read *The Wall Street Journal* article about you, and I am proud to be your banker."

"Wilson, I hadn't seen you for a while. Just wanted to say hello. Are you taking good care of my sinkers?"

"Yes."

Noah walked to his car.

Wilson, looking at his secretary, who'd seen Noah come and go, said, "He's not forgetting his friends."

FORTY-SIX

The spring weather featured some pleasant evenings, and Noah was enjoying one on his porch. An old Buick sedan entered Noah's driveway and came to a stop. Four people alighted, two old and two young.

The older woman asked, "Are you Noah North?"

Noah said, "Yes, and who are you?"

She said, "I'm your Grandmother Porter." Pointing, she said, "That's your grandfather. We're your mother's parents." Again pointing, she said, "That's your Uncle Josh and his wife."

Noah said, "Well, where's Willis?"

"We don't know. We think he is with your father."

"My father is dead." Noah, not knowing where this surprise event was headed, said, "Why are you here?"

Grandmother said, "We just wanted to visit and see how you are doing."

Noah said, "I think you know how I am doing, and that is why you are here."

Noah watched Josh walk over to his Mercedes and peer through one window, then another. Noah stepped off his porch and down to his visitors to get a closer look. He glanced in their car, and on the front seat was the April 11 issue of *The Wall Street Journal*.

Noah asked, "Where do you live?"

Grandmother said, "Grants Pass."

Noah said to the whole carload, "That's about a forty- to forty-five-minute drive from here, and you waited sixteen years for a visit? I'm sorry, but I've struggled my whole life without a family, especially my mother's family, and here you are, twenty years late. Now that I don't need any help, you show up. It's hard to see anything good coming from this visit, but I'll try. I want to have a private conversation with my Grandmother Porter in my house. The rest of you can hang around outside."

Josh said, "We can do that."

Noah looked at his grandmother and said, "Please come in."

They sat in Noah's living room, and he asked her to tell him about his mother, Virginia. Grandmother Porter said she was well liked, attractive, a good mother, and bright, but she wasn't aware of Buster North's flawed character until after marriage. He had been convicted of numerous misdemeanors and never had steady work.

Grandmother Porter said, "Virginia was a waitress. She loved you, and there were times when I babysat you. Virginia and you lived in a small one-bedroom apartment. Virginia worked five and six days a week, and when working, she hired a woman that cared for you in your home. That cost left Virginia with money for essentials only. If it wasn't for her tips, Virginia would have been lost financially."

"Did you help my mother financially?"

"No, we didn't have the means."

Noah asked, "Why didn't you take me when my mother was killed?"

"The family didn't want the responsibility or the expense."

Noah said, "You're being honest, and the precise reason you're here is because I have something to offer, right?"

"That's true about the others." With tears in her eyes, she said, "I just wanted to see you, that's all."

Noah said, "I don't even know your first name."

"It's Susan."

"Tell me about Josh and his wife."

"Josh can't keep a steady job. His wife, June, is a clerk in the post office, and they have no children."

"So you and June are the two responsible members of my mother's family?"

Noah took her address and phone number and said, "I'm going to visit you, but I'll call first. Can you accept that?"

Grandma Susan said, "Yes."

Noah hugged Grandma Susan Porter and whispered in her ear, "Remember, I'm mainly interested in you, and I can't help that."

Noah watched the car disappear down his driveway. No telling what the conversation was in the car.

Several days later, Noah drove home, and there was an old pickup truck parked in front of his house. Noah parked in front of his garage under construction. He walked to his front door, and Uncle Willis stepped out of the truck and walked to Noah.

Noah stopped and said, "What are you doing here? You need to get back in your truck and leave."

Willis said, "My mother was here and told me you were nice to her, so I thought maybe you had changed your attitude about me."

"Willis, nothing has changed. Please, you can't do anything for me, and the only reason you are here is for me to do something for you, and that ain't gonna happen, so goodbye!"

"Can't we just talk about things?"

Noah said, "We're not talking, you're leaving, and if you stay you are trespassing."

Willis stepped toward Noah in a menacing manner. Noah stepped onto his porch, opened his front door, and reached in. Baseball bat in hand, he moved to Willis and said, "I've had to use this once, and I'm ready to use it now."

Noah watched part of his phantom family drive away.

Noah went into his house, shaking his head over the encounter with Willis, when his phone rang. It was Samantha, and she said she had been calling all day.

Sam seemed to be a little agitated when she said, "Noah, Road Victor is not able to fill all orders for our new products, and something needs to be done. I told Sims to run a second eight-hour shift, and he won't do it without board consent."

"Sam, have him call every board member and get consent. Tell him he has my consent. Will you do that and call me? If that doesn't work, expect to see me. April twenty-eighth should be the next directors' meeting, and we can confirm a second shift. Sam, I'm thinking I should be there, so I'll fly up Friday. I have some ideas about employee compensation that need to be in place like yesterday."

Sam said, "As long as you continue to manage Road Victor and run the board, you might as well be here."

"Sam, am I that pushy?"

"It's OK, you haven't made a mistake yet," countered Sam.

"Am I pushy with you? If I am, I don't want to be."

"No, you're good with me."

Noah left the Medford airport Friday morning, and he flew first class, where the distractions were not as great. He was thinking about the visit by his family, if you could call it that. When in Seattle, he had been giving Felix Bronson $25 to keep an eye on his place. This trip he gave him Sam's number.

Sam met him early afternoon on Friday at Sea-Tac, and they drove to the Road Victor offices where they met CEO John Sims. They discussed a second shift. Sims complained that good employees were hard to find.

Noah said, "We have to produce and sell. This is the golden opportunity that we worked hard for, and we're not messing it up. We can offer a high hourly wage with a bonus based on production numbers and maybe a signing bonus. Sims, you figure out a normal production rate, and we pay a bonus to every employee on that shift for every unit above the normal production rate. You get CFO Tom Martin to run some numbers on this so we make money and not lose money. Also, those compensation rules need to be carefully written. Our present employees need to benefit from compensation changes. We might have to raise our prices slightly, but we're off to the races, boys and girls. We do all this immediately and fix any problems later. I'll see to it that the board approves. Sims, you might even get a bonus. Sam, you OK with this?"

Sam said, "Of course, how could I not be?"

Noah said, "I am what I am—hand me a can of spinach."

Sam gently put a hand on Noah's chest and said, "We should leave. You've given John plenty of work."

On their way to her car, she said, "It's amazing how you deal with a problem."

After a business weekend, Noah was on his way home in first class. He was weary of travel to and from Seattle. He would not leave Rock City. Nor would he abandon his business interests in Seattle. His five-thousand-plus acres, his house, his beautiful big cedars, and his friends in Rock City were essential to him. He'd been away too often, and leaving on Thursday for the April 25 directors' meeting would not be easy.

Pleased to be home and comfortable with his life, he was surprised at his overwhelming desire to see and be with Rose Marie. He puzzled about it. Was this some sort of collateral passion from the absence of Sam?

He called Rose Marie and said, "I want to see you."

He opened the passenger door for her. She hesitated briefly, stepped in, and sat on the leather seat. Soon they were driving onto Noah's driveway.

"You're not taking me into your house, are you?" Rose Marie's question lacked strength of purpose, and it seemed programmed by a nineteenth-century mother.

Noah smiled at her and said, "I'm taking you to a magic place, the best place in this world."

They left the car and, grabbing the wool car blanket, Noah said, "Please, follow me. I want to show you something in my forest."

They walked into the center of the grove of huge incense cedars. It was a warm day with little wind.

Spreading out the blanket, Noah said, "We'll sit down here for a while."

Noah lay on his back with Rose Marie at his side. Focusing on the little birds in the treetops, he said, "I love you."

Rose Marie rolled over on her side and, looking down on him, said, "I love you more than you know."

They lay beneath the tall cedars for a while, saying nothing while pondering the new exciting intensity in their relationship.

When they parted at Rose Marie's house, Noah said, "You're going to have to put up with my business work. It can be demanding at times. Just know that you are the most important person in my life. We are young, and we're smart, and we'll outwit any roadblock. I'm leaving for Seattle soon. Seattle will not be in my life forever. I'll be back to you as soon as possible."

They kissed, and Noah walked her to her house.

Before Noah headed for Seattle, he visited Martha, Felix, and his grove of big cedars. The forest there was an enchanted place.

FORTY-SEVEN

Noah left the Medford airport Thursday afternoon, and two hours later he was in the Sea-Tac terminal. A taxi put him at the Olympic. The board meeting was the next day, and everyone was anxious to have the first-quarter financial report.

It was a pleasant experience to walk into the Road Victor board-room in April 1978. No longer were they faced with perilous issues of failure or survival. Chairman Hedges opened the meeting, and Noah immediately said, "Could CFO Martin give us the first-quarter report?"

Hedges was surprised and said, "Might as well. Martin, can you do that?"

Martin handed a copy of the report to everyone, and silence followed as if a judge were about to read a jury verdict in a murder case.

After reading the report, every director clapped.

Noah said, "You need to immediately release that report to the press and mail it to *The Wall Street Journal* with a copy of our minutes approving it. Make certain the press release is mailed to our larger shareholders."

Martin said, "You need to note that our production capacity cannot meet demand. We've added a second shift and may add a third if necessary. Sale of bikes is level and steady. Demand for our patented strollers, golf carts, and walkers is huge, and we upped our price a little to cool sales until we can meet that demand."

Noah said, "You must have solved the welder problem."

"We did, but we pissed off several aluminum boat manufacturers."

CEO Sims said, "The bottom line will allow a modest dividend that, based on present market value of all common shares, could be around a three percent yield, a good return on equity and way ahead of many of our peers. That will light a fire under the price of our shares."

A resolution was unanimously passed, declaring a six-cent-per-share dividend.

Bobby Shaffer said, "Our shareholders' meeting is June 6, and his report couldn't come at a better time. Our major shareholders should be ecstatic."

Hedges asked, "Could we now pay directors' fees?"

Noah sternly said, "Not until after the annual meeting of shareholders."

No one said anything, and the subject was not mentioned again.

CEO Sims asked the board to approve employee wage, bonus, and second and third shift issues, and approval was given. The meeting adjourned, and Noah knew that Sam would have a comment about his meeting demeanor.

Sam had her hand on Noah's arm when she said, "I guess it's OK for you to maneuver the agenda around, but to totally control it and take an issue off the table is astounding. Poor Mr. Hedges wants to be paid, and a twenty-year-old won't allow it."

"Sam, when it comes to Road Victor business, I'm twenty-five."

Sam said, "Guess I'll see you May twenty-sixth."

Noah said, "Maybe not."

Noah was alone at the Olympic. Dinner alone seemed unnatural. He admired the gorgeous piece of salmon on his plate. The salmon dinner distraction passed and he mused, Someday a woman may be here with me. The next day he left Seattle in the rain and landed at Medford in the rain. He drove his car to his house, paid Felix for house-sitting, and called Rose Marie.

At her house, Rose Marie walked to Noah's black car, got in, and said, "I missed you. You left after you told me you loved me."

Noah said, "And I do, and for that reason I plan to miss my May twenty-sixth meeting, but I can't miss the annual shareholders' meeting on June sixth."

Noah and Rose Marie then spent many days together in May. Noah's love and affection for Sam began to fade as common practical sense reared its head. He welcomed the wise reality that Rose Marie would be his mate, if she would have him.

The June 1, 1978, *Wall Street Journal* had Road Victor shares trading at $37. About two years ago, it had been trading at $4⅛. When he read that news at his mailbox, Noah asked the sky out loud, "Did I do that?" Maybe, but with lots of help.

That price put Noah's stake in Road Victor at $1,850,000, and Sylvia and Lila would be overjoyed with their huge equities. He had received a copy of the minutes of the May 26 directors' meeting that he missed. Expansion of manufacturing hours at Road Victor, with Sam and Bobby urging it, had been approved by the board. Comments on mail orders were a fascinating tribute to the company's success. His work at Road Victor was nearly complete—or was it?

Did he dare leave Road Victor in the hands of a board without him? Should he move on to something that would keep him close to Rose Marie? He thought there might be job offers as news of Road Victor's success made its rounds. The concept of a twenty-year-old corporate president and director having saved a dying corporation might excite the headhunter species. Noah never had a job, not even a paper route, and he wasn't going to work for anyone, not unless he was at least 90 percent in control. He knew that leaving Seattle would limit his opportunities, but he didn't care. He wanted his business life to be in Oregon. Besides, he had to personally distance himself from Samantha O'Leary.

He visited Rose Marie and told her that he needed to be in Seattle for a shareholders' meeting and that he would be back and with her as soon as possible. She didn't understand, but she trusted Noah.

The June 6 annual meeting at the Seattle Hilton conference room was crowded with excited shareholders, some who had never attended such a meeting. Sylvia and Lila found Noah, Sam, and Bobby Shaffer standing together, and they administered huge hugs to those marvelous young directors.

The directors were seated at a table in front of the shareholders. Chairman of the Board Oliver Hedges called the meeting to order. There was a record of nearly four million shares present. Hedges stood at the microphone and said, "We were recently told by our attorney that this company needed a president. We unanimously elected our

youngest director, Noah J. North, president. He and our young directors have accomplished more for our company than was thought possible. Noah North was the catalyst for change, and he will speak to
you."

Noah stood before the shareholders and waited for the applause
to stop.

Noah said, "Three years ago I stood here and told you what was
wrong with Road Victor. You believed me and put me on the board
with Bobby Shaffer, and then Samantha O'Leary arrived. The three
of us forged the change in management, and soon Directors Oliver
Hedges and Walter Morrison were in our camp. We manufacture and
sell four products with a high demand that we will be meeting and answering with a second and maybe a third eight-hour shift. Our shares
were at four and one-eighth two years ago; now they are at thirty-
seven. We declared a dividend equivalent to a three percent yield on
the share price—the first dividend in fifteen years. There are still no
directors' fees and no management bonuses; however, a few bonuses
are appropriate, as are reasonable directors' fees. You now have something unusual: working directors. The last thing I have to say is that
we have developed a great management team, our hourly employees
are acquiring new skills, and I believe our directors have proved themselves to you. It has been a marvelous experience, and we thank all of
you. A word of advice: Don't sell, buy. You still ain't seen nothin' yet!"

The applause was loud and long, and again, tears came to many
eyes. Following the shareholders' meeting there was a brief directors'
meeting. Shareholders and directors stayed for conversation after the
meeting. When the meeting ended, Sam and Noah congratulated one
another. Sylvia Latimer, with her 560,000 shares, found them and said,
"Noah, I can't possibly thank you enough for what you have done for
our shareholders and particularly me." Sylvia had her eye on Sam. "A
word of wise, grandmotherly advice, Noah: Don't let business trump
your personal life. Without a mate, no matter how long you live, you
will live only half a life."

When the meeting ended, Sam and Noah stayed seated at the directors' table until the other directors left and they were alone. There
were still few shareholders milling about.

Noah said, "Road Victor is on track with increased sales and little competition. We have accomplished the impossible in three years. What we didn't accomplish was you and me being together forever. As much as we wanted it to work, with different interests in different towns and states, it can't. That is why we have toned things down, and except for our business connection, we will part. I hate it and think you hate it. There's nothing worse than being sensible."

When he left Seattle, twenty-year-old Noah felt as though he was leaving his life.

Samantha O'Leary would not forget the gifted, clearheaded young man who'd invited her to dinner when he was seventeen years old, or a friendship that had turned to love and affection, or a relationship that ended because it could never be.

Road Victor was slowly eating its way into a large share of the bicycle, walker, golf cart, wheelchair, and baby stroller market. Mail-order sales were booming, and factory production was nearing capacity. Share price was still hovering around $40. Was it time for Noah to let go of Road Victor? He couldn't let go. He stayed, but not without Rose Marie at his side in Rock City and in Seattle. They were married in 1980 at a ceremony held in her parents' home. Noah was twenty-two and Rose Marie twenty-one. Felix was his best man, and Jennifer Moss was the maid of honor. Rock City was a good place to be.

At the reception following, Felix quietly, having Noah's attention, said, "Jennifer and I are marrying next month. I want you to be my best man."

"I accept."

Nineteen ninety-three was the year Noah officially resigned as president. *The Wall Street Journal* reported it. The Seattle meetings had become burdensome, and he believed that he didn't have much more to offer. He received many offers to be interviewed by companies seeking a leader with aggressive corporate finance and management skills. Offers came from East and West Coast companies. Noah was intrigued but not ready. He asked for and received financials from several companies. They wanted a CEO or an upper-level manager. They all offered share options, and usually the salary was to be negotiated. Only three offers interested Noah: A startup pharmaceutical in New Jersey that wanted a public offering of its common shares managed.

International Business Machines in California wanted aggressive management in the development and marketing of its new word processor. A giant timber company in Washington wanted timber sales and forest-land acquisition managed.

Noah was flattered by the offers. He thought, I'm thirty-five years old, I'm happily married with two children, and I really don't need a job. He concentrated, swept aside some emotional and some not-so-practical underbrush, and there was the answer, bright and clear. Forget the job offers. The years ahead with my family are more important and will be the best.

Noah North's achievement in the world of finance and corporate rescue and management, and in the limited world of corporate governance, was storybook stuff. During that exciting time, he expertly managed his personal financial affairs and his personal life. He continued to be a Road Victor shareholder and director.

EPILOGUE

Samantha O'Leary married Dr. Charles Turner in 1979 at her parents' home in Boise, Idaho. Marsha was their only child. Sam's husband was killed in an automobile collision.

Cancer caused Rose Marie's death in December 2001.

Except for his two children who were away in college, Noah was alone again and saw no end to it. Feeling sorry for himself was not like him. He'd done that momentarily years ago. Memories of Rose Marie were at first painful, but soon he was remembering only the good things. He continued to live in their Rock City home, a home they had remodeled to accommodate two children.

He occasionally thought about Samantha O'Leary. From 1980 to 1993, Noah was meeting Sam at directors' meetings. They were both married, and their intimate personal conversations at those meetings had ended. The last time they met was at the 1997 shareholders' meeting. For Noah and Sam, the emotional torment continued to linger.

Noah's business interests required attention. He read his *Wall Street Journal*s, kept in touch with Bobby Shaffer, who'd continued on the Road Victor board, maintained his friendship with Wilson Marston, and nurtured his friendship with his old guardian and friend Martha Webb and his friends Felix and Jennifer Bronson. Managing his forest assets was important, and staying knowledgeable about events at Road Victor to protect his million-plus equity was essential. He knew he should spread that investment to other companies, but he was in love with Road Victor shares and couldn't sell.

Noah had two relatives that he liked and with whom he had

fostered a decent relationship. Margo North in Buffalo, New York, and Grandmother Susan Porter near Grants Pass, Oregon, were good people. Twice, he and Rose Marie had visited Margo in Buffalo. Margo had married and divorced. Her brother, Thomas, had nearly destroyed her inheritance, as well as his own, coming from their grandfather's estate. As a direct result of Noah's financial rescue, Noah ended up with six million, less taxes, after he managed the sale of North Marine. After Margo's divorce, Noah bought her a house in Buffalo. She was no longer the fiery young woman she'd once been, and she had been the key to Noah's meager relationship with some of the North family.

Grandmother Susan Porter's family lived from welfare check to food stamp. Noah and Rose Marie frequently visited her, and with respect for her, they tolerated her family. Following Grandfather Porter's death, Noah built Susan a modest house whose design she helped plan, and he deeded it to her. He filled it with modern appliances, paid her property taxes and insurance, and, with her approval, kept her family at arm's length.

TOGETHER

Early in May 2003, Noah received notice of the Road Victor's shareholders' meeting to be held June 7, 2003, at the Seattle Hilton. He immediately reserved a room at the Olympic. He was excited and lost in mixed emotions for a few moments, but he regained a clarity that urged him to call Bobby Shaffer to find out if anything new was going on in Seattle.

Bobby reported that Road Victor was healthy and didn't need any help from Noah, but if it did need help, he would call.

Noah asked, "How is Samantha?"

Bobby said, "Well, you just had to ask, didn't you."

Bobby then told Noah about her husband's death and said he didn't know if there was a man in her life. He also said, "For whatever it's worth, she's still as bright and beautiful as ever, and she has one adult child. She resigned from her directorship, but you knew that. I'm pretty sure she hung on to all of her Road Victor shares."

Noah thanked Bobby and said, "Maybe I'll see you at the annual meeting."

Apparently, no one at Road Victor knew about the death of Rose Marie, or Bobby would have said something. Sam hadn't known, or she would have called.

It was then that Noah realized this and asked himself, What the hell was the matter with me? I should have called her. I never called her. I thought I would just sound pathetic, and the past was ancient history, so I left it alone. He and Sam had exchanged Christmas cards for two or three Christmases, but that ended years ago.

When Noah's plane lifted off the Medford airport runway on June 5, 2003, for Seattle, Noah worried about leaving home, and he worried about seeing old shareholder friends and what that would be like. He whispered to himself, "I'm Noah North, and I am what I am, and I think I'm on the right track." He never admitted that, when facing the unknown, he talked to himself.

His plane was held in a landing pattern because of wind and rain. He could barely see the ground. After landing, there was of course no one to meet him, and the rain turned into a downpour. It was depressing, and Noah felt a flash of remorse about his long absence from friends in Seattle. He thought, What am I doing? What's left of my life is in Rock City and my two children. So why am I in Seattle? I want to be at this shareholders' meeting for one reason, and there is no certainty that she will be there.

He felt better after he settled in his room at the Olympic. Noah's contact with Samantha had ended, but not everything had ended. He seated himself in the great Olympic dining room, remembering that many years ago, he'd had dinner at this very table with a bright young woman who'd captured his affection.

Even though neither he nor Sam were now directors, he had hoped she would attend the shareholders' meeting. He wanted to see her and hear about her life, but he knew he wanted more. He was dressed in a white shirt, tie, and sport coat. After he left by taxi for the Hilton conference room, he thought, If she's not at this meeting, I will call her. How could I do otherwise?

Noah walked into the annual meeting and directly into Lila

Jameson, Sylvia Latimer, and George Newton, about 1,500,000 shares in the aggregate. They crowded around Noah, each saying, "We've missed you." Noah was ultimately cordial.

Noah said, "You couldn't miss me too much at $46 a share."

Sylvia threw her arms around Noah and said, "Next presidential year, I'm writing your name on my ballot for president."

He walked over to the secretary/registrar and discovered that over five million shares might be present. Samantha hadn't registered. He then found Bobby Shaffer, who was still a board member, and it pleased him to learn that all the board members were knowledgeable and keen on the governance culture and the products whose diversity Noah had established.

Noah asked, "Do you know if Samantha will be here?" Bobby didn't know.

Oliver Hedges, still chairman of the board, called the shareholders' meeting to order. Nearly everyone sat down, and Noah was disappointed. He had not seen Samantha.

After the meeting formally commenced, Noah saw Samantha walk in and sit in one of the few remaining chairs in a back row with a vacant chair beside her. She was indeed beautiful, smartly dressed, and attracted some attention. Noah was seated at the edge of the room. He slipped out of his seat, mostly unnoticed, and he walked around to the back row and sat down beside Samantha O'Leary Turner and said, "Remember me?" For a fraction of a second, Sam was shaken, but she gently grasped Noah's arm with both hands and partially collapsed against him with her head on his shoulder. She gently tightened her grip, pulling herself closer, and not a word was uttered. Noah pulled his arm loose and put it around her and held her close. After a respectful time, they turned, facing each other, devouring the message contained in their eyes and body language.

Noah said, "Let's get out of here."

Sam said, "I could, but you can't. You're married."

Noah said, "I apologize. I didn't tell you. Rose Marie died a year and a half ago, and my excitement in this moment caused me to speak as I did."

Sam said, "My husband was killed some time ago when a car ran a red light and broadsided his car. There is no man in my life except you."

They again sat in silence, pondering their bad fortune and good fortune.

Noah said, whispering, "I'm alive, in good health, and emotionally ready for what has just been laid at our doorstep."

Sam quietly said, "You know that in situations like this, people are vulnerable to making mistakes."

"I don't make mistakes."

Sam thought, My God, he's still Noah.

"Sam, when I was seventeen years old and you were twenty-two, we said no to the possibility of acting on our love for one another and parted. Now, at fifty and forty-five, we're not parting, ever."

Their continued conversation disturbed the couple in front of them, who turned and scowled at Noah.

Noah removed his arm from Sam, and he said, "Sam, let's leave."

"OK, let's leave. Noah, the real reason I came here was the likelihood of seeing you, and if I did see you, I had a wishful idea of what might happen."

Noah said, "The only reason I came here was to see you."

Sylvia saw Noah and Sam leaving together arm in arm. Sylvia nudged Lila and said, "There goes Mr. and Mrs. Road Victor. About twenty-five years ago they saved our now-very-old financial asses. I'd die to know what's going on in their lives."

Noah and Sam said goodbye to Sylvia and Lila and walked to Sam's car in silence, both sensing what was going to happen.

Sam unlocked the passenger door, opened it, and momentarily blocked Noah's entry; looking him in the eye, she said, "You know this is forever."

Sitting in Sam's BMW and looking at Sam, who was now sitting behind the wheel, he said, "It is absolutely forever."

Sam, with her mouth close to Noah's ear, whispered, "That is why we are driving straight to the King County Courthouse, where you are buying us a marriage license, and a judge there will marry us."

"I'm good with that. Looks like you're in charge."

"Can you live with that?"

"Maybe, but you are on thin ice."

"You'll mellow with age."

"You've overlooked a small detail. I haven't asked you to marry me."

"Well?"

"Sam, will you please marry me?"

"Yes, a thousand times yes."

The next morning, the sun rose on two renewed lives.

ACKNOWLEDGMENTS

The following resources and people were helpful during the writing of this book: *One Nation Under Gold: How One Precious Metal Has Dominated the American Imagination for Four Centuries* by James Ledbetter; *20th Century Day by Day* by Sharon Lucas; Clete Smith and Kim Kent, two great editors; and Helen Slack Miller, my daughter, whose help was essential.

ABOUT THE AUTHOR

Harry Slack is a retired lawyer with a degree in political science from the University of Oregon and a law degree from Willamette University College of Law. He owned a commercial-fishing enterprise in Alaska for twenty-five years and served on the board of directors of a community bank for twenty-five years. He now lives in Bandon, Oregon. He is also the author of *Lost in the Surf.*

www.ingramcontent.com/pod-product-compliance
Lightning Source LLC
Chambersburg PA
CBHW050030120726
47903CB00006B/1982